THE SECO[ND ...]
CAME TO [...]

"What do you think will happen," William asked, hoping that they might actually have stumbled on the solution.

"I don't know," Carter admitted softly.

The numbers flashed on the screen of the enclosed computer. Those standing around the protective shell did everything they could to conceal their tension. Each was aware that if their theory were right, and their precautions were not adequate, they would realize their success as they burned to death.

There was a quiver in the computer vacuum chamber and a bright feather of flame appeared at the back of the monitor where the cable attached to the electrical power. It flared, now becoming a small banner of fire, and flapped against the computer terminal, growing larger.

"Oh my God," one of the technicians whispered...

FIRECODE

**Also by
Chelsea Quinn Yarbro**

To the High Redoubt

Published by
POPULAR LIBRARY

ATTENTION: SCHOOLS AND CORPORATIONS

POPULAR LIBRARY books are available at quantity discounts with bulk purchase for educational, business, or sales promotional use. For information, please write to SPECIAL SALES DEPARTMENT, POPULAR LIBRARY, 666 FIFTH AVENUE, NEW YORK, N Y 10103

**ARE THERE POPULAR LIBRARY BOOKS
YOU WANT BUT CANNOT FIND IN YOUR LOCAL STORES?**

You can get any POPULAR LIBRARY title in print. Simply send title and retail price, plus 50¢ per order and 50¢ per copy to cover mailing and handling costs for each book desired. New York State and California residents add applicable sales tax. Enclose check or money order only, no cash please, to POPULAR LIBRARY, P. O. BOX 690, NEW YORK, N Y 10019

FIRECODE

CHELSEA QUINN YARBRO

POPULAR LIBRARY

An Imprint of Warner Books, Inc.

A Warner Communications Company

This story is fiction. All characters, events, and locales are either the product of the writer's imagination or used fictitiously. Any resemblance to actual persons, places, or events is wholly coincidental.

POPULAR LIBRARY EDITION

Copyright © 1987 by Chelsea Quinn Yarbro
All rights reserved.

Popular Library® is a registered trademark of
Warner Books, Inc.

Cover art by J. K. Potter

Popular Library books are published by
Warner Books, Inc.
666 Fifth Avenue
New York, N.Y. 10103

A Warner Communications Company

Printed in the United States of America

First Printing: April, 1987

10 9 8 7 6 5 4 3 2 1

For
the every-other-Monday-night gang
—all of you—
with love

Thus it has pleased Allah (may His Name be praised forever and ever) to give all things in and beyond the realms of earth a number, from the beginning of all things to the end of all things, in all dimensions of things; and whosoever commands the number also commands the thing that owns it, be it benefic or malignant... and by the number is the thing which owns it summoned, from the least to the greatest of all things."

> Dabir Ibn Jamil, mathematician
> (Fl. A.D. 940–955)

August 19, Baltimore, Maryland

Convenience be damned, thought Marianne Jenkins as she searched through the instruction booklet for the right combination of numbers to program her microwave oven. No wonder the thing was a bargain, given its impossible-to-remember programming.

"All right," she said to the appliances in her kitchen as she opened the instruction book for her oven. "This time I'm going to get it right." She switched the toggle to Delay and then read down the page. First there had to be the five-hour delay. That much was easy. Then there was a thawing sequence—she punched in the numbers for that—and after that, the cooking.

Outside there were shrieks on the street as a wedge of eight- and nine-year-old children raced down the block.

Marianne glanced toward the window and listened for Tony's voice, but if he was part of the group, she could not hear him clearly; the hum of the air conditioning was too loud for that. She sighed and went back to her microwave oven. Her parents were coming to dinner and she wanted it to be right, to prove to them that she could handle her part-time job and her marriage without either suffering. She consulted the page once more and continued to punch buttons.

All that was left to do now was to program the last warm-up sequence. She checked the page for a third time and then put her fingers on the keys.

A sudden, acrid scent of charring filled the kitchen.

"What the hell . . . ?" Marianne demanded, her patience exhausted. She reached for the cord to unplug the oven, but never touched it.

Consuming as a volcanic eruption, flames filled the kitchen, turning the tile countertops to slag and engulfing most of the apartment before a jerking, scarecrow figure that had been Marianne Jenkins collapsed to the molten linoleum.

In less than ten minutes, half of the apartment building was burning.

August 24, Phoenix, Arizona

It always came easier when he was stoned. Gary Winters crooned along with his keyboard, hearing the lovely, lovely notes blast out through his four enormous speakers. He had the first half of the melody, a nice, plaintive thing that would put him back at the top of the charts where he was two years ago. His hand-rolled cigarette gave off bitter smoke, and he paused to take another hit before working out the rest of the tune.

He leaned back, bringing the electronic keyboard from his knees to his lap. It was coming so easy now, one note right after the other, every single one of them right. He'd call Mike as soon as he was done and play it for him, so that they could get to work on lyrics. Just like old times.

He liked the pattern that was building—short, double-short, long, double-long—as much as the melody.

The joint was still in his fingers when the speakers exploded as fire engulfed Gary Winters and most of his house.

September 1, Chicago, Illinois

Although the Labor Day holiday was just over twenty-four hours old, the casualties had been coming into the emergency room in an ever-increasing stream; this year threatened to break all records. Pete Washington and Gloria Symons already had more than their hands full processing the claims through the huge, new billing computer that took up a good portion of the basement, across the hall from Pathology.

"There's two more drownings and burns from a runaway barbecue fire," Gloria said as she looked over the paperwork that the harassed clerks had rushed to them.

"How many of them have insurance, do you know?" Pete asked. Outdoors, Chicago was a humid ninety-six degrees, but here both of the programmers wore light sweaters under their lab coats; it was sixty-three. "Computers and corpses do better in cold," the chief adminstrator had quipped when the installation was complete.

"Most of them do. There's also half a dozen more cases of that stomach flu. I suppose we'd better notify Atlanta. I'll flag the charts going in." Gloria reached for a cigarette but stopped herself in time.

"How many days is it now?" asked Pete as he started to work out the codes. He was not yet used to the new system.

"Twenty-four and nary a cigarette. I've gained five pounds."

She patted her lean hips. "And who wants to jog in this weather? Besides, there's as much crap in the air as there is in cigarettes."

"So join a gym," suggested Pete.

Gloria was tired enough to be grouchy. "Fine thing for you to say—you play basketball three times a week and you're skinny as a pencil."

"Uh-huh," said Pete. "What's the code for noncontagious and noninfectious diseases?"

"Nine-forty-three, I think," said Gloria, reaching for their manual. "Yeah," she confirmed. "Nine-forty-three. Which case is that?"

"Crohn's disease," said Pete with sympathy.

"You tack another three onto the list. Christ, all these numbers! I tell you, one of these days, I'm going to the deli and ask for a six-six-two with nine-seven-four and a fifty-one to go." She sorted through the stack. "Here're a couple more you can add to the current run. The first is a two-three-one."

"Poor kid," said Pete. "That's anaphylactic shock, isn't it? And a pediatric admit?"

"Right. Bee stings, I'd bet. The last is an eight-nine-eight. The cops must have brought that one in."

"Gotcha," said Pete, typing carefully and watching the monitor screen to be sure he had the order right.

"What's that?" Gloria asked as the room began to smoke.

Her question was never answered; the entire basement was filled with an expanding fireball that roared and ravaged through most of the hospital before it was brought under control by almost a third of the city's available fire fighters and their equipment.

PART I

September 5, near San Jose, California

Traffic had slowed almost to a stop on Highway 17. To the commuters bound for home in Felton, Scott's Valley, Santa Cruz and Cabrillo this problem—overheating engines and tempers in the afternoon crawl—was familiar enough to be infuriating.

Carter Milne shifted down to first gear and adjusted her sunglasses, resigned to inching forward for the next ten miles. She had a low-grade headache, but it had little to do with the delay. Ever since her boss, Jeremiah Patterson, had dumped the Murchison Hospital fire on her desk that morning, she had been caught up in an ill-defined but persistent dread.

"Look, Carter, the fire department thinks that it might be sabotage, and that makes it our business," he had said when she asked what the fire had to do with Patterson Security Systems.

She had spent three hours going over the file, and could find nothing in the preliminary material to justify sabotage as a cause. The trouble was that there was nothing to rule it

7

out, either. She honked at a shiny Mercedes that prodded in ahead of her. What worried her was the report that had come in at 3:48 that the Coglin Optics factory near Fort Worth had caught fire, and the profile—sudden and almost total "involvement in flame"—was the same as the Murchison Hospital fire.

In the next hour, as the snake of cars wound over the summit and down toward the northern end of the glistening crescent of Monterey Bay, Carter reviewed all that she had read that day, looking for similarities and dissimilarities. When she finally reached the turnoff for Highway 1, she had done nothing more than escalate her headache.

At her house in Aptos she noticed that Greg's car was not in the driveway. No lights shone in the house, and she could hear Winslow, their four-year-old Chow, whining at the back door.

"Just a minute, fella," she called out as she locked the Mazda's door. Automatically she tucked her brief portfolio under her arm and paused at the mailbox to see what was there. It was empty; she assumed that Greg had been home earlier.

And the house was empty. The Macintosh in the alcove off the living room was where she looked first, since it was Greg's habit to leave her notes on the computer.

> Hi, hon, it said as she turned it on. *I'm taking off a day early for Reno. Stanton is coming with me, so I can't lose. If nothing else happens, I'll clean him out. Be back late on Sunday. I'll call you if I change my plans. Have a good weekend.*
> *Love and kisses, Peanut.*
> Greg

She sighed as she filed the note in the electronic innards. Peanut. The old nickname used to please her, and seemed amusing. Now, she thought it was inappropriate. It wasn't as if they were still grad students. As she let Winslow into the house, she had to hold back vexed tears. Why did Greg insist on living this way? There was no point in crying, she told herself. Greg was the way he was, and that was all there was to it.

"Here, fella," she called to Winslow, patting his black ruff. She had filled his bowl with food and now stood back to watch him eat. As the dog started to gulp down his food, she heard two plaintive feline voices; Pyotr and Modeste, her Russian Blues, were waiting anxiously at the back door. She went to let them in, glad to be of use to someone, even if it was only a pet. "Come on, guys," she said as they raced into the kitchen. "Suppertime."

When the pets were fed, Carter turned her attention to something to eat for herself. Nothing really interested her, and she could not bring herself to get into the car and drive a mile or two to a restaurant. Finally she took out a cup of yogurt and made a supper of it, talking to her cats to keep the illusion of company.

A little later she wandered into the living room and turned on the TV, catching part of a baseball game. Who was playing whom did not matter, since she ignored it while she read through the reports in her brief portfolio until the game was over and *Simon and Simon* came on. She set her work aside and watched Jameson Parker and Gerald McRaney romp through a lighthearted adventure, her worries momentarily upstaged by the entertainment.

At ten she put the dog and cats out and went to take a bath, the TV set still on but the sound turned way down. The flicker of the screen and the occasional buzz of dialogue was oddly comforting, taking some of the loneliness out of the evening. She lay back in the tub, indulging in honeysuckle-scented bubble bath, and did her best to unwind. She had almost succeeded when the spot-announcement of news caught her attention.

There was a brief follow-up about a bank fire in Santa Fe that the reporter implied was a mystery. Carter heard this with growing apprehension that made her body turn chilly in the warm water. Another fire. She got out of the tub and wrapped herself in her terry-cloth robe and padded into the living room.

At eleven, she watched dutifully while the nightly news team recapped the major stories of the day and added a report on a five-car pileup on Route 101. Finally the Santa Fe story came on, and Carter listened to various speculations about the origin of the fire. The consensus was that it was an attempt to influence the New Mexico State Legislature in some way, but there was no agreement as to who was doing it, or why, or how.

Carter listened attentively to the baffled comments of the Fire Marshal and a few of the politicians. Everyone decried the act and vowed that those responsible would be dealt with severely. So far no person or group had claimed credit for the blaze, but it was only a matter of time until someone came forth. The FBI was already looking into it. Fires aren't accidents, happening for no reason, said the Fire Marshal. It was very suspicious.

"It sure is," said Carter to the television screen. She hit the off switch and stood staring at the darkness. "It sure is," she repeated as she wandered toward the bedroom.

Patterson Security Systems occupied three buildings in the northwest corner of an industrial park that boasted two creeks, over fifty oak trees and a small stand of young sempervirens redwoods. The buildings were all low and inconspicuous, the largest three stories tall, the others, two. They were done in what Carter called "California natural," with large exposed wooden beams and a great many windows, some of them oddly shaped. Each had an atrium in its center, with huge potted plants reaching past the gallery of the upper floors to the skylights above.

Carter's office was in the largest building, and boasted two windows, one overlooking a creek, the other facing the atrium. She was one of six statisticians with so favored a location, and it still gave her a touch of pride to open her door in the morning.

There was a note on her desk, the slanted emphatic handwriting as familiar as it was illegible. Her boss wanted to see her at eleven, she deciphered. Under this memo was a new stack of printouts, more information on the Coglin Optics fire. Carter put her brief portfolio down and took her place at the desk. "No rest for the wicked," she remarked to the air before she buzzed the secretary she shared with Hank Edwards and asked for a large cup of coffee.

"Right away, Doctor Milne," said Dena Ottermeyer, sounding even brisker than usual.

Carter had long since given up trying to get the girl to use her first name. "Thank you, Miss Ottermeyer," she said, and drew the new material toward her. With a shift of mental gears, she started to read.

At ten minutes to eleven, Dena interrupted Carter with the reminder that she had a meeting with J. D. Patterson. Carter thanked her and gathered up her notes and the printouts. She wondered who else would be there, and how urgent the meeting was. With Jeremiah Dermott Patterson, there was no way to tell.

At the elevator, she found Cynthia Harper waiting, which relieved her. "You, too?" asked the attorney.

"Me, too," said Carter. "Do you have any idea what this is about?"

"The Coglin Optics fire. Apparently there's some doubt as to cause, and the question is whose responsibility it is. I've already had a long talk with Glen Lewis."

"What does he think?" Carter had tried to like the head of the legal department, but had never quite succeeded. She often wondered how Cynthia stood him.

"Oh, Glen thinks six impossible things before breakfast, just for the hell of it," she said. "He won't have anything so concrete as an opinion until we have more information."

"Well, from what I've seen, we still have a long way to go." The elevator doors opened, and the two women stepped in. Cynthia pushed the button for the third floor, and they started their upward journey.

"Why's that?" Cynthia asked.

"There was a lot of destruction—and you know what that does to evidence. Apparently, most of the usual signs of arson are lacking, but that could mean a very experienced professional set the fire, for some reason or another." Carter tugged on the knot of the silk scarf she wore loosely over her lacquer-red blouse. "I don't know what to make of it yet."

The elevator doors opened and they stepped out together. The door to J.D.'s office was only a few steps away and the outer door was open.

"Good morning," called out Phylis Dunlap, looking as neat as her office.

"Morning, Phyl," said Carter. "How's the boss?"

"Irked," said Phylis succinctly. "But not too annoyed."

Cynthia rolled her eyes upward. "Can we go in?"

"He's waiting," said Phylis as she buzzed them through.

J.D. Patterson was not behind his wide redwood desk as the two women came in; he was making espresso by the wet bar; he waved them to chairs, saying, "Want a cup?"

"Please," said Carter.

"No thanks," said Cynthia.

"Barry and Scott and Dave Fisher will be joining us," he said as he cut a section of lemon peel. "The meeting should be lively."

"Wonderful," Cynthia said to the air.

At fifty-four, Jeremiah Patterson had learned to take such remarks in stride. "Be nice, Cynthia. The man can't help it if he doesn't understand the law."

"No, and he makes no effort to change," said Cynthia with a pained expression. "His last mistake cost us a lot of money, J.D."

"And I've told him to be more careful." He said this affably enough, but it was no secret that Scott Costa's job was on the line if he bungled again.

"Why anticipate trouble?" asked Carter. She had taken one of the straight-backed chairs and was sitting at attention. She hated meetings like this—they always made her feel ten years old.

"We don't have to anticipate it. We've already got it." J.D. came away from the wet bar carrying two demitasses. He held one out to Carter. "It's hot."

"Good. Thanks." She inhaled the penetrating aroma that rose in steam from her cup. She watched J.D. as he took his place behind his desk. There were times she almost envied his supreme self-confidence, but today was not one of them, because she knew he was as baffled as any of them.

"We're going to have to get some more figures from various of the fire departments who have dealt with inexplicable fires and find out what similarities they have, if any. I leave that to Dave's crew of merry men, but I expect you, Carter, to sift it for us." He folded his hands on the desk in front of him. "That's for openers."

"But we haven't got nearly enough data yet. I wouldn't rely on anything I could learn from the little we've got. I've spent a couple hours on it already, and—" She was cut short as the door opened and two of the men came in.

"Morning," said Dave Fisher. "Nice day for a fire."

"Not funny," Carter murmured.

Scott Costa waved uncertainly and took the chair farthest away from J.D.

"We had a call from Coglin yesterday that worried me, and I want you all to get to work on it before the weekend," said J.D. without any introduction. "That means I want all of you to be aware of what the others are doing, so you'll know who to call without wasting time and energy."

"Isn't Barry supposed to be here?" Dave Fisher asked, not truly interrupting—he was not the sort who interrupted—but concerned enough to speak up.

"He will be," said J.D. "He's checking on something for me now; there's a Fire Marshals' Task Force in the East that he's been trying to reach. That's more in his line, in any case." He looked over the four people in his office. "You're not going to like some of this."

"Why?" asked Cynthia.

"Because it's messy. And from what little we've found out so far, it's a real mystery." He leaned back, shifting his focus and emphasis. "It's never easy, trying to find the best way to address a security problem where fire is concerned. So much of the evidence you need isn't there anymore. And fires are so costly, in every sense of the word. Coglin Optics won't be able to operate for at least three and possibly four months, and that is going to be hard on many of their employees. Their insurance company is trying to claim that they aren't protected, and naturally there are questions about the fire itself."

"Two men died," Carter said in the silence. "A nightwatchman and a fireman."

"That's the worst of it," J.D. said. "Anytime someone is killed, it's a very dicey thing. I wouldn't want to think that we had been lax, or that our security had in any way contributed to the loss of life or property. For what it's worth," he added thoughtfully, "the alarm system in the smoke detectors worked, but the fire spread very rapidly and was extremely hot."

"The system was destroyed before it could do any good, really." Dave Fisher shook his head slowly. "I saw that in the report this morning."

"That appears to be the case," said J.D.

"Appears?" Cynthia asked, more attentive. "Whole cases have risen or fallen on appearances. Why is there a question?"

Finally Scott Costa spoke. "They haven't been able to determine what started the fire, and in this case they're discussing materials. Whatever was burning burned very fast and hot, and there was nothing in that part of the plant that ought to have done that. According to what we know about the plant, the fire couldn't happen at all."

"And unfortunately for Coglin Optics, it did." J.D. got up and went to the east end of his office where he had a blackboard concealed behind tall redwood panels. As he slid these panels open, he said, "We mustn't overlook any possibility. We want this client satisfied that we took every reasonable precaution against the fire, and that so far as it was possible, our systems worked. Otherwise, there might be a hint of culpability. Mightn't there, Cynthia?"

"It's possible," she said. "There's also the case of Westminster, where it was discovered that the company was causing minor security problems that would magically stop when their systems were installed."

"High-tech protection racket," said J.D. with disgust. "I know it's possible, but it galls me to think about it. We don't want the least hint of that to touch us, and therefore, I'd like it if you'd all bend as far over backward on this one as you can. I want to be ready to assist anyone researching this fire or any similar to it, I want every one of you to take time to develop every possible lead to the fullest. If you have other projects, pass them on to someone who can handle them. Is that clear?"

Dave Fisher cleared his throat. "What about the mine-safety study we've been doing, and the security development?" This was his pet and he had already devoted close to a year to it, trying to show that with proper detection and security devices, mine safety could be improved at least thirty percent, and loss of life reduced by forty percent. It was just beginning to show real promise.

"I don't like to ask you to do it, but frankly, Dave, I have to." J.D. was truly sympathetic, but it was clear he would not tolerate any questioning of his orders.

Carter thought of the material waiting on her desk. "I think I'd like to spend some time getting more information on these unexplained fires," she said abruptly. "It's clear that something is going on here, and I want to take time to find out what it is."

"How do you mean?" asked J.D.

"You said you wanted me to go over the incidents of fires with profiles similar to this one at Coglin," she said, flushing as she spoke.

"Yes. And if you've found a pattern, tell me now," J.D. ordered.

"I don't know if it's a pattern, but it is something that bears examining further, I think," she said with a trace of a stammer.

"Tell us more," J.D. said, giving her his full attention.

This was the sort of thing she hated, but she tried to

sound and appear unconcerned. I'm not a child, she said inwardly, and this isn't Miss Manning's class. "I went over the various reports on recent fires, and about half a dozen, scattered from one end of the country to the other, have started suddenly, been unusually hot and the cause is still in question. That's enough like the Coglin fire to make me think that there might be other bits of data we can use. I can give you a rough statistical profile on Monday or Tuesday."

"You do that," J.D. approved. "Now, that's what I'm hoping for from all of you," he went on expansively. "I want you to try to find something that we can use."

"You mean that can get us off the hook," Cynthia said, not at all cynically.

"That's a factor," J.D. allowed. "And it's more than that. If there are going to be any more of these fires, if there's the least *hint* that there might be more of these fires, then we're going to have to take the possibility into account with our clients. Anything less would have some very unpleasant repercussions."

The others nodded, and Scott Costa looked upset. "I hate fires," he said. "I just hate them."

"No one likes them," Dave said, stating the obvious.

"Arsonists do," J.D. pointed out. "If this turns out to be arson, then Coglin will have some claim against us, and rightly. I don't want to deny any client damages if those damages are our fault, but I'm damned if I want to shell out a dime for a fire that has nothing to do with Patterson Security Systems."

His four employees were nodding in agreement when the door opened and Barry Tsugoro walked in, saying, "I'm sorry the calls took so long."

"Did you reach anyone in the Fire Marshals' Task Force?" asked J.D.

"I talked to one of the administrators in Detroit, and he's agreed to share information with us in return for anything we come up with. He said that they were worried."

"I can imagine," said Dave.

J.D. clasped his hands together, in what Carter thought

of as his battering-ram position. "We have to work hard on this one, and I can't reiterate that enough. Barry, we have to get everything the Task Force will let us have, as quickly as they will supply it. If it might speed things along, send them everything we've got and any developmental material we've got."

"All right," said Barry with a quick glance at the others for signs of their cooperation.

"I also want each one of you to be very careful about checking out any questionable new fires, no matter where they are. I want to have all the information as up-to-the-minute as possible, and I want your efforts coordinated so that no one will be left behind simply because no one gave them the morning update. Is that understood?" He paused, not expecting an interruption, but he had one from Scott.

"J.D., what if there are political implications? You know that the feds could put a lid on the information faster than a hooker's—" Scott stopped himself as he saw Cynthia's warning gesture.

"That might happen," J.D. conceded. "If this is the result of terrorism, then there's a good chance that one of the federal agencies will get involved. Hell, if a pattern shows up, they're likely to take a hand, no matter what. Which is all the more reason to get as much done right now as we can, so that if anything develops that way, they'll have to include us in some way." He reached for a piece of chalk and started to sketch one of his organizational charts, labeling boxes and connecting them with lines. "Anything with legal implications goes through Cynthia, no matter who else might be involved. Got that? All facts and figures, and I do mean all of them, go to Carter. Barry will get all the information he can from all the outside sources we can find. If there are any marginal cases, check them out with me, Barry."

"Fine," said Barry.

"And Dave, I want you to go to Texas and run a complete check on as much of our system as there is left. I want a thorough going-over of the site, and I want reports with every single witness you can get your hands on, including the firemen and the factory workers who had jobs in that part of the building. I expect to have a full report by next Tuesday at the latest." He squinted at the blackboard. "We also have to develop our contingency plans, and that means you, Scott, will have to get together with Cynthia this afternoon and come up with something that will get by for the time being."

"Right after lunch," Scott promised.

Ordinarily, Cynthia would have objected to the wait, but Scott was diabetic and had to eat at regular intervals. "Okay, I'll be waiting for you in my office."

"There are a few things I want all of you to keep in mind," J.D. said, beginning his closing. "Lives were lost in the Coglin fire. We have more than a professional obligation to determine the cause and responsibility, we have a moral one." He met the eyes of each of the others in turn. "If you find yourself getting stale, keep that in mind, will you."

"How often are we to report to you?" Barry asked, his manner as serious as J.D.'s.

"I want to hear from each of you at least once a day. Call in on Saturday and Sunday; I'll tell you what I've heard, and you can arrange any necessary conferences."

"You're shooting down the weekend," Cynthia pointed out.

"Yeah," J.D. agreed. "I sure as hell am. And I'll probably go on doing it until we know what's the cause of these fires and we've established responsibility once and for all. And then we can start adapting our security to cover contingencies of this nature, so our clients won't need to worry about being burned out."

"I don't mind the extra work," Carter said, more to herself than the others.

"Good," J.D. said, his face creasing as he smiled. "Listen to her."

"I've got relatives coming for the weekend," said Cynthia in a measured tone. "I'll try to work around them, but no promises."

"Do the best you can," said J.D. "Barry? Dave? Scott? Any problems from you?"

Barry shook his head, Scott looked troubled and Dave said, "I'll be in touch while I'm in Texas."

"Good, then it's under way," said J.D., clearly wanting no argument about it.

"J.D.," said Scott, "how much staff will we need?"

"Who knows. You ought to be able to determine that for yourself, and if you have to make changes, so be it."

Carter looked out the window, toward the trees and the cool green swath of lawn. She had planned to spend her lunch hour sitting outside, enjoying the sun, but she supposed now that she ought to cut that short and spend as much time in her office as possible.

"That's it," said J.D. "Get to work, everyone." It was his standard dismissal.

The first one to rise was Scott, who hesitated, glancing once at the blackboard as if hoping to memorize what J.D. had written there. He checked his watch and gave a terse nod, as if satisfied that the time was proper for leaving.

"J.D.," said Dave, "should I ask Phylis to arrange my tickets, or would you prefer I call Executive Travel?"

"Phylis will take care of it; she's faster. I'll have one of the company drivers standing by to take you to the airport whenever you need to leave." He cleared his throat. "If you don't mind, I'll arrange for your family to have dinner on me while you're gone."

"Why should I mind?" Dave asked. "Just call Jeannie and make your plans. The kids are going through a pizza-and-calzone phase, by the way. They like pesto."

"I'll keep that in mind," said J.D. "Gary's the same way." Gary was J.D.'s son by his second marriage and unlike his other two children, lived not far away, with his mother in Los Gatos.

"I should be ready to go by midafternoon if I pack right now. If I stick around for a couple more hours, then a flight after seven would be better—it would get us behind the commute traffic." Dave moved restlessly, unwilling to leave without settling his plans, but at the same time preoccupied with what was coming up for him.

Carter caught Cynthia's eye and the two of them rose together.

"Back to the law books." Cynthia sighed. "You have time after work for a drink?"

"Sure," said Carter.

"I'll stop by your office when I'm through," said Cynthia, then addressed J.D., who had just arranged with Dave that he would take an evening flight to Houston. "If it's all right, I'll call you in the afternoon tomorrow and Sunday. I'm pretty sure I'll have a little spare time then. Is that okay?"

"Certainly," said J.D. "I don't mean to break up families, Cynthia, but I do want the job done."

They were drifting out of the office, and J.D. was already going back to his desk, running one large hand through his thick, graying hair. "J.D., what's so special about this fire? You don't usually pull out all the stops this way."

"I don't like fires," J.D. said. "And fires like this give people ideas."

"What kind of ideas?" Carter asked, trying to imagine what she ought to be looking for in the figures that were crossing her desk.

"Panic, for one; imitation for another." J.D. folded his arms and looked at the two women. "And a fire, when it's done, takes almost everything with it, including a lot of evidence. We can make security systems that guard against many things—thieves, sabotage, intrusion, malicious mischief, industrial espionage, breakdowns, tapping, computer raiding, production hazards, and the like—but fire, unless the cause can be identified and traced, is one of the things that we're not well prepared to handle, no matter how advanced the system. When I was in the Navy, we had one bad fire at our base, and I don't think I'll ever forget what I saw then."

"We've got one of the most advanced sprinkler systems

and smoke alarms around," Cynthia pointed out. "Everyone agrees."

"Everyone can agree as much as they like; it obviously isn't good enough or Coglin Optics would still have that building." J.D. paused. "I know you're more concerned about the legal aspects, and that's what I pay you for, but there's more going on than the chance of a lawsuit. That's why I want Carter to get all the material she can, because the more we know, statistically, about this fire and others like it, the better chance we have to make sure it never happens again, not to Coglin and not to anyone else."

Cynthia clapped lightly. "Great speech, boss."

"Because I mean every word of it," J.D. said, unruffled. "Now, get back to your law books and find me some legal parameters."

"You bet," said Cynthia, executing a smart about-face and winking at Carter as she did.

"J.D.," Carter ventured, hesitating near his desk.

"What?"

"How far back do you want me to go for statistics? A year? Two? Five?" She fiddled with the end of her scarf as she waited for her answer.

"Use your own best judgment. Check our records and see what else we have on file about fires, okay? And Carter, don't worry if you can't come up with the analysis you'd like to prepare. Statistics deals in generalities, not absolutes, remember." He had taken a stack of printouts from the top drawer of his desk and had set them out in front of him. "You're conscientious to a fault; don't let that keep you from giving me information simply because you're afraid it's incomplete. I expect it to be incomplete."

"And the Murchison fire? What about that one?" she asked, raising the question of the hospital yet again.

"By all means. There's a limit on the information we can get until the Fire Marshal is satisfied that they're not dealing with terrorism, but I'll see if we can get some cooperation through our Cleveland or Madison offices. Murchison is a special case until we hear otherwise."

"But it is an unexplained fire, just like Coglin Optics," she reminded him. "What if they're connected in some way?"

"A hospital in Chicago and an optics plant in Texas? I hope you're not on to something," said J.D.

"Let me run a comparison, will you please?" Carter asked, the end of her scarf now hopelessly knotted.

"Fine. Go to it. I just hope you come up empty on that hunch." He tapped the printouts on his desk. "I'll go over the Murchison Hospital material, too. Just in case."

"I'll call you tomorrow," Carter promised, satisfied that she had enough leeway in her work to present a reasonable report.

"Good hunting," said J.D., waving Carter to the door. "I have work to do, and so do you."

Cynthia was waiting in Phylis's office, her impatience showing in the vertical line between her brows. "What was that last all about?"

"Nothing, probably. But I reviewed the Murchison fire yesterday, and now this . . . I can't help feeling that they're similar, somehow," said Carter inadequately. When she was developing a line of thought, she often had trouble putting her notions into words.

"Don't forget that drink. The traffic's going to be awful in any case, and I think we ought to talk." She gave a thumbs-up sign to Phylis as the two women left her office.

"I've got a dog and two cats who'll be hungry," Carter warned Cynthia, but it was not a serious objection.

"They'll be hungry if you sit in traffic or if you have a drink with me; big deal. I'll come to your office, otherwise you might forget that it's quitting time." They were at the elevator and as Carter pressed the button, Cynthia added, "If you're feeling guilty, call Greg and ask him to take care of the animals."

"Greg's out of town," Carter said in a neutral voice.

The elevator doors opened so Cynthia's silence passed unnoticed.

* * *

It was cool and inviting in the restaurant where Cynthia took Carter. The waiters were not too busy to be attentive, so the drinks and the appetizer that Cynthia ordered for them arrived promptly.

"Ah!" said Cynthia as she sipped at her generous strawberry daiquiri. "Andy can say what he wants about girl drinks, but this is wonderful." She indicated the plate of nachos. "Have some of these, Carter. I'll make a pig of myself if you don't."

Carter, who was staring into the middle distance, gave herself a little shake and obediently took one of the chips. "They've put everything but sweet-and-sour sauce on these."

"Um. That's what makes them so good." Cynthia set her drink down and said, "Okay: what is it? You look like Little Orphan Annie on a bad day." She kicked off her shoes and tucked her feet up under her.

Carter's eyes were forlorn.

"I don't know what to say—it's just more of the same, and after a while it bores even me." She picked up her drink but did not bring it to her lips. "It's no better and no worse than it was a month ago, or a year ago."

Cynthia tossed her head, her dark hair swinging around her face. "I remember that part. That was when I kept telling myself that it wasn't as if I had a *bad* marriage, and that I could handle almost anything Wally did, and that I never expected marriage to be perfect anyway, et cetera, et cetera." She regarded Carter seriously. "Now listen to me: you're kidding yourself. You don't have a good marriage; you have a rotten marriage and there's nothing you can do about it. You can't go back to being happy grad students together. You're thirty-eight—"

"Thirty-nine," murmured Carter.

"Okay, thirty-*nine* years old, and you've been married for sixteen years, nine of which were okay and seven of which were the pits, am I right?" She paused without expecting an answer. "You've said that Greg doesn't want to get counseling, and when you've gone, he's been angry about it. Carter, that's very bad news. I know what I'm talking about. Wally told me everything was just fine until the day I took the overdose of sleeping pills."

"You did what?" Carter asked, startled out of her inattention.

"Took an overdose of sleeping pills," Cynthia said in the same even tone. "That only made him mad, because I was embarrassing him. I was so depressed that I didn't care." She ate another nacho chip, studying Carter. "I'd dropped out of grad school the year before, it seemed such a waste of time, and Wally needed me to help him, or so he insisted."

"You've never told me about this," Carter said, aghast.

"You didn't need to hear it. And it's not a part of my life that I'm very proud of. I don't like advertising my problems any more than you do." She took a deep breath. "J.D. knows, of course. He asked me about it when he interviewed me. I thought I was a goner when he did, but he was in the middle of his third divorce, and I guess he had some understanding."

"I guess," said Carter. She continued to watch Cynthia, feeling almost unreal.

"Anyway, what I'm saying to you is that you can't get away from your problems with work. It's no answer. All you'll do is end up exhausting yourself and it will still turn out the same way—one or the other of you will leave." She leaned back against the upholstery. "Right now you've got the Coglin and Murchison Hospital fires to deal with, and that gives you a place to hide. But what about next weekend when Greg takes off for Reno or Las Vegas again? What then?"

"I don't know," said Carter. "He doesn't usually gamble more than a weekend a month."

"That you know of," warned Cynthia.

"I think he's being honest." Carter was feeling very defensive. "We had a real showdown last year when he lost his car in that twenty-one game. Now he's more careful; losing the car really scared him." She could hear the petulance in her own voice and it shocked her. She remembered all the times her mother had insisted that "your father is really a very good man, Carter" when Carter had fought with him. All her life she had sworn she would never become like that.

"Oh, that's swell." Cynthia made no excuse for her sarcasm. "And just how do you think you'll manage if it turns out that he's lost something else, like the house. And don't," she went on without permitting Carter to interrupt, "tell me that it can't happen. You know better than I do what it's like to live with a compulsive gambler."

"He's not a compulsive gambler; he just likes to gamble," said Carter, repeating what Greg had told her so many times.

"Yeah, and the Great Pyramid is a real neat headstone." Cynthia glared at the food between them. "You know better than that. You are much too bright to kid yourself, no matter what you say to me. But it just makes me furious at Greg—and you—to see what's happening to you. Damn it, Carter. Why don't you leave him while you've got something to hang on to?"

"What's that?" Carter asked. "Two cats and a dog?"

"A career. A house. Self-respect." She took a deep breath and had some more of her drink. "If I hadn't been through it myself, I wouldn't talk to you like this. At least Greg only gambles. Wally did coke, and after a while, it was costing him over twenty thousand dollars a year. To say nothing of what happened to his job and everything else. Maybe gambling isn't as bad as coke, but it's just as much a habit. And in the end it will eat up everything. I just don't want it to eat you up along with the cars and the house. That's all."

"It's not going to come to that," Carter said, not nearly as confidently as she would have wanted.

"I hope you're right," said Cynthia. "But don't get yourself too far out on a limb. And if you need a place to get away from it all, you know where to come. Ben would be happy to have you for a weekend, and so would the kids."

"He's a nice guy," Carter said, glad to be shifting the subject.

"Ain't it the truth?" Cynthia asked of the air. "Sometimes I want to pinch myself, just to be sure I really have found him. He says the same thing about me, and that floors me." Cynthia hesitated, then recklessly said, "That's one of the reasons I'm talking to you. I'd like you to have the same chance that I did."

"With Ben?" Carter laughed.

"Someone as good for you as he is for me," Cynthia said at her most unperturbed.

"I . . ." Carter wanted to be able to say that Greg was that, but the words would not come. Her face turned scarlet, and she looked away from Cynthia toward the door as if seeking escape.

Cynthia gave her a weary smile and said, "I know the feeling. You're not being disloyal, or whatever you're afraid you're being. You can tell me to shut up and mind my own business, if you want."

"Shut up and mind your own business," said Carter without anger.

"Okay. What about the fires?" She gave a quick, short sigh. "You have any ideas about that?"

"A few," said Carter, picking up her drink. "They all scare the hell out of me. There was another strange fire last night in Santa Fe, at a bank. I want to know about that one, as well." Now that she was on safe ground, she went on with more force. "I think there's a pattern, and if there is, then the problem is a lot worse than it appears right now, because who knows how many other fires are involved?" She helped herself to the nachos. "I hope that we can get enough information that I can prepare some figures that have some bearing on the case."

"And what do you thing it is?" Cynthia asked, a glimmer of professional curiosity in her large brown eyes.

"It could be terrorism. It makes a certain kind of sense. A hospital, a factory, a bank, all potential targets for various of the weirdies out there. If the figures hold, then I think we're going to have to look at a vast and well-organized terrorist conspiracy." The words, now that she spoke them aloud, sounded so melodramatic that she almost laughed. "Sounds like a Stallone movie, doesn't it?"

"I hope it does," said Cynthia, the beginnings of a frown creasing her forehead. "If you're right, it's not going to be pleasant."

Carter had more of her drink, wishing that Cynthia had made a joke or told her she was crazy. "I'll know more by Monday," she said.

"Figures all weekend?" asked Cynthia.

"Probably. I might go for a walk on the beach. Providing it's foggy. Somehow it's hard to be reflective with surfers all over the place." She had more of the nachos. "These sure are good."

"Filling, though," said Cynthia. "I still have to do something about dinner. Maybe I'll stop on the way home and pick up a pizza or . . . oh, I don't know. There's that Hunan place on El Camino."

"Does Ben like Hunan food?" asked Carter. Small talk, that was what she hoped for. Between her worries about Greg and the new problem of the fires, she needed a diversion.

"Anything edible. It's one of the nicest things about him. He knows what the good stuff is, but he's not a snob. I wish we didn't have relatives coming tomorrow, or I'd say stay the weekend with us right now, and the hell with walking on foggy beaches." Cynthia set her glass down. "That's enough. I'd rather have my calories in corn chips and cheese." The glass was little more than half empty, but she moved it aside. "Now, that's one thing about Ben that I *do* dislike; he can stuff himself and not gain an ounce."

"Unfair," said Carter.

"Hey, you're another of the skinny ones," Cynthia said, though she was as slender as Carter. "Sometimes I wonder why I bother about it, but I guess vanity has a price, and it's paid in calories, at least for me." She took another small helping of nachos. "Thank goodness I'm almost finished. I have to cook for our visitors this weekend, and that's always dangerous."

Carter, who had not done much entertaining at home for the last three years, said, "It can be a problem, can't it."

"What's your method of dieting? I do all kinds of salad without any dressing but vinegar." Cynthia had her last bite of nachos and resolutely moved the plate aside. "You want the rest?"

"I just don't eat," Carter said, answering the first question. She put her glass down. "That's enough for me, too."

Impulsively Cynthia turned to her. "Look, why don't you come with me? We'll stop at the Hunan place, you can have dinner with us, we can go over the fire material one more time, and then you can head for home. Your pets can stand waiting a few hours, can't they? I hate seeing you going off by yourself."

"Why?" Carter was touched and for a second or two she was afraid she might start to cry. Talk about overreacting, she chided herself.

"Because you're all alone in that house most of the time, and Greg wouldn't give a damn if it burned down around you, or half the crazies in the state broke in and wrecked the place." Cynthia saw Carter straighten up, and went on, "I've been in practice long enough to know things like that do happen, and with what we're doing at P.S.S. I've got fire on the brain." She cocked her head. "If you want to take a rain check, that's okay, providing you redeem it before too much time goes by. But if you decide to go home now, call me when you get home, will you?"

"Because I've had about half a drink with you?" Carter inquired politely, to show that she felt insulted.

"Of course not," said Cynthia. "Because this is a Friday and there are all kinds of nuts on the road. Because I want to make sure that you're all right. Because I'm a fussbudget. Okay?"

Carter nodded, feeling relieved and faintly chagrined. "Sure. If you like being den mother."

"It's my nature," said Cynthia gruffly. "And no wise-cracks about that, if you please."

Carter was able to grin for the first time that day.

At nine-thirty, Carter sat down to go over the printout that she had prepared from the first rough statistics. Reading glasses perched on her nose, she sat on the king-size bed, Pyotr and Modeste curled up in a bundle near her feet. With her pencil in hand, she stared at the columns and let her mind drift. At first nothing occurred to her, but gradually she began to get a sense of the questions she would have to ask next. She did not have anything close to enough data to work with, but she decided that there were a few avenues that would not be worth exploring at the moment. Almost all the unexplained fires she had studied had been in institutional buildings—a hospital, a factory, a bank—and that one fact stuck out, as it had from the beginning. Other than their institutionality, Carter wanted to find things that the buildings had in common. Slowly, almost playfully, she began to make lists, starting with the first and most obvious similarity: all of them had security systems.

Sometime after midnight, when the house was chilly and the cats had grown restless, Carter put her pages aside and wandered into the kitchen, vaguely hungry. Nothing she saw appealed to her, and she finally settled for a cup of camomile tea. She sipped at it, prolonging the moment before she would return to the empty bedroom. Her throat ached and her eyes felt scraped and raw. "I must be getting a cold," she muttered, and at the sound of her voice in the stillness, she started to cry.

Winslow's barking woke Carter; she sat up abruptly, her thoughts jangled. She had the vague impression that she had been dreaming or that someone had been speaking to her, but this faded at the dog's insistent clamor.

"All right, fella," she called, reaching for her worn terry-cloth robe as she got out of bed. She glanced at the clock as she tied the belt and was appalled to see that it was nearing eleven. "No wonder," she said, trying to account for her long and heavy sleep. "I'm coming, Winslow!"

The Chow was scratching at the back door, showing more animation than usual. His black tongue lolled over his teeth and he whined as Carter let him in.

She had given him his breakfast and was about to turn on the shower when the phone rang. She heard it with dread, and hurried to answer it.

"This is Scott checking in," said the voice on the other end. "Are you okay? You sound out of breath."

"I was outside," she lied. "What is it?"

"Just following Jeremiah Douglas' orders, that's all. Do you have anything you want to tell me, or am I off the hook for today?"

"You're off the hook so far as I'm concerned," said Carter. "But you'd better talk with J.D. first."

"I'm saving him for last. These days, I don't like to push my luck with him." Scott hesitated. "Did you come up with anything that could help?"

"I've got a few early guesses. Nothing concrete, but I think there are a few things we can eliminate, and that could speed up our investigations."

"God, Carter, I don't know how you do it. You take all the crap Patterson dishes out and chug along as if there's nothing wrong with what he demands. Taking up a whole weekend, just like that, no question about convenience." There was an aggrieved sound to his voice now, and he was clearly about to launch into a tirade. "He's too hard to work for, that's what I think."

"No one's insisting that you *do* work for him," said Carter softly. "If you have so much trouble, you might consider changing jobs."

"And you think that Patterson would give me a recommendation? Not on your life. He likes his little fiefdom the way it is and he won't let anyone leave it, that's for damn sure. He likes his serfs in place."

"Scott," Carter told him in a sharper tone, "you

shouldn't be saying these things to me. I wish you wouldn't."

"Why? Corporate loyalty and all that bullshit? What's the risk for you? You've got a safe job, a doctorate and a husband. What have you got to lose if Jeremiah Dermott kicks you out?" He paused and then said, "You can tell him everything I said, if you want to get a few more points with him. Not that women have trouble doing that."

"That's enough, Scott." It was all she could do to continue her work with her own life in turmoil; she did not need to listen to Scott's complaints as well.

"'That's enough, Scott,'" he mocked. "Very good. Patterson will be proud of you." Without warning, he hung up.

Carter stared at the receiver, her hand beginning to shake. "Good-bye, Scott," she said to the air. She thought fleetingly of calling Cynthia, and then changed her mind, remembering that her friend had weekend guests. Finally she went and took her shower and did her best to return her attention to the figures and notes she had worked on the night before.

About seven-thirty, when it was starting to grow dark and the redwoods cast their tall shadows across the deck, Carter put aside the adventure novel she had been reading —not that she had paid any attention to the predicament of the hero—and went into the house. She fed her pets and turned on the TV. The sounds it made were comforting, better than music or the radio in making her think she was not entirely alone.

She was making an omelette when something caught her attention. She hardly dared leave her eggs and cheese to burn, but the random mention of fire brought her up short. She hurried to the living room and hoped she would catch the end of the news bulletin. All she heard were a few words, indicating that authorities in Las Vegas were investigating.

"Las Vegas," said Carter to herself. "Las Vegas." While she went to salvage her supper, she wondered if she ought to call J.D. and ask him to get her information about the fire, and decided that might be misinterpreted. But the notion that this new fire might be connected to the others would not leave her, and finally, when she had washed her few dishes and set them to dry, she phoned Phylis Dunlap.

"Goodness, I didn't expect to hear from you, Carter," said J.D.'s secretary when Carter identified herself.

"How's it going with you?" Carter asked, hoping to make the call sound less urgent.

"Well enough," said Phylis. "We've got a mare with a problem, but that's Carol's worry. These Arab-Saddlebred crosses can be hellishly delicate. But you're not calling to find out about the horses, are you?"

"No, that's not why I called, though I hope the mare's all right."

"She will be. The vet's on his way, and Carol's out there with one of the stablehands. What's the matter?" Phylis managed to maintain an attitude of good humor in the face of almost any crisis, and this was one of the many reasons she had been J.D.'s secretary for as long as she had.

"I heard on the news that there was another fire, this one in Las Vegas. Do you think that there's any way I can get information on it, if it turns out that it's like the others?"

"I don't see why not, unless the authorities there put a lid of one kind or another on it. Why?" Phylis asked.

"Because I don't want to create more alarm than we're already feeling. I don't know how to broach this with J.D.: Murchison and Coglin are bad enough, but I keep thinking that there's much more to it, and if this latest fire fits the profiles, it could give more needed information as well as adding to the pressure. It might mean things are worse than we think, but I don't want to cry wolf."

"Unless it's justified, of course," appended Phylis. "Yes, I understand your caution, but I think that perhaps you need not be so reluctant to follow up on your hunches, at least not right now. Jerry has always said that you're the only one who doesn't overreact when the pressure is on."

"That's very kind of him," said Carter, more touched by this unexpected vote of confidence than she was willing to admit even to herself. Was her life so barren, she asked herself, that a minor compliment seemed terribly important?

"Nonsense," said Phylis. "It's nothing more than good sense. So, in answer I'd say there's no reason not to check with him and request as much information as can be had. You could tell him what you've developed so far, if you don't think it's too early." There was a commotion on her end of the line. "Excuse me a sec, Carter."

Carter waited, hearing a garble of conversation, then she heard a door slam. "Phyl?"

"I've got to go lend a hand," said Phylis to her. "The mare kicked the stablehand and Carol needs someone to take up the slack, as she puts it. I'll talk to you on Monday. In the meantime, call Jerry and don't worry." Without a word more, she hung up.

"Okay," Carter said to the receiver. "I'll call... Jerry." Never in the world could she bring herself to call J.D. Patterson Jerry. As she dialed his number, she caught herself rehearsing her opening remarks, trying to find the most diplomatic way to phrase her questions to him.

"Pattersons," said the young voice answering the phone.

"Uh..." Carter responded, unprepared. "This is Carter Milne. I'd like to speak to Mister Patterson?"

"Just a sec." There was a muffling sound, and then, "Hey, Dad! It's your statistician!" This was followed by a clatter as the girl set the phone down.

A short while later, Carter heard it moved again, and then the familiar growl. "Hello, Carter."

"Yes, J.D.," she said, now almost completely flustered.

"Don't mind Cheryl—she's right at the age when everyone over twenty-five makes her impatient," her father said proudly. "What can I do for you? Do you have any more suppositions you want to try out on me?"

"Not exactly," Carter ventured. "I have a request, though."

"Oh? What is it?"

"There was another fire; I heard about it on the news. It took place in Las Vegas, and it sounds like it might be like the fires we're investigating. I was wondering if it would be possible to get the basic information on the fire. I know that it isn't one of our cases and that it—"

"If it has a bearing on the fires we're investigating, it's one of our cases whether we did the security for the building or not," J.D. cut in. "It sounds as if you're staying on top of the whole thing. I'll make a call this evening and see what we can get to you before Monday. You'll be home tomorrow?"

"I might go down to the beach for a while in the afternoon, but other than that . . ." She let the words die.

"All right, I'll do what I can to get the figures to you in the morning. Does the office have the access codes to your computer at home?"

"I think so. I'll call and give them, if you like." She was glad that she had insisted on the modem when she and Greg had purchased their computer.

"That would be good of you. Talk to Jack; I'll put him in charge of handling this for you. Is there anything else?" He was abrupt without being brusque.

"I don't think so, not yet. We'll see when we have the meeting on Monday morning," she said, wanting to apologize for the lack of answers.

"Great. You're doing a fine job." He paused long enough to let her add something, and when she did not, he said, "I appreciate your call, Carter. I'll talk to you tomorrow and look forward to hearing your report on Monday."

"Thanks. Yes, thank you, J.D." She took a deep breath. "Well, good-bye."

"Till Monday," he said as he hung up.

Carter ran his few words of praise through her thoughts.

J.D. had actually approved of what she was doing. Part of her mind, the older, more experienced and sophisticated part, chided her for being worse than a little girl, lapping up Daddy's casual flattery as if it were sustenance in a wasteland. "Pull yourself together, lady," she said in her sternest manner. "You've got work to do, and there are lives at stake. It doesn't matter what your boss says if you can't deliver the goods. Got that?"

Self-chastened, she called Jack at the office and gave him the access code for her fire files, and reminded him of her telephone number, in case he did not have it handy. That done, she fought down the urge to go out for some ice cream, and instead took Winslow on an extra-long walk.

Fog snuggled against the bluffs and hid the beaches. Only a few adventurous windsurfers and skin divers were venturing into the chill waters of Monterey Bay. Carter could barely make out their shapes in the gathering mists, but she could hear the surge and splash of the ocean. Winslow kept her company, sometimes loping beside her, occasionally running off to investigate promising scents and people.

"Winslow," she called out to him when he had been gone longer than usual.

A soft bark answered her, and shortly afterward, he came at her out of the fog, a large garland of seaweed clamped in his jaws and trailing after him.

Carter got this prize away from him with a little effort, and then resumed her walk along the beach, lost in thought. Her running shoes were soaked and cold from the occasional kiss of the spent waves. That morning, she had learned of a fire in Dearborn, Michigan, that had taken out most of a warehouse storing imported glassware. From the first reports, she assumed that this was yet another unexplained fire, and one that fit the information curve she was trying to establish. The warehouse was a total loss.

Winslow came bounding up to Carter with another trophy: a piece of a tire.

"Good dog," Carter said absently as she took this from her pet and flung it away, watching the Chow disappear into the fog as he chased joyously after the treasure.

Coglin Optics, Murchison Hospital, the bank in Santa Fe, the Las Vegas thing, and now Steiner Imports: they had their fires in common, but what was the rest of it? Commercial and business implications, certainly. Carter could see why terrorists might want to do away with a bank, and possibly a hospital, but an optical factory and importing firm? She knew that she had to look deeper, and perhaps from a different perspective. "I'm overlooking something," she said to herself, in the hope that hearing the words aloud, she might shake herself into a more receptive frame of mind.

Winslow emerged out of the enveloping whiteness with his piece of a tire in his jaws, carrying his head up the better to show off. Carter took it from him and threw it again, watching as Winslow leaped after it.

It was chilly, and Carter began to feel the cold turning her face stiff and making her huddle more deeply in the Irish fisherman's sweater she had pulled on over her shirt. She would have to end her walk soon and return to the warmth and solitude of her house. In a way she was disappointed to have gleaned so little from the information she had assembled, and in spite of her patterns of the past, this time the walk at the water's edge had not shaken loose an intuition for her to pursue. Reluctantly she turned back and watched for the narrow trail to the parking area.

Black tongue lolling, Winslow padded after her, his piece of tire abandoned for the time being.

Greg's TransAm was in the driveway when Carter got back to the house, and she found herself regarding it as an intruder, another reminder of the problems that surrounded her. She did her best to fix a welcoming smile on her face before she went inside.

There were flowers and a bottle of champagne on the

dining room table, and Greg caroled out a greeting as Carter came through the door. "Hey, Peanut, guess what?"

"You won," she said, wishing that she could imbue her voice with enthusiasm.

"Thirty-three thousand, eight hundred seventy-three dollars and twenty-one cents, to be precise." He strolled in from their bedroom in a new and obviously expensive robe. "My best to date."

"Congratulations," said Carter, dread settling in her chest like a lump of ice.

"Not bad for two days' work," he boasted. "I've got two perfect filet mignons in the kitchen. Or is that filets mignon? And the fixings for a salad. Where've you been?"

"At the beach," said Carter, indicating her shoes, which squished with every step she took.

"Have a good time?" he asked without waiting to hear her reply. "I tell you, honey, I was hot. I couldn't do anything wrong. Another couple weekends like this one and I can retire."

"Oh?" Carter was careful to keep all feeling out of her tone.

"It was something else, Reno was. You should've been there. Every card was perfect. I tell you, there were people making bets on my bets because they knew I couldn't lose. I wish I had another day to spare. Maybe next month." He went into the kitchen and began opening cupboard doors. "Where do you keep the wineglasses?"

"Second shelf over the sink," she said as she finally managed to untie her soaked shoelaces. "I have to get out of these clothes and I need a bath."

"Champagne first. Then you can have a bath while I make dinner for a change. How's that?"

"Fine," she said, holding her shoes in one hand and going through the kitchen to the laundry behind it.

Greg caught her around the waist as she passed behind him. "Hey," he said, turning her toward him. "Don't I get a kiss?"

Carter felt their mouths touch with almost no emotion, and tried to bring some passion to their embrace. She was subtly ashamed that she could not respond to Greg as she had done before, when they were younger.

If Greg noticed her lack of response, he gave no sign of it. "Get out of those things," he whispered. "There're wet."

"And I'm half frozen," added Carter.

"If you can wait a while for dinner, I can warm you up," he suggested.

"Umm," said Carter. "Let me put these in the wash, okay?"

"So long as you don't put anything else on." He nuzzled her neck and slid one hand down her back and over her buttock. "Better hurry up."

"I will." As she opened the door to the laundry, she paused, her mind still on the fires and figures that had haunted her for the last three days. It was strange, she thought, that she could not awaken even the most perfunctory desire for Greg. Whenever he won, she recalled, he had been eager to make love, to celebrate his victory with her body. When he lost, he was sullen and withdrawn. Perhaps it was the pattern, she decided, that had taken so much of the joy from their intimacy, and turned it into something else.

"Hey, I'm waiting for you, Peanut," he called out.

Guiltily, Carter peeled off her clothes, stuffing all of them into the washing machine. Naked, she was colder than before, and she felt gooseflesh rise on her skin. She did not like the feeling. "I'm coming, Greg," she said, going back into the kitchen.

"Not bad for the brink of middle-age," approved Greg as he stared at her. "You've lost a few pounds; I like that. It looks good not on you."

"Thanks," she whispered, stifling her anger.

"Let me look at you," he ordered, holding her off from him so that he could inspect her with a lascivious eye. "Not bad—not bad at all."

"But damned cold," she said, hoping he would take the hint.

He did not. "I want to open the champagne now. I want

to lick champagne off your nipples." It was clear that his words excited him and he quickly bolted for the dining room to grab the champagne bottle. "Wait a sec," he told her as he struggled with the cork.

"Greg—" she began.

"Almost got it," he said, cutting her off. The cork popped and foam welled out the top of the bottle. Greg whooped and reached for one of the wineglasses he had set out.

"I'm *freezing*, Greg," she protested, but not very loudly.

"Almost ready," he said as he filled the two glasses and took the champagne bottle by the neck. "Come on. Let's go to bed."

With more relief than she expected, Carter nodded. "Good idea," she said with feeling, anticipating the warmth.

As he led the way through the house, Greg went on, "I want you to lie on top of the bedspread, just lie there and let me do all the work. You'll like that, won't you?" He grinned back at her. "All you have to do is lie there. That's all."

This choreographing was something new that had come into their lives little more than six months ago, and at first it had been a pleasant diversion in a foundering marriage. Carter soon saw that Greg was fascinated with setting his ideas in motion, in the scenario and its enactment, and at first she found it amusing; now it was starting to repel her. Yet she tagged along after him, as much out of habit as hope that there would be any change.

"Go lie down, face up," Greg said breathlessly as he held out a half-filled glass to her.

"Greg, can't we just—"

"Go on," he said sharply. "Lie down. I'm going to get undressed." He had set the champagne and his glass aside and was busy trying to get out of his clothes. "Face up. Just lie there," he reminded her.

Sighing, Carter did as she was told. She wished she could get under the covers, but that would only make things worse.

Greg tossed his clothes aside and pulled his robe out of the closet as he came toward her.

"Hey, Greg, I'm cold, too," Carter said in what she hoped was a provocative tone. Sometimes that worked with Greg.

"I'll warm you up in a little while," he promised her as he picked up his glass of champagne. He dipped his finger in the fizzy wine and then pinched her nipple, watching the bright drops slide down her breast. "Turns you on, doesn't it?"

"Damn it, Greg, it's *cold*," she hissed.

He paid no attention to her as he prepared to anoint her other breast. He smiled as the wine ran over skin and traced its progress with one finger. "Feels great," he said dreamily.

"It feels like ice," Carter said bluntly. "Greg, please—"

"Give it a chance; it'll turn you on," he said, tipping his glass and grinning as the champagne dribbled along the arch of her ribs.

"Greg, stop." She moved back. "I'm cold and if I don't get under the covers, all I'll do is shiver."

"Shit!" Greg burst out, pushing away from her. "You're turning into a first-class ball-breaking bitch, you know that, Carter?" He threw what was left of the wine at her. "Satisfied?"

"Greg, don't—" she began, but he cut her off.

"Turning up nice now, the real prick-tease, right?" He strode the length of the room, his face darkened with anger. "I want to do something nice for us, something out of the ordinary, and you ruin it. Makes you feel good? Is that it? You like to spoil things between us? If you don't want to fuck, just say so." His words were hurled at her like rocks, and most of them struck home.

"I didn't mean I didn't want . . . to have sex with you. I only wanted to get warm and to . . ." She could not go on faced with his scorn.

"What?" he asked when the silence had dragged out.

"So get under the covers and get warm: who's stopping you?"

Obediently she reached behind and dragged one edge of the comforter around her shoulders. She wanted to cry, but would not let the tears come for fear of the contempt Greg would show for them.

"When do you think you might condescend to let me touch you? Carter?" He rounded on her. "And what makes you think I'd want to?"

She shook her head, trying to put her thoughts elsewhere. "I hoped we could—"

"Don't give me that. It's bullshit and you know it." He came and picked up the champagne bottle by the neck and swung it suggestively toward her. "I'm going to finish this myself, since you aren't willing to celebrate with me. Go on, get warm. I'll come to bed later." With that he stormed out the bedroom door and noisily went to the living room.

A little while later while Carter was blotting her tears with the edge of the pillowcase, Winslow came in, whining softly, and curled up on the bed—which was strictly against the rules—by her feet.

Listening to the news on the car radio the next morning, Carter learned that there had been a large and unexplained fire in Toronto: three blocks of warehouses destroyed, and the losses well into the millions of dollars. Two of the warehouses had belonged to U.S. companies, and the Canadians were handling the matter with a great deal of caution.

Listening to this, Carter gratefully turned her attention from the breakfast-table discussion she had had with Greg, who was full of plans to quit his job in Silicone Valley in order to gamble full-time. It was easier to think about these appalling fires than worry about the shambles of her marriage.

When she arrived at work, she found a note on her desk; J.D. Patterson wanted to see her at once.

September 9, near Tacoma, Washington

Jack Middleton watched the figures on the screen, studying them intently. "Tulsa, Tulsa, Tulsa," he said softly, waiting for the records from the offices there to appear. He had promised the Otterlys that he would have a choice of listings for them by noon, and it was after eleven now.

"Hey, Jack," called one of his associates at the next desk. "Are you handling that four-bedroom with detached garage, or is Hilda?"

"Hilda's got it," Jack said curtly. He had to make this sale; his commissions for the last two months had been low, and with Sandra's mother living with them now, he needed every penny he could earn. Making that sale for Tulsa and the listing in Tacoma would help a lot.

"What range of price are we talking about for that Tulsa deal?" the senior manager asked Jack as he came out of his office.

"They're pretty well off. He brings in about sixty-five thousand a year and she has a partnership in a catering business," Jack answered, grudging his superior so much information about his own clients.

"There's a listing for a three-bedroom on last week's sheet. It hasn't been picked up yet." Chuck Andrews, the senior manager, gave his very best friendly smile, the sort of smile that had sold hundreds of houses over the years. "Why not check it out? If it looks like it fits the bill, then get ahold of Tulsa and get the information on it."

"Thanks, Chuck," said Jack, who knew he ought to have thought of it himself.

"Any time," Chuck said, and went back into his office.

Jack inhaled deeply in order to keep from being angry. For some reason, the sympathy he received was more irritating than a reproach. He hit the codes for last week's listings and then for the Oklahoma listings. He ran the material through as quickly as he could, needing to be busy.

Finally he saw something promising—not the one that Chuck Andrews had mentioned, he saw with satisfaction—and started the process to get the current status of the house and the asking price.

Somewhere in the sequence of numbers there was a short in the system, or so the fire department guessed later on, and in the next instant, the office was caught in a firestorm that gutted most of the south end of the mall.

September 12, Miami, Florida

Dale Albermay was pleased as could be with the changes in his factory. It wasn't simply because he was gadget-happy—although he was—but he felt that he had taken a very important step in automating the more hazardous processes of his plastics business. He was convinced that his workers would benefit and he would be able not only to show off the waldos as the state of the art in remote assembly, but also to show how the human workers were being protected.

"Smithers is on the phone," said his secretary, breaking into his mood of self-congratulation.

"What does he want?" Albermay asked, knowing full well that the man was determined to spoil his day. With a sigh he picked up the phone. "Yes, Smithers?"

"We want to know if you're really going through with it," said Smithers in the sullen tone that had become habitual.

"You know the answer to that. Is it really necessary for us to pick at the scabs again?"

"Scabs is right," Smithers declared, and Albermay

winced at the opportunity he had provided the other man. "That's all that you've got left, Albermay, and all you'll ever get unless you're willing to arrange compensation for those workers you're putting out of business with your damned toys."

"They are not toys," Albermay insisted, knowing that Smithers would ignore this.

"Waldos, then. They're nothing but electric trains for grown-ups." Smithers jeered.

Since Dale Albermay's wife had said much the same thing, he reacted with more heat than he might have done. "You reactionary imbecile! You ox-headed nincompoop!" He knew worse things to call a man but even now, at age fifty-two, he could not break away from the soft-spoken tyranny of his childhood.

"Mister Albermay," Smithers began, sounding huffy.

"You listen to me, Smithers. Your men were offered retraining, and they refused. They were provided generous severance pay, and I've had the office here doing what they can to find jobs for all those who want our help. If you want to blame the machines, go ahead, but if I hadn't brought them in, we'd have all gone down the tubes, thanks to foreign competition." His face was flushed now and his collar felt unusually tight. "Do you understand what I'm telling you, Smithers?"

Smithers replied with equal indignation. "Fine. You get us jobs, and in two years at the most the new job goes pffft, and then what? Everyone in management has an obligation to see that we're not turned out to pasture on a pittance so that you can play with your robots. That's what this country is all about."

"Oh, patriotism, very good, Mister Smithers," said Dale Albermay with enormous sarcasm. "And next it will be God and apple pie I guess. It won't change the fact that industry is feeling the competition and if we don't go with the future, we'll be gone with the dinosaurs. So you might as well learn to build and repair waldos, because they need as much care and maintenance as any other machine around—more than many. And you will remember that one of the options I've given my laid-off workers is the opportunity to study waldos and their maintenance. It's a pity you decided to refuse this offer. We wouldn't be having this unnecessary discussion and we would not be wasting each other's time." He wanted to slam the receiver down, but it was risking too much.

"You wait and see, Mister Albermay; you might have to change that tune of yours." With a soft and unpleasant laugh, Smithers hung up.

Dale Albermay was infuriated. Not only had the little twerp had the gall to phone him, but he had made it worse by getting the last word. It turned his day of triumph very sour, and that, as much as anything, ate at Albermay as he went to inspect the rest of his plant.

At the second inspection station, he stopped to talk to the operator of the waldos, hoping that an affirmation of progress would soothe him.

"Going fine, Mister Albermay," said the operator, immaculate in his pale-green dust-and-lint-resistant suit. Against the pastel shade, his black features stood out sharply. "You want to give it a try? I'll show you how."

"Well..." Albermay demurred.

"Have a seat and I'll show you how to do it." He moved aside for his boss and stood over him, indicating the various sequences of orders that operated the spot-welding waldo.

"It's marvelous, isn't it?" Albermay said, his good mood beginning to return.

"It's a good machine," said the operator. He had a guarded respect for the thing, but thought it looked like a giant spider. He hated spiders.

"What else can it do—anything?" Albermay inquired after a short time.

"Well, there are a few alternate commands. One of them is for aligning the parts if they're not right, and one of them is for changing the timing on the weld. I haven't had to use either of them yet." He punched in some numbers. "Let's say that the top section of the frame was out of trim by, oh, point five one-hundredths of an inch. First we correct that, and then put it in the right place, like this, and then we add these increments, so that the whole frame is in the right position. The computer works out what the right sequence is, and it shows up there, on the LED display."

"Splendid." Albermay beamed.

"And if what we want to do is adjust the length of time on the weld, then we do it this way..." He began punching another series of numbers. "And the computer will say what the results will be"—he indicated the LED again—"and we add that, so that when those tolerances are reached, the machine will know to stop." He was repeating what the instructor had told him; he had never actually used either of those commands. "And then, we go back to the original commands like—"

He was stopped by a popping sound and a sudden unexplained wind.

"What was—" Albermay cried in dismay just before the fire gouted around him.

September 13, Bozeman, Montana

Lorna Deerhurst read through the letter accompanying the transcript and sighed. A transfer student from New York who needed to know if there was provision for handicapped students—in this case an amputee—at Montana State University. Lorna clicked her tongue and tried to decide what was best to do.

"Lorna," called Molly Bolt from her adjoining office, "how many late registrations do you have?"

"About two dozen yet," Lorna answered, still trying to make up her mind about this new application. "How about you?"

"More than that," Molly answered, sounding discouraged. "Would you mind taking over a few for me? I want to get out of here before five this afternoon; I have to get Dori to band practice."

"Oh," Lorna said with a shrug, "sure, why not? Listen, do you have any idea where Flanders, New York, is?"

"I don't know," Molly answered after giving it a little consideration. "Maybe Long Island, but I'm not sure."

Lorna tapped the letter one more time. "I guess I'd better call. Do I put the admission file number before or after the phone number?"

"After, so that we've got it with the billing. You know what they can be like in the accounting office if we screw up." Molly could roll her eyes heavenward with just the sound of her voice. "Who wants to come here from Flanders, anyway?"

"Some guy with a handicap. I think I'd better check out the problem before sending him the rest of his material, don't you? If he's got more than one limb missing, we'll probably have to make special provisions in the dorms." Lorna pursed her lips. "Flanders is area code five-one-six."

"Yeah, that goes first," Molly said, already losing interest.

Lorna picked up the telephone and punched in the ten-number sequence, then waited for the signal to add the seven numbers of the admission file. As always, she tried to find a melody in the progression of beeps from the receiver, and was still puzzling it out when the first snout of flame poked out of the telephone. "What on earth—?" she marveled, not believing what she saw.

Then there was a sound like a muted explosion as the office filled with fire, devouring Lorna Deerhurst's and Molly Bolt's offices before the sprinkler system could spring to life, and by that time, the pipes carrying the water were starting to melt from the heat.

PART II

September 16, near Oxon Hill, Virginia

Norman Haley squirmed in his heavy fire-resistant suit and gave an apologetic look to Frank Vickery. "We're trying to find what caused the fire; you know that."

"Don't worry about it," Frank responded as he stared down at the ash around his feet. "You're not the only one." This was his fifth investigation in as many days, and he was beyond exhaustion. He rubbed his face, remembered the gloves on his hands, and stopped at once, leaving a smear on his jaw.

"We've had half the staff out here. We're getting a lot of community pressure. We're about half government employees here, and when something like this happens"—he cocked his head at the rubble around him—"we get paranoia."

"Not without reason," Frank allowed. "There are four men on the task force who are convinced that the fires are the work of terrorists, urban guerillas." He still remembered the last meeting he had attended the day before yesterday, when he and Perry Bennington had ended up yelling at each other.

"That's what the Mayor told me yesterday. Why else would a repository burn to the ground? The security here was pretty tight, and they had every protection known in the business. Still, according to the official records, they only kept Customs records here, most of it on tape." Norman looked around once more, helplessness in his stance. "What next?"

"Not another fire," Frank said to himself. He rarely prayed, and when he did, he had the uncomfortable feeling that there was nothing and no one listening but himself, and so it had ceased to comfort him; since his wife's death the sense of isolation had grown stronger.

"We sure hope not," Norman said. "There's quite a rash of them going on, isn't there?" He began to pick his way out of the destruction. "Looks like a bomb site, doesn't it? I remember the snapshots my dad brought back from Europe in 'forty-five. Most of it was just like this."

"I know what you mean," Frank agreed. "I've seen some of those pictures, too."

Sodden ash slid around their boots; the air was acrid with the aftermath of burning.

"Has your arson squad started work out here yet?"

"As soon as it was cool enough to move. There's a two-man team from your Task Force, too. But you can see as well as I can, Frank, and if this is arson, it's the fuckingest case of it I've ever come across. As far as anyone can tell, this place went up on its own for no reason. Spontaneous combustion." His laughter was bitter and tinny in the protective clothing and mask. "There's no such thing, they tell us, or it's so rare that it hardly counts. Then this turns up in my backyard, in a government building of all places." They had reached the crumbling outer wall, and Norman said, "Watch yourself," to Frank as they went gingerly past it.

Frank let the Fire Marshal precede him, thinking as he did that Norman Haley was being unfairly treated. He had taken the brunt of public outcry since the fire struck. "How many of the locals think that this is arson or terrorism?"

"Most of them. They're scared, and what they see on the news isn't helping." Norman indicated his car, parked some distance away. "Enough?" He had already started walking.

"For the moment; I'll have to come back later, but no need to stick around." He could tell that Norman was anxious to be away from the place and he could hardly blame him. "If this is arson, I'd love to know how they're doing it, and why."

"Careful; you might find out," Norman said, trying to make light of it and failing. "Get out of that suit and I'll put it in the trunk."

Frank was glad to comply. He unfastened the mask and took a deep breath, then ran his large, big-jointed hands through his graying brown hair. He unzipped the suit and peeled it off expertly, untangling his rangy limbs from the slick fabric with practiced ease. Last were the boots and they came off quickly. He tossed the whole outfit into the open trunk. "I always think of a snake shedding its skin when I get out of those things."

"Can't stand snakes," said Norman, panting a little; he was a much squarer, heavier man than Frank, and he wrestled with the suit as he got out of it.

"Do you have any idea what's going on?" Frank asked, cocking his head toward the charred skeleton of the building.

"Well, it's a local legend that the Customs people store confiscated drugs here, but they wouldn't burn it down for that, they'd break in. So it's arson, I guess. What else can it be?" Norman asked miserably as he lugged his 260-plus pounds into the driver's seat.

"I don't know," Frank admitted. "I can't figure it out."

"Too bad." Norman started the car with an irate twist of the key, and the ignition ground a protest.

As they backed out of the parking lot—now forlorn and unused because of the destruction—Norman indicated the barriers. "They're being strict about this. The cops are helping out. Just as well. No one takes a fireman that seriously when they can't see a fire."

Frank had heard this complaint before, and he could not argue. He kept silent, as they drove away through the curve of the hills. It was too early for fall color, but there was a hint in the air that the seasons had shifted. In three weeks, or four at the most, thought Frank, the hills would be aflame—he flinched at the word—with red and golden leaves. He was sorry he would miss it.

"There's some FBI types waiting to talk with you," Norman said when they had gone a little way. "Call came in this morning. They're following the investigation."

"McPherson and Bethune." Frank sighed. "They're on this case. Someone in the department is convinced that this is a conspiracy and wants to make sure they don't miss it." He folded his arms, his hazel eyes flat with resignation.

"They're the ones," said Norman as he swung off the main road onto a cross street lined with small shops and restaurants done in a modified Federal style. He pulled up in front of a small office building and stopped the car. "What are you going to tell them?"

"As much as I know," said Frank, "which is nothing. No trace of arson, no trace of bombs, no trace of sabotage. As far as we can tell, the only thing going on there when the fire started was that some of the catalog of records was being revised, and suddenly, spontaneous combustion." He stared out the window of the car, not seeing the people in the street or the facade of the buildings. "It's the same thing as Baltimore and Philadelphia and Santa Fe, from what we can tell, and they're as—" He stopped abruptly, opening the door and getting out of the car.

Norman did the same, not bothering to lock the door after he slammed it. He lumbered into the building, Frank following in his wake.

Unlike most government offices, the walls here were neither beige nor green; the hall was Wedgewood blue, and in Norman Haley's office, light-colored corkboard served as decoration and a place for tacking memos, letters, pictures and receipts. Norman's desk was flanked by filing cabinets, and it was something of a feat for Norman to get his bulk between them. Once seated, he waved Frank to one of the two visitors chairs.

"Where are Bethune and McPherson?" Frank asked as he chose the chair nearest the window.

"They'll be here shortly," Norman promised sadly. "What a pair."

"They're supposed to be like that," said Frank. He held the case with his protective clothing in it on his lap, feeling very much like a job applicant waiting for an interview. "I don't have anything more to tell them now than I had two days ago; I've got a hell of a lot more questions to ask."

"Any theories?" Norman asked hopefully. "Anything I could give the Mayor to get the heat off?"

"Not really," Frank said, his voice distant. He hated not being able to find the reasons, and these fires were by far the most puzzling he had ever encountered.

"Is that all?" Norman asked with obvious annoyance. "Not really is the best you can come up with?"

"I'm sorry," Frank said. "I'm not going to try to explain something I haven't figured out yet. I don't want to be stampeded." The warning was clear, but Norman chose to ignore it.

"You mean you want your ass covered at all times, Frank. Look, this isn't like the shopping mall two years ago, this is something much worse, and I have to have something to say to the Mayor, or this whole town's going to be in deep shit." He put the slab of his hands on the table and leaned forward to make his point.

It took Frank a few deep breaths to control his temper enough to respond. "This town isn't the only place, and that's what the trouble is," he said. "These fires are cropping up all over, for no reason. No one has taken credit for them, at least not that's believable. We've had one group say that they're doing it with death rays, but that's about it. The other claims are not sensible and they don't check out. That's what makes them so fucking—"

Norman swung his chair to the side. "That's not good

enough, Frank, and you know it. I need something better than that."

"It's the best I can do," Frank insisted. "McPherson and Bethune don't like it any better than you do, and I don't blame them." He fingered the cuff of his tweed jacket; it was a nervous habit he had acquired only recently and so he still noticed when he caught himself doing it.

"There's another person in this, too," Norman said with a wagging of his massive head. "An insurance adjuster. One of those pinstripe-suit women."

"Great," said Frank with no enthusiasm.

"They're looking for a way not to pay off," Norman added.

"Naturally," Frank agreed. "Is there any way to get a cup of coffee around here?" He thought about asking for some of the bourbon that he knew Norman kept in a flask in his filing cabinet, but thought better of it; it would take a clear head to deal with McPherson and Bethune. And the insurance adjuster, he appended in his thoughts.

"I can give you something stronger than coffee," Norman suggested, as if reading his mind.

"Not this time; thanks anyway," Frank said.

"Patty, bring us two cups of coffee and a couple of those bear claws, okay?" Norman bellowed into his intercom.

"Right away," his secretary said with a hint of exasperation.

"Good broad, Patty, but not soft-tempered," Norman remarked. "What are you going to say in your report? Have you made up your mind about that yet?"

"How can I?" Frank asked, staring out the window once more.

"Don't you have to say something?" Norman pressed.

"Anything I say would be inconclusive. That's what makes this so difficult." He turned as the door opened and Patty brought in a tray.

"Great," Norman said to her. "Just put it here on the desk and we'll take care of the rest."

"Your meeting is in twenty minutes," Patty reminded

him with the same tone of voice she would use with her six-year-old son when giving him his galoshes.

"We'll be ready," Norman said and waved her out of his office. "Cream and sugar?"

"Black," Frank said, taking the nearer mug before Norman could add anything to it.

"Have the bear claw," Norman recommended, pushing the paper plate toward him.

"No, thanks," said Frank, sipping his coffee.

Norman shrugged and bit into his own pastry. "It's good," he said, the words muffled by the food. "What's with the FBI? Think they'll have anything I could tell the Mayor?"

"Probably," said Frank with resignation. "But it won't mean much of anything."

"That bad?" Norman joked.

"Yes" was Frank's bleak answer.

Aside from the difference in age, Simon McPherson and Myron Bethune were virtually interchangeable. Both were slightly over six feet tall, with athletic frames and bland expressions. Both wore glasses, although McPherson's were more fashionable. At thirty-one, McPherson was a bit more impatient than the forty-two-year-old Bethune.

"Good to see you again, Vickery," said McPherson holding out his hand to Frank. His smile, showing perfect teeth, went no farther than his mouth.

Frank took the agent's hand. "Hello, McPherson. Hello, Bethune." Next to these well-groomed and efficient men he felt disheveled and grubby.

Myron Bethune brought out a small tape recorder and set it conspicuously on the conference table. "I don't suppose you'd mind having this meeting on tape?"

"Of course not," said Frank, far more cordially than he would have liked. He wanted to tell them to leave him alone to do his job, but the words stuck back of his tongue.

As Bethune sat down, he said, "We've been talking to Burt Williamson."

"How's he coming with the fire in Buffalo?" Frank

asked as affably as he could. Burt Williamson was also on the Task Force and was being run as ragged as Frank was.

"So far so good," said McPherson. "It looks like a pretty straightforward case of arson now." He had a smug, I-told-you-so expression, and he could not resist adding, "You wait until the full reports are in—you'll see this is more of the same. They're clever, but we'll find out how they do it."

"And how many more fires will we have?" Frank wanted to know. "I'd like to be as confident as you are, but how?"

"It's arson," said Bethune with conviction. "It's very well-executed and they're going to great pains to make sure that we can't detect it easily, but you can be sure that they will make a mistake, and then we'll have them."

Norman Haley, who had hung back in the doorway, suddenly and incongruously intimidated by the soft-spoken men from the FBI, now came into the room and sat down. "It isn't like any arson I ever saw."

"There are many kinds of arson," said McPherson. "With the kind of fire load that repository had, it might take a little longer to locate its point of inception, but in time we'll manage it."

Frank turned toward Norman. "I don't think you'll find it no matter how you look." He saw Norman sit straighter as he went on. "Whatever the method for starting the fires, it leaves no detectable trace, or none that we've been able to determine and identify. You either have to accept that there is a way for starting a fire at a distance that leaves no trace whatsoever, or you have to consider that there might be a pattern here that we don't understand that is the result of an agency we don't understand."

"UFOs, perhaps?" sneered Bethune.

"It's as good an explanation as any," Frank said seriously. "Do you have a better one?"

McPherson rolled his eyes toward the ceiling. "Mister Vickery, you're not being much help. You may not realize this, but the President is very concerned, and many of the members of Congress are getting pressure from their constituencies. That in turn brings pressure on the Bureau, and we are putting it on you, and will continue to put it on you, until we know what the cause of these fires is and have put a stop to them. Is that clear?"

"Very," said Frank.

"And you!" Bethune said, shifting his baleful gaze to Norman. "Chief Haley, we expect you to treat this whole miserable business with diplomacy. No newsmen, no TV, no grandstanding of any kind. That arson inspector in Bozeman made an ass of himself; we'd hate to see you make the same mistake."

"You don't need to worry," Norman said, avoiding looking at Frank. "Anything I can do to help you and the Bureau, you let me know and it's as good as done."

"We appreciate your cooperation, Chief Haley," said Bethune in a very pointed way.

"Well, you men at the Bureau, you're the ones we're all relying on to put an end to this." Norman looked from Bethune to McPherson, his uncertainty increasing as he tried to appeal to the two men. "I already told the men checking for arson to keep anything they find under their hats until you give the word."

Frank folded his arms and stared hard at the tabletop.

McPherson lowered his voice. "We are classifying eight fires so far as part of this rash of sabotage. And that is what we believe it is—sabotage. We are up against a clever and ruthless enemy."

Norman nodded several times.

"We need to keep the rest of this interview confidential, Chief Haley," Bethune went on, "and for that reason, we'll be happy to have one of our drivers take you back to your office. We appreciate your help and your discretion."

"Otherwise known as a kiss-off," Frank muttered.

"Mister Vickery has reason to feel dissatisfied," said McPherson smoothly. "He hasn't been able to accomplish much and it weighs on him; as you might expect."

"Frank and I talked about it a little," said Norman as he got to his feet. "I'm grateful for your help, gentlemen, and

I want to tell you that I'll do all that I can to help out. All you have to do is let me know. It's a privilege to—"

"That's good to know," said Bethune, cutting short the effusion.

As Norman left the room, he called back to Frank, "I'll talk to you later Frank, okay?"

"Sure," said Frank as the door closed.

"He'll do as we tell him," McPherson warned Frank as soon as they were alone.

"I know that," Frank agreed. "And so will the others. All you have to do is come up with a theory to fit the facts and you can call the case closed, and never mind that there are more fires. You will both have your arses covered, and that's what this is all about, isn't it?"

"You're out of line, Vickery," warned Bethune.

"Out of line?" Frank repeated. "This isn't a matter of close-order drill or politics, this is about fires, about human beings burned to death for no apparent reason, and the destruction of property. Where's the politics in that?" He knew that his anger played into their hands, but he was tired enough that it no longer seemed important.

"There are politics," said McPherson with certainty. "If you look in the right place, there will be politics."

Frank held himself in check. "In the meantime, the fires go on. And that's my job."

"Not that you're doing it," said McPherson. "You don't have anything more to tell us than you did after Baltimore."

"There isn't anything more to tell, except that there have been more fires." Frank hesitated. "You think that I'm holding something back, don't you? You think I've found some kind of ace in the hole and that I want to save it for a more advantageous occasion. For Chrissake! there are people getting killed! What kind of ghoul do you think I am?"

"We don't think you're a ghoul," said Myron Bethune smoothly. "We are a bit concerned that you're in over your head. You've been working very hard—"

"With good reason," Simon McPherson went on, this

sudden change of tactics making him appear almost like a different person.

"Oh yes," seconded Bethune. "You've done more than your share, and that might be the problem. You may need some time off. Take a weekend with your family, unwind."

Frank gave Bethune a hard stare. "My wife died three years ago and her sister in Toronto is taking care of my daughter. If you'd taken the time to review your files, you'd know that."

McPherson coughed. "Uh . . . that wasn't quite what we meant. You could visit your daughter. That would give you the time off you need and—"

"Look," Frank said. "Let's all cut the shit, okay? I am not going to leave this case simply because I embarrass you. Is that plain?"

"Under the circumstances—"

"If I am ordered off the investigation, that's another matter, but until I am, I'll do the best job I know how to do for as long as I have to do it. Is that clear enough for both of you? Faking answers will not stop the fires. And that is what I want to do—stop these damned fires."

Bethune and McPherson exchanged glances and then Bethune spoke. "You've made yourself clear, Vickery. And at the first opportunity, we will get you off this Task Force, or we'll move you sideways. Do you understand that?"

"Certainly," said Frank with relief. "What's next on the agenda?"

"This flippancy—" McPherson said and stopped himself.

"It isn't flippancy," said Frank more seriously. "I have trouble worrying about your little dance when I think about the fires. You're trivial; the investigation is deadly serious. What's next on the agenda?"

McPherson made a sound like a snort, then answered the question. "A Ms. Lois Hillyer is waiting to talk to us. She's an insurance adjuster, and she had a few questions to ask you."

"Is she coming to us, or are we going to her?"

"She's waiting in the outer office," said Bethune. "She's already spoken to Chief Haley."

So that was the pinstripe-suit woman Norman had referred to, thought Frank. "Let's get it over with."

"And tomorrow," Bethune went on, "you are scheduled to spend two hours with Howard Li." Since this young statistician was known to be as irascible as he was brilliant, few of the investigators on the case looked forward to their appointments with him.

"Maybe he'll have turned something up," said Frank. "Why don't we go and find out what this Ms. Hillyer wants?"

McPherson pressed the intercom and in an irritated tone asked that Lois Hillyer be sent in.

She was younger than Frank had expected, certainly no more than thirty, a very polished young woman in a double-breasted pinstripe charcoal-gray suit and deep-red high-necked silk blouse. Her hair was short, straight and glistening, and she carried a leather attaché case. She paused in the door as if sensing the atmosphere in the room, then walked in.

"Good afternoon, gentlemen," she said, holding out her hand to Simon McPherson, who was nearest to her. "I'm Lois Hillyer."

"Simon McPherson," he said, studying her with an appraising eye. "This is Myron Bethune and Frank Vickery."

She acknowledged the others and made her way to a chair near the head of the table. There she opened her attaché case and took out three files as she sat down. "My company has told me that you are the ones investigating the burning of the apartment house in Baltimore on August nineteenth. There are two other fires you have under investigation that our company would like to be kept abreast of as you work."

"So far as we know," said Frank, "that August nineteenth fire was the first of the series you mention."

"We're checking out every suspicious fire," added McPherson, taking the seat next-but-one to her. "It's part of the assignment."

"What our company needs to know is whether or not the fires are the result of arson or accident. Obviously we do not wish to make any settlements if there is culpable arson involved. As long as your investigation is in progress, we need not make payment. Of course, if there is reason to assume that the building was burned for other reasons, such as negligence in maintenance, that would also be a factor in our settlements." She turned to McPherson. "I'd appreciate any information you're at liberty to pass on to me."

McPherson smiled at her. "Certainly we're trying to find the cause of the fires, but so far, we have no firm recommendations on procedure."

"Then, technically, it's still a mystery?" asked Lois Hillyer, a bit of color mounting in her cheeks.

"For a little while yet," McPherson conceded.

"And why is the FBI taking an interest in this fire?" she asked. "There are a number of fires you're investigating, aren't there?"

"Yes. We've concluded that two of them are arson and have advised the appropriate authorities of our conclusions." He indicated Myron Bethune. "We're only part of the team, but—"

"I've already talked with your supervisor," Lois said firmly. "He was very cooperative."

"I hope we'll be that, too," said McPherson, managing to put greater meaning into the words than they warranted.

Lois blinked twice, but this was the only sign that she was flustered by the attention Simon McPherson was giving her. "There has been loss of life in the fires our company is concerned about," she went on, addressing herself to McPherson more than the others.

"Yes," he said slowly. "There are forty-nine confirmed dead in the Baltimore fire alone. The Murchison Hospital fire, well, you must have read the papers."

She shuddered and it was not for effect. "Over three hundred, I heard."

"Three hundred eighty-six, with another two hundred injured or harmed," said Frank with very little emotion.

"Ms. Hillyer, if you think that your company is entitled to withhold funds for damages, then you have the power to do so. However, I am convinced that these fires are not caused by those you have insured, and some kind of settlement is advisable."

Lois looked at him with alarm mixed with respect. "How many of these fires have you investigated?"

"Seven so far. There are another four on my list." He paused. "I was a fireman at first, and then I became a Fire Marshal, and now I'm on the Task Force. I've been on the Task Force for three years. You can check that if you like." This last was an indirect challenge to the two FBI agents.

"No one questions your credentials, Vickery," Bethune said ponderously. "A few of us are uncertain about your methods and motives, but there's no doubt that you have the experience."

"You're the one who was called in on the Baltimore fire, aren't you?" Lois asked.

"Yes. The Fire Marshal put in a call to the Task Force and I was the one who was available."

"Luck of the draw," said McPherson. "We were assigned two days after he was."

"All for an apartment-house fire?" Lois inquired. "That seems odd, if you will allow me to mention it."

"A large fire with no discernible cause is reason enough to call in the Task Force," Frank pointed out. "That's what we're there for. Our labs and our members have the greatest combination of state-of-the-art equipment and experience that exists on the East Coast. We cover eighteen states and the District of Columbia, and are available to other states upon request."

"We're familiar with the Task Force," said Bethune.

"I've never dealt with the Task Force before," Lois Hillyer said primly. "I've heard about them, but most of the cases I've handled for the company weren't as . . . vast as the Baltimore fire, or the others."

"What sort of cases were they?" asked McPherson in a bid to regain Lois's attention.

"Not as . . . complex. Reasonable settlements based on

official determinations. I was promoted last June, and this was the first major... fire I've handled." She stared hard at the files in front or her.

"I'm sorry it had to be this one," said Frank. "It's very unsettling."

"Yes, it is," she said.

"Which is why we're involved," McPherson reminded Lois. "And you can rest assured that we'll get to the bottom of it. These investigations take time and the waiting is difficult. For what it may mean to your company, we've almost ruled out any culpability on the part of the owners. Arson was very likely the cause, but as far as we have been able to determine, it was not... typical."

Bethune looked at her with sympathy. "We are as anxious as you are, believe me, to see this at an end."

For once, they were all in agreement.

At twenty-seven, Howard Li had held his Ph.D. for eight years. He was used to being deferred to, and he took flagrant advantage of this. His office staff—one secretary and two research assistants—were in awe of him, both for his astonishing mind and his acid tongue. He regarded Frank Vickery with undisguised contempt. "And what makes you think that my methods could be useful in these cases?" he asked after the most perfunctory of greetings.

"There's something we're not seeing, and so much is going on that we don't have time enough to stop and evaluate the problem. You got to the bottom of those metal fatigue cases and you determined the source of the toxic waste leakage last year; we hoped you could do something with these fires."

"There was another one last night, wasn't there? Near El Paso. According to what I have here, they lost a goodly section of the courthouse."

"Yes," said Frank, having had no time to study the material he had found waiting for him in his temporary office that morning. "It fits the profile."

"And what is that?" Howard demanded. "Specifically."

"Until now, all buildings have been professional and

commercial structures. They have all had security systems of some sort and the local requirements for fire and smoke detection. All fires have been very hot, have spread unusually quickly, as if a huge, superheated blowtorch had suddenly gone off for no reason." He paused. "Whatever the method for starting the fires, we have not yet been able to trace it."

Howard nodded, pushing his glasses back up his nose. "And you want me to make sense of it for you."

"If you can," said Frank.

"If I can't, then no one can or will," Howard told him in his most matter-of-fact way. "I will need all the information, no matter how trivial, about all the fires, especially where they appear to have originated. I also want full weather reports for the areas and some indication of the nearness of roads as well as air traffic overhead. That is for a start. I also want a complete set of plans for all the buildings, including any and all modifications that have been made since the structures were built. I will have to have records of energy consumption for the last two years at least, and all complaints or similar filings against the building and its owners for each and every structure. All insurance policies, all payment records, everything that can be gathered. And I wish to have it within the next forty-eight hours. If there is anything more I require, you and the Task Force will be informed."

"You'll use your NSA status to obtain the information?" asked Frank, fully aware that he was not empowered to gather these data.

"If necessary," said Howard, surprised by the question.

"All right; I'll see you have everything we've got and I'll do what I can to supply the rest, or as much of it as I can. If you need to contact the FBI, it's Myron Bethune you should talk to." He regarded Howard Li thoughtfully. "There are going to be more fires."

"What makes you so certain?" Howard asked with genuine interest.

"Feeling," he said, shrugging. "Something at the base

of my spine. Not very scientific, but if I didn't have it, I'd be dead by now."

"You're right, it isn't scientific," Howard said. "Yet experience and rapport can do this thing. Most who experience it do so without any judgment or sensitivity, but I will allow that there are those who have more critical faculties where these feelings are concerned. You may be one of them."

"Thanks," said Frank.

"You shouldn't be offended that I am skeptical. No one can always trust these things, and I, for one, would prefer to err on the side of reason. You've suggested that there are sensations you have come to rely on, and I believe that; what those senses are, neither you nor I can tell." He favored Frank with an evaluating look.

Frank couldn't bring himself to like the arrogant young man watching him, but he had to give him respect. "I'll give you all the information I can, and when there are more fires, I'll see you get any additional data as soon as possible. That's the best I can do."

"I expect nothing less," said Howard. "If there are any delays, I will hold you responsible for them, Inspector Vickery, and I will act accordingly. These fires are very serious problems, and if there is any attempt to bias the investigation, I will see that my complaints are heard."

"No doubt," Frank murmured. "Is there anything else?"

"I don't want the FBI interfering, and I will not tolerate being deliberately misled. In order to accomplish my work, I demand unquestioning forthrightness."

"I'll do my best," Frank promised wearily. "It's in my interests to cooperate with you, Doctor Li."

Howard looked amused. "In Chinese the word 'Li' means 'fire'." He had given the word the proper inflection. "A curious synchronicity."

"You mean coincidence," Frank said.

"I mean precisely what I say," Howard corrected him. He held up an admonitory finger. "Keep that in mind while we work together."

"I will," Frank vowed, having heard about Howard's

eruptive temper. "Is there anything else I need to get for you?"

"I will notify you if there is. I have my staff trained to work efficiently and to respond quickly, and you may consider that a request from them is a request from me." He tapped his blunt fingers on the desk. "If you think of anything that might be germane to what we're doing, feel free to include it, along with any notation you believe may assist us."

Frank knew that for Howard Li, this was a generous offer. "I'll be as concerned as you are, in my way," he said, adding the last to placate the temperamental man who was the only true genius he had ever met.

"If each of us does his job, then we can be confident that we will unravel the mystery," Howard proclaimed, for all the world as if he expected to hear this broadcast to the troops or repeated on the evening news. "I have yet to be given a problem that could not be solved. I do not intend to have that happen now with these fires. Whatever the cause and whatever the motive, we will find it."

Frank nodded. "If there's nothing else . . ."

"I will notify you. Thank you for acting so quickly." He looked toward the door leading to his computer room. "I will get to work." With that he rose and left the room.

Frank heard his voice beyond the door calling to someone named Haskell. He picked up his notebook and left the office.

Myron Bethune met Frank Vickery at the airport. "Knoxville, a hotel, apparently started at the reservations desk. All the usual indications." He indicated the open door to the small jet. "We were called in at once this time."

Frank ducked going into the plane and took one of the six passenger seats, thrusting his overnight case under one of the others. "I heard that there were over a hundred dead and another sixty in the hospital."

"First figures. I've already sent the basics over to Howard Li and his people so they can add it to their data."

Frank found himself wishing, as he had many times before, that he could bring himself to like the FBI agent. "Did Howard have anything to say?" he asked as he buckled himself in.

"Nothing so far. He did tell me it was more perplexing than many cases he's seen. For Howard, that's strong language." He disapproved, judging from the tone of his voice.

"He's just got started. I don't think this is something that can be solved overnight."

It was early morning, and the shadows were fresh and long. The jet plunged down the runway and then angled sharply into the sky. It glistened on the eastern wing as it began its turn toward the southwest.

"When did the fire break out?" Frank asked as the plane leveled off.

"Around eleven-thirty last night. It spread very quickly. The reservations clerk was processing a block for members of a church choir; there was some confusion about when they would arrive. The travel agency in Baton Rouge had one person working late on the problem, and he said that the line went dead at eleven twenty-seven." Bethune was reading from his notes. "The first alarm reached the Knoxville Fire Department at eleven-twenty-eight, so this sounds about right."

"How much of the building did they save?" Frank asked, dreading the answer.

"Almost none of it. At least half of the guests were in bed and asleep, so the first order was to get as many of them out as possible, and that hampered some of the fire fighting. I suppose I don't have to tell you about that."

"No," said Frank. "How many alarms did it go to?"

"Four. There was some damage to two nearby buildings, a department store and a theatre." Bethune closed his notebook. "The immediate supposition is that this is arson, but you and I know that this might not be the case. I'm becoming more and more convinced that this is terrorism. It fits the techniques—public and commercial properties, no apparent motive."

"Except that there have been no demands, no sensible

claim of credit, and no one has announced what these fires are supposed to accomplish." Frank turned toward Bethune as far as he could manage it in his seat. "Isn't that more typical of terrorists?"

"Most of the time," Bethune allowed. "But there are exceptions, particularly when the eventual demands are extreme. They want to be sure they've softened us up before they tell us what it will take to get them to stop."

"What about informants?" Frank pursued. "Hasn't anyone heard anything? Don't you think that by now one of the informants would have picked up something? You admitted that no one has any solid information to offer, and I gather that's unusual for something this big."

"Some of those terrorist groups are very, very closed, and they deal harshly with anyone suspected of informing. That's my theory; any informant has been killed. It's not unreasonable to make such an assumption. Anyone who would set the kinds of fires we've seen wouldn't hesitate to kill one of their own." He cleared his throat. "Unless you have a better idea."

"I don't," said Frank. "But I'm not prepared to buy your terrorists, either."

"Well, we'll see what Howard turns up," Bethune said, becoming huffy. "I don't suppose you've had much experience with terrorists."

"Not much, no; there was a bomb factory in Detroit, but I only saw that after it blew up. And there was an investigation of a series of fires set in Corpus Christi, where some Central American revolutionaries were trying to keep certain ships from sailing. That was very basic and very simple, and the bombs they set were obvious and meant to be. That's what puzzles me about these fires—they may have a message that makes sense to someone, but I'm damned if I know what it is."

A dark-tan Dodge was waiting for Bethune and Frank when they arrived in Knoxville, and the driver looked very much like Simon McPherson, except that his hair was blonder. He drove well and said little, answering only those questions that were put to him directly; when Frank asked him about kudzu, he scowled.

By the time they reached the site of the fire, Frank was getting hungry, and he told Bethune that he would need some breakfast before they got down to work.

"Isn't that a little callous?" Bethune asked with a trace of contempt.

"Probably," Frank said, unflustered. "But I won't do a good job hungry, and a case like this needs all the attention I can give it, and then some."

Bethune shook his head, but told the driver to take them to a good restaurant. "We don't want Mr. Vickery to be put off his stride."

"Thanks," Frank said, and made no apology.

The day proved more difficult than either Frank or Bethune had anticipated. The Fire Chief and the Fire Marshal were at loggerheads over the loss of the hotel, and required placating. Once that had been taken care of, there were reports to examine and a second inspection of the gutted hotel to complete before their initial work was over.

When Frank finally got back to his hotel room, it was almost nine o'clock. He sighed as he took out his address book, though he did not need it; he had dialed the number many times.

"Hello?" said the voice on the other end of the line after four rings.

"Anne?" Frank said. "How are you?"

"Frank," responded his sister-in-law. "Good to hear from you. I'll call Melinda."

"Not quite yet, please," Frank forestalled her. "Look, I'm going to have to disappoint her again, and I hate doing it."

"You've had more of those fires." It was not a question. "We've been watching the news."

"Yeah," Frank said with difficulty. "I know I said I'd be there this weekend, but... I can't get away. Not the way things are going."

"Melinda will understand," Anne told him, but there was doubt in her voice.

"No, she won't," Frank said. "And I don't blame her. She has a right to expect her father to visit when he says he will, and when I let her down like this, she's going to be hurt. Hell, I'm hurt that I have to do this, but—"

Anne cut him off. "Where are you?"

"Knoxville. A hotel burned here last night, and we've been called in to check it out."

"Is it like the others, this fire?"

"Apparently. They'll be carrying out tests and examining what's left to find out if there's any clear indication of cause, but if you ask me, I'd say that it was like the others." He hesitated before going on. "I want to talk to Melinda now, if you don't mind."

"Fine. I'll do what I can to help her out, you know that. She realizes that there is something serious happening, and that makes it less hard for her." Anne called out her niece's name, then said to Frank, "You're trying to be a good father, and at least you've had the sense to let Melinda stay with Stan and me; if she were alone and you were gone, it would be harder on her."

"That's what I keep telling myself," Frank said, as much for his own benefit as his sister-in-law's.

"Here she is," said Anne.

"Daddy?" came Melinda's breathless voice.

Frank swallowed hard and forced himself to sound cheerful. "Hi, Pumpkin."

"How are you, Daddy?" There was a guarded sound to the question.

"Busy, honey. There've been more of those fires I told you about on Monday night." God, how he missed her!

"Uh-huh. It's been on TV." There was even more caution now.

"We had another one last night. I'm in Tennessee right now, on the investigation." He wanted to tell her he was sorry, that he never intended to disappoint her in this way. He wanted her to understand that because she mattered so much to him he could not bear to leave her exposed to the risks that were being faced by almost everyone. Instead he said to her, "It's going to take a while, Pumpkin, and that means that I might not be able to visit you this weekend."

"Oh, Daddy," she sighed, a rebuke in the forlorn sound of the words.

"I wish it didn't have to be this way, but the fires are very bad, and you know I have to do my job, don't you?"

"I guess," Melinda said slowly. "You've been very busy, haven't you?"

"There's been a lot of fires, honey, and you know what the Task Force has to do." He cleared his throat. "Melinda, honey, I don't know how long this is going to take, but the first chance I get, I'm going to come and visit you and we can take a vacation together. I wish it could be right now." He knew he was explaining badly, but he could not stop himself. "Melinda?"

"I want to see you, Daddy," she said quietly.

He had to take a deep breath before he trusted himself to answer. "I want to see you, too. I wish there were some way I could take the time and we could spend more time right now, just being a family."

"Isn't there any way?" she pleaded.

He could picture her face so clearly: her hazel eyes framed by long, pale lashes, her light-brown hair a little untidy, the corners of her mouth starting to turn down. "Melinda, I'm going to try to get a day off. It won't be much, but we'll be able to have dinner together, or have a talk."

"They're real bad fires, aren't they, Daddy?"

"Yes, honey, they're real bad. People are getting killed; I want to stop them if I can." What could he tell her that would salve the hurt she was feeling?

"If you have to work to stop them, then you don't have to see me until you do." She sounded the way she had just after her mother went to the hospital, when she had been told that she was too young to visit intensive care.

"Yes, I do," he insisted. "And I'll find a way. But please, honey, don't be too mad at me if I have to stay away for a while. Please."

"I won't be mad, Daddy," she said very softly.

"Even if you are, it's okay. I'm not staying away because I don't love you, but these fires..." His voice trailed off.

"You find out why they're happening, Daddy. You have to do that." She sounded resigned now. "Aunt Anne explained it all to me last week. Uncle Stan tried to show me why the fires were so strange, but I didn't really understand it."

"Neither do I, honey," Frank said gently.

"And Cindy and Louise are real nice. I'll be okay here. You don't have to worry about that."

He could hear the tears in her voice and it tore at him. "Listen, Melinda, I will get up there to see you. I'll call you as soon as I've arranged it. You take care of yourself. I love you, Pumpkin."

"I love you, too, Daddy," she said obediently.

"Let me talk to Anne again, okay?" He felt the tightness in his throat spread to his chest. He wished he could fly to Toronto that night, or get drunk.

"What's the trouble, Frank?" Anne said, cutting through the self-pity that threatened him.

"The usual. Never mind. I'm going to try to get a day off to come visit, but it won't be long, and I probably won't be able to give you much notice."

"Fine," said Anne as if it actually was. "Call us and we'll meet you at the airport."

"You're a good egg, Anne; thanks for everything."

"I'm glad to do it, Frank. You ought to get some rest, by the way—you sound exhausted." This last bit of advice was brusque, but Frank had long since recognized the affection behind it.

"You're right. I'll try." He hated saying good-bye, and so he told her, "I'll see you soon."

"I'm looking forward to it. So is Stan. Take care of yourself, Frank." Then she hung up and the phone had no sound but the hum of the receiver.

* * *

Flames scoured the night sky and the wail of sirens, eerily like shrieking voices, filled the air. Ambulances, fire trucks, police cars, all of them in a tangle, gathered around the twelve-story building in frenzied desperation. In the foreground, an ashen-faced reporter tried to give a coherent account of the rescue efforts.

"The local NBC affiliate let us have this tape," said Bethune to Frank as they watched the screen together. "We've got the CBS and ABC ones as well, if you want to compare them."

"I doubt they'd be significantly different," said Frank. "But keep them on tap. How soon after the fire broke out was this report made?"

"About thirty to forty minutes," Bethune answered after consulting the log the TV station had provided. "They're trained to hustle."

"Thirty to forty minutes," Frank repeated, staring at the screen. "It spread fast."

"And it was hot. There's almost nothing left of the reception-desk area. We've been going over the residue and whatever started it—as usual—left no trace. We don't even know what fueled it." He glowered at the picture in front of him as if it were a personal insult. "We're gonna find out one of these days, and when we do, it's all over for the firebugs."

"We hope," amended Frank.

"Hope, shit!" Bethune jeered. "How many places in the world can you find something that ignites like whatever they're using? A dozen at most, right? It's just a matter of tracing back, and we can stop every one of these conscienceless bastards."

"If we're lucky," Frank said, his eyes still on the screen.

"Excuse me," said one of the secretaries, opening the door, "but you'd better switch on the news. Another fire has broken out. Manhattan."

Bethune turned the TV from VCR to regular transmission. "They're really stepping it up."

"Harlem?" Frank suggested. "Hell's Kitchen?" He had seen slum fires before and the thought sickened him.

"Skyscraper," the secretary said with some difficulty.

"Which one? Do you know?" As Bethune rapped out his questions, the screen filled with a pylon of flame.

"Six-sixty-six Fifth Avenue," said the woman, and then she left the room.

Howling sirens were muffled by the roar of the flames. A reporter, shouting into his microphone in order to be heard at all, said something about the problem of evacuating all the enormous buildings near the conflagration. "Traffic is being diverted and everyone is ordered to stay out of the area. Everyone! Keep away from this fire. If you can leave Manhattan, do so at once. Do not come to look at the fire. Stay at home."

"Most of those buildings have daytime populations the size of small towns," Frank whispered.

A helicopter trying to pick up some people huddled on the roof of a nearby building got too near the fire—the wind generated by the flames enveloped it, making it stagger in the air before it toppled and fell, glancing off the glassy sides of two buildings as it plummeted to the pavement.

"Oh, Christ," Frank muttered.

Then the picture returned to the local newsroom where a young man with a mustache and stricken eyes tried to find something to say.

Bethune turned off the set. "I'll call the airport."

"Perry Bennington will handle it," Frank said, thinking of how much his superior on the Task Force would resent more interference.

"Not on his own, he won't," vowed Bethune.

"And I am telling you," Howard Li said to Myron Bethune, his face darkening with rage, "that until we have sufficient data, we cannot produce the results you are demanding!"

Bethune folded his arms, looked at Simon McPherson

on his right and tried to stare down the man on the other side of the desk. "Seven skyscrapers gutted, two totally destroyed, over four thousand casualties, property loss in the billions, and you tell me that you can't come up with some consistent pattern we can act on?"

"That is precisely what I am telling you. Unlike you, I refuse to give in to scapegoating and panic. You are already making a number of dangerous assumptions, and have decided that they are correct. I am doing my best to keep from making similar mistakes." He picked up a memo, his hands shaking. "You have the audacity to question my capability and my integrity, you cast doubt on my procedures, you attempt to undermine the work my staff and I have been doing, and you now confront me with this... this calumny!" He tore the memo in half and rose to his feet.

"Listen, you bastard," McPherson began, but Howard cut him off.

"You will listen to me for a change," he said in so forceful a tone that both agents fell silent. "You have gone out of your way to make my work difficult, and you have made irresponsible accusations. You are wholly incapable of grasping the magnitude of this problem." He slammed his hands down on the desk for emphasis. "What are you seeking to achieve? Do you want to prolong the problem, compound the disasters? Because what you are doing will achieve precisely that end."

Bethune had taken as much of this as he was willing to endure. "You're out of line, Mister."

"Doctor," Howard corrected him haughtily.

"You high-handed Jap—" Bethune sputtered.

"Chink, if you please," Howard shot back. "And if you want to indulge in racial slurs, do it elsewhere if you want to have my cooperation." He turned to the two men who had remained silent through all this. "Have either of you anything to add to this shoddy display, or am I to be permitted to return to my work."

"Nothing," said Perry Bennington at once.

"Not a thing," added Frank, secretly pleased that Howard Li had taken on both McPherson and Bethune.

"Doctor, these terrorists have to be stopped. If you will not help us do it, then we will have to find someone who will." It was meant to be a threat, but it did not succeed.

"Mister Bethune," Howard said condemningly, "you have already heard my opinion of what you have done. Do you seriously expect me to continue to entertain the notion that this is simple terrorism in the face of growing evidence that it is something worse than that—possibly much worse?" He indicated the door. "I still have work to do, and you are all wasting my time."

"That little fart," McPherson grated as the four men left Howard Li's office. He nodded to himself then turned to Bethune. "What do we do now?"

"We have to go along with him for the time being. Everyone higher up expects a miracle from him, and we might as well give him rope enough to hang himself once and for all," said Bethune levelly.

Perry Bennington tapped Bethune on the shoulder. "I want to talk to you for a minute, please. Frank, Mister McPherson, come with me." He indicated an open conference room at the end of the hall.

"What's on your mind?" McPherson demanded.

Perry stood aside so that the other three could enter the room before he closed the door. "I am still officially in charge of the Task Force investigating fires," he reminded the three men. "We are supposed to be helping each other, not interfering. If you aren't willing to do this, then perhaps the FBI should let the NSA take over entirely, and be content to do the cleanup later on." His remarks were calculated to sting, and they succeeded.

"I've had about all I'm going to take!" McPherson burst out. "First that arrogant Chinese Ph.D., and now this! What are you trying to prove?"

"We all have frayed nerves," Perry went on. "That's to be expected. Given what's been going on, you'd be less than human if you didn't. But you're both getting in the way of the rest of us doing our jobs, and that means that we're going to have to arrange something different than the way we've been doing things."

"You know, Bennington," said McPherson, "there's already talk about replacing you, or putting you under someone in a more . . . responsible position."

"When that happens, I'll be willing to do anything and everything I can to aid the transition. Until that time, I am in charge and I am telling you to stop interfering. Is that plain?" In spite of the even tone, it was clear that his patience was almost exhausted.

"We hear you," said McPherson. "Is that all, or do we have to listen to a lecture from Vickery as well?"

"No lecture," said Frank.

"Then we've got work to do," Bethune announced, getting to his feet and moving toward the door. "There's a special meeting scheduled for three-thirty this afternoon." He said this last as if it were a surprise.

"An emergency," Perry agreed. "Your boss and I both requested it. We're looking forward to what you have to say."

"I'll bet," muttered McPherson as the two agents left.

"You having trouble with them?" Perry asked Frank when the others were gone.

"You could say that. They're wedded to their terrorist conspiracy theory, and they're insisting that we investigate that way." He pinched the bridge of his nose. "Trouble is, I'm not sure they're wrong. I don't make any sense out of this at all."

Perry nodded. "None of the team does. Haegerston and Molichoff aren't getting anywhere; Wood and Linquist aren't getting anywhere; LoMonico hasn't turned up anything; Espinz says he's baffled. The whole Task Force is in the same predicament. They aren't going to want to hear that this afternoon. The President said on television last night that we will put a stop to these fires and punish those responsible for them. When the White House makes promises, we are expected to deliver."

"Great." Frank sighed. "So you're going to give me the party line, is that it?"

"No, I'm not. I want the fires stopped more than I want my job. The Task Force is my baby, but I can't measure that against the damage those fires are doing. What I *am* going to suggest is that we involve the private sector more in our work, and I'll suggest that we farm most of you out to insurance and securities companies, as well as letting the NSA and the FBI have one or two of you to help out. That will spread the pressure around a little more, and give us, I hope, a little more freedom to continue our investigations."

"I see," Frank said, once more thinking that Perry Bennington was a very canny man.

"I'm offering you the chance to stay with the FBI or get farmed out. I have to warn you," he added before Frank could speak, "that I won't have much control in where you go, if you decide to get out of the main arena here. The companies I'm proposing we work with are all over the country. You might find yourself in Denver, for all I know."

"You're thinking about Melinda?" Frank guessed.

"Yes, in part. But I can tell that the strain is taking a toll on you, and that worries me. I don't want to lose a good man at this time. We're under siege, and we have to think about making the most of what we have." Perry stopped, fished a cigarette out of the pack in his pocket, stuck it in his mouth, but did not light it. "How much sleep have you had in the last seventy-two hours?"

"Oh, probably sixteen, seventeen hours," Frank said, a bit guiltily.

"Uh-huh." Perry nodded. "And you're how old?"

"Thirty-seven," Frank growled.

"Just how long are you planning to keep this pace up?" Perry inquired with an amiable smile.

"Okay, okay, point taken," Frank said.

"I hope so," Perry said. "I'm counting on you." He finally lit his cigarette and took a deep drag. "Big fires." He put his lighter away. "Little fires."

"Just one thing," Frank said as an afterthought.

"What?"

"You're forty-seven, forty-eight?"

"Forty-eight," Perry said, guarded now.

"You want to see fifty-five?" He indicated the cigarette and shook his head.

"Get out of here," said Perry. "I'll meet you at three."

"You got it," said Frank.

September 20, Fresno, California

The building was impressive, more like a headstone than a place of business. It was the western regional center for the IRS, and it was busy with processing the flood of quarterly installments.

Elena Montez had been working at her computer terminal for three hours straight, flagging those payments that had reason to be reviewed. She was heartily bored and it occurred to her that she might be coming down with a cold.

"How much longer are you going to be on that batch?" asked her supervisor, a thin, harried man in his forties.

"I don't know, Mister Quarrels. Not more than a hour, I hope."

"Well, I don't want to rush you, Elena, but we are running behind." He held up a fistful of computer printouts. "Dauntry has most of his done."

"Good for Dauntry," said Elena Montez, thinking of the zealous new assistant Gordon Quarrels had acquired only three weeks ago.

"He's an example to us all," announced Quarrels.

"Look, I'm doing the best I can. If you want me to be thorough, you have to give me some time with this, Mister Quarrels. Otherwise I could overlook something important, you know?"

"Of course, of course," Quarrels backpedaled.

"Look, Mister Quarrels," Elena pressed on, "it's Friday; we've all had a difficult week. You said yourself that it is going to be hard work a while longer, and that's okay with me, but I need to do it at my own speed. You said it was fine at my review."

Gordon Quarrels nodded several times. "I don't want to interfere with your work."

"Thanks," Elena said, and waited until he walked away. She couldn't stand being leaned on, and it seemed that was all Quarrels ever did when the quarterlies came in. She turned back to the screen and continued to study the columns of names and figures that moved across it.

Finally something caught her eye, and she stopped the information. Yes, she decided, this was one to be checked. She began to type in the code to pull out the records of Carla Gorsich, who sold marine insurance.

Somewhere in the process, something went dreadfully wrong; almost at once Elena's small office was filled with flames that gouted from her terminal. The last thing she heard was screams, not all of them her own.

By the time the first fire truck careened up to the building, fire was lashing at the broken windows on three floors and smoke was towering into the sky.

September 22, near Homer, Alaska

For months everyone in the neighborhood—which extended to isolated houses for more than five miles in all directions—had been laughing at Jerry Wells's contraption, but now the dish antenna was in place and Jerry was smug. Today he would be able to pick up the football games off the satellite. At least that was how he thought it worked; he was not very good with ideas but was known to be a wizard with machines.

"It looks weird," Sandra said, as she had said every day for four months.

"You won't care when you see what we can get with it," Jerry promised her.

"What about when winter comes? won't that mess with the reception?" It was a question that had faded into ritual.

"It'll be fine," said Jerry, who had no idea whether it would or not, and did not much care.

"Well, I hope you know what you're doing," Sandra said as she watched him working with the controls.

"Honey, you wait; you aren't going to believe what this'll be like." He began to align the dish with the coordinates he had been given by the company that had sold him the antenna. "We'll be able to watch everything with this, just everything."

"I'd rather have a good VCR," Sandra said softly, not wanting to spoil his fun.

More numbers were fed into the system, and Jerry waited to hear the shifting of the antenna. Instead there was a curious popping sound, and then fire erupted over the antenna and through the coding board he had been using.

Sandra, halfway to the tiny kitchen, felt rather than saw the voracious flames. Jerry's right, she thought in the last instant of her life. I don't believe what this is like.

September 23, Bismarck, North Dakota

McKinley Junior High School was all but deserted by 3:45, which was when Scott Polnik and Tyler Bates crept back into Room 242 where Mister Conners taught mathematics and computer science. Without the lights, the room seemed unfamiliar to the two boys, and Tyler hung back.

"Don't be an asshole," scoffed Scott, who had only recently discovered the power of profanity and obscenity. "We can do it."

"But, Scott..." Tyler could find no words to express his worries, and hated to think that he might appear cowardly to his friend. "What do you want me to do?"

"Wait till I get into something. I saw it in a movie. It was *gross*!" His eyes shone with excitement. "We could bust the codes for the Pentagon, maybe." He did not actually think that was possible, but just the sound of it was exciting.

"Do you think—I mean, Mister Conners is gonna be mad if he catches us." It was the one sensible objection that the boy could find that did not make him out to be afraid.

"Mister Conners won't know anything about it. We'll reset the times and everything." He was already pulling up a chair to the nearest monitor. "I was watching how he did it the other day, and I know I can do it, too. Besides, it's fun." He had turned on the machine and he stared avidly at the screen as it came to life.

In spite of himself, Tyler was interested. He came over to stand behind his friend. "What are you doing?"

"Well, first, I gotta get us out of this program and start looking for good stuff. Get me that file of floppies that Mister Conners keeps in his desk."

"But it's locked," Tyler protested.

"So unlock it," came Scott's exasperated reply. "You know how to break into lockers, don't you? This is the same thing."

Reluctantly Tyler did as he was told. "I don't know if this is such a good idea," he said as he handed the plastic container to Scott. "If Mister Conners ever finds out—"

"He won't," said Scott with the absolute confidence of an eighth-grader.

"But if he does—"

"Shut up," Scott cut in. "Let me think." He began to flip through the file and at last drew out one of the disks. "I think this is the one."

Tyler watched as Scott slipped the disk into place. "It's not that I—"

"I'm thinking," Scott interrupted, his fingers playing over the keys. "I want to find out what we can access."

"But what if—"

"Not now!" Scott was becoming excited. "Jeez, will you look at that? I bet I could get the frigging DMV." He had yet to find out what "frigging" meant, but his mother had been shocked the first time he said it, and so he liked to use it every now and then.

"Scott—" Tyler was becoming frightened. If they were caught they would be punished, both by the school and by their parents, and he was afraid that this would be more severe than usual. It was one thing to set fires in trash cans, but something else to break into a schoolroom.

"Hey! I'm getting something. I think it's some kind of code." Excitedly he began to type in numbers, hoping that he would find the right combination.

The school was an old one, made of wood often painted and varnished, and when Room 242 ignited, the rest of the wing flared almost at once. The destruction was so total that it was only the missing-persons reports filed by the grieving parents that led to the eventual and tenuous identification of the few bits of bone as being parts of the two boys.

PART III

September 25, Lansing, Michigan

One fluorescent tube over William Ridour's desk was sputtering, and he cursed it as he typed his story into the computer. Deadline for the first edition was in fifteen minutes and he was anxious to finish.

Galen Murphy, the managing editor, stopped by William's desk and read his screen over his shoulder. "What makes you think that it was the latest in a series of mysterious fires?" he asked in mildly curious tones.

"Because it is, so far as I'm concerned. That fire in Flint was just one in a chain. Go back in the files if you doubt it." William continued to type as he spoke.

"What's mysterious about a fire in a DMV office?" He waited for an answer, and William realized that Galen was fishing.

"There have been more than a dozen fires since mid-August that have been investigated by the Fire Marshals' Task Force that are admitted to have no known cause, including arson. This looks like another one in the series. There was also a hospital in Chicago on Labor Day weekend, and a factory in Texas, as well as that terrible fire in Manhattan."

"The one the President wants investigated," Galen said.

"That's the one."

"How do you know this is more of the same?"

William turned toward the editor. "How do you know it isn't?"

"Has the cause of the Flint fire been determined?" Galen dodged William's question.

"Not yet. For what it's worth, most of the standard indications for arson haven't been established, which makes it like the others." He glanced at his watch. "Almost six. I have to finish this."

"When you're through," said Galen as he stepped back, "come by my desk and tell me some more about this. There might be something worth following up."

William managed not to grin, but it was difficult to keep his pleasure contained. He had been trying all day to find a way to convince someone at the *Lansing Morning Sentinel* that there was a series of features in the fires. "How about an open-ended assignment? Think you could arrange that?"

"Can't and won't," said Galen succinctly. "How about a week?"

"It'll take more than that." He folded his arms and squinted up over the rim of his glasses. "And while I'm gone, you can get someone to fix that damned light."

"Gone?" Galen sounded truly astonished.

"I can use the phone for a lot of basic stuff, but if I want hard information, I'm going to have to go to it. You know that and I know that, which," he went on, taking advantage of the momentum he had built up, "you know and I know will take more than a week to do properly. Let me have five weeks and I can give you something really good."

"Two," Galen offered, as if he had extended himself beyond all reason.

"Four," William demanded, his expression that of a man driven to the greatest limit.

"All right, we'll find a way to get you three, but that is the best I can offer unless you really blow the top off the story in the meantime, and that means something more than giving us what the wire services are carrying. Do you get my point?" He folded his arms and did what everyone in the city room called his Ivan-the-Terrible look.

"I'll have to travel," William said, making it a flat statement rather than a suggestion.

"We'll cover reasonable travel. Listen to the word carefully: reasonable." Galen waited for what might come next.

"What about entertainment? I'm going to have to do some of that if I'm going to get anyone to open up." This was always the most difficult area, and the one where the greatest acrimony arose.

"I'd want to clear it first," Galen said, as William expected he would.

"Not possible. What if I get to someone after a meeting or there's an unexpected opportunity? You can't always anticipate how things are gonna break. Don't tie my hands, Galen. Give me a little breathing room."

This area of conflict was almost a ritual. "You know I can't do that."

"Galen, I'm not asking you to underwrite a holiday in the Swiss Alps, for Chrissake. I just want to know that I can do a bit of courting if it can help me get the story and information I want." He waited. If he were stopped now, that would be the end of it.

"Yeah?" Galen said.

Relieved that he had not been turned down flat, William went on. "I want to get the information no one else has uncovered, and I want to know that you're not going to shoot me down."

"Tell you what: you get ten days of discretionary entertaining funds, and then we'll review." He reached down to pat William on the shoulder. "You could be on to something, and if the little old *Lansing Morning Sentinel* can get the drop on the *Post-Dispatch* or any of the macho *Times*es then I want to do it. I'll make sure that Parke understands." Galen Murphy always talked about Litton

Parke, the *Morning Sentinel*'s owner, as if he were a bit dim mentally and had to be led by the hand.

"Thanks," William said, knowing that he had been given a great opportunity, but knowing also that if he did not succeed in delivering something of significance that he would very likely be out of a job.

"We're counting on you," said Galen, making the point doubly emphatic.

William went back to filing his story, but he was already thinking of how he would break the news to Elinore, who never liked him to be gone for any longer than overnight.

By the time he had come back from dinner, William Ridour had a number of notes jotted to himself. He was determined to get a quick start on his assignment, to prove to Galen that he was not going to waste any time or energy on this project; Galen was known for his conviction that everyone had to be serious and capable to gain his support and approval. He handled one minor story for the late edition, and then left, making sure that he thanked Galen on the way out.

Elinore had that look about her when William got home. Her face was more lined, her eyes more sunken than usual, and she greeted him with more feeling than she usually showed when he came in the door.

"What's the matter?" William asked after he hugged her.

"They've cut our funding again."

"How much?" He sent with her toward the living room, his concern for her also extending to the school where she worked.

"Almost twenty percent, and we were just eking out what we had." She sat down beside him, her face averted, her close-clipped Afro emphasizing her boyishness. "The trouble is, most of the kids in the school are pretty hopeless, or they wouldn't be there. The brightest kid we've got has an IQ of seventy-eight, and the thinking seems to be that since they aren't going to get much beyond what they are now, why throw the money down a rathole?"

"Elinore!" William stared at her in shock.

"I am quoting the secretary of one of our foundations—that's where the cut is coming."

"Didn't Powers talk to them?" William watched her nod as she wiped her face where the tears were. "And?"

"They've made their minds up, and nothing can be done, at least that's what they told Georgia. It isn't a question of mostly black teachers, either, which is what Bobby Sampson thinks, it's just that they see the kids as pretty much a waste of time and money."

"You mean because they are— what's the phrase?"

"Learning impaired," Elinore supplied with distaste. "Most of these kids have to work like hell just to be good enough to get by. Most of them will never do more than menial work, they won't be able to compete in the marketplace, and that foundation has decided that they want to back winners. I don't blame them, but we need the money so badly, and those kids need it more than anyone if they're going to be able to be anything more than a drain on everyone. If they become apathetic, then we're probably lost anyway." She leaned against him and let herself weep.

"Let me talk to someone at the paper, to see if there's anything we can do." He did not hold out much hope, but could not tell his wife that.

"We're waiting to hear what the education budget will let us have, too. The state is feeling the pinch as well as everyone else, and we're not the highest priority in the area." She made no excuse for her distress as she might have done three years ago. She had decided that she could trust William not to trivialize her hurt and frustration, something that had never happened to her before in a relationship.

"Still . . ." William said, wishing he had a way to comfort her and reassure her.

"In this time of self-sufficiency, you'd think they could see that self-sufficient retarded adults are as much a part of the scheme as anything." She slammed her fist into the sofa. "William."

"It's a rotten thing they're doing, honey. And I don't

know how you hold up under the pressure, but you sure as hell do, and you amaze me." He kissed her forehead. "I'm sure that if anyone can find a way to get this mess straightened out, you and Georgia can."

"Glad you think so." She sniffed ruefully. "Now all we have to do is convince the rest of the world."

"You'll manage." He hoped she would, but he saw enough of bureaucratic indifference that he was not convinced.

"If you were the one we had to deal with, it would be a cinch," she said, then she reached over and touched his face. "You really do look a lot like Dumas Pere." It was a special memory for both of them, and her way of thanking him.

"The next trick is to write like him." He kissed her. "Want to go out to dinner tonight?"

"A consolation prize?" she asked wistfully.

"That, and something to celebrate," he said, hoping she would not be angry with him for leaving on a story when she was under so much stress.

"William! What's happened?" She clearly welcomed the diversion of his good news, and she wrapped her arms around his neck.

"I'll tell you over fettuccine and prawns," he promised her. He smiled, thinking again how much he loved her face, her skin, the marvelous darkness of her, the shape of her head like an Ethiopian goddess. He was always astonished that she had chosen him, for it seemed to William that she was too beautiful to be happy with anyone less than a man as extraordinary as she.

"You and your Italian food," she said, laughing but resigned. "Let me wash my face. My eyes feel puffy."

"You look wonderful, but go ahead and wash your face if you want to." His eyes followed her as she walked down the hall.

"It sounds like a real opportunity," Elinore said as she held up a spoon of dark-chocolate gelato.

"It is," William said, relieved that she was not too disappointed.

"And those fires are the hottest thing since AIDS," she said, puzzled when Willian gave a comic wince. "What is it?"

"Didn't you hear yourself?" he asked, and repeated what she had said.

"Well, I didn't mean it quite that way," she admitted when they both stopped laughing. "I'm just a little . . . well, you know . . . sad that you'll be gone for so long. You know I like it better when you're home. But that doesn't mean much."

"It means a lot," he said with feeling. "And unless I believed, really believed that this story could make a big difference in my career, you know I wouldn't do it. But I can't turn down a chance to work on something big, something that might be able to make a difference."

"I know that," she said, though there was an undertone of regret in her voice she made no effort to disguise. "You'll do a good job, and Galen Murphy will have to admit it. I'm glad you're doing something that doesn't have to do with blacks either directly or indirectly, or with community relations." She ate more of the gelato.

"Galen's only got two black reporters," William said, not quite defending his boss.

"And Jim is on sports, big deal," Elinore said, dismissing the other man. "You're doing the right thing, and I'm sorry if I sound like a wet blanket. I'm tired, I've had a bad day, and I sometimes think about my stepfather and the way he'd string my mother along with promises about the next big thing he was going to do. It never quite came off, but it always took every bit of money we'd saved."

"If you'd rather I—" William said with an effort.

"I'd rather you go out there and turn the assignment into a Pulitzer Prize," she interrupted him. "But I just wish you could come home at night, too."

"Me, too," William said, relaxing at last. "And I will try to get someone at the paper to cover your funding crisis. You're doing a major community service at the very least, and it's being endangered. I'll suggest Potter, but there's no saying Galen will put him on it."

"Potter'd be nice," said Elinore. "We need a firebrand."

"Potter qualifies," William said, relieved that the touchy moments were over at last.

As the waiter brought the bill, William reached over and took Elinore's hand. "You're one fine lady."

"Takes a real gentleman to know that," she responded, lowering her eyes and looking at him through her thick lashes.

"Outrageous, too," he added as he helped her on with her coat.

"Good God, I hope so," she said.

They were half an hour away from the local evening news, and Brad Gordon was pacing nervously, reading over the stories that were to go on as leads while keeping an uneasy eye on the wire-service displays, as if expecting a story to break that would toss all his carefully laid plans into the wastebasket. He did this every night and so far, the evening news had gone off without a hitch for the four years he had produced it.

Nina Foss, fresh from makeup and looking as if she had spent the day shopping instead of in a lightplane, came over to Brad, smiling at him with the dazzling ease that had kept her popular even though she was over thirty.

"I saw your film. It'll be fine. That fire took out most of the hillside, by the looks of it," Brad told her.

"Give Ray most of the credit; he filmed it." She made a point of giving credit where it was due—it assured her the continuing goodwill of the men she worked with.

"Your commentary tied it all together, though," Brad said, although he was clearly distracted.

"Thanks." She smiled again, her considerable charm in full operation. "Brad, about the fire. It could be tied in to those other fires that have been popping up all over the place. I think it might be worth doing more about them; I think we could be on to something."

"Which fires?" Brad demanded, as if he thought the building was starting to smoke.

"Like the ones in Michigan and that terrible fire in Manhattan. I think that this was like the others—the Fire Marshal has already said that they have not been able to determine the cause—"

"Hell, give them time. They'll find out." Brad looked around almost frantically. "It's twenty-one minutes to air."

"Let's talk about it later, okay? When you've had time to think about it. I've got a file on the fires and it's on your desk."

"Hey, we're local news. We leave all that big stuff to network." Brad often used this as an escape from things that he disliked; he disliked fires very much.

"Maybe we could nudge them," said Nina, who was determined to give it a shot first. "Let's have a drink after the show."

"Yeah. Fine." Brad might have promised her his oldest child at this point. He swiveled around, trying to find Patrick Fenton. The anchorman rarely walked through the door until they were ten minutes away from starting, largely because Brad's antics made him nervous.

Nina took her place at the news desk and chatted with the camera crew as they made their adjustments. She exchanged jokes with the sound man. All the while, she was thinking about the fires and trying to find the key to convincing Brad to let her do a series on the fires. At thirty-one—well, thirty-two for almost a month now—she knew her days were numbered unless she could get one or two big credits to her name that would more than compensate for the laugh lines and crow's-feet that were beginning to change her face.

"Hi, Snookins," said Patrick Fenton, sliding into the chair beside Nina. "Ready to lay it on 'em?"

"Sounds good," said Nina, hating Pat for being forty-six and admired for his maturity.

Their weatherman, a lanky kid from Taos by way of Washington, D.C., ambled on and clipped his mike to his sports coat. He coughed once, gave a general wave, and then stared vacantly toward the monitor.

"Heard you had quite a plane ride today," Pat said to Nina. "Riding over a fire is pretty dangerous."

"Is it?" Nina would have flown over the fire in a box kite if it had been necessary for the story.

"Weren't you frightened?" Pat inquired as if he were interviewing the survivor of a disaster.

"A little," Nina admitted, concealing the wrenching fear that had gripped her the whole time the lightplane had bounced and skidded through the smoky sky.

"Intrepid girl reporter, is that it?" Pat teased, then gave his attention to the Teleprompter.

Nina adjusted her smile for the third time.

They had been given a table near the front of the restaurant, where diners could see them, which irritated Nina more than she wanted to admit. Her smile stayed firmly in place, and she made sure she appeared animated and interesting while she talked with Brad Gordon, who squirmed whenever he noticed that they were being observed.

"The way I see it," Nina said when she had succeeded in wangling the conversation around to the fires, "is that there has to be some kind of cover-up going on. That fire in New York can't have been an accident, can it? and the others are just the same. Damn it, I want to find out what's going on, what's behind it. For all we know," she went on, aware that Brad was a great believer in conspiracies, "it's the government that's behind this and they're trying out something on us before they use it on the Russians or the Chinese or the Arabs, or whoever they're after these days."

"You can't be certain of that," Brad said, but a keenness of eye denied this.

"No, I can't," Nina said promptly. "But it might be right. And," she launched into her pitch with all the skill she could muster, her face shining with sincerity, "there are private security companies, and there are insurance companies, all of which must be feeling the effects of this change in the statistics. You know what this could do to underwriting, if it turns out that the fires really have a cause other than the 'Act of God' kind. There are bound to be lawsuits and the courts will be tied up for . . . decades."

"Decades?" Brad interrupted.

"Years, anyway. Someone is going to have to pay for the damage, and no matter who it turns out to be, it's going to make an impact on everyone, if in nothing more than higher insurance rates."

Brad pursed his lips. "And what does this have to do with the story you have in mind?"

"Well, if we can't get any solid information out of the government—and it's pretty clear that we can't—then I propose to go to the security companies and the insurance carriers and find out just how much they know and what they're planning to do about the mess we're all in." She braced her elbows on the table, flanking the shrimp cocktail.

"And?" Brad said, clearly considering the possibilities of her venture. "What do you want to get out of it?"

"Well, I'd like to find out what the scope of this thing really is, and if it is terrorism, the way some officials are saying, of whatever kind. If it's not, then I think we have an obligation to the public to find out what the cause of the fires is, for their protection and for our own." She did her best earnest-girl-reporter smile for him and waited impatiently for him to respond. "Brad?"

He had plunged his fork into his dinner salad. "I'm thinking," he said after a moment. "Eat something, for God's sake."

Obediently, Nina attacked her shrimp, not tasting it. She finally had to ask, "Well?"

"It could be an angle," Brad allowed. "You're right in saying that we haven't got enough information, and it's our job to go after it. You do realize," he went on in a more avuncular way, "that we could get the door slammed in our faces if we guess wrong on this?"

When Brad said "we," it meant that he was thinking about the proposition. Nina concealed a relieved sigh and said, "It could happen, but until it does, I think it would be good for us and good for the country to go after the story. The Manhattan fire alone should be enough for a major investigation, and from what I can tell, there have been more than a dozen such. I checked with the National Fire Data Center in Washington."

"Let me sleep on it," Brad said as the waiter removed their first course. "It sounds good, but I want to be certain before we tie up time and money."

Nina took a sip of her Sauvignon Blanc and did her best to appear calm. "I want to get to work on this as fast as possible. I know I'm not the only reporter who sees the possibilities in these fires."

"I'll give you my answer in the morning," said Brad at his most methodical. "And in the meantime, can we talk about something else? You've made your point already, and I don't need you to trot out all your reasons for wanting to do the story, okay?" He winked at her, which Nina thought only made it worse.

William Ridour took a taxi from National Airport to the Sheraton Hotel. Although he did not want to admit it, he was worried that he might have taken on more than he could handle.

By three that afternoon, he had an appointment with the FBI to find out more about their investigations, and had already spoken to three analysts at the National Fire Data Center. So far, he was unable to find the thread he wanted that would tie all his stories together. As he finished a late lunch, he decided that he would have to be more cautious than he had planned at first.

Honoria Pearson was the receptionist who did her best to impress William with his surroundings when he walked into the office of Myron Bethune.

"Special Agent Bethune is on a very tight schedule," she said as if she were addressing a sixth-grade class. "I have to ask that you keep within the time limits of your interview."

"I will," William assured her. "Do you know if Special Agent Bethune will permit me to use a tape recorder?"

"You will have to ask him," she said, peering over the top of her glasses in her most intimidating way.

"Is there a general policy?" William was determined to be polite to Special Agent Bethune's door dragon, and he refused to be put off by her manner.

"It is in the best interests of all concerned to keep the most accurate records for the sake of proper and responsible dissemination of information." She ended this with a disapproving sniff, making it clear that this was not the way she would handle it at all.

"Then I'd guess he wouldn't mind a tape recorder." William sat back and waited for ten minutes, using the time to thumb through his notes once more.

"I'm pleased to meet you," Myron Bethune said as he caught sight of William. "Mister Rider, isn't it?"

"Ridour," William corrected diffidently. "Thank you for taking the time to see me."

As Bethune ushered William into his office, he signaled to Miss Pearson that he would want to be interrupted in seven minutes. As he closed the door, he directed William to the straight-backed chair facing his desk. "I'm glad to know that you're taking a responsible attitude about this dreadful situation. Not everyone is as conscientious as you are. We of the Bureau want you to know we appreciate this."

William was on guard at once, and as he began to probe Special Agent Bethune, he decided that his apprehension was well-founded: no new information was forthcoming.

"Do you, or does the Bureau believe that this epidemic of fires is in any way associated with international terrorism?" William asked, trying to keep the disappointment from his voice.

"Well, *we* certainly haven't ruled it out. There has been too much damage for us to ignore that possibility." He leaned back in his chair. "I think that when we separate the nuts from the crazies, we'll find that there is a well-organized action behind the fires."

William had caught the emphasis on "we" and was curious to know who disagreed with the Bureau, but he postponed that question. "The nuts from the crazies?" he inquired.

"As you can imagine events of this sort generate all kinds of mail and phone calls. There are those who claim that this is a judgment of one kind or another across the whole religious and political spectrum. Most of them can be dismissed as lunatic ravings or well-meaning cranks, but there are a few who have a more serious aspect, and those are the ones where we concentrate our activities for the time being." He folded his hands, a subtle gesture of denial to William.

"How do you differentiate them?" William asked, permitting himself to be sidetracked.

"Most of the crazies are obvious. The UFOs are doing it, the Martians are doing it, the devil is doing it, ghosts are doing it, spirits are doing it, astrology is doing it, geomancy is doing it. And all the rest of those ologies and isms that spout nonsense. The rest, well, that's another matter. Some are generally angry—the ones that say God is mad at the blacks or the women or the gays or the military-industrial complex, or the Arabs, or anyone else they don't like. There's the flip side of that: the blacks or the gays or the women or the Arabs are getting the devil to do it. We rank those with the crazies, too. Then we have things like those who claim that this is a secret weapon that they have learned about through various means. We might check one of those out just in case. We leave the more extreme alone and concentrate on what might be viable. Then we get to the groups that think this is a good idea and either want to promote it or take credit for it." Myron Bethune cleared his throat. "I can't tell you too much more. Ongoing investigations. You understand."

William thought that probably meant that the FBI had not the least clue about the actual cause of the fires. "May I check with your office while I'm on the story, in case you may have an update for me?"

"Certainly, but we're not going to show favoritism. Our

work will be available to all the news media when it is complete." He glanced at his watch. "Is there anything else?"

Ordinarily, William might have tried to find out more about any disagreements that concerned the fires, but this time he knew he would not do well to push his luck. He stood up and extended his hand to Bethune, who took it reluctantly. "Thank you. You've been very helpful. I hope that you're able to solve the case soon." But not, he added to himself, before I can get my stories in print.

"The Bureau is always eager to help responsible journalists," Bethune said stiffly. "It was good of you to take the time to come here first."

Again William sensed disagreement and rivalry, which pricked his curiosity, but he kept that to himself. "Good afternoon, Mister Bethune," he said as he went to the door.

An inferno filled the television screen, and in front of it, backed by fire trucks, ambulances and helicopters, Nina Foss addressed the nation. "This most recent in a chain of fires that have created near-panic in the nation has damage estimates upwards of twenty million dollars. The condominium complex had been open for less than a year and had only a sixty-percent occupancy. Even then, there are nineteen known dead and more than fifty missing. What the final toll of this latest catastrophe will be can only be grimly estimated at this time. This is Nina Foss in Phoenix, Arizona."

Nina sat at her little glass-topped coffee table watching herself on national news. She grinned as she saw her name under her image. Perhaps she was finally getting the break she had been waiting for.

The phone rang less than five seconds after the national anchorman replaced her on the screen, and she answered as calmly as she could. "This is Nina Foss."

"It sure as hell is," said her ex-husband. "You did a terrific job, Babe. I want you to know I'm proud of you."

Nina had expected Brad or Pat Fenton, not Aaron Fitzsimmons. "Thank you," she said coolly.

"Yeah, Martha and I were just saying that you're doing a better job of carrying the ball on this fire thing than anyone else. It's great." He sounded genuinely enthusiastic, and for an instant, Nina could almost forgive him for leaving her in favor of his latest protégée.

"How nice of you and Martha." She wished she had nerve enough to hang up on him.

"Really, Nina. We mean it. You're a hell of a reporter, and we just wanted you to know we're really pulling for you." There was a slight hesitation. "You going to do any more on the fires?"

"As long as they keep happening. I'm doing a series of features about the whole problem." She could not resist feeling smug as she told him this, wishing she could see Martha's face when she learned of it.

"Good for you. That's the way to keep on top. And you can do it, Nina, if anyone can."

Mercifully, Nina's other line rang and she was able to say, "I'm sorry, Aaron; I have to take another call."

"Great. More of your fans, I hope." With that he hung up, and Nina had to pause for three deep breaths before she picked up her other line. "This is Nina Foss," she said with all the authority she could muster.

"That was quite a job you did, Nina." Brad sounded as close to enthusiastic as he ever did. "A little sensationalistic, but not out of line. We're proud of you at the station."

"Thanks," she said, trying to sound modest and almost succeeding.

"I think you're right to keep at this thing. And that security and insurance approach looks like a good one. The impact on the public in general, never mind the direct victims, is going to be important and it's part of our job to cover it." Brad often sounded stuffy when he wanted most to be encouraging.

"I think so, too, Brad; that's why I brought it up." Nina wanted to ask him how much time he was willing to devote to her coverage, but this was not the time to do it. "I'll give you a list of companies I want to talk with tomorrow morning. I think it will keep us tuned in."

"Sounds good," Brad assured her as her first line rang again. "You'll want to take that. I'll let you go. Just wanted you to know that I'm very pleased with your work." Without waiting for her to say anything, he hung up, leaving Nina to take the next call.

"Hi," said Pat Fenton with a slight edge to his voice. "I bet you're in the catbird seat."

"Almost," Nina admitted, and grinned at her anchorman's forced compliments.

"Why didn't you talk to that woman?" Myron Bethune demanded of Simon McPherson the next morning when the two met for conference with six other men.

"How was I supposed to know she'd get national coverage? How do you expect me to control the press and the media, anyway?" McPherson's face was pale and there were dark patches under his eyes. He sounded as if he had the beginnings of a cold.

"This could be a question of national security." Myron's tone implied everyone in the room had better remember that fact.

"'Could' is the operative word," said Frank Vickery quietly. He was growing increasingly impatient with the attitude of the FBI and the NSA. "They have a right—"

"Don't start that First Amendment crap again. I've been hearing that for the last two days and I'm tired of it." Bethune clapped his hands once in irritation, then did his best to be more composed. "I know they have rights, but in a case like this, they should be exercising restraint and judgment. The people are frightened enough as it is."

"We refused to give them any additional information," McPherson offered by way of excuse.

"And they're making it sound as if we're withholding vital information," Bethune reminded everyone. "That's just great. It helps the whole thing, doesn't it?" His sarcasm caused the other men to bristle.

"I think you're being a little high-handed," said the chief arson investigator from New York City. "We're trying to be candid about the fire at Six-sixty-six; when you refuse to cooperate, it hurts our investigation."

"You want to be deluged with nut mail, and phone calls about spacemen with death beams?" Bethune demanded. "That's all we've been getting for the last two days, and it's getting worse all the time. We've logged in well over four thousand letters on this in the last eight days, and the largest increase was in the last two. That Foss woman is using the whole emergency to further her career." He thumped the conference table with the side of his hand. "It's bad enough that we have to endure the speculations in the press, but when some broad with false eyelashes starts implying that we're falling down on the job—"

"Wait a minute," said Howard Li, who had been silent since the meeting began. "You're trying to find someone to blame, and it isn't good sense to choose the press, or the other media. You're acting as if they're contributing to the problem—"

"They are," muttered McPherson.

"—instead of enlisting their aid in combating a common enemy." Howard's face clouded briefly. "I don't blame that Foss woman for making the most of this. This crisis is a real opportunity for someone ambitious and hardworking."

"You sound as if you admire her," said Sidney Rountree, the most academic of the Presidential advisers.

"In a sense I do," Howard said condescendingly. "She has great perseverance and tenacity, and I admire that. She's grandstanding, but that is part of the entertainment side of politics, isn't it?" He smiled slightly and looked over at the two Fire Marshals.

Sidney Rountree cleared his throat, the most diplomatic signal he could give the meeting. "Perhaps we ought to concentrate on the fires. How do you see the situation at present?"

"We're still trying to find out which groups are claiming credit and how they say they've done it," Bethune said. "We're not getting much cooperation from the CIA or the DIA, but the NSA has been"—he gave Howard a nod—"more reasonable."

"We're analyzing the patterns, trying to coordinate all known information for the commonality. Still." Howard folded his arms "I think that we're overlooking certain obvious areas of exploration."

"Don't start again," pleaded Bethune.

"What is it?" Marshal Rountree asked, ignoring Bethune. He leaned forward, elbows braced on the polished mahogany.

"By this time all of you are aware, I trust," Howard began with a contemptuous glance at the two FBI agents, "that your standard methods are failing. As I understand it, the only explanation you've been willing to accept is terrorism or other subversive activities in spite of a complete lack of evidence that this is, in fact, the case."

"Oh, for Lord's sake!" McPherson said loudly enough to gain the attention of the group. "You're not starting that old saw again?"

"I'm saying," Howard went on with hardly a pause, "that we have been ignoring the basic theories of investigation—and I am assuming that in spite of my Bureau colleages this is still an investigation."

"Howard, shut up," Bethune said.

"What do you mean, Doctor Li?" Frank Vickery asked, ignoring the interruption.

"You can find it in Sherlock Holmes: that once the impossible has been eliminated, whatever is left, no matter how improbable, must be the truth. And no matter what the Bureau wants to think, we have, to all intents and purposes, eliminated terrorism as a valid factor in this investigation, and that leaves us with certain inescapable conclusions, little as anyone here may like it."

Sidney Rountree held up his hand. "What are you saying, Doctor Li?"

"I'm saying that spontaneous combustion is a very rare phenomenon until now, and we are in the middle of an unprecedented outbreak of it. Since no one can account for it, I think it's time that we take another look and approach the matter from a different perspective." He opened the notebook in front of him. "There are now thirty-two fires ranked for certain as being part of these fires, with another fourteen questionable. The areas of commonality are not apparent in terms of ownership, function, purpose, geographic ownership, insurance, employees or designers. Any link between any of the fires is more than tertiary at best." He looked down at his notes.

"How can you buy into this nonsense, Li?" asked McPherson. "Afraid to admit that you can't figure this out?"

"Let him go on, please," said Rountree.

"And considering the lack of success in preventing, predicting, controlling or containing these fires, it is appropriate to accept the fact that we need to expand our realms of investigation to include what you want to call paranormal elements."

"Oh, for Chrissake!" Bethune scoffed.

"What do you mean?" Rountree said, sitting a little straighter, "paranormal elements?"

"Spooks," said McPherson. "That's what he means. He thinks that this is some kind of grade-B movie and that the devil or alien or who-know-what has been causing the fires, and we're going to have to hire an exorcist to get rid of it."

"Why not?" Rountree murmured. "We're not getting anywhere with anything else."

"Sid," Frank warned him softly.

"I see that none of you are prepared to give this any legitimate consideration." Howard Li got up from the table. "And if that is the case, then I won't take up your time. I hope that you are confident that you can stop these fires, since you're gambling with lives and property in a very cavalier way." He reached the door and took a last, scathing glare at Myron Bethune. "I need to return to my office."

"Fine," Bethune said, and when Howard was gone, he looked at the closed door for a long moment. "Howard has a bee in his bonnet, and he won't give it up. It's a shame; he's got a first-class mind, but you know what these far-out types can be like." He looked at Sidney Rountree.

"What about the Fire Marshals' Task Force? Have you any theories we ought to know about? Anything that makes sense, that is."

"For the time being, we're still trying to find out what's causing the fires. Spontaneous combustion is the apparent cause, and that's pretty damned unlikely. One case, maybe, but a dozen?" Rountree put his wide, square hands flat on the table. "We've got to be overlooking something, and that's why we're expanding our area of operations to include the insurance companies and all the businesses involved in these catastrophes." He had prepared this announcement in advance but stated it badly.

"That's what the Bureau has been suggesting for more than a week," McPherson said without a trace of diplomacy. "High time you decided to agree with us."

"The Bureau, if you'll excuse me saying so," Frank Vickery said, goaded beyond his patience, "has been going out of its way to keep us from obtaining the information we need to complete our work, and what little we know about this . . . mess has been dished out in dribs and drabs by you people, and only after it has been requested time and time again. If you were willing to meet us even a quarter of the way, we might be able to make some progress."

"That's uncalled for, Vickery," McPherson said, bristling.

"Is it? Then how come you haven't yet released your report on the Manhattan fire? How come I've had to call twice and three times every day to renew my request, when I ought to be out doing my job, instead of playing footsies with you fu . . . fellows." He stopped abruptly, conscious of Rountree's hand on his wrist.

"You have a complaint to make about our staff?" Bethune asked in a soft, forbidding voice.

"I already did, in case you weren't listening." Frank turned to Rountree. "Sorry, Sid. I didn't mean to screw this up for you. But there are problems and we aren't getting the help we need; you know this and I know it." He looked at the others. "I guess that's why you're assigning me to that security company in California."

"Frank," Rountree stopped him. "You'd best wait in the reception room."

"Yeah," he agreed, nodding once before he picked up his notebook and started for the door.

He found Howard Li sitting in the reception room as well, two bound reports open on his knees. "I thought you'd left."

"I had planned to," said Howard. "But unfortunately my superior instructed me to remain here until he can finish dealing with Messers Bethune and McPherson. He has an appointment with them as soon as this travesty of a conference is over." He scribbled a note in the margin of the larger report.

Frank sat down and stared at his hands, his notebook between his knees. He looked at the opposite wall, wishing he were back at the Task Force headquarters in Philadelphia where he did not feel such an intruder.

"Tell me, Marshal... Vickers?" Li broke into his thoughts.

"Vickery," Frank corrected.

"Vickery. Vickery. Are you as convinced as those agents that these fires are acts of terrorism?"

"I don't know what they are," Frank said. "I've been on-site for eleven of them, and I can't find a trace of a reason why they happened, or what caused them. Maybe you're right—it's spooks."

Howard drew a pained breath. "If you want to make jokes, that's all there is to say."

Frank ground his teeth together. "Okay."

"If you are annoyed, Marshal Vickery, so am I. I have done everything I can think of to change the methodology being used by the investigators, and the only reception is derision." He closed both the reports.

"Why?" Frank asked after he had given it his consideration.

"I am worried," Howard announced, not looking at Frank. "We could be on the brink of a major calamity, we might have ruinous fires day after day after day. Have you the slightest notion what that could do to this country, to its economy, to its security? I've been trying to find what the parameters are for these tragedies and the only thing I find consistently is that these buildings all were reasonably modern, which is not a significant statistic. I do not want more of the fires to happen. I don't care what is causing the fires so long as I can find it and establish the means to stop or contain them." He flung the pencil he was holding across the room. "I am not too narrow-minded to admit that there are reasons for things that are not yet codified by science. And since there seems to be no other explanation that fits the facts, then I have to suppose that we are dealing with something we do not understand."

"Is that what has Bethune so worked up?" Frank hesitated. "I've seen what these fires are like. I don't care what the answer is. I just want one. Maybe you're right and it is spooks."

Howard looked away. "Don't use that word, Marshal Vickery."

"All right, if you like that paranormal word better, then that's what I'll use." Frank opened his notebook and took a pen from his pocket. He hated the three-piece suit he was wearing, hated the building, hated the whole charade of meetings and conferences. He was not even sure he had any business talking with Howard Li.

"How much math background do you have?" Howard's tone indicated that whatever Frank knew, it would not be enough.

"I went to a two-year college, and picked up other units over the years, if that's what you're trying to find out. I don't know much about statistics except that they lie." He found it impossible to be polite, but that brought its own satisfaction.

"Well, then I won't waste time trying to explain the theory." Howard opened the larger of the reports. "Do you see this? It is a compilation of all the information we have on file about the fires, and I have gone over it so many times that I see it in my sleep. I can find no sensible reason, no significant data, in this information, and that might mean that there are things we must examine, things that are not within the usual realm of science." He gave Frank a mocking look. "Hence, spooks, as you choose to call them."

"No argument," said Frank. "I hope that it's something we've overlooked, something simple like a pattern of shorts or... maybe a case of a bad batch of wiring, or phone lines, or who—"

"You haven't grasped the point at all," Howard interrupted him. "You're as bad as the rest, seeking simplistic answers in a complex case. You might as well think about spooks, after all." Howard got up and started to the door. "I'm going to wait for my superior in the lower lobby. Tell him for me will you? if you should see him."

Frank shrugged, deciding that it was one of those days. By the time Sidney Rountree came out of the meeting, Frank had sunk into gloom.

"It's for you," said the waiter as he brought the telephone to William Ridour's table.

William looked up from his shrimp salad and blinked at the waiter. The only person he thought might be calling was Elinore, but she had told him the night before that she would be at a meeting until nine-thirty tonight.

"William Ridour?" said a man's voice.

"Yes," William responded cautiously.

"You're the one who's been doing the articles for the Lansing paper?" There was an edge in the question.

"Yes," William said with less confidence than before.

"This is Simon McPherson. I'm with the FBI, and I believe we ought to talk."

William had seen the name on several reports. "Why?"

"Because we believe that the tone of your articles has been damaging to the investigation now in progress, and we would like an opportunity to explain to you why your stories have been irresponsible."

William was surprised at how quickly he became angry. "If you want me to file a story giving your side of the question, I'll be happy to do that—" He looked down at the lettuce that surrounded the mound of little, tight-curled shrimp, thinking that it looked like a very odd wig.

"You don't understand me, Mister Ridour," said McPherson without apology.

"Explain it to me, then," said William, anticipating what was coming.

"We'd like to speak with you in person, and we can show you what it is we're trying to accomplish here."

"And precisely what is that, Mister McPherson? From what I can see, you're doing your best to keep the news media from doing their jobs. Is that what you want to explain?" He felt his jaw tighten as he spoke and his appetite faded to nothing.

"Now, you don't have to do the standard knee-jerk response, Mister Ridour," McPherson recommended. "You don't understand the scope of the problem—"

"And I won't if you fellas have anything to say about this," William interrupted. "If you've found any error in fact in my stories, I'd like to know about it, if not, then—"

"Mister Ridour, the nation is on the edge of panic and most of you reporters can only spend your time trying to make points for the most horrific coverage. Do you have any idea the kind of reaction your irresponsible coverage is generating?" From his tone, it was apparent that McPherson was nearly as upset as William was.

"Don't try leaning on me, McPherson," said William. "I'll put this in my next story if you keep on this way, and then you might have more questions to answer than the ones I've been asking." He wondered if he could get into trouble for hanging up on an FBI agent.

"I'm not leaning on you, I'm trying to keep the country from coming apart, which you, Mister Ridour, are not. You are a big part of the problem."

"Thanks. No one ever accused me before of being able to throw all the country into collapse. That is what you're suggesting, isn't it? Well, I think you're trying to find someone to put in the pillory in order to shift blame from your own culpability."

Even as he said it, he was afraid that he had overstepped

himself and was preparing to back off when McPherson said, "You say that in print, Mister Ridour, and you will be in more hot water than you can possibly imagine."

"I hadn't intended to make any statements that I can't back up. What about you, Mister McPherson? Can you back up your statements with facts?" He felt heat mount in his face, and was glad that this was a telephone conversation.

"If you're going to start throwing around charges of irresponsibility, you'd best be prepared to change occupations in a hurry." There was a brief pause, and then McPherson said with obvious difficulty, "I didn't mean to take out after you this way. It's the strain of the case. You can comprehend that, can't you?"

"I can comprehend strain, if that's what you're asking," William said, wondering what the change in manner meant.

"There are a number of issues that we really ought to make clear, so that you have a better picture of what we believe is at stake here. Surely that will interest you, Mister Ridour." McPherson's attempt at good-fellowship only increased William's mistrust.

"Mister McPherson, if you don't mind my asking—and off the record, of course—how many of these calls have you made today? How many more are you planning to make."

There was silence on the line, and then McPherson said tersely, "There is going to be a briefing at the Bureau tomorrow morning at nine. There will be a pass in your name if you want to use it."

"Thank you, Mister McPherson. You might have said that at the beginning and saved us both high blood pressure." William was about to hang up, but could not resist adding, "What did you expect to gain with your tactics?"

"Tactics!" McPherson made the word ugly. "We're simply trying to avert more problems, but I can tell that averting problems isn't your cup of tea. You'd rather add to them."

"You can't be sure of that, McPherson, and unless you

are, I'd suggest you keep your accusations to yourself." He was ready to hang up again, but this time he decided to add a gibe. "I could make a case for this being a race issue, McPherson, unless you've been hassling other newsmen and women, in which case we're back at the First Amendment, aren't we?"

"You son of a bi—" McPherson burst out, then brought himself under control. "Be here for that briefing if you know what's good for you. Understand that?"

"Yes, I understand," said William with false sweetness. "And if I can fit it into my schedule I'll come by." With that he gave himself the satisfaction of hanging up.

"Is there anything wrong, sir?" asked the waiter when William had sat without eating for a good ten minutes after his phone conversation had ended.

"Not with the food," said William in a distracted way.

"Nothing wrong, I hope," the waiter said before leaving William to himself.

"I hope so, too."

"I'm tired of this shit," said William in an undervoice as the briefing ended.

"They didn't give us a hell of a lot," agreed the man beside him whose clip-on badge said he was from the *Chicago Sun-Times*. "They're all fucking terrified."

"So?" William asked. "The government is always frightened about something. This time it's fires, and for once I can understand what's bothering them, but still—"

"Look, file the story and find out where the next fire is, and give it all you've got." He gave a cynical smile before striding out the glass doors, to become lost in the company of other journalists.

William hesitated, shaking his head at the few notes he had taken. There was nothing new to report; the hour had been a waste of time.

"Where's the phones?" asked one of the journalists, lighting a cigarette.

"I think they're over there on the left," William said, indicating the hall at the end of the lobby.

"Thanks." The other was gone, walking nervously.

William slipped his notebook into its carrying case and was starting out the door when he saw one of the Fire Marshals hurrying for the door. On impulse, William went after him, calling out to him, "Marshal. Wait."

In the door Frank Vickery turned and saw a tall, lean black man with a press badge clipped to the lapel of his jacket coming up to him. "I'm sorry, but—"

"Let me buy you a cup of coffee, Marshal . . . ?" He left the last name open for Frank to fill in.

"Vickery. Your badge says William Ridour." He held out his hand and had it gripped at once.

"I saw you in the briefing," William said, and noticed the expression of distaste that went across Frank's features. "I gather it wasn't to your liking, either."

"It's what the official line is," Frank said, his eyes slightly averted. "The basic theory is that this is the work of terrorists and some new type of incendiary device that we have not yet identified."

"Bullshit," said William cordially as they started down the street. There was a smattering of rain and both men turned their collars up.

"Yes," said Frank reluctantly. "But it's all we're giving out."

"Do you know where we can get a cup of coffee?" William asked. "I'm from Lansing."

"I'm from Philadelphia," Frank said. "There's bound to be somewhere near. All these government employees have to eat somewhere."

They found a restaurant down the next street and hurried into it. They were shown to a banquette and offered four-page menus.

"We really only want coffee," Frank said with a hint of apology.

"Speak for yourself," William declared. "I think I want a sandwich. I skipped lunch today."

Frank chuckled. "You could be right. I was in meetings right up to that briefing."

"So have a sandwich. The paper'll pay for it." William

opened the menu and earned a disgusted look from the waiter when he turned to the quick luncheon section.

"Is this going to be on the record, then?" Frank asked, suddenly hesitant.

"I don't know; it depends on what you have to say that I haven't heard before." Admitting this was a relief to William; he was tired of the endless games that had been the mark of this investigation so far.

"I don't have much of anything to say." Frank stared down at the menu blankly. "Nothing so far has made any sense and I don't blame you for being frustrated—I've never been more frustrated in my life, and I've been fighting fires since I was twenty-one."

This brought out a little interest in William. "So you've had practical experience with fires?"

"I was in the department for eleven years, and then I was moved up. At the time," he went on strangely, "I hadn't understood how much I'd miss being a fire fighter. I missed it more than I thought I could."

"Do you still miss it?" William asked, falling automatically into the pattern of interviewing.

"Yeah," Frank said slowly. "Yeah, I do. Especially now. Going around to see what happened afterward, all it does is remind me of how inadequate we are to handle this. If I were fighting the fires, really there and doing something, I don't think I'd feel as much like a fifth wheel as I do." He stopped. "You're very good, Mister Ridour. You're making me think about things—"

"How do you know it's me." William signaled for the waiter. "Maybe it's you. Maybe you just needed someone to talk to."

"And I chose a reporter," Frank said, not entirely pleased.

"Someone as confused as you are," William suggested.

Frank looked over at William, one brow rising quizzically. "And you want some hints from me?"

"Do you have any?" William stopped and looked at the waiter. "I'll have the Rueben sandwich and coffee. What about you?"

"Uh . . . I don't know. Make it ham and cheese on rye with a slice of onion." He looked at William. "I'll buy my own, if you don't mind."

"Less worry?" William inquired.

"Conflict of interest. I'd want to give you something for the lunch and this way I can be a real bastard and you won't be able to make a case about it." Frank paused. "They're very security conscious, and we're expected to go along with it."

"I gather you don't approve," William said as the waiter brought two cups of coffee.

"Not entirely, no. I can see the reason, but I think they're making a mistake in keeping such tight wraps on the case. I think that if the public were better informed that they would not panic, and we might get information that would help us." Frank stopped. "That's got to be off the record, I'm afraid."

"Can you be an informed or highly placed source? I wouldn't have to say who you are." William watched Frank closely. "I think I can make your case for you, if you'd let me."

"It's damned tempting," said Frank. "Let me think about it while we have lunch, okay?"

"Fine by me," said William, feeling a burst of optimism that added savor to his meal.

"I'll make a deal with you," said Frank when he had finished his sandwich and was on his second cup of coffee. "I'll go over my notes and I'll give you a call to outline what the most pressing problems appear to be. I'm willing to be an informed source, but I can't have any more identification. I'm in enough trouble as it is."

"Is that why they're sending you to California?" William asked. Frank had mentioned his assignment during their meal.

"Part of the reason, anyway. For what it's worth, I think it's a good idea to bring in these other companies and methods. Anything is better than what we're doing now. Or not doing." He let his breath out slowly, not quite a sigh.

"If you were in charge, what would you do?" William had wanted to ask that question since they sat down.

The waiter refilled their cups and left them alone.

"Shit, I don't know," Frank said with a shake of his head. "Not what we are doing. I'd make sure we didn't hold back information from the public, and I'd get rid of the terrorist theory until there was some sort of real proof that was what's going on. As long as we're not certain that this is terrorism, there's no reason to assume we have to take the kinds of precautions that the government is taking right now. I think the lack of candor has made the public more apprehensive instead of less. No one likes to admit that they're stumped, but, Christ Almighty, we might as well admit that we are."

"What good would that do?" William asked.

"I don't know for sure. End the rumors of cover-up, maybe. There are people who think that the government is behind the fires, some experiment that got out of hand and they're trying to cover up their blunder." He stirred his coffee absently. "I've heard versions of that theory on talk shows in eight different cities, and it's only going to get worse unless we come clean."

"I guess the FBI doesn't agree," William prodded.

"Nor does the CIA and the DIA. The NSA is leaning in this direction but they're the only one so far, other than the Task Force, but we're a minority voice."

"What's your guess on the chance that they'll come around to your point of view?" William wished he could take notes, but knew that if there was any sign of this, Frank would be much less willing to speak.

"I think it's got the chance of the proverbial snowflake in hell," said Frank, feeling very tired. He reached into his jacket for his wallet. "What do I owe you?"

William waved the question away. "If you feel you have to, give me a five and that's fine."

Frank shrugged and took the bill out. "Here. Thanks. I didn't give you very much."

"You gave me more than the FBI just did." William signaled the waiter and handed over payment. "We'll call you an informed source or a source close to the investigation or something of that nature, and don't worry. I'll do my best to make sure that you don't catch any flak from this."

"Thanks, but they'll guess who's done this, and... They're pissed already; it won't really matter. I want to see progress made, and the way things are going, it isn't going to happen unless someone gives 'em a nudge. I'm out of line, but so are they." He drank the last of his coffee. "Let me know if it helps."

"You're more likely to know than I am," said William.

"Not after you publish. They're exiling me to California as it is." He rose. "Do you have a card? Just so we can keep in touch."

William handed it over. "Give me a call when you get settled. I think we're going to want to compare notes on this."

Frank nodded. "It's coming down now," he said as he reached the door. "I should have brought my raincoat. Or my umbrella." With a shrug he turned up the collar of his jacket and went out into the wet.

September 30, Portland, Oregon

Louis Miller was so tired that he felt wrapped in layers of cotton batting. He had been reviewing reports for more than ten hours and he was beginning to think he would not recognize a discrepancy if it leaped off the page and seized him by the throat. If only he had not volunteered to examine the Customs forms. He had merely wanted to establish himself on a better footing with the boss, but he never imagined that the simple chore would turn into such a grueling ordeal. This was his third day of twelve hours' working and he was no closer to finding where the missing bills of lading were than he had been when he started.

"I ought to call Hill and admit that I can't do this," he said to the screen in front of him. "I ought to give up."

But he knew, even as he said this, that he would not give up. He had taken on other assignments like this in the past and had always managed to find what he was looking for. It galled him that the first time he had a challenge like this in Portland, he had failed.

He glanced at the clock, thinking that another two hours and he could go home without feeling he had shirked his duty. With a sigh he entered another date—May 16—from the forms at his elbow. He was beginning to suspect that Hill's worst fears were true and that there was more to the problem than simply missing bills of lading, and that troubled him.

On the ninth entry, Louis noticed a strange smell in the room, like a cigarette that had been left burning in an ashtray. He stopped working long enough to look up, wondering if someone else might be working late.

Before he could shove his chair back from the screen, the first sliver of fire had lodged itself deep inside the monitor, and within three seconds it festered; the room filled with smoke and the alarm skirled its warning briefly but heat and flame silenced it, as it joined Louis Miller as a victim.

October 2, Kansas City

All of the third- and fourth-grade classes would be on the field trip, and Mary Higgins worried that she didn't have enough adults with her to watch over the children properly.

"I think you're being overcautious, Mary," said John Bemis, the principal of her school. "We've got Lois going along, and there are six adults for each of the three buses. That is supposed to be sufficient according to the Board of

Education. You're always nervous about these field trips, Mary."

"I'm sorry, John," she said, holding her clipboard more tightly. "You don't seem concerned."

"I'm not. You're taking the children to the museum with proper chaperonage. You have the docents to help you if you need them and—it's not as if you've never done this."

Mary smiled a nervous apology. "I don't mean to be a nuisance."

"Oh, that's not it, Mary," John said, softening. "It's early in the morning and I'm not awake yet." He straightened his tie and smoothed his thinning hair back from his forehead. "Come on down to the cafeteria and we'll go over the agenda, okay?"

Mary smiled her relief. "Thank you, John. I'd like that."

The two left the principal's office and went across the courtyard to the oldest part of the school. The cafeteria, located in the basement, was a vast, echoing, ugly room with fifteen long tables set up in ranks.

"I think that this field trip is very important to the class, don't you?" John went behind the serving counters and picked up two cups beside the large urns. He filled both with tea and came back around the end. "Doughnuts?"

"Please," said Mary, taking two quarters from her change purse. "When is the faculty lounge going to be ready again?"

"The painters ought to be finished tomorrow," said John as they sat down at the nearest table.

"Next week, do you think?" Mary said, sipping her tea and scalding her tongue.

"I'm sure," said John. "Think of the next few days as being like hazing in college. You can get through it."

"Hazing," said Mary, who had never had any personal experience of hazing. "I suppose you're right."

"Oh, come on, Mary; there's nothing to worry about. You know how to run this field trip. You've done it dozens of times before. You always get nervous and you always manage perfectly. Now, drink your tea and let's go check up on the buses."

Obediently Mary did as she had been told, thinking that there were times she acted more like her students than the sensible woman of forty-one she was. "I want to call Lois, too."

"Fine; fine," said John. "If you'd like, we can check with the museum."

"I always do," Mary said, doing her best to make a joke of it.

"So you do."

They left the cafeteria together, going across the courtyard once again, this time finding the first few students wandering through the walks between buildings.

"Oh," said Mary as they reached the library, "I just want to stop in and take out a few of the books to show the students—the ones on art and the masters."

John nodded; this had been part of Mary's ritual for several years. "Remember, we did get in those new books on the Flemish masters and one on El Greco. And there is that book on architecture. You might find that useful, as well."

"Yes; thanks for suggesting it." She touched her temple with one finger. "If it weren't attached, I'd probably leave it somewhere."

"I doubt it." He gave her a thumbs-up sign and moved away from her, going back to his office with a sense of satisfaction.

Mary entered the library and found Leeann restoring order to the shelves. "Hi," she called out to the librarian.

"Oh, hi, Mary. I swear that Miss Wharton's class is harder on books than any of the others." She made a face and went on with her work.

"I'm going to pick up the art books and that new one on architecture." Mary was already making her way to the shelves, reaching for the eight titles she usually took out, and pausing to consider a few of the new titles. "I've got five of them."

"Check them out on the computer, will you? I don't want to stop now," Leeann said over her shoulder.

"Okay." Mary stepped behind the tall desk and flipped the switch for the monitor. "Name and number, or just number?"

"Just number's enough, and put your code in afterward."

Mary nodded as she flipped open the cover of the first book and copied down the identifying code, repeating the process for the next book, and the next. She hesitated, saying, "I know I've requested this before, but will you do me a favor and do a display of books about art?"

"Don't I always? Just relax, Mary." She laughed, a light, flirtatious sound that was out of place with her high-necked Victorian blouse and midcalf skirt.

"I didn't mean—" Mary said and went back to punching in the codes for the books.

The library, with its thousands of books, took to the flames as eagerly as a professor takes to footnotes. In less than three minutes the library was enveloped in fire and the first wails of fire sirens rose over the bells and whoops of the school alarms and the shrieks and screams of the students attempting to flee.

October 4, Atlanta, Georgia

By four o'clock the Friday-evening commuter traffic was building up on the runways as well as the freeways. Sam Reinhart was busy with keeping track of the smaller planes connecting Atlanta with Baton Rouge, Charleston, Knoxville, Louisville, and all the rest of the cities of the South. His relief, Nicky Hoyle, was tied up in an enormous multicar snarl on Peachtree and Sam had given his word that he would stay on until Nicky arrived. He was already regretting it.

Two international flights were due in, which only added to the confusion. Sam began working out alternate approaches for the lightplanes and commuter lines. Most of the time he liked this part of the job, and it satisfied him to know that he could help eliminate risk for so many thousands of people. When he considered his work, he often thought of himself as an unsung hero. He was content to be unsung, but when he was as overworked as he was right now, he found it difficult to keep his sense of heroism.

There were six commuter flights due in in the next fifteen minutes and an additional five going out. At least two of those would be leaving late because connecting flights from Dallas and Chicago had been delayed. He did not trust himself to juggle any of the figures in his head, and he went to the computer terminal for a status update. He watched the information flicker on the screen and then began working out runways for each of the incoming planes, allowing for the shifts in schedules that he had just seen.

Like most large airports, Atlanta is a vast, sprawling place with long spokes poking out in many directions. The fire that erupted without warning in the control tower ate up most of two concourses before it could be brought under control. Among the casualties was an Eastern Airlines jet that was just pulling away from the gate when the flames reached it and ignited the fuel in the fully loaded tanks.

PART IV

October 6, San Jose, California

Hazy warm sunshine greeted Frank Vickery as he stepped off the plane. He noticed that security had been tightened at this airport as it had at all others. He shifted his garment bag so that it hung more comfortably on his shoulder, then walked into the terminal. He had been told that someone would meet him.

The woman was carrying a sign with his name on it. She was dark and attractive, with an easy smile. "Frank Vickery?" she asked as he paused in front of her.

"That's me," he said.

She held out her hand. "I'm Cynthia Harper; I'm in the legal department of Patterson Security Systems."

"A lady lawyer. In jeans and a sweater."

"Hey," she said, taking mock offense. "It's Sunday afternoon. I save the pinstripes for work. This is for trimming hedges." She had started walking and he fell in with her.

"I understand we're scheduled for a meeting tomorrow

129

morning at eight." They approached the baggage-claim area and found a convenient place to wait.

"That's right. That FBI agent has been driving J.D. crazy since yesterday. Eight Monday morning was the earliest that J.D. was willing to confer. As much because of the travel problems as any."

Two uniformed policemen walked by them, their eyes constantly moving over the travelers gathered there.

"Which FBI agent?" asked Frank. "McPherson or Bethune?"

"Youngish guy, tall, looks like he played football in college. McPherson, I think. The other one arrives around midnight. Phylis is picking him up."

"Phylis?" prompted Frank.

"J.D.'s secretary. She's been acting as coordinator for this project, unofficially, of course. She would have picked you up, but her partner is having trouble with two new mares and—"

Frank laughed and held up his hand. "Wait a minute. What do mares have to do with this?"

Cynthia grinned. "Phylis's partner raises horses. Phylis is giving her a hand with a new mare and she called me and asked if I could pick you up. In a way, I think it's for the best. Our best statistician is at my place, and you two will want to compare notes."

"Okay," he said, thinking that he would not have any opportunity to enjoy California. He had promised Melinda he would look around to see if this was a place they might want to come for a vacation sometime.

"It's not that bad. Carter's gathered a lot of material, and I know that if you go over your material together you're going to come up with something worthwhile."

The baggage carousel clanked into life, and Frank moved closer to it.

"I'm going out to get the car," said Cynthia. "I'll meet you in front. I've got the hatchback, yellow, license plate BENSCAR. You just go out those doors"—she pointed—"and I'll be waiting. See you in a couple minutes."

She was as good as her word, and Frank emerged to

find her parked at the very edge of the waiting zone, her engine running. The hatch was up in back and the passenger door was open.

"Thanks," said Frank as he got in beside her having put his luggage in the back.

"Pleasure's all mine," said Cynthia as she swung into traffic.

The drive to her house took little over half an hour and most of the way they discussed the investigation PSS had under way. Both of them agreed that terrorism or conspiracy did not fit the nature of the continuing tragedy.

"A cousin of mine was burned in Manhattan," said Cynthia as she turned onto a quiet residential street. "Everyone I know knows someone who was killed or left homeless by these fires. I want them stopped."

"So do I," Frank said, noticing their surroundings for the first time and realizing that the lady lawyer in sweater and jeans who was driving a two-year-old Nissan was clearly prosperous.

The house was modified Spanish–style, built in a U shape with a live oak growing in the courtyard. The garage, off to the side of the house, held a BMW and a small four-wheel-drive pickup. There was another car in the driveway, a pewter-colored Mazda; Frank found himself curious about the car.

"That's Carter's," explained Cynthia.

"I hear they're temperamental," Frank remarked.

"Probably," Cynthia said. "Most expensive machines are."

As they got out of the car, a tall, lanky man came around the end of the garage. He held out his hand to Frank, introducing himself as Ben Harper. "Carter's inside; we just made ice tea."

"You can leave your bags in the car if you like; I'll take you to your hotel later on, after supper." Cynthia made a point of locking the car before taking Frank into the house.

Carter Milne was seated at the coffee table, busily scribbling in her notebook. She looked up, a bit startled, when Cynthia came into the living room. "You're back," she said, looking embarrassed, as if she had been caught cheating on an examination.

Frank made no attempt to conceal his surprise. He had been expecting a man and to find that Carter was a woman, and very appealing in an unpretentious way, startled him. He remembered all the times Barbara had teased him for being a sexist, and how they had laughed. He decided to make a clean breast of it. "You're not what I—"

Carter offered her hand. "You're Fire Marshal Vickery, aren't you? We'll be working together, so my boss tells me. It's a pleasure to meet you."

Frank took her hand, surprised at her firm grip. "And you're Carter Milne. I'm looking forward to it."

She drew her hand back. "I've just been going over the records again. This is all the information I've been able to gather on the series of fires. Incidentally, I understand the Las Vegas fire has been determined as arson. I've taken that off the list." She sat down again, her head lowered as she reviewed her notes.

"Yes; they found two pieces of timers in the kitchen storage room." He took his tone from her, a little puzzled at her coolness. "Perhaps the Toronto warehouse fire is also arson; they've got some evidence that might indicate that fire was set, but it hasn't been established for sure yet." He considered sitting next to her on the couch, then changed his mind and drew up a chair to the coffee table. "If you'll give me a couple of minutes, I can get my briefcase from the car and we can start going over our material."

Charter looked up, her cheeks suffused with color. "I'm sorry," she said with a slight stammer. "I . . . it's just that I've been so wrapped up in this mess, I didn't think—"

Cynthia came to the rescue. "That's Carter; half the time she forgets to eat unless someone reminds her. Let's have some tea and a bite to eat, and we can get to work then."

"Sounds good," said Frank, glad to have a chance to work out a schedule before tackling figures. "I'm a little jet-lagged and I don't know how much use I'm going to be, but if you're willing to make allowances for that, I think we can get through the preliminary comparisons tonight."

"I didn't mean to be so... preoccupied," Carter said, and once again she sounded slightly upset. "Really, Mister Vickery."

"Frank," he said automatically, deciding that Carter was one of those brainy, skittish women who never learned how to act in company. He hated to admit it, but there was something daunting about her.

"Frank," she said. "I'm Carter. I was named for my mother's family." She rubbed her palms on her slacks, awkward and looking a trifle lost.

"Thank goodness that's over," Cynthia said. "I hope you'll make yourself at home, Frank. I've also got some papers you might want to look at, after we eat." This last was directed at Carter.

Ben came in from the kitchen carrying a tray with tea and sandwiches laid out. "I hope this is enough." He set it down and poured out two cups.

While they ate, Frank noticed that Carter began to relax, but there was still an air about her that he could not identify, an elusive tension that earned an occasional covert warning glance from Cynthia.

I'll take care of the dishes and I'll pick up the kids," said Ben when all that was left of the sandwiches was crumbs. "You guys get to work."

"God, I love him," Cynthia said as Ben set about his self-appointed tasks. "And not only for this. He's my salvation."

Frank could think of nothing to say to such a heartfelt statement, but he noticed that Carter blinked nervously while Cynthia spoke. What was going on with her, anyway?

"I've brought my compilations," Carter said abruptly. "I think the Coglin Optics is the most complete, but there are some good facts on the Murchison fire as well." She put a stack of computer sheets on the table.

"Carter, for Lord's sake, we can't read through three or

four hundred sheets this evening," Cynthia protested. "Can you sum up the basics?"

"I'd like to have a copy of your printouts," said Frank. "I might be able to collate our findings—or some of them—tonight."

"But I was hoping we'd have a good preliminary report for tomorrow," Carter said.

"J.D. isn't expecting that, and who knows what other information we'll get tomorrow. Ease up, Carter." Cynthia put her hand on Carter's shoulder. "I know you want to figure it out. But Carter, you aren't Superwoman."

Carter got up and walked away from the table, her face set in hard lines. She paced between the window and the baby grand piano. "It's not that."

"Look, why don't we call it an evening," Cynthia suggested. "You're worn out and I'll bet Frank could use some sleep." She got up and went over to Carter. "You okay?"

"Sure, okay enough," said Carter. "You're right. It's time we quit. Besides, Ben'll be back with the kids soon and I don't want to cut into family time." She passed her hand over her eyes. "I'll get my things and I'll meet you in the morning. You'll call J.D. for me, won't you?"

Cynthia looked vexed, but she accepted the idea. "I'll be in early tomorrow. Glen wants to go over possible liability claims before we go into the meeting with the FBI men." She went to her hall closet and took out a light jacket which she gave to Carter. "Look, I want you to give me a call when you get home, just so I won't worry."

"Oh, don't be such a worrywart," said Carter trying to make light of the request. "I haven't had any trouble in years, and you know it."

"There's always a chance, and I'd feel better. Let me hear from you, or I'll call your place in an hour or so." She waited while Carter gathered up her material and handed a stack of papers to Frank. "Drive safely, okay?"

"You know I will." Impulsively Carter hugged Cynthia. "Sorry I've been such a drag, but... well, thanks." She hurried to the door and went out without saying good-bye to Frank.

"Don't mind her," Cynthia said as they heard the car start out in the driveway. "She's been under a lot of pressure."

"Just work?" Frank asked.

"Not entirely," said Cynthia. "Let's go over that second report of yours before I take you to your hotel."

Frank was pleased to oblige, but could not entirely set aside his questions about the elusive Doctor Carter Milne.

By the time Cynthia and Frank had finished, Ben had come back with the kids and Carter had called to assure Cynthia that she was home safe.

"I didn't mean to take up so much of your Sunday," said Frank as Cynthia walked out to the car with him.

"Nonsense, it was time well spent." She got in and opened the passenger door for Frank. "We need the time to get organized. There's so damn much information coming in and we haven't the least idea what might or might not be germane to the investigation. You've been very helpful and I want you to know that I appreciate it." As she drove him to his hotel, she gave him a succinct report on what had been going on at Patterson Security Systems.

"You're being very candid," Frank told her at last.

"Someone has to be," Cynthia responded. "My boss suggested that it might be a good idea to put most of our cards on the table. He thinks that we need a hell of a lot more cooperation than we've had so far. I don't think you're as convinced as some of the others that we're on the right track; everything you've said supports that, and so I want you to be on our side."

"What makes you think there are sides in this?" Frank asked, becoming guarded.

"You mean there aren't? You could have fooled me," said Cynthia as she turned into the parking lot of a modern hotel.

"Well, it's possible," Frank admitted. "I haven't always been willing to go along with the party line." He watched the doorman as he came up to the car. "Thanks for the ride. I look forward to seeing you tomorrow morning. And I do appreciate all you've done."

"Wonderful," said Cynthia as Frank got his bags out of the car. "We'll make quite a team if we keep our heads."

"Yeah," said Frank before turning away from the car and going into the hotel lobby. For the first time in weeks he felt only tired and not discouraged.

"Carter?" J.D. said for the third time. "What do your records say about the Atlanta fire?"

Carter looked up sharply, meeting her boss's eyes reluctantly. "I'm sorry; I was—"

"You certainly were," said J.D., cutting off the comments of Bethune and McPherson. "I would like you to review the figures you've gathered on the Atlanta Airport fire."

"Well, they aren't very complete, sir," said Carter. "We've only got the first evaluations and they're not really very clear. There has been no proof of arson, which means that it is still ranked with the mystery fires. But according to the report we have now from the Canadians, the Toronto fire is not arson, at least not in the conventional sense. The devices they found apparently have been analyzed, and it seems that they exploded as a result of heat, but they have reason to think that they were not the cause of the fire. I've already relayed a request for more information."

"Good," said J.D. "I'm certain we'll get cooperation from the Canadian authorities." His tone was sharp, and he was clearly criticizing the federal authorities.

"What have you determined in regard to the cause or triggering of the fires?" J.D. saw the look of dismay that crossed Carter's face and he went on, "I don't expect anything final."

"Well, the best I can say is that we've still made no determination of commonality between the fires beyond the fact that the buildings were modern and most were large." She rubbed her eyes. "I'd like to have access to the NSA records; I might be able to do more if I had them."

"That information is classified," McPherson said.

"I'm aware of that, Mister McPherson," said Carter. "I only wanted you to know that my work might be more useful if I had that information you haven't been willing to release."

"What's your security clearance?" demanded McPherson.

"Please," J.D. interrupted. "This won't accomplish anything. If you aren't willing to let us have the figures, you aren't, and we'll do our best without them." He cleared his throat. "What is your opinion, Mister Vickery?"

Frank was surprised, but he answered without hesitation. "If it were up to me, you'd have the data. As Special Agents Bethune and McPherson know, I don't agree with the high level of secrecy they've imposed on this investigation. I don't believe we're serving the best interests of the country by withholding this information from those legitimately involved in the investigation."

"You know our position on that, Vickery," Myron Bethune said as he stared at J.D. Patterson. "And you don't make our job any easier by sounding off in this way."

"When and if your policy changes," J.D. said blandly, "we'd appreciate being included in your informational chain."

Cynthia scribbled a note and passed it to Glen Lewis, who headed up the PSS legal department. *What about a court order for the information? Would there be a chance we'd get it?*

"Good question," Glen whispered. "We might give it a try."

"Anything you want to share?" asked J.D.

"In a while," Glen replied.

"We expect you to pass on any data you acquire through independent sources," McPherson was saying. "If you do not, we will request that you be withdrawn from the investigation."

J.D. gave the FBI men a sardonic stare. "I see; we have to cooperate and you can mete out such portions as you see fit. Very equitable."

"Your attitude isn't making any of this easier," said Bethune. "We're trying to conduct our investigation as best we can."

"And be damned to the rest of us," said J.D. "That's your position; we understand that. I think you're mistaken, and I want it on the record. As much for our protection in court as anything else."

Bethune sighed. "All right; we'll make sure it's in our reports and if you insist we'll file our reports with you as well as with the Bureau."

J.D. sighed. It was going to be a very long meeting.

"So what are we going to do about the Bobbsie twins?" J.D. asked Cynthia and Glen as they sat over lunch in the executive room of the PSS cafeteria.

"Find a way to get them out of here," Cynthia said without looking at Glen.

"Cynthia suggested we try to get a court order to obtain the federal records for the fires. I think it's a good idea. If nothing else, we can bolster our position in any lawsuit. I'd advise you to authorize it."

"Okay; I'm advised." J.D. looked down the room to where Carter sat by herself. "What's wrong with her, do you know?"

"Same thing as before," Cynthia said, lowering her voice. "Greg has been gambling. I found out yesterday that he lost heavily and she took money out of her savings to cover his losses."

"What kinds of amounts are we talking about? Don't betray a confidence, but if you can let me—"

Cynthia cut into this. "It's over twenty thousand, that's all I know."

"That's serious," J.D. said, frowning. "How long has this been going on?"

"I don't know," Cynthia answered honestly. "I'll try to find out, if you insist."

"I'm going to need Carter at her best if we're going to do any good in this investigation at all. Yes, I'd like to know what's happened to her. It's necessary." J.D. shook his head. "Gambling. That's not good."

Cynthia hesitated, then said cautiously, "She's under a lot of pressure."

"We're all under a lot of pressure." He fell silent then said, "My aunt is in intensive care in Atlanta. She's badly burned and they don't expect her to make it, not at her age. And my second wife's brother was killed in the condominium fire. I want to end this. I want to make this the top priority of this company immediately and I want us to be the ones to break it. I take these deaths and injuries personally. To me the fires are not disasters, they are also personal attacks."

Glen nodded. "It's your company. I'd recommend you not make statements like that in public—it might create problems for you as well as for the company."

"Point taken," said J.D.

"I hope so," said Glen. "It's not the kind of thing I'd want those two from Washington hearing. They're territorial enough without you giving more—"

"Territorial!" Cynthia exclaimed. "That's it, that's exactly it. They don't want anyone trespassing on their fires. They want to keep the investigation to themselves and that's what's getting in the way."

J.D. cocked his head. "Do you think it might be worth putting a little pressure on my contacts in the capital and see if we can get McPherson and Bethune out of our hair earlier than planned? I can tell they're putting a damper on Vickery, and I've got a hunch that *he's* got a handle on how to go about this."

"You're confident about that?" Glen asked.

"I'm more confident about Vickery than those two FBI clones. He's had practical experience fighting fires and he's been on the scene of most of the fires." J.D. got up from the table. "Cynthia, I want you to have a talk with Carter, and soon. Before we get any further into this thing. If she needs replacement or a backup, I want to know about it. I don't want her coming unglued in the middle of things."

"Okay," Cynthia said, a bit uncertainly. "I don't feel quite right about this."

"Would you feel any righter if she buckles?" J.D. said, and did not wait for Cynthia to answer. "I'll talk to you later."

Cynthia nodded and watched J.D. leave the room. "He's got so much on his mind."

"We all do. You might work on pacing yourself, Cynthia," Glen suggested. "We're all in this for the duration."

Cynthia shoved her chair back from the table and stood up, smoothing her skirt as she did. Little as she liked it, Glen was right. "Carter," she said as she approached the table where the statistician sat.

"Oh, hi," Carter said, looking up from the report she was reading. "The fire in Portland is definitely one of the tribe. I had confirmation waiting on my desk when I got out of the meeting. There's been a fire in Great Falls that might also be in the running. It happened last night, and so far they haven't been able to turn up any sign of arson. I put in a request for data."

"You don't have to report to me," said Cynthia, taking the chair across from Carter. "Look, I don't want to seem nosy, but if you want to talk, all you have to do is let me know."

"Like we did over nachos?" Carter asked bleakly. "What's the use?"

"You can't know until you give it a try," Cynthia said. "I'm afraid you're in over your head."

"Tell Greg," Carter said. "Maybe he'll listen to you; he won't listen to me." She shook her head. "Forget I said that. Greg would be furious if he knew I'd talked about this at all."

Cynthia felt a twinge of guilt as she heard this and at the same time, she had to bite back an angry outburst against Greg. "I can't do that," she said firmly. "You couldn't either, in my place."

"No, I guess not," said Carter.

"We need to be prepared to handle a lot more activity in

the fire investigation. Keep that in mind." Cynthia glanced at her watch. "No rest for the wicked."

"There sure isn't," Carter said, shoving aside her plate with her sandwich only half-eaten.

"You're going to dry up and blow away," Cynthia warned as she went to the door with Carter.

"Don't I wish," Carter said with a botched chuckle.

Bethune was in J.D.'s chair and McPherson was standing by the window. Both wore the same conservative suit and regimental-looking tie.

"We have to talk to you," Bethune said as Frank came through the door and regarded them in a puzzled way.

"Sure," said Frank, wondering why they had chosen J.D.'s office for a meeting that might have taken place anywhere in the PSS building.

"We're very dissatisfied with the way these meetings are going, and we think that PSS is derelict in their responsibilities in this investigation." Bethune's face, usually neutral in expression, was set in hard and angry lines.

"Why?" asked Frank, startled.

"You know why; they are not proceeding in a professional manner; they are disregarding our guidelines and they are demanding material we cannot release without compromising our national security." He ticked these complaints off on his fingers, looking at Frank between items as if waiting for an argument.

"In other words, they aren't doing it your way," Frank said, fatigue coming back to him in a rush. "What does this have to do with me? Are you taking PSS off the investigation?"

"Unfortunately, we're not able to do that," Bethune said. "But we don't believe any good purpose will be served by our remaining here. We're leaving it to you to keep some semblance of control over Jeremiah Patterson and his company while we return to Washington where we can take a greater hand in the investigation."

Frank thought that he probably ought to call Sidney Rountree and warn him that Bethune and McPherson would be returning, but kept his face impassive. "What do you expect me to do?"

"Keep Patterson from trying to run the operation," Bethune said with heavy emphasis. "He's a menace." He tapped impatiently on the desk. "We rely on you to keep us informed on any and all developments on this front. You already report to the Fire Marshals' Task Force; you can now report to us as well."

"And when do I get any work done, with all this reporting and observing? I have a stake in ending these fires, too."

"You will have to use your best judgment, but we require information in order to continue our investigation. We are developing leads—"

"Oh, cut the crap, Bethune," Frank said. "There aren't any real leads and we all know it. If I were you, I'd go talk to Howard Li and find out if he's gotten anywhere with his theories and then I'd give him all the help I could." He went to the end of the room where J.D.'s chalkboard hung behind half-open redwood panels. "I will do everything I can to keep the Bureau and the Task Force abreast of what goes on here, but not because you want me to—because it's good tactics." He took a deep breath, knowing he had already said too much.

"We have to return by way of Dallas," said McPherson as if he had not heard anything Frank said. "There was a fire in a shopping mall; it looks like a copycat to me."

"Great," Frank said sarcastically. "Now there are two bunches out there who can do the same impossible thing. Catch the copycat, why don't you, and ask him how he does it and then see if you can find the original arsonist."

"If this is how you mean to work with us, then we may ask the Task Force to reconsider your assignment," Bethune warned.

"I'm getting real tired of your threats, Bethune. Instead of wasting your time and mine with them, why don't you try to get more investigatory agencies working on this. I'll bet that the insurance adjusters have all kinds of data you could use." He started toward the door. "If that's all..."

"Vickery," McPherson said, growing more angry, "I'll make sure there's a note about your attitude in my report."

"Good," said Frank cordially. "And that way they can compare it to my observations in my report. It ought to make interesting reading for someone." Before the two could detain him longer, Frank left the office, moving rapidly.

"Is there anything wrong, Marshal Vickery?" asked Phylis Dunlap as Frank strode through her office.

"Not really," he called back to her, not stopping. He took the stairs instead of the elevator and when he reached the ground floor, he went out of doors into the sunlight and the rustle of the trees, keeping up a vigorous pace in order to work off his mounting fury.

He had completed two circuits of the PSS building when J.D., looking almost jaunty, came up to him and fell in stride, apparently unfazed by the speed Frank established. "You've got a problem?"

"Not once they're on their way back to Washington, I haven't," Frank said brusquely.

"Ah, yes, Bethune and McPherson—a remarkable team, I'll say that for them. I remember encountering men like them when I was in Navy Intelligence, back in Korea. I used to think they'd drive me crazy." He pointed out one of the oak trees growing near the creek that cut through the industrial park. "There's a family of squirrels living in that tree, tame as puppies."

Frank put on a burst of speed. He needed time to figure out what Patterson wanted of him.

J.D. caught up with him. "Men like Bethune and McPherson," he resumed, "you know they're sincere, but they're also pigheaded, don't you agree?" J.D. might have been talking about gardening for all the feeling he gave the words.

Frank had to stop himself from laughing. "Yeah. You could say that all right."

They rounded the end of the building and approached

the larger parking lot. "You know, Vickery, they aren't the only ones with connections in Washington; they aren't leaving because they've asked to, they're leaving because I requested it."

Frank slowed down. "And what does that mean?" He regarded J.D. narrowly.

"It means that no matter what you might hear from them, you will not and cannot be held personally accountable for what this company does or does not do in regard to the investigation of these fires. If they did the guilt number of you, forget it." J.D. stopped walking and waited for Frank to speak.

"You're right; they did try to put the whole thing on my shoulders," he admitted. "I resent it, but the thing is, I do feel I have a responsibility in this thing, and I can't excuse myself if I shirk my job." He walked back to where J.D. was standing.

"Of course not," J.D. said. "You are on the Fire Marshals' Task Force and that means you're committed to do what you can to find out how and why these fires are happening, and then to find a way to prevent any more from occurring. That's legitimate. The rest is pure bullshit. The way Bethune and McPherson have been carrying on this morning, everyone in my office is supposed to be responsible for the state of the investigation and anything that goes wrong is by definition our fault. It's more spite than good sense, Vickery."

"You said there's a family of tame squirrels in the tree back there?" Frank asked.

"They'll eat out of your hand if you offer them food. They've been there three years." The two men began to retrace their steps at a comfortable amble.

Carter glared at the figures in front of her and shook her head in frustration. "I know it has to be here somewhere," she said to the columns of entries on the screen. The cities, dates, locations and types of businesses were displayed, along with the loss of life and property in the case of each fire.

Frank put down the computer sheets he had been reading. "Maybe we'd better give it a break. You're so close to it you don't know what you're looking at."

Carter closed her eyes, her face showing harsh lines of fatigue. "I thought it might be apparent but so far, nothing. I've been over the material and over it and over it. Nothing makes any sense. It doesn't make sense for terrorism, not with the targets that have gone up." She stifled a yawn. "I don't know where else to look."

"One of the men working on this at the federal end thinks that it might be... paranormal." Frank felt silly saying this, and his manner was apologetic.

"Makes as much sense as anything else we've come up with," said Carter, not giving him much attention. "I suppose I might even try something like that, eventually, if I don't get anywhere with the other figures. Did you notice anything in your inspections of the fire sites that you haven't mentioned already, anything that might help us?"

"Other than there was no reason for the fires and no trace of how they started, no. I've gone over every note I've taken and tried to remember everything I've seen, but nothing sticks out." He watched Carter, then said, "Look, it's after five; why don't we leave it alone for the day. We'll get a fresh start tomorrow."

"There's still time to get some work done," Carter said, not really looking at him.

Frank was a bit nonplussed. "If you want to come back after dinner, maybe we could do something then."

"I don't need to be sweet-talked," said Carter, sounding like a chastised child.

"Who's sweet-talking?" Frank said, puzzled by her reaction. "I'm hungry, and if you want to work longer, I've got to get some food into me or I'll turn into a grouch."

"Go ahead. I'll ring you in when you get back." She sounded stiff now.

"I can bring something back for you, if you'll tell me what I can get for you." He hesitated. "Is there anything you'd like? I don't know what's close, but there must be good take-out food around."

"Oh, anything." She managed a shy smile. "It's been a long day, you're right, and if it weren't so important, I might knock off—"

"Well, it's good to see you're so dedicated, but use a little sense. You can't keep up this pace if you don't take reasonable care of yourself. I'll get you a sandwich or a salad from the deli. We can go for another three or four hours, but then we'll both need sleep. I learned that much when I was still fighting fires. You don't do anyone any good if you wear yourself out." He noticed that she was more at ease, and it piqued his curiosity.

"You've convinced me. I'll have whatever you recommend, so long as it isn't fried. And while you're gone, I'll try a different sort on the data. I haven't compared brands of electrical equipment, or telephone equipment. That might tell us something." Her face brightened a little. "Maybe I'm grasping at straws, but it's better than doing nothing. Isn't it?"

"Yeah," Frank said, encouraged by her attitude. He went out of her office and to the elevators. A few stragglers were leaving the building, and Frank was surprised to run into Cynthia Harper, who had a stuffed portfolio tucked under her arm.

"Through for the day?" Cynthia asked as they rode down in the elevator.

"Nope; just taking a dinner break and then back to the computer with Doctor Milne." He indicated the case. "It looks like you're going to have a full evening yourself."

"Luckily Ben is willing to shoulder many of the chores. He likes working with the kids and he's very worried about the fires. He's afraid it's going to happen here and that we won't be able to stop it. Ben would be up all night with me if I asked it—I don't, but it's good to know he's willing."

As the elevator doors opened, Frank asked, "Do you know where I can get good take-out food? I told Doctor Milne I'd bring something back for her."

"There's a good place about a mile and half down the road. It has a garish sign, but don't let that put you off." She hurried out the door, going to the parking lot.

Frank followed Cynthia's recommendation and found the restaurant more easily than he had expected, and discovered that the fare was not fancy but tasty and good. As he ordered chicken salad and a denver sandwich for himself and the same to go for Carter, he found himself beginning to relax, his mood improving. He was still curious about her, but did not find her as maddening as he had at first. She was conscientious and dedicated, which he admired. Would he ever know her well enough to like her? If they found the key to the fires, he supposed it wouldn't matter one way or the other, but having to work with her, he wanted more rapport.

When he got back to the PSS building, Carter was deep in study of her printouts. She thanked him in an absent way for the meal and told him to take the money for it out of her purse. She handed him a copy of what she was reviewing and asked him if he noticed anything in the patterns that suggested a similarity.

"I've gone over these so many times already—" he began.

"Well, I think it has something to do with equipment. All of the burnings took place in buildings with fairly sophisticated electronic equipment. Suppose someone found a way to trigger shorts in the machines; that could cause fires, couldn't it?"

"It might," he said, giving the question consideration. "But it's not that easy to do. Whoever was doing the triggering would need pretty impressive equipment to manage it, and whoever was controlling it would need to have very specific information about the types of electronic systems in operation and what the power sources and uses might be. That's off the top of my head, but it should be pretty accurate."

"All right, but suppose someone had enough information to do at least some of the fires. Couldn't that be what they have in common?"

"I suppose it could," said Frank. "But why? What's the motive?"

"God, I don't know. Why does anyone want to cause a fire?" She tossed the stack of sheets onto her desk. "But it's the only thing that looks even superficially consistent that I've been able to come up with." She opened the paper sack and took out the container that held her supper.

"Fires are set for any number of reasons," Frank said, frowning at the numbers on the sheet. "Gain, most often, and a desire to be rid of something. There are those who set fires for sexual reasons, but these aren't even in the same ballpark. Sabotage, terrorism, blackmail, subversion. If there was a group using a device like the one you suggest, they'd have made demands by now, I should think."

"Maybe they just like fires," ventured Carter.

"That's really stretching it," Frank said, though he had no better idea than she did.

"Do you think it might be worth finding out about power surges from the local utility companies for these fires?"

"Anything's worth a try," Frank said. "But don't expect too much. Big fires create their own kind of havoc with utilities."

"How encouraging." She began to eat the salad and between bites, she made notes to herself on a large yellow pad.

"What are you doing?" Frank asked when she had been at it for several minutes.

"Adding to the list; phone companies, water companies, alarm companies, and all the rest of it."

"You seem to like the idea," Frank commented without changing his tone.

"It's the only thing so far that fits." She met his eyes. "Why? Do you disagree?"

"I haven't got enough information to agree or disagree. I'm still very much in the dark." He read disappointment in her face and modified his stance. "You're right that it could fit the circumstances. But what does this trigger? Shorts don't usually burn down a whole building, it just wrecks one machine. What causes the short to take out whole city blocks and large buildings? If there were a secondary device, it could explain it, but then, how does the secondary device get into place, and why can we find no trace of it?"

"Another dead end?" she asked, her mouth turning down at the corners.

"Maybe not," Frank said. "Maybe if we could find out the focus, then we could tie in the electronic systems and deliberate shorting in a provable and workable pattern. We might as well give it a try."

Carter was starting on her sandwich. "You want to work late tonight?"

"What about you?" he asked, a little surprised at the suggestion.

"I've got to get home to feed the dog and cats sometime this evening, but there isn't any hurry. I wouldn't mind staying a couple more hours, to find out what kinds of systems were in place in the buildings that have burned so far."

Frank shrugged. "If I can call Toronto from here, okay."

"Go ahead. What's in Toronto?"

"My daughter," he said. "She's living with my sister-in-law and her family." He picked up the phone and started to dial, his thoughts full of Melinda.

"What does your wife think of that?"

"My wife's dead," Frank told her brusquely.

Carter looked up, clearly shocked and embarrassed. "I'm sorry; I didn't know."

He made a dismissing gesture as he listened to the telephone ring, and was rewarded when he heard Stan Bragondette answer the phone. "Hello, this is Frank. How are things in Canada?"

"Canadian," answered Stan. "How's the investigation going?"

"We're keeping busy. Is Melinda there?" He glanced over at Carter and gave her a reassuring smile.

"Melinda and our girls are at the movies. Anne went with them. They should be back in a couple hours at the most."

"I'll try to call back then," said Frank. "How's she doing, Stan?"

"Melinda? Pretty well. She has bad days, just as you'd expect, but in general she has a good outlook and her state of mind is improving."

"You'll tell her I called and say that I'll call again in two hours?" Frank asked, though he knew it was not necessary.

"Certainly. Good luck with the fire fighting," Stan said adding good-bye.

"It sounds as if your daughter misses you," Carter said in order to make some comment.

"I hope so. I miss her. She had a hard time when Barbara died, and it was recommended that she spend time in an established family. My sister-in-law has two daughters and Melinda really wanted to live with them for a while. It's been good for her; I can see the improvement every time we get together. She still remembers that firemen get burned, and she wants to know there's some security in her life. Her therapist said that in another year she might be ready to live at home with me again, but until she gets to that point, it's important for me to be patient. And right now, it's probably just as well."

Carter was silent, and when she spoke, her tone was much more sympathetic than Frank had ever heard. "It must be hard on you to have lost your wife and then have to share your daughter. You're a lot more generous than many people are."

"Generous?" Frank repeated, surprised.

"Yes," Carter said, watching him. "There are many people in your position who wouldn't be able to give up a child so soon after the death of a spouse. They'd want to hang on no matter what."

"Melinda was very depressed and frightened. I couldn't stand to watch her suffer so when there was something I could do about it."

"That's what I meant by generous," said Carter.

At eight-fifteen, Frank called Toronto again and spoke with Melinda for twenty minutes. She was curious about California and carefully avoided most questions about fires. Frank reminded her that he loved her and promised to call again in two days. When he hung up, he saw that Carter was putting her sheets into a portfolio.

"Are you through for tonight?" Frank asked incredulously.

"Not really; I was going to suggest that you might want to come over the hill with me. There're several nice motels in Santa Cruz where you can stay, and we can get more work done. You could have a bit of a break from here, and we'd—"

"Hold it," Frank said, puzzled once again by Carter. "Why this shift? Because you found out I love my daughter?"

"That's part of it," Carter said. "We can take my car and leave yours here for the night. That could save on your charges, couldn't it?"

"What's this all about?" Frank probed. "You're up to something."

Carter sighed. "No, I'm not. I just thought that we might be able to be friends. I'm not making a pass at you, I'm not trying to flatter you, I'm not anything. I've got to take care of my animals and I want to get more work done tonight. I thought that if we were working together we might save ourselves wasted effort, but if you don't agree, then so be it, and I'll see you in the morning."

Frank shook his head. "It doesn't make much sense, but okay, I'll go along with it. I'll let you find me a place for the night in Santa Cruz and we can go over the material in the car."

"Thanks," said Carter, resuming her packing. "Bring along that last sheet of printouts, okay? It has local utility companies listed for all the major fire locales, and tomorrow I want to start making inquiries there."

Obediently Frank picked up the papers. "Is there anything else?"

"Whatever you think you might need. I don't know how much stuff you want to go over for the comparisons." She found her purse and took out her keys. "It takes about forty-five minutes to get to my place, and I'll make sure you're at a motel before midnight."

"I'll need a razor and other things like that," Frank reminded her. "Where do I get those?"

"I've got things in the guest room you can use. I'd say sleep over at the house, but I don't think Greg would like it. Or you, for that matter. I don't want you to feel awkward about coming to Santa Cruz. I'll give the local motel a call from here and arrange a room in advance, if that's what you'd like."

"I'll take a chance, since it's October." He paused, and when she did not offer a smile, he went on, "You don't have much tourist traffic at this time of year, do you?"

"Oh, that. No, not really." She was almost ready to go. She checked her monitor one last time and as they went out the door, she tried the knob twice to make sure it was locked.

"You're very careful," Frank said as they took the elevator down to the main floor.

"J.D. encourages it," she remarked, taking care to let herself out of the building through the security system.

"Have you ever had any problems?" Frank asked as they crossed the parking lot to her Audi.

"It would cause a lot of red faces if we ever did, considering the business we're in. J.D. likes us to set an example so that he can demonstrate our methods on the spot." She opened the passenger door for him, then went around to the driver's side. "Be sure your seat belt is fastened," she reminded him as she secured her own.

He was impressed again with how cautiously she lived, and though he said nothing more about that, he once again was puzzled by her.

Once over the crest of the coast range they encountered fog.

"It isn't likely to get very thick at this time of year,"

said Carter as she decreased her speed. "If there's anything I like less than fog, it's heavy rain."

"It must make driving hard on a road this twisty."

"Especially if it's windy. I've had—" She broke off with a shriek as a TransAm hurtled up behind and swerved around her.

"Problems," Frank said, deliberately keeping his voice level.

"If that was Greg—" she said, then stopped. "That would be part of the whole thing, I guess."

"Part of what whole thing?" Frank asked her, hearing desolation in her words.

"Oh, the risks, the gambling. He might as well drive like a crazy man." She shook her head. "I don't mean to speak against him. He's my husband and we've been married a long time. Sometimes marriages go through rough stretches. Sometimes there are problems and you have to work them through."

In the shine of approaching headlights, Frank saw that she was crying. "Carter, what is it?"

"Nothing. Truly. We're having a few difficulties is all, and with the strain about the fires, I don't have the time I need to work with him so we can make things better."

"Um," said Frank, not knowing what to say, but aware that he needed to let her know he was listening.

She continued to drive slowly, her eyes on the obscure bendings of the fog-shrouded highway. "It's been hard on Greg, no longer being the wunderkind he was for most of his twenties. He was more in the limelight then, and he got used to it. Now that it isn't so much the case, he looks for more excitement. It takes time to adjust to changes like that."

"It sounds like a tough time for him," Frank said, wanting to say that he was more concerned about her.

"It has been," she said gratefully. "I think that's why the gambling—you see, it has some of the same fascination that his work used to have, some of the recognition and thrill, some of the ways of winning." Her words faltered, but she made herself go on. "It scares me, sometimes, the gambling. It used to be for smaller amounts, nothing over a hundred dollars. Then it was nothing over a thousand, and now I don't think he has any limit. He says it isn't interesting unless it's worth money. It might be true. I don't know."

"I don't know much about gambling," Frank said by way of apology. "If he's hooked on it, maybe he can get into a support group or see someone about it."

"He doesn't want to. He tells me he likes gambling." She took one hand and tucked a stray lock of hair behind her ear. "He wants to gamble."

"How do you feel about it? It's none of my business, I know, but if you'd like to—" He was not sure himself if he ought to hear any more, but in the fog, they seemed so isolated, so removed from the world that they were exempted from the usual barriers.

"I don't know how I feel about it," she said as she swung onto a connecting ramp. "I used to know; I could deal with it and when he finally tired of it, I was planning to be ready to help him find a new direction. Not like a martyr, you understand, but . . . I don't know."

"Like a friend?" Frank suggested.

"Yes, that's it," she said, her expression lightening.

"What makes you doubt that now?" Frank asked.

Carter signaled for her exit. "I don't think he wants a friend, at least not now, and maybe not later. He's more interested in the money and . . . if I'm willing to give it to him, that's all he wants. I don't know what to do with that."

"You can't be sure," he said, watching two fuzzy lights approach and pass them as Carter signaled for a left turn.

"Yes, I can," she said sadly. "He told me that was what he wanted from me and all he wanted from me. I gave him what he asked for, and I still don't know if I ought to have done it." She drove along a town street, pointing out a large motel. "I'll bring you back here later."

"If you don't want to tell me, that's okay, but how much money did you give him?" Frank felt awkward, but he could not assess his reaction unless he had a general idea of what her husband had taken from her.

"Twenty-six thousand, seven hundred dollars," Carter said flatly. "Please don't tell anyone."

"Twenty-six thousand?" Frank repeated, his throat constricting.

"It took most of my savings. He used his up in July and—" She stopped at a red light and at last turned to look at him. "I'm really frightened."

"Jesus Christ, that's a lot of money." He rubbed his face with both hands.

"It took me almost fourteen years to save it, and there isn't much left in the bank. If he has another big loss, we'll probably have to take out a second mortgage or sell the house, or..." She could not bring herself to go on.

"Oh, Carter," Frank said, having no words or comfort to offer, and no suggestions for help. Her faint air of distraction and preoccupation was no longer a mystery. "Is there someone who could help out, talk to your husband? Explain the risks?"

"I don't know. If you mean family, he was the brilliant kid in a blue-collar family, and they don't get along very well. His mother calls on his birthday to remind him that the higher you climb the longer you'll fall. He has a few friends who pal around with him at work, but I don't know most of them." She sniffed once. "It wasn't like this five years ago. Five years ago there were people we knew together and things we did for fun." She made another turn. "I'm sorry; I didn't mean to dump all this on you. It all caught up with me a couple days back and you were unlucky enough to be around when the dam broke."

"Hey," he said, "we're working together and how you feel about what we're doing could have some bearing on how well we do it. It's one of the hazards of an emergency." He noticed that the road they were on was narrower, threading between tall trees. "You had to tell someone."

"But it isn't fair to expect you to—"

"Give a damn?" he finished for her when she did not go on.

"I guess so."

"Since when does an emergency cancel real life? Did couples suddenly make up because it was Vietnam? Did Germans stop having trouble with kids during the World War II bombing raids? The best you can do is put those things on hold: they don't go away."

At last Carter turned into a driveway and onto a parking deck. "Well, here we are. The barking you hear is Winslow."

"He's a hungry dog." Frank got out of the car, taking care to lock his door while Carter took her portfolio out of the back seat along with his papers.

"Yes. Winslow gets nervous when dinner is later than eight at night."

"Nothing unusual in that," said Frank as he followed Carter to the door. It was a pretty house, he thought. It would be a shame if she lost it.

"There's a light switch on your right," said Carter as she went into the dark room.

Frank found it and blinked as the brightness struck his night-widened eyes. "It's a nice place, Carter," he said with sincerity.

"I love it," Carter said simply, and pointed toward the living room. "Have a seat and I'll be with you. I want to call Fred at the motel to let him know I'll be bringing you over later this evening." She ducked into the kitchen and opened the door for Winslow and the cats.

When the call had been made and the animals fed, Carter joined Frank in the living room, bringing a pot of freshly brewed coffee with her.

"Not all the buildings that burned had computers in them," Frank said as he held out the printed sheets. "And some of them had several. I don't know what to make of that."

"Well," Carter asked, "do you find any matchup? What about modems, telephone connections, long-distance services, and all the rest of it? I think there has to be a connection." She had taken mugs from the cupboard and poured out coffee. "I'm out of milk. If you're desperate, I can put a little ice cream in your coffee, but the only flavor in the freezer is chocolate."

"Black is fine," Frank said. "I think that we'd better concentrate on the computer and security equipment. You're bound to have better information about that than anything else."

"True enough," said Carter as she put down the mugs. "Fred told me he'd have a key waiting for you at the office, by the way. He gave you the end room, with the best light."

They spent the next half-hour going over the printouts, making notes about electronic equipment and security systems. It was painstaking work and very frustrating, complicated by Pyotr and Modeste's determination to curl up on whatever they were working on.

They were interrupted by the sound of a car arriving, and Carter looked up in dismay. "That's Greg," she said as the engine fell silent.

Frank felt suddenly awkward. "Is that a problem?"

"I don't know," she said.

The car door slammed and urgent steps came to the house. As Carter rose to answer the door, it swung open and Greg Milne shoved his way into the house, his face set in irate lines.

"Greg," Carter faltered, seeing his expression.

"The fuckers were cheating," he said. "They were cheating."

Carter's face fell. "You were playing cards?"

"Just a company game, after hours. Hoopes won all night. I was having lousy luck, but that wasn't what made the difference; he was cheating. The bastard won over three hundred bucks from me." He caught sight of Frank, and his face grew thunderous.

Carter intervened. "Honey, this is Fire Marshal Vickery from Philadelphia. He's been assigned to PSS for the investigation of these terrible fires. Frank, this is my husband Greg Milne."

Frank rose, extending his hand. "Good to meet you, Greg."

Greg did not accept the handshake. "You're working mighty late," he accused. "Or do they give you extra for entertaining visitors, Carter?"

Frank bristled, but Carter did her best to laugh. "Over a nice romantic stack of printouts," Carter said, with a wave to the papers strewn over the coffee table.

"Finding out anything interesting?" Greg asked nastily.

"Don't I wish," said Frank, looking resigned. "About all we have to go on is that the fires may have something to do with electronic equipment."

Greg laughed harshly. "Not shining, are we, Carter? No magic statistics? Are you baffled?"

"Yes, Greg. And so is everyone else working on the case. We've been trying to find the key, if there is one, so we can stop the next fire from happening."

"God, you sound prissy when you talk like that," Greg told her as he flung himself into the largest chair in the living room. "And all you've got so far is that it might have something to do with the electronic equipment? What about the uses of the equipment? What about codes?" He nodded to himself. "You got your hands full, don't you?"

"I have had since early September," she said, exasperated.

"And you're just getting around to the electronic equipment?" He picked up the sheets of figures. "Coglin Optics. Four different security codes. That's pretty impressive, and one for after hours, as well as a special code for the executive wing. Quite a thorough display for PSS. And a sign-out code for after hours as well. Not bad."

"Greg..." Carter said with an uneasy shake of her head.

"And you haven't been able to figure it out. Pity." He looked from Frank to Carter. "All the brains at PSS and everywhere else can't get to the bottom of it? Well, there has to be a system, doesn't there? Everything has a system. It's just a matter of finding it. That really isn't hard, Carter.

Kids work out systems every day." He looked at the sheet. "Tell you what: I'm going to be home tomorrow and I'll spend a few hours on this. I can probably come up with something, don't you think?"

"I hope you can, Greg," Carter said with genuine feeling.

"I'll bet you haven't looked for the system. You're probably still trying to figure curves and commonality, right? It's always the system." He waved his finger at her, then winked at Frank. "She's pretty bright, but she doesn't have much creativity. It hampers her."

Frank could think of no good answer to this taunt, so he said, "If you can come up with something, you'd be doing the whole country a service."

"Sure," Greg said. "Great to hear it. Just make sure they have a good reward, that's all I ask." He cocked his head toward Carter. "Want me to solve this for you, Peanut? Want me to work it out?"

"If you can, that would be wonderful," said Carter with feeling. "I don't care who finds the answer so long as it's found before too many more people die."

"God, aren't you noble?" Greg mocked. "Maybe I should license the system when I figure it out, let the government have it so they can use the fires. They might like that as a new secret weapon or— what do you think of that idea, Peanut?"

Frank decided to end the evening. "Carter, if I'm going to be worth anything in the morning, maybe I better get down to the motel. I'd appreciate the loan of a razor."

"Loan of a razor, is it? How cozy." Greg bowed to Carter. "Too bad you'll have to postpone whatever extras you had planned for tonight."

"We had work planned for tonight." Frank's voice was far more sharp than usual.

"Whatever you say," Greg jeered. "I'll help myself to the leftovers." He got up and ambled into the kitchen.

"Come on. I'll get the razor and a toothbrush. I usually have two or three in the linen closet, for guests." She shifted her gaze to the kitchen door. "I'm sorry about this. It's really been very inexcusable and I—"

"Carter," Frank interrupted her gently, "he's the one who has bad manners, not you. I don't expect you to be his teacher or his mother. You don't need to say anything more."

"It is just bad manners, Frank." It was more a plea than a defense.

"So let's go, and let him do what he wants." He indicated the door.

Carter accepted the offer at once. "I'll get the things for you."

As Frank waited, he stared at the kitchen door, still trying to fathom Greg's malice.

It was almost four o'clock the next afternoon when two uniformed police officers showed up at the PSS building and asked for Carter Milne.

"Is it urgent?" Dena Ottermeyer asked, giving the two policemen her most daunting stare.

"Yes, it is," said the older.

"I'll ring her; she's in conference." Dena picked up the telephone and dialed J.D.'s office. "This is Ms. Ottermeyer. There are two policemen here who say they have to speak with Doctor Milne. Can they be interrupted?"

Phylis Dunlap, who was a good deal more flexible than Dena, rang through at once, and reported that Carter would be right down.

The two policemen thanked Dena politely, and that continuing politeness put Dena even more on her guard. "May I ask what this is about?"

"It's an emergency. Doctor Milne is needed at home at once." The younger officer shifted from one foot to the other as he spoke, not willing to meet Dena's eyes.

Dena sighed noticeably and went back to typing request letters to various insurance companies.

Carter returned to her office in less than five minutes, her face pale but composed. She was afraid that Greg had got into trouble gambling and might be in jail, or the hospital. "Hello," she said to the policemen, extending her hand to each of them in turn. "I'm Carter Milne. I understand you need to speak with me." She found it difficult to breathe, and she refused to meet either man's eyes.

"I'm afraid we have bad news, Missus Milne," said the older man, sounding awkward and troubled.

"Oh, dear," Carter murmured, glancing once at Dena. "Should we talk in my office?"

"If you prefer. There's been a fire."

Carter looked puzzled, then almost laughed. "Another one? How many does this make? I didn't realize we'd had one in San Jose yet."

"I beg your pardon?" the older policeman said, more confused than Carter was.

"It's about a fire. Since we're doing a project on these fires, I— It's not about that kind of fire?" She had the oddest sensation in her chest, as if her ribs had turned cold and hard, made of steel or stone.

"The Fire Department in Aptos called us—"

He was interrupted as Cynthia Harper came into Carter's outer office. "If you need me, Carter." She, too, had assumed that Greg had finally got himself in over his head.

"The Fire Department in Aptos?" It was small and staffed by volunteers. She frowned.

"There's been a fire. At your home." He tried to say this gently, but Carter stared at him in the dazed way accident victims stare. "We're sorry."

"A fire at my home?" She repeated the words as if they had been in a foreign language.

"They're requesting that you return at once. We're here to drive you, if you need that, and escort you, if you want to be escorted. We'll arrange it with the Highway Patrol."

"But—"

Cynthia took charge at that point. "I'll drive Doctor Milne's car; we'd appreciate an escort. It was good of you to offer." She put her arm around Carter. "We have a Fire Marshal from Philadelphia working with us on our current project, and if you don't mind, I'd like to ask him to come with us. I'm sure he could be of help." She eased Carter into one of the two chairs provided for visitors, then turned to Dena. "Ring J.D.'s office, tell him what's happened and ask for Marshal Vickery to join us at once."

The two policemen exchanged looks.

"Then if either of you officers will tell me how serious the fire was?" She intercepted the covert glance one of them threw in Carter's direction. "Whatever it is, she'll have to know sometime."

"Her house and three others were destroyed. Apparently there are four serious burn cases and at least five fatalities. The fire started around two-forty-five and spread very fast." The younger officer cleared his throat. "One of the fatalities was at her house. The assumption is that her... husband was at home. There was no way he could have been rescued, according to the report we've seen. The house just... went up, like a torch. That's what the men in Santa Cruz said. They had fire fighters from Cabrillo and Capitola and Santa Cruz all working on it."

"Greg?" Carter said, still dazed.

"He was in the fire, Carter," Cynthia said, going to put her hand on Carter's arm. "He was in the house, they said."

"He was working on the computer. He said..." She let her voice trail off and began to cry.

Dena, speaking in an undervoice, informed J.D. Patterson of what had occurred and gave Cynthia's request for Frank Vickery with more reservations than usual. "Pardon me, Ms. Harper," she said as she put down the receiver. "Mister Patterson extends his condolences and says that Marshal Vickery is on his way down right now."

"Good," said Cynthia, adding, "I need to use your phone." She had to let Ben know that she would not be home at dinnertime.

* * *

One of the worst things about it was the smell, Carter thought as she stood on the road and looked at the wreckage of her house and the houses on either side. The landscape was no longer familiar, and only her memory was able to trace out where the rooms had been, where the parking deck had stood, where the trees had sheltered the back deck. The fire had consumed everything down to the creek and on the far bank several of the bushes were scorched and charred.

"Doctor Milne?" said an exhausted fireman. "I'm sorry, but it isn't safe to get much closer."

"I understand," she said, stepping back. The pictures she had seen had not brought so much shock to her, not even when they were of huge buildings eaten by the flames. The pictures did not convey desolation so totally as the sight of her vanished house, and the destroyed houses of her neighbors.

The burned-out shell of Greg's TransAm was half buried in the ashes. Carter stared at it, trying to make herself understand that Greg was dead.

"Doctor Milne," said another official, "we're going to need a report from you as soon as possible. We're still trying to establish the cause of the fire. If you have any idea what your husband was doing, we'd like to know. We made some calls, and—"

"He was investigating the fires," Carter said, choking on the words. "PSS, the company where I work—"

"We're aware of where you work, Missus Milne," the man said curtly.

"We're involved in the investigation of the unexplained fires that have been going on all over the country. We're trying to coordinate the information. Greg's a mathematician, and he thought that as long as he was home for the day"—she could not bring herself to remember their last, bitter conversation—"he'd go over some of the material, in case he might spot something,

something we'd missed." She stared at the ugly ruin in front of her.

"And how long had he been out of work?" the official asked.

"He wasn't out of work. He told me that he was planning to quit in the next three months." She was surprised at the question, and found it frightening.

"We called his company half an hour after answering the alarm on this fire; they told us he was fired two months ago."

"He can't have been," she objected. "This is ludicrous. Call Jim Morris and ask him." The lethargy of shock gave way to a hard surge of indignation and energy.

"We already talked to Jim Morris," the man said patiently, following Carter as she turned and walked back to the police cars blocking the road. "He said that Greg Milne had been warned several times and they had reluctantly fired him."

"I'll call him myself." She approached Cynthia, her face set. "Can you imagine that? He says that Jim Morris told him that Greg doesn't work for him anymore. Didn't," she amended softly.

"Since when?" Cynthia wanted to be more outraged, but knew that it was quite possible for Greg Milne to keep his firing a secret from Carter. "How did they find out?"

"They say they made some calls," Carter answered vaguely. "It sounds like they've been real busy."

"What 'they' are we talking about?" Cynthia asked.

"One of the fire officials," Carter said.

Cynthia did a little rapid calculation in her head and decided that the two hours the fire department had had was more than enough time to gather basic information on the Milnes. She looked around. "Which is he?"

"Over there," Carter said, pointing out the official who had questioned her.

As if invited, the man strolled over to Cynthia. "Let me introduce myself," he said to both women. "I'm Henry Broeder, of the Santa Cruz County arson squad," he said, watching her closely to see her reaction.

"You think this was arson?" Carter demanded, her control all but shattered. "You think that my husband set the house on fire because of some misunderstanding about his work? Is that it?"

Cynthia, hearing this, came over to intervene. "Hey, is this the time or the place, buster?" she asked of Broeder. "Where do you get off hassling this woman?"

Broeder said, "This fire certainly isn't like the electrical-failure fires we see in most houses. Since Doctor Milne was out of work and had large gambling debts, we figure he arranged this, with or without his wife's knowledge, and gave the electrical failure a little help. And if that's the case, the insurance company is going to want to know as soon as possible so that they can decide what to do about their policy." He folded his arms and looked at Cynthia.

"We'll see about that," Cynthia said, as much to Carter as to Inspector Broeder. "You're going to have to be able to prove that, and if you don't, you might find some interesting litigation awaiting you." She handed her card to Broeder and waited for his reaction.

"I've got a job to do. We lost lives and property in this fire, and so far there's no good reason for it to have happened. What would you do in my position? Especially given the facts."

"You mean your allegations. I don't know that what you say about Greg is true"—though she admitted to herself that she would not be surprised to learn that Greg had lost his job through his gambling—"but until it is established one way or another, you have no business treating this woman the way you have."

"There's always the possibility she helped out," Broeder said, opening his hands to show that he was at the mercy of his profession.

"Carter might do a lot for Greg, but believe me, there is no way she would burn her house, or start any fire. We've been investigating fires and—"

Broeder interrupted her. "Yeah, we know that. It's what got me to thinking that there might have been a plan to make this another one of those mysterious fires and then get out of any questions that way. I'm sure by now that she knows enough about them to fake it pretty well."

Carter, who had been standing dazed and silent, looked up, and her face was contorted with fury. "What kind of a ghoul do you think I am? Or Greg... was? How can you believe that anyone, after seeing what one of those fires can do, would ever, *ever* want to have anything like that happen again, to anyone, anywhere? How can you think this? What's wrong with you?" She had started to sob.

Broeder gave Carter a measuring look. "We also thought that perhaps it wasn't supposed to happen while anyone was at home." He raised his voice defensively. "Look at it from my point of view. We get a fire that causes a lot of damage and destruction, for no apparent reason, or none that makes sense, and we have to do something to find out why it happened. With all the work you've done with fires, you ought to be able to appreciate my problem."

"Look at it from her point of view—she's been trying to determine how those fires start for over a month, and now she seems to have lost her husband to one." Cynthia looked over her shoulder, hoping to find Frank Vickery, but he was not in sight. "We've got a Fire Marshal from Philadelphia with us, and if you have any doubts about the role Carter might have played in this, you talk to him. I guarantee you that you'll find out your suspicions are wrong." She had taken her best firm tone and waited for Broeder to back off.

"You read it one way, I read it another. You can't say for sure you're right, and for now I can't prove—and I understand about proof, counselor—that this was arson, but if there is the least little bit of evidence, you know I'll find it, and when I do, anyone who had any association with this fire will be in a lot of trouble." He looked very much like a bulldog just then, and Cynthia was fully convinced that he was as good as his word.

"Inspector," Carter said, the words coming badly, "aside from Greg, did you find anything else in . . . in the house? We have two cats and a dog."

"There was one cat. I don't know about the other one, or the dog." He answered with genuine confusion, and decided that Carter was still in shock. "You might want to ask some of the fire fighters, or the neighbors. Maybe you should try the animal shelter or the pound."

"Thank you," Carter said, breathing deeply and shakily. "I will." She scanned the brush on the other side of the creek, now an indistinguishable mass in the gathering darkness. "Winslow!" she called in a thread of a voice. "Here, Winslow."

"Carter," Cynthia said, choking on her friend's name. "Come on. We'll find him later." This last was a polite fabrication; she assumed that the dog and one cat would never be found.

"But . . ." Carter said, trying to break away. "He's frightened and might run off if he can't find anything he knows." She called the dog, more loudly, going as close to the ruined buildings as she was allowed. "Here, Winslow!"

Once again Cynthia took her arm. "Come on. We'll tell the fire fighters and some of the others to be on the lookout for him."

"He won't come to them. Chows are very aloof. *Winslow!*"

"Carter, come on. Tomorrow we'll look again, if you want, and we'll make sure his description is left."

"I have to wait awhile," said Carter. "I have to make the effort. I have to save something." She pulled away from Cynthia and began to walk along the road, still calling for her dog.

Inspector Broeder looked after her. "If it makes you feel any better, I don't think she wanted the fire to get out of hand. I think that she expected interior damage and no one hurt." He turned to regard Cynthia. "That's the direction the investigation is taking right now, and until I find reason—"

"You're being generous to tell me," Cynthia said sarcastically. "I think I'll stick with my original premise, that this was an accident, or one of the unexplained fires. And if you don't do your best to check that possibility out as well, you can explain the omission in court. I trust you understand me." She started after Carter, going toward her.

Carter had gone beyond the three burned houses and was looking toward the woods beyond the road. She was still calling her dog, her voice high and thin, sounding almost like a child. She walked slowly, as if she were lost.

"Carter, let's go. Leave the firemen to finish up. If there's anything they find, they can call my place." Cynthia held out her hand.

"But...oh, God, Cynthia, I don't have anything!" She faced her friend. "I thought I needed a change of clothes, but I don't have anything but these and the jeans in my trunk. Do I?" This last was the only trace of hope she could maintain.

"You can get some more. In the meantime, we're about the same size. I'll loan you a nightgown and something for tomorrow. Everyone will understand." She approached Carter as if she was uncertain of how she would be perceived.

"Thanks," she said, forlorn. "Winslow!"

"We'll come tomorrow morning," Cynthia promised her, unwilling to take away this one last hope.

"Wins-low!" she shouted.

Over her shoulder, Cynthia could see one of the firemen coming toward her, and she knew she would have to take Carter home soon. She gave the man a signal that might give her a few more seconds of privacy with Carter. "I'll call the credit-card companies and arrange for a leave of absence with J.D.," she continued. "And we can go shopping. There are some sales at the Pruneyard that will tide you over."

"I'll have to go to the bank," Carter said in a distracted way. "I don't have much right now, but..." She looked back toward the woods, then sighed and started toward

Cynthia. "Okay; tomorrow morning we can come back and I'll try again."

"I'm sorry, Carter. I really am," Cynthia said, tears standing in her eyes.

"I know," Carter said simply, and with a tiny, regretful sigh followed after Cynthia.

Then, down the road from the woods, there came a soot-colored dog with a singed ruff, his black tongue lolling. He favored his right front paw, and when he was near enough, he whimpered; Carter rushed to him, dropping down beside him, her hands locked in his coat while she cried.

Frank Vickery sat at a formica-topped table at the back of the Aptos Fire Station, a mug of beef broth cooling in his hand. It was almost eleven at night, and he was thinking that this was the first time that the unexplained fires had come so close to the investigators. He was exhausted, but it brought nostalgia with it, for it reminded him of the years he had spent actually fighting fires instead of coordinating fire-fighting information.

"Is there anything else you can tell me about these fires?" Inspector Broeder said, as he drank the dregs of his coffee. His jaw was dark with stubble and he was getting hoarse.

"You've got the gist of it: they're sudden, hot, and large. I can arrange for a full profile to be sent from the Fire Data people in Washington, as well as give you everything Patterson has on them." He had convinced Broeder that he had been hasty in suspecting arson, but not that Greg Milne had somehow stumbled onto the cause of the fire and it had been the death of him.

"But they can't go around booby-trapping every single computer in the country, Vickery; that doesn't make sense." He had been voicing variations on this complaint for the better part of three hours.

"None of it makes sense," Frank reminded him. "But I'm beginning to think that Greg was right, and there is some kind of system to them." He drank the last of the broth, but still felt cold.

"System!" scoffed Broeder. "You might as well account for it all by witchcraft."

"That might have something to do with them as well; I'm prepared to believe it." Frank stood up. "Any chance of getting a ride back to San Jose at this hour?"

"I'll check with Haskins. He said he'd make sure you get back to your hotel." He tucked his pages of notes into a small briefcase and reached for the wall phone. "We must look pretty rinky-dink to you, with volunteers and these small stations."

"Actually, it makes me want to be back fighting fires." He was quiet while Broeder talked to Lloyd Haskins, arranging Frank's ride back to San Jose.

"How long have you been on the Fire Marshals' Task Force?" Broeder asked when he had hung up.

"Just over three years. We didn't have much to do until these fires started." He stood up and carried his mug to the sink at the back of the room.

"Bet you got your hands full now," Broeder said.

"More than any of us could have thought," Frank said heavily.

"Nice thing that Missus Milne's dog came back," Broeder said by way of small talk.

"Yes," Frank said, hoping that Winslow was not badly injured. He knew that Carter could not sustain another loss in her life without even more serious repercussions than she had already experienced.

"Too bad about the cats, though." He looked around as there was a knock on the side door. "That'll be Lloyd."

"How—?" Frank began.

"He lives two houses down," Broeder explained.

"Ah," said Frank, reaching for his jacket. "Thanks, Inspector. I'll make sure you get all the information I can."

The two shook hands before Frank left with Lloyd Haskins.

* * *

In San Jose it was seventy-six degrees; Lansing had been forty-three in the chill autumn morning when William Ridour had started his journey west, going as far as Denver in the first leg, and then changing planes in a ninety-minute layover. He had never been to northern California before, and was curious about this fabled Silicone Valley, the Santa Clara Valley, once filled with more orchards than microchips.

His first phone call to PSS had not been encouraging.

"Mister Patterson," said Phylis Dunlap in her most neutral tone, "believes he cannot show preference to any member of the news media, and therefore he is refusing all requests for such information. I'm sure you understand."

"Yes," said William at his most polite. "But I don't agree. I intend to do my job and pursue this story with or without Patterson's cooperation."

"You're well within your rights to do so," Phylis said. "We have no intention of interfering."

William had to give Patterson full marks for that; anyone attempting to muzzle a newsman without a gag order from the courts was asking for serious trouble.

When he had tried a few more offices at PSS, he decided to change tactics. He rented a car and drove out to the PSS industrial park, then scouted the area for restaurants where employees might be expected to eat. He decided on three and a possible fourth, and began to plan his rounds. Eventually he would find someone who wanted to talk, and when he did, he would be ready.

The second restaurant was the most elegant in an informal way, with dark beams and brass accents and a menu featuring such items as fresh grilled fish with almond-and-olive butter. William requested a table near the bar and deliberated over his order, in part because of his plan and in part because so much of what was offered was unfamiliar to him. What on earth was Orange Roughy?

"The salad for the day is Bibb lettuce with goat cheese

and a raspberry vinegar and extra virgin olive oil dressing," his waitress informed him. "The soup is spicy black bean."

"Thank you," William murmured, trying to overhear a comment at the bar. There was a man talking with a well-dressed and attractive young woman, and William had heard him say Patterson. "Is there any way to get a hamburger?"

"If that's what you want," the waitress said, clearly offended. "Would you like creole spices or plain grilled?"

"Whichever you think is better," William said. "And I'll have one of your salads, too." He did not want the waitress giving him a bad time.

"—but it's not like simple shock, and you know it," the woman was saying. "All right, you and I both admit that this is a very high stress time for all of us, without anything like what she's going through, but I think you're mistaken in keeping her away from the project."

"It's only been two days since the fire; her husband's memorial service isn't for three days yet. You're jumping the gun, Cynthia." The man ordered red wine for both of them and asked that their table be ready in twenty minutes.

"I still say that she'd feel better, and handle things better, if she were back on the project. All she does now is brood, and tranks aren't the answer. She has to have something to do, something that gives her a sense of accomplishment. It isn't enough to have the dog, she's got to help us." The woman picked up her wineglass and made a vague gesture that might have been a toast while her companion spoke.

"You might be right, but I can't go along with the idea that it would be good for her. She's been through too much, and the pressure is too high right now. She could fall apart without warning, and that wouldn't do anyone any good." He waited for the woman to make her next argument.

"She's depressed; I know that. You'd be depressed too, if you'd been through what she had. But that doesn't mean that she's not up to working."

The waitress arrived with William's salad and put it in

front of him with a flourish. "Would you like anything to drink? We have a very nice French Colombard we're pouring at three-twenty-five the glass."

"Coffee, please," said William, not wanting to fuzz his mind.

"Caffeinated?"

"Please," he said, wanting her to go away and let him listen.

"There's milk and sugar on the table. You can request milk substitutes and sugar substitutes if you like." Her smile was more of a smirk.

"I take it black."

"—too much of a reminder," the man was saying to the woman. "You admit that this is my area of expertise, and I want you to know that your concern is really terrific. You're being supportive without intruding. That's quite an accomplishment."

"She's my friend," said the woman.

"But what do you think could happen to her, being forced to relive these fires every day? Even though she and Greg had problems, they were still married, she is a new widow and she has just lost everything. I don't think I can give her a clean pass to come back to work for a while. If you guys insist, then the only thing I can do is be sure my reservations are on record." He was half finished with his wine and signaled for a second glass. "You want one?"

"I've got to do some assessments for Glen, and I have to have my mind sharp." She had set her wineglass aside with less than a third of it gone. "Still, it helps to have a break like this."

"All part of my job, the way I see it. J.D. expects me to minimize the stress he puts everyone under, and I do the best I can. It's not easy to be a shrink for a company full of compulsive overachievers." He gave a gesture of mock surrender. "If you're determined to go back into the front lines, the only thing left for me is to remind you that you're taking a risk."

"Randy, in your heart of hearts, you're the last of the swashbucklers. The only place you can still get a kick from plundering is minds, and that's what you do." She kissed him on the cheek and then said, "Come on, let's have lunch while we can."

William was disappointed when he realized how far away from him the two would be seated. He had heard just enough to be tantalized, but not enough to proceed.

When the woman left, the man came back to the bar and ordered another glass of wine. He drank slowly and with relish, more pleased now than he had been earlier.

Taking a chance, William got up from the table and took the stool two away from the Patterson psychiatrist. He ordered a glass of red wine and opened up his notebook, reading through all he had been able to gather since coming to San Jose, which was not much. He made no attempt to talk to the middle-aged man.

"Problems?" asked the psychiatrist when almost fifteen minutes had passed.

"Everyone's got 'em," William responded.

"True enough," the psychiatrist said, adding as he held out his hand, "I'm Randall Whiting."

"William Ridour." He found Whiting's handclasp firm but not crushing. "I'm a journalist. You?"

"Shrink," answered Whiting. "I thought you'd figured that out earlier when you were watching Cynthia Harper and me."

"Was I that obvious?" William asked in dismay, knowing he had not been.

"You were restrained." He lifted his glass. "You're not pushy, though, and that's a pleasant change."

"Here's to soft sell," said William, a glint in his eyes.

"You've been doing responsible reporting, too," added Whiting. "I've seen most of your articles, including the one two days ago about that fire in the naval shipyards. You say that it doesn't fit the pattern. You all but said it was espionage."

William felt off balance, which was rare for him. "I'm flattered, I think. Most people don't pay much attention to bylines."

"Well, I had a little help there. We've got a Fire Marshal Vickery on loan to us, and he—"

"Frank Vickery's here?" William said with satisfaction, thinking that at last he had a chance to get somewhere with PSS.

"He's supposed to liaise with us and the other investigators, like the FBI. He told me about you, and I have to admit that broad-shouldered tall black journalists aren't all that common. Would you like another glass of wine? I should warn you that I'm switching to coffee." Whiting had a breezy way of talking, and William suspected that he cultivated it to put others at their ease.

"Coffee's fine," William said, smiling in spite of himself.

"I gather you've been getting the usual blank wall from the company? It's the policy toward newspersons, ever since that Foss woman tried to waylay J.D. in the parking lot three days ago."

William had heard about that, and had not quite believed it, though it seemed the sort of thing she might do. "She's a very tough lady. She's going to ride this to the top if it kills her."

"I wouldn't say that in jest, young man," Whiting warned. "The fires have cost too many lives already."

William faced Frank over the desk in his temporary office at PSS. "I don't think it was wrong to put forth another theory, and from what I've heard, you've considered it yourself. So what's wrong with me saying and printing what you're kicking around?"

"The trouble is, it's going to make most people more paranoid than they already are, and it could cause serious problems. And all that might not make one jot of difference where the fires are concerned, because we're guessing wrong. Or because we're grasping at straws." He had been glad to see William when Randall Whiting brought him to Frank's office three days before, but he was aware that the newsman was searching for answers and pieces of answers, and that might not work out well between them.

"I understand that the Santa Cruz County Fire Marshal is saying that the fire at Doctor Milne's house was caused by faulty machinery, that there was something wrong with the computer itself and it malfunctioned." William was aware that this was a very touchy subject with Frank, but they would come to it eventually and he decided that now was better than later.

"That's what the official decision is." Frank had read the report the night before, and had given it to J.D. with the note that they might consider it a possibility.

"Judging from your tone of voice, you're not convinced."

"Nothing convinces me right now about these fires. And, since you're curious, yes, I think that the fire at the Milne house was caused by whatever is causing the other fires; I think that Gregory Milne got too close to an answer and it killed him. How and why I don't know." He read increased interest in William's face. "I'd prefer you don't quote me yet. If it turns out that we can get something—anything—to support the theory, then I give you my word that you'll have the whole thing, okay?"

"Not entirely," William said, "but acceptable. And for what it's worth to you, I don't blame you. Ever since McPherson came out with his death-ray explanation last week, everyone's treating all suggestions as crackpot."

"McPherson's idea *is* crackpot," Frank said. "That's off the record, too."

"Would you mind if I say that a highly placed source in the investigatory team believes that McPherson's death-ray theory does not quite account for what we've learned about the fires? Remember, Nina Foss has already pointed out that the notion of an invisible death-ray satellite that homes in on industrial equipment is too farfetched even for nineteen-fifties science fiction."

"That woman," Frank said, shaking his head, "is a barracuda and I hope she never goes after me the way she went after McPherson. Not that I didn't enjoy it, but—"

"Yeah," said William. "But."

They sat in silence for a couple of minutes, each following his own thoughts. Then Frank said, "William, I've got an idea that might get you some more stories without putting anyone here in jeopardy, or doing things that might upset the public more than it already is."

"Sounds great. What is it?" William could not keep the skeptical edge out of his voice.

"I think that we can let you know how we are going about the investigation from this end, and how it fits in with other aspects of the investigation. I'll call J.D. and see if he'll approve it, but it might be the answer for all of us. You get your story, we get to do our work and no one gets hassled too much... or no more than we're already being hassled."

"Aren't you stretching a point? Why would you do this for me?" He liked Frank well enough, but he did not believe that the Fire Marshal from Philadelphia wanted to have a journalist checking up on him.

"Because I think that you're already getting a lot of information from Randy Whiting, and he doesn't understand half of what he hears about the fires. He's a good shrink, or so they tell me, and he's got some kind of spectacular record for dealing with patients under stress, but that isn't the same thing as knowing what the fire investigation is really like, is it?" He stood up. "Costa and Fisher are both talking to Whiting, but neither of them has the full story, and Costa's in trouble as it is. That is also not for the record."

"Suppose that Patterson goes along with this. How much do you think they'll permit me to print? That's what matters to me—no offense, Frank."

"Of course not. I think you'll get stories, and good ones, if you don't push your luck." He started to the door. "Come on; I know where J.D. has lunch and we can do better over a sandwich than waiting in his outer office."

* * *

"I wish," said Carter Milne as the man across the conference table averted his eyes, "that all of you would stop acting as if I'm an invalid. I'm a widow. My husband died in a fire. There are a lot of women in my position these days, and a lot of men. You can say fire, you can say victims, you can talk about the number of people killed or injured and I will not fall apart. Is that clear?"

Dave Fisher looked to J.D. for support. "I don't want to offend anyone," he mumbled, not willing to look at Carter.

J.D. braced his arms on the table. "Carter's right." He paused and let this sink in. "I think that most of you have been coddling her, forgetting that she is back at work at her own request so that she can do something to end the fires like the one that killed Greg." He was using harsh words deliberately, and went on in only slightly gentler tones. "If all of you spend your time looking for acceptable euphemisms to keep Carter from being upset, we're not going to do the job we're all here to do, and that includes Carter."

"Thank you," Carter said.

Randall Whiting, who had been attending these meetings for the last week, nodded. "This is like a war, and the fires are the enemy. Using words to soften the destruction does not help Carter. It makes the enemy seem less real, less lethal, and that can only serve to blunt her purpose. All of you need to remember that those figures you read represent real loss to real people. Keep that in mind." He was looking at Scott Costa as he spoke.

"What makes any of you think that we're going to be the ones to find the answer?" Scott demanded, his face darkening. "And even if we do, what makes any of you think that we'll be able to do anything about the fires?"

"We think that, Costa," J.D. said in his most conversational manner, "because we have to. If we don't think that, then we're lost already."

There was an awkward pause while no one in the room felt they belonged there. J.D. tapped the intercom and asked Phylis to come in to pick up their notes so far, and this simple routine ended the worst of the tension.

When the meeting resumed, the topic was the fire that had broken out in a prison in Ohio. "In the typesetting room," said Barry Tsugoro, reading from his annotated report. "The pattern is the standard one for the fires; starts without any warning and the spread is rapid and hot, there's no fire trail to show any evidence of how the fire started, what the initial fuel was or where it started, though my guess is one of the machines."

"It appears to be the case," Dave Fisher agreed. "And there hasn't been any more information on that fire in the fish-packing plant in Maine. That means it stays on the list, striking workers be damned."

"What about the medical lab in Norman?" asked Frank. "That one had questions."

"That one is apparently arson, done to mimic these other fires. There were signs of a timer and plastic explosives in the computer room. The insurance investigators just turned in their report this morning. There wasn't much left, but it's conclusive enough." Barry handed around copies of the report.

"We're being sued by Murchison Memorial," Cynthia announced when J.D. directed his attention to her. "They're claiming our security devices were not adequate. For the time being, we have very little to worry about, and we can regard this as routine. Both Glen and Halmon Ringer agree that the court could not support the claims."

"Not even on the preponderance of evidence test?" J.D. asked.

"Since there is no example of any equipment, no matter how sophisticated, being able to provide any warning at all, and the conditions have been such that very few companies have been able to find a pattern of negligence, we're likely to be safe. Murchison Memorial needs to make the effort, however, for their own protection, since there were many lives lost in the fire and some of the survivors are suing for negligence on Murchison's part. It's my opinion that these cases come under national-disaster definitions and that the sooner we can get an official ruling on that, the sooner the... heat will be off us and other companies like us."

"What do you think we can do to speed that along?" J.D. inquired not only of Cynthia but of all his employees.

"We can find out what the real cause is," said Carter. "We can prove that this is being caused by something we could not anticipate or provide warning or protection against."

"And if we can't do that, we can demonstrate that no one has had adequate protection and warning against these fires," Barry said. "That might be the most effective argument for the time being, because so far as we know, no one has been able to stop one of these fires once it gets started, not in any preventative sense. Once they start, that's it."

"If we could show that our security systems minimized the damage, that would be even better. If it could be shown that the response time for rescue equipment was cut to the minimum and that those areas of the buildings not immediately affected were damaged less than buildings without our systems, we'd be pretty much in the clear." Cynthia turned to Carter. "Is there any way you can do that with statistics?"

"You can do anything you want with statistics, if you just select your samples right," Scott Costa said.

"That is true enough," J.D. agreed with displeasure. "And no matter what we show, there will be ways for others to show a different situation, but it would not be a bad idea to have that comparison available, using the National Fire Data information to make the curves as analytical as possible. Don't adjust the curves to suit our purposes, but do straight plotting, so that they can stand up to close scrutiny."

"If that's what you want," said Carter, making a note in her large pad. "Is there anything else?"

"I'll let you know," J.D. assured her. "And I want a good thorough check made on all fire information available for the last six weeks. If we've missed any fires, I want the information about them added to what we already have. I also want a compilation of all brands and sorts of electronic equipment used by all the various organizations we've done security for, so that if there is the least significance, we'll be able to spot it, and that means everything from copying machines to coffee makers as well as typewriters and computers and phone-answering machines. Got that?"

"Anything else?" asked Dave Fisher.

"If you think of something important, then by all means include it. And if the Navy will release figures on the fire they had, then incorporate as much about that as you can."

Everyone nodded, making notes to themselves. Scott was the first to gather his materials together to leave.

"I hope that every one of you will stretch your minds for this project. I've seen many things go wrong in our business, but nothing so complete and consistent as these fires have been." J.D. hesitated. "If you have questions or doubts or anything else that you want to talk over with me, don't hesitate. I don't want to learn that you have an idea three days after the fact. That's it. I'll see you all tomorrow at the same time."

"And be damned to us," said Scott in what was supposed to be an undervoice but was not.

"That man can't take much more of this," said Whiting to J.D. when the rest had left the conference room.

"I know. He's angry with me already, and this pressure has not made it any better for him." He waited for Whiting to go on.

"If you're trying to get me to estimate how much more of this he's going to be able to handle, I'm sorry. He has been on the edge long enough that anything could prove to be too much for him, and when that happens, I can't begin to predict what he'll do." Whiting cleared his throat. "Psychiatry is not an exact science, J.D., and you know it."

"Okay," J.D. said, giving in. "But it baffles me, to have a man like Costa, under moderate stress, ready to fall apart while Carter, who in theory is going through much more severe stress, is eager to work, and appears to be able to handle as much as we can give her."

"That's the way things are," Whiting said, shrugging. "You figure it out."

"For the time being, I'd rather figure out the fires," J.D. said to him as the two men left the conference room.

"That's typical; take the easy way out," Whiting joked feebly, and accepted the annoyed stare J.D. gave him with equanimity.

October 9, near Wichita, Kansas

Clay Selby was almost through for the day, and it was not an instant too soon. His head ached, his back was sore and he had stopped enjoying off-loading his hogs by three in the afternoon. Robbinson was almost through weighing up the hogs and once that was done, Selby could start back for home, his stock bound for the slaughterhouse and meat-packers.

"We found eight piggy sows," said one of Robbinson's men. "They're separated from the rest."

"Only eight?" Robbinson asked. "You're as close to being an honest man as any livestock dealer I've ever met, Clay," he quipped. "We've got just over five hundred head, then."

"Five hundred sixteen," one of the others corroborated.

"A respectable number. And you got good weight on 'em. We'll just get this routing and receipt for you, and we're settled."

"Good," Selby said, trying to decide if he ought to call Samantha and tell her to get ready to have dinner out for a change. This was the best sale they'd had in well over a year, and after all the scrimping and saving they'd done, it was time to celebrate. He didn't think she'd mind an evening at Whister's Restaurant. The last time they'd been there was their anniversary the year before last. It was high time they went back again.

"It looks like the market is holding for you," said Robbinson as he fed figures into his computer and watched the answering figures appear on the screen of his monitor. "It's a lot simpler, doing the brokering this way. My daddy, he never had anything so easy."

"Yeah," Clay said, thinking that a check would be a great way to begin the evening.

"Okay, I think we're set up. Just let me get a confirmation on this and we can all go home." He started to run his seller's code through the wires, but the last two figures were never entered.

Over five hundred hogs escaped from the weighing pens of Robbinson's Livestock Brokerage as the main building went up in flames. The terrified livestock, maddened by the fire, blocked the roads and as a result, the fire trucks that might have arrived in time to save at least a portion of the huge warehouse were stopped or delayed, so that nothing was salvaged.

October 12, Washington, D.C.

Almost no one was in the building when Howard Li entered his office at seven-thirty on Saturday morning. He had decided that he would test out his theory on his own.

Webster, who managed security on the weekend, was used to seeing Doctor Li in the building at all manner of unlikely hours. He had long since stopped wondering about the Chinese mathematician and had decided that he was typical of those strange intellectuals who lived in worlds of their own. He disliked Li only slightly, which was unusual. "Where'll you be?" he asked as Howard signed in.

"In my computer room, 237A. I'll be working alone and I don't expect to leave the building until much later today. If you have calls for me, please request that the caller leave a message."

"If that's what you want." He took his log back and noted the time.

"Thank you," Howard said, Webster already forgotten as he went to the elevator bank. As he rode up alone, Howard wondered how he would explain his actions if his theory proved to be wrong. There had to be an explanation he could give that would not compromise his position within the NSA and therefore limit what he would be allowed to work on in future. He could not stand the idea of being shunted to the side, to the less crucial projects where he could be monitored and protected but prohibited from doing what he loved the most.

His office was chilly, the small terminal for the computer in the next room topped with a small green light, like a bug, that showed the power was on and the machine functional. Howard went to the terminal and punched his personal lock code into the machine, gaining access to the next room and the enormous machine that resided there.

"Hi there, Napoleon," Howard said as he went into his computer room, using his pet name for the machine. "How's tricks?" He knew some of his staff thought he was a bit cracked for his occasional conversations with the computer, but for Howard, it made the thing more accessible. He was convinced that by speaking to the computer, he gained a greater sense of the capacity of its circuits and chips, of its processes and memory.

"I have a theory," Howard announced when he had taken his seat in front of the main monitor screen. "My theory is this: there is a sequence of numbers or letters that for some reason triggers the fire capacity of the machines being used. It's like using an equation to summon a demon. A spell is nothing more than an equation. Therefore, this may appear to be the worst kind of twentieth-century demonology, but I believe that this is the key, and Napoleon, you and I are going to prove it."

For the next four hours, Howard fed in every combination of numbers and letters he could find that were in any way associated with the fires. He used bank-account numbers, insurance-policy numbers, DMV and IRS codes, passport numbers, social-security numbers, credit-card numbers, any and every numerical code he could find in the few records that had been gleaned from the wreckage.

Then he rose, putting three supersensitive smoke alarms around the room and bringing two fire extinguishers within easy reach. He felt prepared and excited, anticipating success within the next few hours. He was confident he had taken reasonable precautions, and he sensed victory approaching.

"Go to it, Napoleon," Howard said as he switched on the computer. Printout paper began to pour from three high-speed printers, and Howard spent the greater part of the next three hours scanning what the machine had done.

As time dragged by, he felt frustrated, and while the printing continued, he switched to another set of records, this one compiled from other records that had been sent to him by the NSA and the FBI.

"It has to be here somewhere," he declared. "There is a simple set of letters and numbers that brings about the hazard. It isn't terrorists and it isn't sabotage, it is a question of triggering, that's all." Thinking aloud often helped him to clarify his ideas. He originally developed the habit out of his solitary life, and now hardly noticed he was doing it. As he muttered, he made more entries, and was so caught up in finding his way through the lists that he did not notice when the first sign of malfunction halted the circuits of his beloved machine. In the next fraction of a second the smoke alarms shrilled and he lifted his head sharply, reaching for the nearest of the extinguishers. For the first time he felt that he might be in some danger from his experiment.

A bouquet of fire blossomed on the front of the largest console. Howard stared at it, mesmerized by what he saw;

his hand closed on the red cylinder of the extinguisher and he pulled it around to aim it at the invading flames.

And then the fire was everywhere and Howard Li no longer saw or held anything at all.

October 13, East Orange, New Jersey

For Lola diMaggio, the view of marshes out the window was as familiar as the faintly soapy smell of the air, and she had long since ceased to pay attention to either of them. Her mind was on the stack of account records that were yet to be processed. She had been working on the receipts for yesterday's sale more than three hours now, and she was growing tired.

As she gave herself a coffee break, she thought of Jonathan, her husband. She had promised to visit him later today, to bring him something new to read. Ever since he had been transferred from his jail cell to the psychiatric facility, he had been more and more eager for things to read.

Lola sighed. It had been one thing when Jonathan was certain to be out in eight years, possibly five if the parole board could be convinced that he would not be so lax with other people's money. The psychiatric evaluation had stunned Lola, and for two weeks she had not been able to tell her two children or Jonathan's family about the new development in what everyone was calling "the difficulty with Jonathan." Only three days before she had attended another hearing of the hospital board, and their prognosis was not promising. In fact, once Lola had got them to speak plain English, she had found out that Jonathan, instead of getting better, was getting markedly worse. She did not believe them, but after half an hour with her husband, she knew that they had been being kind to her and that Jonathan had gone far away from her.

Before coming into work—she was always glad to pick up a little overtime, with the cost of raising two kids being what it was—she had stopped off at St. Phillip Neri to talk with Father Curran about the possibility of annulment, but as usual, the priest's answers had been discouraging. There was no doubt the marriage was valid when she and her husband entered into it, and the vows they made were binding.

"In sickness and in health, Missus diMaggio," said the tight-lipped cleric when Lola tried again to plead her case.

"But how can you be sure he wasn't starting to . . . go crazy when we married?" she had asked, her desperation giving her impetus that she would normally have lacked. "It's not only myself I'm thinking of, Father, but our children. It was bad enough when their father was a crook, but now they say he's a nut, and they're ashamed of him."

"God never sends us burdens that we cannot carry," the priest reminded her sternly. "You and your children should pray for more guidance. You are turning away from the Church at the very time it can offer you a haven, and that, Missus diMaggio, is a very sorry thing for an old confessor like me to witness."

"But you don't know what it's like," she had protested, and as she drank her lukewarm coffee, the sound of her voice in the echoing, incense-scented gloom came back to her, and she felt a new stab of embarrassment.

The phone rang, jarring her out of her unhappy reverie, and she went to pick it up. "Winston's," she said, knowing that it had to be one of three people calling her.

"This is Clara Winston," said the voice on the other end of the line. "My husband asked me to see how you are coming along with the receipts."

Actually, Lola thought, Art Winston was probably in the den, shoes off, feet up, watching his twenty-eight-inch television and drinking lite beer. He was not very concerned with the business as long as Clara was willing to take care of it for him. Lola had seen the pattern before, and it puzzled her. "I'm about two-thirds done," she said optimistically and stretching a point. "You had a very good day yesterday."

"People need things to fix up the house for winter," said Clara with the same logic that had dictated the sale. "Hardware is cheaper than union labor."

"I don't think it will take me more than another two hours at most." If she had to, she would fudge her time card a little, so that Clara Winston would not dispute her overtime. She would rather let them have a free hour than lose the opportunity to work next time.

"I hope you're right. My husband doesn't like paying for laziness." She paused, and softened the blow. "How are your boys? I understand that Alan is doing very well in school. You must be very pleased."

"Yes, he's getting excellent grades," said Lola, thinking once again that she didn't know how much longer she could afford to keep him in parochial school. "Matt's playing with a band now."

"Electric guitar?" asked Clara, trying to feign interest.

"Saxophone," Lola corrected, taking a strange satisfaction in catching the formidable Clara in a mistake.

"Noisy?"

"Sometimes. Luckily they don't rehearse at our house." Lola sensed that there was something more on Clara Winston's mind, and so she offered an opening. "Have you heard from Stephen?"

"Just yesterday," said Clara. "He was . . . in the hospital."

"Oh!" Lola was genuinely sympathetic, and she added with a touch of fear, "Nothing too serious, I hope?"

"I . . . I don't know. But I was hoping that perhaps you might be able to stop by later? I might . . . like to talk with you."

So there was something wrong, thought Lola. Little as she liked Clara Winston, her heart went out to the woman. "Of course. Would three-thirty be all right? I have to pick up a few things."

"Any time. Just give me a call before you come." There

was relief in Clara's voice. "I never thought we'd . . . have to deal with something like this. You understand, Lola, don't you?"

"I understand," said Lola, not without bitterness.

"I didn't mean . . . I know every situation is different, and I . . . well, I thought . . ."

Lola took her off the hook. "No one ever knows how they'll react to a crisis until they have one. I'll see you at three-thirty, and I'm sorry about Stephen, whatever the trouble is." She wondered if she sounded sincere or not, but could not bring herself to care.

"Thank you. Art isn't up to talking about it. You know how he is." She swallowed audibly. "Thank you, Lola."

"Sure," she said, hanging up. As she put her unfinished and cold coffee aside, she puzzled what might be wrong with Clara's boy. But she wouldn't get any work done if she let that take over her thoughts, so she sat down and put her mind on making the entries on their bookkeeping program which included inventory control. The only thing that Lola disliked about the software package was the long strings of numbers she had to copy.

When the fire started, she could not get to the telephone before flames caught her in their devouring embrace.

The fire had destroyed all of the office and most of the enormous hardware store before the Fire Department could bring it under control and add it to the number of unexplained fires that plagued the country.

PART V

October 15, Pittsford, New York

Lois Hillyer was having second thoughts about the interview. When Nina Foss had contacted her, Lois had been flattered, even pleased that of all those Nina might have selected, she was the choice. But in the last few hours her confidence had eroded and she was convinced that Nina Foss had selected her because she thought she could manipulate her, get her to reveal more than another executive might. This isn't girl talk, thought Lois as she wandered about her brother's house.

The crew arrived before Nina did, setting up lights and other equipment with an automatic aplomb that startled Lois. When the makeup woman came to Lois and reminded her that something had to be done, Lois sighed and led the way to the downstairs bathroom.

Last to arrive was Nina, driven in a limousine with a uniformed chauffeur and a good-looking male assistant who never strayed more than ten feet from his boss.

"Now, Lois," Nina said in her coziest voice, "I don't want you even to *think* about the cameras and the lights.

You keep your mind on me, and leave the rest to them; that's what I do. They know their business, and you can leave them to it, just as you know your business and you can be left to that."

Lois had never been around anyone with such high-voltage charm, and it dazzled her, as it was intended to do. "All right," she said, trying to match professionalism for professionalism.

"Do you think that you have anything a little less... boyish to wear?" Nina suggested gently. "We're not trying to sell the audience a policy. We need to find a little gentler note, since the subject is so dreadful." She put her arm around Lois's shoulder and nodded to the makeup artist to come with them. "If you have something in a dark blue, perhaps like that jersey dress you wore at the... you know, the funeral."

Until that moment, no one had alluded to the death of Lois's brother and family, who had been in Manhattan when 666 Fifth Avenue went up. They had been a building away, but were killed when hit by falling panes of glass from the skyscraper. Lois felt her face go red then white, and she was very certain that she had been foolish to grant the interview.

"You see," Nina was going on, "you're one of the few people in the investigation who has direct experience with the fires. You've had the most direct, the greatest loss, and you've elected to continue on the case, which is very brave of you. Everyone will be fascinated to hear your reasons, how you've been able to keep going." She had found the door to the main bedroom and indicated the closet. "If you and Marci take a little time, I'm sure you can find just the right thing to wear, and make sure that it looks good to the camera, Marci; we want to show Ms. Hillyer in the best light possible." She stepped back, pulling the door closed behind her, then went briskly to her cameraman. "Lenny, I want you to check the house for the best location. We don't want this to be too formal; that makes Hillyer look heartless. If there's a summer porch in the back, or a family room, one with pictures—we'll need pictures in any case

—we'll be able to show the audience the whole sad story without too much time for background question."

Lenny, who was used to the manner Nina employed, let her rattle on as he went about his business. He had been in the business more than twenty years and had seen newsmen and newswomen come and go. He knew his job and that was what mattered to him. "There's a family room," he told her as he motioned to his assistant.

"Good. Are there pictures?"

"Enough," Lenny said, paying little attention to the smile that Nina lavished on him.

Marci came toward Nina. "We found a dinner dress, and there was a nice scarf. Navy blue and amber, conservative. It looks a little dressy, but I told her only simple earrings, and that should be about right." She inspected Nina's face. "Let me put something under your eyes; you're looking tired."

"I want to look like I've been working," Nina said.

"You don't want to look worn-out or the network might think that you're not up to the pace." Marci was another veteran and had that quality that long ago had been called savvy.

"You're right; something under the eyes. And if there's a briefcase or some official-looking papers we could put around."

"There's a PC in the family room," Lenny said, although neither woman had been aware that he was listening.

"No," said Nina decisively. "Everyone's becoming paranoid about computers. Ever since that FBI freak said that thing about the death ray and computers, no one wants to use them. There are people who won't even go near buildings where there are computers being used—they're afraid they'll get burned to death." She turned to her assistant. "Doug, make sure no one sees that PC and warn Ms. Hillyer that she's not to say she's using computers for any part of her business. We don't want this place deluged with phone calls and crazies."

Looking bewildered, Lois Hillyer came into the living

room and stood, transfixed by the chaos she saw. She lifted her hand to her throat where she had tied an amber scarf. "Ms. Foss?"

"Oh, Ms. Hillyer—can I call you Lois?—I know what this looks like, and you don't have to be concerned. We'll neaten everything up before we leave." She had been told this was always done, but never remained long enough to make sure for herself.

"I . . . I didn't think there would be so much—" She made a gesture.

"I know how it must appear. You wonder if all these people are necessary for a seven-minute spot on the news. But seven minutes, that's forever for newspeople, and I can promise you that you can do more good and reach more people in that time than you can imagine." She was being chummy again, exerting all her personal persuasive abilities.

"That would be wonderful," Lois said with a frown. "My brother and his family would want this thing ended."

"To say nothing of everyone else in the country, and in Canada and Mexico. We've had reports of similar fires in Calgary, Montreal and Nanaimo, as well as in Sonora and Puerto Vallarta."

"Does that mean it's spreading?" Lois asked, sounding like a girl at a dance without a partner. Her eyes were moist.

"Either that, or we're finally getting full reports of what's been going on in other countries. I understand an official request has been made to Interpol for statistics on any unexplained fires of similar . . . profile in Europe." Nina had led the way to the family room and looked at the furniture. "That couch would be a good place to sit. We can put your portfolio on the coffee table, put a few of your reports out so that everyone can see you're keeping up on your work." She beamed at Lois. "It's a great morale builder, having you take the time to do this. A lot of viewers are so frightened that they're afraid to take any action."

Lenny came and stood beside Lois. "You want to do this

on the couch? Fine. I want to get it lit. Can you sit down, please?"

Nina took her place at once, and indicated that Lois should sit on her left. "Don't pay any attention to this while they get the lights right. Just talk with me. Did you know that long-distance phone calls are down more than fifty percent since August? Almost everyone is trying to use the mails, since they're afraid of the phones. Some people have gone so far as to remove phones and phone lines from their houses entirely. The Post Office is going crazy, with a thirty-two percent increase in mail over the last month." She waited a moment, while Lenny stepped between them and checked his light meter. "And then you should hear the airlines. There's almost no tourism, thanks to the airport and hotel fires, and anyone who can postpone business travel seems to be doing that. Most planes are flying almost half empty."

"I've seen something about that," Lois said in a dreamy voice. She was trying to make herself believe that this was real.

"On the other hand, some movie theaters are doing well, and they say that branch libraries, especially the old-fashioned kind without computers, are doing a land-office business, which ought to make some people very happy. Newspaper sales are much higher than usual in part because many people don't want to turn on their TV sets for very long." She chuckled, to show that this amused her.

Lois nodded. "But what does that do for you?"

"Oh, the one thing they don't stop watching is the news. They want to know the bad news as soon as it happens." Nina grinned. "And that's where we come in."

It was almost two hours later when the last of the television crew left Lois alone. She was more exhausted than she ever thought she could be, and she went around the empty and messy house like a sleepwalker. She would have to do something about the disorder in the morning, but she could not bring herself to undertake the job yet. She had decided that she had made a mistake in granting the interview, but everyone had been so certain that it would be the right, the sensible thing to do, that she had submerged her own reservations and gone ahead with it. She hoped that she would find she was wrong, but amid the shambles of the living room, with the dark lines on the pale carpet where the cables had lain, she could not imagine she would.

"And I tell you, it's sabotage, and it comes under the protection of discretionary powers!" Myron Bethune slammed his fist into the conference table and glared at Sidney Rountree. For once his smooth exterior was shattered and his calm control had deserted him. The two representatives of the Joint Chiefs flanked him, but he took no sense of support from their presence.

"And I remind you," Sidney Rountree said in a tone that suggested that he had said this many, many times before, "that there is no evidence that this is sabotage, arson or any other illegal act."

"Setting fires is illegal!" Bethune shouted.

"Yes, but being on fire isn't," Rountree said. "And if you keep a lid on this, any chance we might have of determining what the real cause is vanishes; we might as well throw in the towel. The exchange of information is crucial —*crucial*— to ending these fires. If the Joint Chiefs don't agree with me, then I must insist that we bring it to the Supreme Court for adjudication."

"And if we go to the court, we open up everything we're doing to public scrutiny," Bethune said, with a little more control. "And whoever is doing this can see what our position really is."

"If there is some kind of foreign power behind these fires," said the Chief in an Air Force uniform, "they know already. Their agents would make this a top priority, as you know that very well, Inspector Bethune."

"General Sinclair," said Bethune in a very respectful tone, "I don't see why that means we have to open the door for them and invite them to help themselves."

Admiral Waltham cleared his throat. "While the Navy has no reason to be proud of itself in this regard, I can't see that trying to withhold information for reasons of national security will make any difference in terms of the frequency and severity of the fires. In this case, I believe the Bureau has been a thought overzealous and might be better employed gathering data instead of interfering with the inquiries and procedures of the Fire Marshals' Task Force. You've attempted to support your contention, but you haven't demonstrated consistent sabotage to my satisfaction."

Myron Bethune was floundering. "Your services have been the most damaged by these fires; I would have thought you'd welcome a security blanket over the troubles you've had."

"We have a modified one right now," General Sinclair said at his most amiable. "And we've decided to lift it in order to aid the Task Force." The General enjoyed dropping these conversational bombs, and he gave his famous Cheshire-cat grin when he had finished.

"Does the Navy agree?" Bethune had lost and he knew it, but he could not give up entirely. "Or are you going to be more sensible?" This addition was a serious tactical error, for it hardened Admiral Waltham's attitude.

"The Navy will open its records to the Task Force no matter what the other services do."

"And what about the economy? You've seen the predictions for the GNP if these fires continue and workers refuse to do anything they think might contribute to another one? The nation is in serious trouble, and what you propose to do will only add to it." Bethune had saved this for his trump card, but he was playing it in the wrong game.

"Frankly, Inspector Bethune, it is likely that the more information we can provide the public, the less problems of the sort you mention will occur. It is what the people *don't* know that is causing the greatest problems, those who think that working around anything electric, for example, and those who think that there are sorts of forms that are dangerous. Obviously the problem isn't nearly as rampant as the workers' fear or we'd have half the country in ashes by now." For Sidney Rountree, this was a long and impassioned speech, though he spoke calmly enough.

"Fire Marshal Rountree has made an excellent point," said General Sinclair. "For the time being, we're going to go along with him and see what a more coordinated effort can do."

Myron Bethune hoped that this indulgence would give him rope enough to hang Sidney Rountree from the top story of the tallest office building in Washington.

"That's enough," Cynthia said as she came into the dining room of her house. It was after one in the morning and Carter, wrapped in the bathrobe she had bought two days ago, was sitting amid papers and reports, Winslow curled up at her feet, his coat looking a bit neater since it had been trimmed of the worst singeing.

"I've only got a little more to do tonight," Carter said, her glasses perched on her nose. Since the fire, she had not taken the time to wear her contacts, and it was Cynthia's private opinion that she was using the glasses to hide behind.

"Randy Whiting said you're to get plenty of rest, or he'd invalid you off the investigation for two weeks. He meant it, Carter. You ought to see yourself. You can't tell me you're doing your best work; I won't believe it."

"But Cynthia—"

"Not another word. I won't have any 'But Cynthias' from you. You're going to bed right now, and tomorrow, we're going to have a talk with Randy and J.D. I don't want you coming apart at the seams when we need you the most. I'd rather have you off the case for a couple of weeks than in treatment for a couple of years. You don't need that experience, do you?" She had come over to the table and had started gathering up papers into a neat pile.

"Don't do that," Carter snapped, seizing one of the stapled sheets that Cynthia had taken.

Cynthia became still. She looked down at Carter, her expression concerned. Winslow raised his head, his brow wrinkling.

Slowly Carter raised her hand. "Point made," she conceded.

"You still have a lot of shopping to do—you can't manage with two pair of slacks, a pair of jeans, three blouses and a sweater. Oh, and two pair of shoes. You're going to need something more. And,"—she went on, launching herself into the most crucial argument—"you're going to need a house."

Carter scowled. "I'll look for an apartment soon."

"I said a house." Cynthia braced her hands on her hips. "You need to have a house, and between the insurance money and the state of your mind, I think it's the best thing you can do."

Carter shrugged as she got up from the table. "It's hard to do," she said. "It's . . . a constant reminder that the other house, my house isn't there anymore."

"Then all the more reason to get another, and make it your house," Cynthia said, putting her arm around Carter's shoulder. "And don't worry about the paperwork end of it; leave that to me. I did all the negotiating for this place and Ben said that he couldn't have got half the deal I did. That's what lawyers are for." She had guided Carter to the bathroom across from the guest room, and turned on the light. "Why don't you draw a bath and I'll heat us up some milk. How does that sound?"

"Fine," Carter admitted.

By the time Cynthia returned from the kitchen with two mugs, Carter was sunk in bubbles and Winslow was curled on the bath mat. "You look better already. I think I'm going to throw in one other chore for you—I'm calling Tony in the morning and seeing if he can take you on short notice." She had sat on the edge of the tub and held out one of the mugs to her friend.

"I don't need a doctor," Carter growled as she took the mug in both slippery hands.

"What doctor? Tony's my hairdresser." She raised her hand to stop the objection she could see in Carter's eyes. "On me, an early or late birthday present, whichever seems right."

"I didn't—" Carter began.

"I don't want to hear that, either. Shopping, house, and

Tony, and you'll come down off the walls where you've been and start to make the kinds of decisions and evaluations that you've done in the past. Don't worry about the job, and don't worry about J.D. He can handle this, and he'll appreciate your recognizing your limitations and doing the sensible thing. Got that?" She was half done with her milk now.

"Have you talked this over with him already?" Carter guessed, ready to argue.

"Yesterday, as a matter of fact," Cynthia admitted. "At least having you take a couple weeks off to look for a house of your own." She paused. "You want to stay on the ocean side of the hills?"

Carter thought it over. "Yes, I think I do," she said after giving it her consideration. "I like the fog."

"Okay, I'll make some calls tomorrow and we'll see what turns up."

"Cynthia, there's one thing," Carter told her in a more assertive tone than she had used so far. "You've got to give me your word that if there are more serious fires, really serious, that you'll let me come back and work on them."

"You said yourself that all fires are serious," Cynthia reminded her.

"You know what I mean. Big fires, lots of damage, the kind that no one can ignore." She noticed that her bubble bath was fading.

"Okay; if something really big happens, or it looks like we're on to something, we'll arrange for you to come back. Is that a deal?"

Carter nodded, then said, "I talked to Greg's father today. He was pretty upset. Greg borrowed five thousand dollars from him. He said it was seed money to start a business of his own—consulting. His father didn't know about the gambling, and I didn't know what to say." She emptied the mug and handed it back to Cynthia. "I'll see you in the kitchen in a little while."

"Fine," said Cynthia, accepting the mug. "You're going to have to decide what you want to do about that loan. Technically this is a community-property state, and therefore his debts are your debts, but under the circumstances —" She started for the door. "Let me do some homework on this one."

"It's not the money," Carter said. "At least, it's not *just* the money. He and his family didn't get along, and the idea that he used them as much as he used . . . everyone else. It galls me." This last Cynthia almost missed as she closed the bathroom door and went down the hall to the kitchen.

"At the bottom line, what does all this add up to?" William asked Frank as they pored over the latest figures released by the government.

"Damned if I know," answered Frank. "I see more facts, more figures, and they mean zip to me." He looked at the reporter. "And if you quote me, I'll come after you with . . . I'll think of something."

"Why do you think the FBI changed its policy on releasing information at all? That has me puzzled."

"Because they can't support their espionage and deathray theories with the evidence. Hell, you can't support much of anything with the evidence." He glanced out the window at the first sullen drizzle of autumn. "I think someone's putting pressure on the Bureau to be more forthcoming about what they've got."

"The President?" William guessed.

"Maybe. Maybe the other intelligence services, maybe the Congress, how do I know? I'd like to think it was the Task Force but we didn't have much luck before and I can't imagine that we'd get a change at this point."

"Have you ordered breakfast yet?" asked William. "It's quarter to eight and if you're going to—"

"You're right. Why don't we go downstairs and get something in the coffee shop? You can tell me what you've come up with that has you so excited."

"What makes you think I've come up with anything?" William asked as Frank picked up his jacket and briefcase.

"This is the first time you've called me and suggested breakfast. Lunch and dinner, yes, but breakfast, no." Frank indicated the phone. "Better let your editor know that you've made contact."

"I don't have to. He says that I've been doing well enough. And that is in large part thanks to you. Why'd you do it?" They were going out the door, Frank taking the time to be certain that it was properly locked. It was noisy in the hall—through an open door three voices were raised in an argument about plane schedules—and so Frank and William gave up talking until they reached the lobby.

"What do you think about the satellite theory?" William asked as they reached the coffee shop.

"I think it's nuts. I think all the explanations are nuts, but since the fires are nuts, what can you expect? By all rights, they can't be happening." He asked for a booth instead of a table, and then went toward the one indicated by the headwaitress.

"Do you have any ideas yet?" William asked. "I don't want to know what it is if you have one, but I would like to know that you might have some leads..." He left the end open.

"I wish I did. Nothing that we've tried seems to be working. That's not for publication. We've got trouble enough without admitting we're still in the dark." He glanced at the menu and wondered if he had appetite enough for a full breakfast.

William was slow to speak. "You know, when I started this assignment, I thought we'd have a spectacular breakthrough by now that I could cover and get a lot of credit for my journalism. Then I'd be in a stronger position at the paper and might end up with a larger paper with more money and prestige. That was my initial interest."

"Isn't that what journalists want?" Frank said.

"Yes, superficially. But this isn't just a good story, or a chance to move up, it's like covering a war, and there's so much at stake. At first, I thought the fires were... well, not great, exactly, but a wonderful opportunity. Then I started seeing what they did, and how terrible they were, and then I began to get worried for my family, and for my friends. I didn't want any of them to be touched by... anything."

"Yeah. When I saw that apartment house in Baltimore, when we were called in because there was no detectable cause, I got those prickles—you know the ones you get sometime, maybe just before an accident—and they're still with me." He paused as the waitress came for their order. "Just toast and coffee for me. William?"

"Same, but a large orange juice, too." He handed the menu back to the waitress, then said, "Frank, will you let me know when the prickles go away?"

Frank nodded once. "You bet."

Simon McPherson tried to be charming, but he could not keep disapproval out of his voice. "Lois, I can understand your motives for doing that interview, but you ought to have consulted... someone first. You're upset, and no doubt you thought that you could do something by having that interview. But there was so much panic. You have no idea how much panic. We had letters pouring in that were—"

Standing in the living room of her brother's house, Lois felt that she had been abandoned in a foreign country. She stared out the window so that she would not have to see the anger in McPherson's eyes. "If you're through, you don't have to stay."

"You... you misunderstand me." McPherson actually had the grace to flush. "I didn't mean it the way it sounded." He took a step toward her. "You don't know what it's been like."

"I don't?" she asked. "I've changed the phone number twice, and I've had to get my neighbor to do my food shopping for me. My company wants me to stay away for three more weeks because of all the publicity."

"I'm sorry that happened," he said, sounding almost sincere. "You have some idea, then, what we're up against, and maybe you can give us a hand with it. You might not want to think about your position with the insurance company as much as your responsibility as a citizen."

"What a pat little speech; have you given it often?" Lois said, and started to cry, which seemed worse than anything she had done since Simon McPherson had arrived on her doorstep.

"You're too much under stress," said McPherson, his attitude changing slightly as he saw her face. "I don't mean that you're doing anything wrong, exactly, but that you could be doing so much more good." He approached her, his manner uncertain; he did not know what to expect.

"Why can't you leave me alone?" Lois wailed. "It's too much, the fires and the dying and the rest of it."

McPherson put his arm tentatively around her. "Ms. Hillyer, don't let this get to you." He knew it was a mistake as soon as he said it.

"Would you like it better if I ignored my brother's death? And my sister-in-law's? And their children's? Would that make it better? Would you rather I spent my time looking over nice, clean, impersonal figures about pain and loss and ruin?" She pulled away from him and rushed out of the room, her hands clapped over her mouth.

McPherson went looking for her ten minutes later, and found her lying on the bed in the guest room, her eyes puffy and her nose red. "I really didn't intend to upset you, Ms. Hillyer," he said from the door.

"What would you have said if you had?" she asked, her voice lethargic as she stared at the ceiling.

"You misunderstand me." He tried to chuckle and failed. "I botched this one from start to finish. I wanted to let you know how sorry I was about your family, and how baffled I was by your interview and it came out all wrong. I'm sorry. I didn't want to make things any worse for you, and I did. Really. I am sorry."

"Apology accepted. You don't have to stay." She still refused to look at him, and this was more distressing to McPherson than her tears had been.

"Lois," he said, trying to catch her attention, "do you think you could consider giving us a hand in our investigation? Ever since we've opened up our files on the fires, we've been swamped with data from all kinds of sources, and we need help sorting it out. You have the kind of background and experience that would be very useful, and we'd be happy to provide housing and a salary and all the rest while you worked with us."

"Changing your approach?" Lois asked, making no other response.

"I can understand how you feel, and I wouldn't blame you for saying no, especially after the way I've bungled, but I hope you'll forget my bad manners and think of the victims of the fires, and do what you can to help us. We'd all appreciate it. I mean that." He came two steps farther into the room. "Lois?"

"You never stop, do you?"

"It's not like that," McPherson protested.

"It's okay; you're doing your job, I know that." She sat up slowly and looked at him. "You have to do this, and it doesn't matter that it's wrong, because the fires have to be stopped. That's what it's all about, isn't it?" She looked desperately weary as she stood up. "I don't know what good I can do for you, but if you want, I'll come to Washington on Monday and I'll do whatever seems to be helpful. For my brother and his family, not for you, not for the country; for my relatives."

"All right," said McPherson, and was puzzled when he felt no satisfaction in accomplishing his task. He looked around the room. "Is there anything I can help with?"

"You've done all the helping I can endure for a while," said Lois in a flat tone. "Just leave, will you? so I can decide what to pack."

"All right," he repeated, and left her alone.

Lois went to the closet and stared at the contents, trying to make her mind work. But whether she should take gray suits and dark blouses or pinstripes and burgundy blouses or taupe suits and cream blouses seemed so supremely unimportant that she could not think about it at all after a few minutes. She had packed her brother's family's clothes the day before and donated them to charity. In comparison, her own packing was trivial and demeaning to the ones she mourned.

* * *

Cynthia bristled with excitement as she came into the living room where she found Carter dutifully reading real-estate ads in the *Mercury-News*. "I've found a place," she announced as soon as the door slammed.

"What?" Carter looked up.

"I've found what you're looking for, over near Felton." She dropped down on the sofa and beamed. "I'll take you there, first thing in the morning."

"What makes you so sure?"

"Just that I am." Her eyes were bright and she looked about to giggle.

"Tell me about it," Carter said, folding the paper, glad to be rid of it.

"Nope; I'll show it to you tomorrow. I've made an appointment with the realtor to meet us there at ten. I don't want to spoil it by telling you everything now." She threw her head back. "Something's finally going right. I hope." This last addition was her hedge against disappointment.

"I'm curious," Carter admitted, and tried to imagine the kind of house Cynthia had found for her.

"Tomorrow," Cynthia promised, and then broke her own rule and spent the next hour discussing the most recent data supplied by the FBI. Carter listened with interest, and finally said, "I hope that Randy Whiting lets me get back to work soon. I want to have a chance to look all this over."

"We'll see. House first, then psychiatrist."

By the next morning, Carter had developed a sense of anticipation, which surprised her. As she drove with Cynthia, she tried to find out more about the house.

"It should interest you," was all Cynthia would say until they took the turnoff for Felton. "We'll backtrack a little, and you'll have a chance to stop it if you can."

"Fine; if I knew what I was looking for, that would be easier." Carter wanted to sound huffy, but there was more excitement in her voice than she realized, and Cynthia smiled.

Twenty minutes later, Cynthia pulled off the road onto a

private drive that led up to a three-story Victorian house, complete with piazza and turret.

"Oh, my God," said Carter. "You're not serious?"

"Have a look at it. The current owner's the grandson of the man who built it. He's been leasing it to his nephew, who teaches at Cal Santa Cruz. The nephew's moving to Boston, and so the owner's decided to sell, with certain conditions attached."

"What conditions?" Carter was staring at the house. It was well-maintained, a Wedgewood-blue candy box with white trim, all looking crisp and new.

"The property consists of the house and three acres of land, with a small orchard and a little stand of redwoods. They're behind the house, in case you were wondering." Cynthia got out of the car and indicated Carter should do the same. "There are two springs on the property. The condition is that the property will be kept intact and not sold for development. The house was built in 1891, is made entirely of redwood and was rewired in 1969. It has eleven rooms, a basement and an attic. There are two bathrooms, all modern plumbing and fixtures, and the kitchen was remodeled at the same time the rewiring was done."

Carter had walked to the steps leading to the covered porch that ran around two sides of the house. "Is this a verandah?" she asked, pointing to it.

"No, they call it a piazza. There used to be a conservatory at the back, but the nephew converted it to an office. You'd like it." She walked up beside Carter. "The price isn't bad, all things considered, and I think I can get you some benefits in the deal, if you like."

Carter was about to express her reservations when a red BMW came barreling up the drive. "This is the realtor?"

"Her name is Stephanie Frasier," said Cynthia, and turned to introduce the two women.

"You do understand the conditions of sale, Doctor Milne?" the realtor asked Carter as she showed her through the house.

"I think so."

"It's made it hard to move, because most of what has been going on here is development, but old Mister Corvin insists... For the right person this would make a wonderful home."

Carter noticed how Stephanie Frasier avoided all references to family or husband, and she supposed the woman had already been given information by Cynthia.

"It's a hell of a lot of house," said Carter as they made their way to the turret on the third floor.

"Yes, but it's amazing how quickly the space gets used." The realtor had a bright smile and a manner so perky that Carter wondered if she ran on batteries.

The viewing took more than an hour, Stephanie keeping up a running commentary most of the time. "When Albert Corvin—the original builder, not his grandson—first came here, he had a good-size family for the time: eight children. He was in the lumber business, and in those days, that was real gold. He made a fortune, and tried to found a commercial empire. But he had bad luck with his children, and only two of them turned out to be worth anything. Old Albert got strange in later life; he turned bitter and introverted. He developed peculiar interests, and for some time after his death there were rumors about this place that kept everyone away from it. He was into seances and tabletapping and magical rituals, or so the local legend says."

"A house with a history," said Cynthia, winking at Carter.

"Matthew Corvin, the current owner, is in his seventies and he wants to dispose of the property. On his terms, of course. He wants to take it easy for a change."

"Tell me," said Carter as Stephanie paused for breath, "what do the utilities run on the house? What are the annual taxes? I don't want to saddle myself with more than I can afford." She was in the turret room, looking over the high rolling hills. She had to admit that the setting was beautiful and that there was a sense of peace that captivated her. But three acres and eleven rooms, plus basement and attic—that was a tremendous responsibility.

"What do you think?" Cynthia prodded.

"Nothing yet. I'll need some time to go over the figures and to look around. From what you've said, I don't have to hurry on this." Carter smiled at Stephanie.

"Well, if you're going to make an offer, I'd want to be able to present it to Mister Corvin as soon as possible. You know what it's like when a property hasn't moved in some time—the owner gets nervous." She led the way back to the front parlor and indicated the fireplace. "The tiles were hand-painted in Belgium, and there are two boxes of replacement tiles in the basement, or so Mister Corvin tells me. I haven't checked for sure."

Carter strolled through the back parlor to the dining room and looked around it. For a large house, it managed to feel cozy. That was more interesting to Carter than its peculiar history.

"Let me go over the figures with you, Carter," Cynthia suggested. "I know we can come up with an acceptable offer, if you decide you want the house."

"I need a little time," Carter said, staring at the fancy plasterwork on the ceiling.

Stephanie started to renew her pitch, but Cynthia cut it short. "I'll give you a call in a couple of days, after we've looked at a few other places."

"I'm looking forward to your call; I'll make sure you have the figures you asked about. Utilities, water, taxes, insurance, all that kind of thing."

As Cynthia started the car, she said, "Don't make up your mind yet."

"Okay," said Carter, suspecting that she already had.

Myron Bethune faced the press as if he were going to the guillotine. "The radio station . . . has been termed another one of the fires. It has not been determined if the fire in the insurance company was arson or caused by undetermined means. There have been several incidents of arson, disguised to appear like the random fires, but in all cases, we have been able to show that arson was the cause."

"Pardon me, Inspector Bethune," said one of the journalists toward the back of the room. "But how can you be sure?"

"Well, where arson is present," Bethune said in obvious discomfort, "there are distinctive signs. We can run tests and analyses on the various burned objects and buildings and if there was a central cause, it will show up. These random fires don't have any apparent cause." It was difficult to admit this last and he did so very reluctantly.

"Isn't it true that spontaneous combustion is very rare?" asked one of the journalists in the second row.

"Until recently that was what we thought. It is also true that the sophisticated equipment and methods at our disposal have made a difference in how we assess fires and the evidence they leave behind. It may be that in the past there were fires of a similar nature that were not adequately investigated or whose causes were misidentified or not identified at all. These considerations are among those we are currently reviewing." He was waffling, and it showed. He could see it in his audience's eyes.

"Inspector Bethune," said a tall young woman in a tailored black suit, "what about the fire that you claim began in Doctor Li's office? Has the cause of that been determined."

"No," Bethune lied. "Not yet." There had been a great deal of debate about whether it was wise to admit that one of the random fires had struck so close to home. Myron Bethune had argued for secrecy and had prevailed, but he did not know how to deal with such questions.

"When do you think you'll have that information?" asked a bearded young man near the door.

"We...don't know. You have to understand that in a secure building, such as the one where Doctor Li worked, there are a number of possibilities to be considered, and access to all material isn't as easy as it might be." This was not an adequate answer and he wanted to change the subject entirely before he got in any deeper.

"Is there any reason to think that this is not a random fire but sabotage or other cause?" This was as sympathetic a question as Bethune was likely to get and he knew it.

"There are some who believe that the fire was arson that was intended to stop Doctor Li's studies. It was very convenient if there is indeed a sabotage component to these fires, which is still the contention of many of the investigators."

"How do you feel about those who refuse to travel or—" began the lanky columnist from St. Louis, only to be joined by many other voices with similar questions.

"Please, please," said Bethune, raising his hands in the hope that he could restore order. "One at a time. I can't answer more than one question at once."

Finally a middle-aged man with a rumpled jacket and mussed hair overrode the others. "What is the position of the investigators in terms of the safety for workers and the public in general?"

"Well," Bethune said, hoping that he could leave the room as soon as he answered this difficult question. "Yes, we know that most of the fires have occurred in public buildings, at least those we have successfully identified. It might not be reasonable to stay away from work, or disconnect electric appliances, as it has been rumored many people are doing. There is no hard evidence that these fires are entirely part of the electric system, or so it appears. We urge everyone to be reasonable and use good sense. In an emergency like this, good sense can prevail. I want you to emphasize that we have no evidence that it is unsafe to use electrical equipment."

"Do you have any evidence that it *is* safe to use electronic equipment."

That was the question that Bethune dreaded more than any other. "We assume that while there may be an element of risk where some sorts of installations are concerned, we have to stress that we do not believe that all electronic equipment is subject to being the focus of the fires." Hands shot into the air, and several journalists started to ask. "I have to end this press conference. I appreciate your attention." He went swiftly to the nearest door, closing it behind him as if to keep out a pack of rabid dogs.

* * *

Ben kissed Cynthia and reached to turn on the shower. "I wish we had the morning free," he said.

"So do I," Cynthia agreed, leaning against him as he pulled his terry-cloth robe off.

"Hey, unfair," Ben murmured. He touched Cynthia's face, then ran his fingers through her sleep-tousled hair.

"You, too." They kissed very slowly, almost lazily.

"Gotta come up for air," said Ben as they moved apart. "I want a whole weekend with you, no kids, no fires, no work, just you and me in a hotel room with caviar and champagne." The bathroom was steaming up from the shower, and Ben reached out to draw a valentine heart on the fogged mirror. "A reminder."

Cynthia drew the Cupid's arrow through it. "I don't know what I'd do without you, and that's a fact, Ben Harper."

"What's on the agenda today, other than the usual meetings?" He was putting more distance between them as he dropped his robe over the towel rack and opened the shower door.

"We've got a Sidney Rountree coming in from Washington, and J.D. told Carter she could attend the briefing. Frank Vickery already knows Rountree, and he said that the man is levelheaded."

"Aren't you getting tired of all this?" Ben asked over the sound of the water.

"Yes. But I . . . Ben, I feel absolutely helpless. Everyone keeps trying and trying and trying and we still don't come any closer to finding the cause of the fires, and people keep getting killed and buildings keep getting destroyed, and nothing seems to help." She fell silent, and was relieved when Ben stuck his head out of the shower.

"Cynthia, you're doing all anyone can. You're trying to find answers and you're doing your best to keep from giving way to despair. That takes nerve and guts." He had lost the playful tone he had used earlier.

"But just to outline the legal implications—" She found her toothbrush and smeared paste on it.

"It's necessary, honey; you said so yourself." He went back to his morning shower while Cynthia finished brushing her teeth.

By the time they went to breakfast, Cynthia was feeling more composed, and she was able to greet Carter with equanimity, saying, "I've found three other houses advertised in the Santa Cruz area you might like to see. I can't do much today, but tomorrow or the day after we can take time to go see them."

"Actually, I want to make an offer on that Victorian. It kind of grows on me." She smiled as she said this, and it was the first genuine pleasure Cynthia had seen on her face in some time. "Then I can get out of your hair and we can all get back to doing something about the fires."

"You sure?" Cynthia asked. "About the Victorian, I mean. I don't want you buying a house just because you're afraid you can't stay here."

Carter might have answered, but Cynthia's two girls came rushing into the dining room, Pamela still buttoning her outsize shirt over her artistically faded jeans.

Before Cynthia had a chance to renew her question, she and Carter were on their way to PSS for the meeting with Sidney Rountree, the traffic moving slowly but steadily.

"I'm serious, Carter," Cynthia said when she heard her friend talk about the Victorian house again. "Don't rush into anything. You don't have to leave until you're satisfied that you're going to be able to live where and as you like."

"I like that house. You were right about it. I didn't think I would, but it grows on me."

A buff-colored Mercedes slipped into the barely adequate space in front of them, and Cynthia leaned on the horn. "Bastard," she accused the other driver. "You can stay with us as long as you like. Ben and I are happy to have you, and so are the girls. I think you might want to take a little more time, just to check a few things out."

"But you're the one who started me looking at houses in the first place," said Carter at her most reasonable. "And if you can work out a reasonable deal, I think I'd get a kick out of Albert Corvin's place." She saw that Cynthia was about to object, and she pressed her argument. "I know it's very soon after Greg's death and the fire, and I know that the pressure at work has been too much. But I want to have something that's mine, even for a while, something that feels permanent, even if it isn't. That's what I like about the house—it's been around for a while and with the orchard and the redwoods, it has a feeling of durability. I think that means a lot just now."

Cynthia considered this. "Tell you what: if you still feel that way tomorrow, we'll work out some kind of offer. But get through today and sleep on it, okay?"

"Is that your legal advice to me?" Carter said, very nearly teasing.

"Yes, it is," Cynthia answered primly, and then ruined her effect by laughing.

Sidney Rountree was thinner than when Frank had seen him last, and he walked as if he had aged ten years. He smiled wanly at Frank as they shook hands, and seemed grateful to have the chance to sit down. "This job is taking the stuffing out of me, Frank," he confessed as the two of them strolled down the hall of the PSS building toward J.D.'s office. "I used to think I was up to it, but I'm not so sure anymore. Two of the guys on the Task Force are under care, and one of them has had two close calls with a heart attack."

"Who?" Frank asked, troubled to hear this.

"Perry Bennington. He's not in good shape, Frank. In fact, if the national situation weren't as grave as it is, Perry'd be in the hospital right now." He shook his head slowly.

Frank had often argued with Perry, a man he thought too rigid in his attitudes and methods, but the news that Bennington was ill dismayed him. "How's he holding up?"

"Not real well. Day before yesterday he looked the color of sour milk. I've tried to arrange leave for him, but he refuses to take it, unless the doctors say that it's imperative." They reached the door to the conference room adjoining J.D.'s office, and Frank led the way in. "Nice place."

"I guess," said Frank, and noticed that the coffee maker was already on and the little samovar was heating up tea. "That Phylis Dunlap is a wonder."

"Every executive needs a good secretary," Rountree said, though his mind was clearly on other matters.

"What's the rest of the news, Sid?" asked Frank.

"Nothing that would surprise you. Grayson is living on tranquilizers, the FBI clones are driving us crazy with their conspiracies and terrorists. At least now we've got a little room to maneuver." He lit a cigarette with a shaking hand. "It's bad, Frank. Everyone in the country, and Canada and Mexico, for that matter, has been touched by this. We've all lost friends and relatives and money and things and..." He took a deep drag on his cigarette. "I gave these things up for six years, and look at me now."

"You'll stop again when this is over," said Frank, thinking how fragile Rountree had become.

"If it ever is," Rountree said, sounding more ancient than ever.

"Do you think it's that bad?" Frank began gently. "From what I've seen, a lot of causes have been eliminated, including the invisible killer satellite and all its kin. We're not looking for a new kind of plastique, and we know that shorts are the result, not the cause of the fires. That must be worth something."

"Oh, it's helping industry a little, but not much. No one trusts machines of any kind. There are people who work in our building who walk up fourteen flights of stairs rather than take a chance with the elevator." He looked for an ashtray, accepting the one Frank handed him with a nod. "It's grim, and getting grimmer. And nothing we've done so far has prevented one fire, or predicted one. We're getting to the end of our rope, and I don't want to think about what could happen then."

"Is that why the files have been opened?"

"Pure desperation," Rountree concurred. "And the worst thing is that if there is any cause at all, it's probably sitting right in front of us; it's something we've been looking at all along and didn't recognize."

Frank recalled Greg Milne's confident assertion that there was a system to the fires, and right or wrong, he had burned to death while testing his theory. "If you're right, how do we spot it? How do we deal with it?"

"God knows," said Rountree heavily.

"Thanks." Frank looked up as the door opened and Cynthia came into the room, followed by Carter. "How're you feeling?" he asked before introducing the two women to Sidney Rountree.

"I'm doing okay; I think I've found a house." She glanced at Cynthia. "I haven't quite made up my mind, but it appeals to me. How are you? How's the investigation going?"

"It's like making progress backward," said Frank without a jot of humor.

"Nothing promising?" She took the seat she usually occupied and pulled out her notes. "I've seen everything that you've worked up in the last few days, and I'd say that it is a much more complete picture than we had before."

"But a picture of what?" Frank asked.

"That's what I might be able to help find out," Carter said, her attitude pointed.

"Hey, the meeting isn't even started yet," Cynthia chided, but in a light, bantering way.

"Sorry," Carter said, looking at Frank. "I'm edgy, I guess."

"I know I am," Frank said, to excuse his words. "And we're all tired."

"Don't remind me," Cynthia said, then turned as the door opened and Scott Costa came in, looking as if he had slept in his clothes and shaved with hedge clippers.

Frank introduced him—a bit awkwardly—to Sidney Rountree and was relieved when Dave Fisher joined them, then Barry Tsugoro. He continued to make introductions, all the while wondering where J.D. Patterson himself had got to.

"I'm sorry," said Phylis Dunlap, coming in through

J.D.'s office. "There was a fire in Sacramento this morning, and Mister Patterson left to join the inspection team at six-thirty. He called a few minutes ago and said that he would be flying back within the hour and asked that the meeting start without him. He deputized Cynthia Harper to run the meeting in his absence." She smiled, checked the levels in the coffee maker and the samovar, then departed, saying, "If you need me, just buzz."

"What happens now?" Scott asked defiantly.

"We have a meeting, as ordered," Cynthia said calmly. "Well, since I don't know everything going on and since Fire Marshal Rountree is here to speak to us, it seems most sensible to let him tell us what he's come to do."

Barry Tsugoro raised his hand. "I just want to mention that we've been analyzing the amount of power used by all the buildings we know of that have been hit by these fires, and those figures will be ready by this afternoon."

"Good," said Carter. "Let me have them along with everything else you might have."

"Let's give Marshal Rountree the floor," Cynthia suggested in her most diplomatic tone.

The others fell silent, and Sidney Rountree cleared his throat as he stood up. "I wish I had better news," he began, and watched the disappointment on the others' faces.

By the time J.D. arrived, the meeting was almost over, and everyone was trying to think of an approach that hadn't been tried before.

"If that won't work," J.D. said when he heard this complaint from most of his employees, "then start from the beginning and check everything all over again. Look at it again, start fresh if you can and assess it for any and every angle you can think of. I don't want any of you to stop working simply because you don't have new suggestions. Maybe we haven't given the old ones enough of a chance." J.D. had the knack of making such pep talks sound not only inspiring but innovative.

"That's a good approach," Rountree said, trying to bring more enthusiasm to the meeting.

"Well, I want to reexamine all the data we've got and

see if there are any commonalities we've overlooked until now. And don't you dare tell me that I'm not ready to come back to work."

J.D. met Carter's eyes coolly. "I can't turn down the request; I need you too much, but I've got to say that I don't feel good about it." J.D. tapped twice on the table.

"What about the fire in Sacramento?" asked Barry, and the others in the room listened with keener attention than they wanted to admit.

"Arson, radio-controlled chemical explosives, planted in the air conditioning, the junction of the main ducts. Another copycat, looks like." J.D. gazed at his employees. "Henry Traeger is in the hospital," he said evenly. "That means I will have to rely on you more than ever, Carter."

Henry, who was the other top statistician at PSS, was a studious and reclusive man in his late forties. Carter pictured him at his desk, barricaded behind books and papers. "What's wrong with Henry?"

"Jane called from the hospital half an hour ago. They say it's bleeding ulcers, and I wouldn't be a bit surprised, the way Henry works," J.D. told them. "I don't want to see too much more of that. We can't afford to have our staff getting sick, and the longer this mess takes to solve, the harder it's likely to be. Speaking of that, Cynthia, Glen Lewis is going to take two days off. His blood pressure is getting out of hand again, and that means the main thrust of the legal department is on your shoulders."

"I'll call Ben. He'll be thrilled." The sarcasm of her remark was not lost on any of them.

"That's another thing," J.D. said. "I know that this has been playing johnny-be-damned with your personal lives, and I'm sorry about that, truly. But until we've got answers and results with this thing, you're all going to have to bite the bullet. Make me the villain if it's any easier."

"When did you find out about Glen's blood pressure?" Cynthia asked.

"Ten-thirty last night. He called. Said he had gone to the hospital for something to calm him down and they wouldn't let him leave in the condition he was in." He looked at the others in a calm but disquieting way. "If any of you think you're reaching the end of your rope, let me know, talk to me, and maybe we can shift some of the load so that we don't make it that much worse for you and everyone else." He motioned to Rountree. "Is there anything else, Marshal?"

"Not specifically. I want to speak to each of these... uh... people and find out what they've got, if anything, and I must call in to Washington before two o'clock, West Coast time. If that can be arranged." Rountree rubbed his face as if he had just wakened.

"They're at your disposal, and all you need do is ask." J.D. checked his watch. "Okay, it's a little after eleven. Scott, Carter, Dave and Frank, go to lunch. The rest of you take Marshal Rountree to your departments. Then at twelve-thirty, you go to lunch and the first shift can take over with Marshal Rountree. When you're done, he can make his call and I'll take him to a late lunch, where we can talk over everything he's seen."

"Allah has spoken," grumbled Scott Costa, who was the first to rise.

"You bet your ass," Barry Tsugoro agreed, but with much less rancor. "I'll be happy to get my three assistants in order, Marshal," he added, trying to smooth over the note of disruption that had been emphasized by Scott's remark.

"Thanks, Barry," said J.D. as the meeting broke up.

Carter looked at the material she had compiled through the last two days and sighed. She knew more—so much more—about the fires, except the crucial points: what caused them, and why and how. The list of what had not caused them was impressively long, but the fires continued, still apparently at random, and the losses were staggering.

Cynthia stuck her head in the door. "I hate to mention it, but it's almost seven-thirty, and we're late for dinner."

"Just a little more time. I'm expecting some more printouts from Grover What's-his-name over in installation. He has some equipment-failure records that could tell us something."

"I'm sure they could, and you'd understand them better tomorrow. Remember all those little lectures that J.D.'s been giving about pacing ourselves." She touched the light switch and the room fell into near-darkness. "Besides, I'm exhausted."

Carter dropped her papers back on her desk. "You've made your point. Okay. Point me in the direction of the dinner table and I'll try to eat." She reached to find her jacket slung over the back of her chair, and as she tugged it on, Cynthia watched her with a trace of amusement.

"You're going to need to go shopping again this weekend."

"I haven't time," protested Carter, tucking her purse under her arm and reaching for her portfolio.

"Better make time. I called in the offer on the house for you, and you're going to need furniture for it." She paused. "If the offer is acceptable, we can work out an immediate-occupancy agreement, and for that you'll need a few pieces of furniture."

"God, really?" exclaimed Carter as she pulled her office door closed. It was the first sign of pleasure she had shown in the last two days.

"Yes. Stephanie was delighted. She said that old man Corvin has been pushing her to find someone to take the house, and with the conditions he's imposed, she was getting very discouraged."

"I can imagine," Carter said as they entered the elevator. "Do you think I could go over there on the weekend and take a look around? I want to have some idea of what I'll need. I want to measure the rooms and all that, make a record of where the windows are and their dimensions."

"Sounds sensible to me. So long as you don't mess up anything."

Just as they were going out the door and signing out with the night security man, Carter said, "You know, I just thought of something. My uncle Jasper—"

"*Jasper?*" Cynthia asked, trying hard not to laugh.

"Well, someone's got to be called Jasper," Carter said reasonably. They had reached Carter's Mazda.

"Okay; what about Uncle Jasper?"

As they got in, Carter said, "He left some furniture in storage, for Mom; she didn't like it, but Jasper's estate has been paying for it. Uncle Jasper was quite well off, but everyone found him a little odd to deal with, so they left him alone, most of the time." They reached the stop sign and turned onto the road toward Cynthia's house.

"You mean, you might be able to use it?" suggested Cynthia.

"If it's still there and Mom doesn't mind." She thought a little while. "I wonder what it would cost to have it shipped from Tacoma?"

"I didn't know you were from Tacoma," Cynthia said.

"Jasper lived there," Carter said. "Do you mind if I call Mom?"

"Feel free, if that's what you want to do," said Cynthia, aware that Carter was almost a stranger to her family.

"I might as well; so far as I know, no one else is using it." She drove in silence, giving the moderate traffic her full attention. Finally she said, "Have you talked to Rountree today?"

"Not since this morning. He spent most of the afternoon with Frank. You know, I wouldn't be surprised if J.D. offers him a job when this is all over. We've got all kinds of experts, but no one like him, with his kind of experience. He's been a godsend." She eased back in the seat. "Whoever designed these seat belts never thought about how sore your breasts get during your period."

Carter chuckled. "I know." She signaled for the right turn, watching the cross traffic for an opening. "About Rountree."

"Yeah?" She also watched the oncoming cars.

"He's not very optimistic, is he?"

"Would you be?" Cynthia wondered aloud. "Poor man's exhausted, there's no end in sight, and he's got half the Washington bureaucracy coming down his neck. I don't envy him at all."

"Neither do I." She completed the turn. "Well, I guess I'll call Mom and find out what Uncle Jasper left, and if she minds if I use it. He had a big house in Tacoma, and he traveled a lot. Mom said he was a self-indulgent child, but I think it was because he got such a kick out of scandalizing the family."

"Probably just getting even for being called Jasper," Cynthia said. "I'll find out about getting you in this weekend, so you can get your measurements."

They had almost reached Cynthia's house when Carter said, "I was just thinking: this is the first time in my life I'll own something that huge all by myself. That's kind of scary."

Cynthia could think of nothing to say.

The travel agency was a smoking ruin, and the firefighting equipment gathered around it cast bright reflections back at the lights of Nina Foss's television crew. Nina herself stood in front of the most imposing fire truck, trying her best not to look satisfied at the latest disaster.

"So the assertion that these fires are limited to heavy industrial use would appear to be inaccurate," she said with relish. "The fire in the Gulf Coast Travel Agency offices today have shown that. Here was a small business, with no heavy equipment and no other obvious hazard, a business that was run by three partners, located in a small, and fortunately detached building, that has been shown conclusively to be part of the same mysterious fires that have gutted the—" She interrupted herself. "Lenny, can we take it back? I think maybe 'gutted' is too strong a word for the six-o'clock news, don't you?"

"Whatever you say, Nina. It doesn't bother me."

"As far as I can tell, nothing bothers you," Nina countered, and took up her position once more. "We received confirmation today that this fire is one of the series of mysterious fires that have caused such tragedy for the whole nation." She paused with a significant set to her mouth. "This is Nina Foss in Galveston."

"That it?" asked Lenny.

"I think so, don't you?"

"Great. Okay, everybody, we're through." He turned to regard Nina. "I hate to say it, babe, but your jet lag is showing. You better get some rest before we catch the plane back to Dallas."

"I'm fine." Nina said it automatically, knowing that she was pushing her luck. The day before she had had a very close call when she was overcome with dizziness and nausea as she started down the stairs of her apartment house. She had recovered then, but little as she liked to admit it, her schedule was catching up with her.

"Hey, we'll join you at that seafood place you mentioned earlier," Lenny offered. "Go have a good stiff drink."

"Maybe you're right," Nina said as she handed her microphone back to the skinny girl in houndstooth trousers and plaid shirt. "Thanks, Sally."

"Sure," said Sally, not hearing her.

As Nina got out of the way of the bustle, she noticed that three of the firemen were staring at her. She liked being recognized, and so she waved to them and was rewarded with a wolf whistle. At least they don't see the jet lag, she thought as she went slowly back to the limousine that waited for her.

Four notebook pages were covered with dimensions, sketches and notes by the time Carter climbed to the second floor. "I've got to be crazy," she said to Winslow who padded after her, his black tongue lolling over his teeth. "This place is a barn. I won't ever be able to use half of it."

Winslow chose the sunniest of the empty rooms and went to lie in it, panting.

"You want a room to yourself?" Carter inquired, standing in the door. "No reason you can't have one, I suppose." She had been working for nearly three hours, and little as she wanted to admit it, she was enjoying herself. The second floor went more quickly, and she made a note that the closets were all small and that she might want to make some structural changes, since the rooms themselves were large.

The turret fascinated her. It was too small to be a cupola, but its steeple top and extensive view made it a pleasant place to sit as the day sunk into afternoon. Carter opened the door to the attic, shining her flashlight in the gloom. She knew there could be mice or birds or squirrels or spiders in the attic, and she did not want to encounter any one of them.

For the most part, the place was empty, though there were three crates of boxes in the far corner. Curious, Carter made her way toward them, shining her flashlight ahead of her.

They all had the name CORVIN stenciled on them, and Carter noticed that they all contained books. She brought her flashlight close to the slats in the hope that she could make out the titles on the spines.

By all rights, she knew she ought to leave them alone, to send them to old man Corvin. Even as she acknowledged this, she knew she wanted to open the boxes, to see what was inside them. It had been so long since she had had the fun of delving into old books. Using the flashlight to loosen the nails, she started to pull up the slats on the nearest of the crates.

Half an hour later, she sat on the floor of the turret, a pile of old books at her side. They were all unfamiliar to her, written in several languages on esoteric subjects. Three were Kabbalistic, two were grimoirs, and the rest covered a number of occult studies. Carter picked up the largest one—*Computations of Spirits*, "translated from the Arabic by Charles Weihly-Gramm"—and riffled the pages. The book was almost a century old and it was concerned with metaphysical mathematics. Carter set it aside, mildly interested because of the underlying concept of benign and malign numbers. Next was a private publication of the Order of the Golden Dawn, Urania Lodge. A few pages of it was about all that Carter could take. Next she picked up a leather-bound volume called *A Mirror for Sorcerors*. This was written in so abstruse a manner that Carter wondered if she would ever know what it meant. She was just dipping into *The Catalogue of Spirits, Angels, Demons, Elementals and Ethereal Beings* when there was a loud knocking from two floors below and Winslow, still on the second floor, began to bark.

Carter set the book aside and called out, "Who's there?" thinking it was probably the realtor.

"Frank Vickery," came the unexpected answer. "Where are you?"

"Frank!" Carter set the books aside, leaving them in a heap. She hurried down the steep, curving stairs. "I'm up here."

"I've brought a pizza. I got it in town." From the sound of it he had come farther into the house. "I've got a salad, too, and a six-pack. I thought you could use some food."

Winslow was barking, and he rushed down the stairs ahead of Carter.

When Carter reached the main floor, she found Frank standing in the front parlor, his hands full of things to eat and an engaging smile on his face. "Hi. Cynthia told me how to find you."

"Hi," Carter said, a bit bewildered. "How nice of you."

"When I found out you were over here, I thought you could use a hand."

As if realizing that she should do something, Carter came and took the container of salad out of his hands and then stopped. "I hope you brought plates and utensils. I don't have anything here. The house is empty."

"No problem," said Frank. "The salad container has two sections and little plastic forks, there are napkins in my pocket, and we can eat the pizza with our hands and drink the beer from the can, if you don't mind."

"That would be nice," Carter told him, indicating the room. "You've got your choice of where we eat. It's all like this."

"The window in the back parlor looks nice," said Frank. As he made his way toward that room, he went on, "It's nice, this house. Cynthia said you've made an offer the owner will accept if everything else is approved."

The hardwood floors had been well cared for and aside from a light film of dust were in excellent condition. "They're kind of hard," said Carter as she sat down, tucking her legs in tailor-style. "I ought to find a mat or something."

Frank did not complain. "It's okay. I can handle it." He joined her, putting the pizza box between them and opening it. Then he got the napkins out of his pocket and put them down beside the box. "I got everything but anchovies. I hope you don't mind. After I got it I was worried that you might not eat meat or be allergic to something on the pizza."

"I eat meat, sometimes, and I'm not allergic to anything on pizza including anchovies." She grinned. She felt delighted and that embarrassed her. "I don't know what to—"

"Then don't; have a beer and take a slice of pizza or I'll eat the whole thing myself." He took the first slice and caught the long strings of cheese with his fingers.

Shrugging, Carter accepted the beer, and then helped herself to the pizza. "This was very sweet," she said between bites.

"Pizza? Sweet?" Frank pretended not to understand.

"No, you . . . you silly man." She sipped at the beer, and tried to convince herself that the rush of warmth she felt was because of the drink.

"Now tell me," said Frank when he had started on his second slice, "what you're planning to do with this place. I like it, by the way. When we've finished, I want the grand tour." He broke off some of the pizza and offered it to Winslow on a napkin.

"I don't know if he'll eat it," Carter warned, then opened the salad container.

"I didn't know what you liked, so I stuck with the old standards: lettuce, tomatoes and onions. You can give the onions to me if you don't like 'em."

"I like 'em," she said, deliberately mimicking his speech.

Their meal lasted almost an hour, and by the end of it, they were able to laugh together, and only a little was because of the beer. When Carter showed Frank around the place, he admired it without exaggeration, and pointed out a few features himself. "I think that the ceilings in the bedrooms are pretty high: you might want to find a way to lower them, for insulation and saving on heating bills."

"That's possible," Carter allowed. "I'm more worried about having enough closet space."

"Make one of the back bedrooms into a storage room; that'll take some of the strain off the rest. But with the attic and the basement as well, I can't see that you'll have as much trouble as you think you will."

"The attic!" Carter said, remembering her find. "You'll never guess what's up there."

"Ghosts? Bats?" Frank joked.

"A little of both, I think," Carter answered, and told him about the crates.

"You ought to tell the owner. They could be valuable." He indicated the stair to the turret. "That's the way up?"

"Yes. Do you want to have a look?" She was glad to find that she liked his company, that she was able to be comfortable.

"I'd like that." He followed her up the narrow stairs into the turret, and approved of what he saw. He noticed the books, and bent to pick the nearest one up. "*The Catalogue of Spirits*?" he read.

"Don't forget the *Angels, Demons, Elementals and Ethereal Beings*," Carter said, reading over his shoulder. "That's what most of them are like."

"Strange stuff," Frank said, putting the book down again as if he were afraid it might be dangerous. "What else is there?"

"I don't think any of it's much different. I only looked in the one crate." She went to the southernmost window and looked out. "It's getting late. The power isn't on."

"Well, tell me if there's anything I can do to make up for the time I've taken." Frank sneaked a look at his watch and was startled to see how long he had been there.

"You can let me get you dinner in Santa Cruz. It's a relief to have company . . . of my own." This required some explanation, she felt, and so she hurried on, "It's not that I don't love the Harpers. I do. But right now, Cynthia and Ben and Pamela and Fiona are—they don't mean to be, not at all—a constant reminder of not . . . being part of a family anymore. They try not to make it difficult, and it's very dear of them, and I'm more grateful than I can say, but, there's—"

"I do understand," Frank said, stopping her. "I know what it was like when Barbara died, and I don't suppose it was much different than what you're feeling now. You don't have to tell me if you don't want to."

Carter nodded, and whistled for Winslow. "I didn't mean that you didn't."

"I know that." He put his arm around her shoulder. "You've had a rough couple weeks, and it's not strange that you'd feel that way. It's a rocky time, isn't it?"

"It sure is," she said, and felt her eyes sting.

"You're doing the right thing, Carter. You're getting on with your life and you're looking ahead. It's hard not to look back, but it's useless to do it."

"I don't know how to stop, though," she said. "I catch myself thinking that I have to get back to the house, that Greg's expecting me, that everything is the way it was."

"I know; I know," Frank said softly.

"Even today, while I was taking measurements, I kept remembering. Not the fire, or the memorial, but the day-to-day things. I want to tell Greg about this place." She looked at him, chagrined.

"It'll fade, in time. And that can be hard, too. The first time I forgot my wife's favorite color, I felt as if I'd betrayed her. It was green, by the way. I had to read one of her letters to remember, and then I wanted to punish myself for forgetting. Don't let it happen to you if you can help it. It serves no good and it only wears you out."

Carter moved away from him and started down the stairs. "I want to get my things before the house is dark."

"Okay," said Frank, going down the stairs after her.

They made their way to the first floor in silence, and gathered up the trash from their lunch with only a few words. Finally, as they started toward the door, Carter said, "Will you let me buy you dinner?"

"Do you still want to?" Frank asked.

"Yes, I do. I've been poor company, haven't I? I'd like to make it up to you. And I've got an idea; those crazy books got me to thinking—let's compare our notes on the fires. You can tell me everything you think you know, and I'll do the same, and maybe we'll find out we know some of the same things."

Frank could not stop himself saying, "And it's safe?"

"That, too," she agreed.

"Okay; your car or mine?"

"We can each take our own. I'll tell you how to find the restaurant and we'll meet there. I'll leave Winslow in the car; he knows how to do that. And afterward we can walk him, if you like, or you can leave me to do it and head back to your hotel." She was more in command of herself, more in the present.

"Sounds good to me. Tell me how to get there and I'll meet you." He had very little appetite after his late lunch, but knew that it was not the meal that mattered.

"Thanks," said Carter, holding the refuse in her hands and doing her best to smile.

October 17, Glenwood Springs, Colorado

Father Thomas Aldo scowled at the instruction booklet by his elbow. ENTER: b, it said. Very carefully, the priest tried to do what the program instruction said to do. He hated the way the manual assumed knowledge on his part that he did not have. All he wanted to do was balance the parish checkbook, and everyone had chipped in to get the computer for him.

"I'm too old for this," he told the screen, looking at the cryptic messages. He made another attempt, and this time a change occurred and a copyright notice appeared, and then the beginning of the bookkeeping program.

Sister Jeanette brought him some tea, and without thinking he told her to put it down on his desk.

"Oh, I don't think I should Father Aldo," she said. She was twenty years his junior, dressed in a neat business suit with only a small veil to indicate her vocation. She patted the machine. "It doesn't like water, Father. I'll put the tea over here, on the table. You can have some when you're through."

"I'd better stop before then, but I daren't turn this infernal machine off. And I ought to ask your pardon for speaking out of turn, Sister, but the fact of the matter is that that's how I feel about the thing. I'm fifty-four. The most sophisticated machine I've used is the Xerox in the library."

"Well, Father," said Sister Jeanette, "don't be intimidated by it. It does work quickly, but it's nothing more than a machine." She started to pour out his tea. "You're the one with the brain. It can only do what you tell it to do."

"And if I tell it something wrong?" Father Aldo said, resenting the machine even more.

"Then it will do that," said the nun in her calm, energetic way. "It's no more difficult than instructing children —less difficult, since it can't think for itself or talk back. Or throw things," she appended.

"All right then," said Father Aldo with more determination. "The instructions tell me to enter something, but how?"

"You press the return key on the board." She explained this patiently.

"Why can't they say that?" asked Father Aldo. "Why don't they give me instructions I can read. What is the matter with the people who design these monsters that they don't have sensible instructions?" He was more upset at himself for not understanding than at the confusing booklet open on the desk beside him.

"Very likely they're all used to it, and they know that 'enter' means hit the return key. Just as you assume everyone in the world knows the Stations of the Cross, which they don't, Father," Sister Jeanette said reasonably.

"It would be a better world if they did," he grumbled. "What's this entry for May sixteenth?" he asked, looking at the figures on the screen. "That isn't right, is it? Father Taggart said he'd been working on the books, but I think he's got it wrong. Will you get me the ledgers?"

"Yes, Father," she said automatically. "In the desk drawer?"

"Lower one on the right," said Father Aldo, trying to make sense of what he was seeing on the screen. "How do you get this thing to make corrections?"

"I'll try to give you a hand, Father," Sister Jeanette said as she brought him the black, old-fashioned ledger. "You said May sixteenth?"

"Yes," he said. "It looks as if Father Taggart put every donation for the month under May sixteenth."

"He might have done the entry wrong," said Sister Jeanette. "He's less able to use this machine than you are." It was not an expression of exasperation, for she was too devoted for that, but a sharpness came into her voice, the same way it did in her seventh-grade class when one of the youngsters challenged her.

Father Aldo ignored this, trying instead to concentrate on what the screen was saying. He hit the series of keys he believed would stop the display, but saw too late that the cursor pad was still set up to do numbers instead of the cursor functions, and that instead of decreasing the numbers on the screen, he had added to them. He decided that he hated the machine. He would tell his bishop tomorrow that they would have to find someone else to operate the thing, or give it up entirely.

"What's that smell?" Sister Jeanette asked.

"What smell?" Father Aldo responded as the room was enveloped in fire. The last thought that crossed Father Aldo's mind as he reached to bless himself—a gesture that was never completed—was that given the way the computer behaved, the flames were entirely appropriate.

October 20, Helena, Montana

Jill Perry donned her most professional smile as she wheeled Arnold Aubin into the therapy room. "This is a big day for you, isn't it, Arnold?"

"Maybe," he said, not looking up from his wheelchair. Like many of Jill's patients, he lacked a leg. He had been an amputee for three years, the result of a mining accident, and in the time he had been doing physical therapy, he had undergone several bouts with serious depression. He was coming out of such a period now, and was to begin the testing to see if he could be fitted with one of the more sophisticated prosthetics currently coming into the field.

"Remember that this is only the beginning. If things don't work out ideally today, we'll continue testing. We don't want you to feel that we've failed—"

"We?" he demanded without looking at her.

"A series of tests like this, is a cooperative effort. We need you to be as responsive as possible, and you need us to work as diligently as we can." Her pep talk sounded strained and she understood that Arnold did not believe her. "Doctor Paulson will be with you in a few minutes, and it's important that you be ready to help him with the tests."

"Yeah," said Arnold. He was thirty-six and until last year had been married; now he was divorced and saw his twin sons only once a month, when his sister brought them out to the hospital.

"Arnold, you know that we're all on your side, and we want you to show us how well you've recovered." That was a bad choice of words, she realized.

"I haven't recovered. I'd need my leg back to do that," he reminded her acerbically. "We're trying to work out a substitute."

"Yes." Jill nodded several times, hoping she'd keep better control of her tongue. "You're right. I didn't mean to imply that this is the same as a leg, but it's much closer than anything we would have been able to provide even a few years ago."

"Glad to hear it," Arnold said in a very flat tone.

The monitor was at the far end of the therapy room and it loomed like a high-tech gymnasium, all pullies and weights and gauges. As Jill rolled Arnold toward it, she said, "By this evening, we'll have a very good idea of your response curves."

This time Arnold did not bother to speak.

"You'll have to get onto the bench and let me fasten the electrodes for you," Jill went on, feeling frustrated by the man's attitude, though she understood it far better than many of the nurses who worked at the hospital; her father had lost both hands in Korea and was still bitter about the prosthetics that had taken the place of flesh and nerve and bone.

"Let's get on with it," Arnold said, his expression impassive as he let Jill help him out of the chair and onto the bench.

Jill was almost finished with the electrodes when Doctor Paulson came into therapy room. "How's he coming?"

"Almost done," said Jill, troubled by Rupert Paulson's tendency to speak of patients as if they were in the other room. "How do you feel, Arnold?"

"Like a fool," said Arnold from his place on the bench. There were over a dozen electrodes attached to him and there were three more to attend to.

Paulson chuckled. "I understand how you might, but don't let it bother you. When we fit that new prosthetic, that'll change."

"Uh-huh," said Arnold.

Rupert Paulson came to inspect the placement of the electrodes. "What we hope to determine," he said, addressing the middle distance over Arnold's head, "is what degree of nerve and muscle impulses are still viable. If there are good responses, then the prosthetic will have an excellent chance for success. The degree of response is what we are trying to determine. You understand that the greater the response, the greater the chance that we can effect a complete adaptation of the prosthetic to your body."

"You've gone over it before," Arnold said.

"I want you to do everything you can to give the most accurate response you can. We have the electrodes to monitor, but things like pain or itching or similar responses are . . . obscure. We'll keep full records of your levels of response but we depend on you to give us some indication of the quality of the response." It was a speech he always gave before these tests; Jill had heard it several times in the last year.

"Okay; okay," said Arnold. "The goop with the electrodes is cold, if that means anything."

Rupert Paulson laughed without humor. "Very well, Mister Aubin. We'll get started. Nurse?"

Obediently Jill followed Doctor Paulson into the next room where the monitors were mounted.

"Mister Aubin has an attitudinal problem that might prove a detriment. I want you to observe him closely, just in case, to make sure we find out what his reactions truly are." He stared at the screens in an abstracted way. "We'll monitor the levels in the stump and the hip. If there's a better than fifty-percent response, then we have reason to hope. If not—" He shook his head. "There's only so much we can do."

At a sign from Doctor Paulson, the technician began the tests.

"Fifty-one percent," murmured Paulson. "Marginal, but it might be enough if the rest of the curves are good."

The technician activated the second one.

"Sixty-nine. That's more promising."

Jill watched the percentages appear: forty-three, thirty-six, then a promising seventy-two. Next a disappointing thirty-one.

"Touch and go," Paulson said to the machines. "How's the patient doing?"

Jill did not take her eyes off Arnold. "He's nervous and uncomfortable."

"Not surprising." He saw the technician press the next toggle. "Eighty-nine; that's more like it. What is that?"

"The gluteus maximus," said the technician.

Doctor Paulson was pleased as he saw an eight appear on the display. What the rest of it might be he never discovered, for the room was filled with sudden acrid smoke, and then flame followed at once, voracious, insatiable. More than two-thirds of the rehabilitation wing was gone in the first twenty minutes of the blaze, and by the time it was brought under control, three hundred seventy-eight patients, fifty-two nurses, nine interns, eight physicians and six laboratory technicians were dead.

October 22, Wheeling, West Virginia

Yvonne Quok had been working in the Welfare Department for almost six months, and she had finally lost her idealism. She had at last become inured to pinched faces and empty eyes. She found herself wanting to shake her superiors and to yell at the men and women who appeared on the other side of her desk. She also recognized their suspicion of her, of her slanted eyes and accented English that had nothing of the softened cadences and upward turns of the ones who came to her.

"Now, Missus Russell," she said to the hollow-eyed woman of twenty-nine who huddled in the wooden chair before her. "How many dependent children do you have living with you?"

"They's all depend . . . ent." She wore an ancient cotton dress and a homemade sweater; her cheeks were hollow and there were bruises on her face and arms.

"How many of them?" Yvonne asked with less patience than she would have shown a few weeks before.

"I got six kids," said Leona Russell.

"All living with you?" Yvonne asked, to make sure they both understood.

"Well, Lee stays with m'sister sometimes, but mostly all six of 'em are with me."

"And what are their ages?" Yvonne said, going on to the next line of the form.

"Well, Lee's the oldest. He's almost ten. Then Matthew, who's eight. Sarah and Sue're twins, they're five. I had a miscarriage between Matthew and the twins. And there's Alice, she's three. The doctor says I'm gonna have another one." She lifted her chin.

"And when is the baby due?" Yvonne asked, continuing to fill in the form and keeping her opinion to herself.

"Let's see, I think he said early March. Yeah. I told my husband and he said that he wanted me to see about getting it taken care of. He don't want more youngsters around the place."

"You mean an abortion?" said Yvonne.

"I don't want an abortion. It's wrong. I want this taken care of." She looked across the desk at the form Yvonne was filling in. "What're you saying there?"

"Missus Russell, if you're willing to sign a release . . . a permission form, when you have this next baby, the doctor can take care of you then, make sure you don't have any more children, if that's what you'd like. If it isn't, then he won't do anything, but he can." She knew that it was not encouraged, telling the women who came for aid and food stamps about sterilization, but she saw the desperation in the woman's face, and she decided that the poor creature should know that there was a choice.

"It don't put anything in? The preacher says that using things is a sin." She looked worried but interested.

"No, it's more a permission to take something out. It won't change anything about you except that you won't have any more children." Yvonne waited while Missus Russell thought this over.

"What about my husband? It won't do anything to him,

will it?" She caught the edge of an already ragged fingernail in her teeth.

"No, he won't even know it's happened." Yvonne thought of what her supervisor would say if she could hear her, but she refused to be deterred.

"I'll think on it," promised Missus Russell, and Yvonne concealed a resigned sigh. "Who is the doctor you're seeing?"

"The clinic hasn't given me one yet," said Missus Russell, then hurried on. "I know you're a lot closer to where I live than the offices downtown, and I know that you're trying to do a good job, but you're just a ... branch office, aren't you?"

"Yes, we're a branch office," said Yvonne, wondering why this was important to the woman.

"What I mean is, you being out here on the edge of things and all, you might not get things as quick as they do downtown, and we have to have the food stamps soon or we won't be eatin' for a time. If it would mean getting the food stamps faster, then maybe I ought to go downtown."

"Don't worry, Missus Russell, we'll get the food stamps to you as quickly as possible; just as fast as you could get them from the central office. Now, what does your husband do?"

"He don't work steady. He got cut up five, six years back, and it makes it hard for him to do anything steady." She had a defiant edge to her voice now, and she held the sweater more tightly around her thin shoulders.

"I see." Yvonne decided she had better have a look through the files when she was through with Missus Russell to find out what the story was on the husband.

"He gets some part-time work fixing engines and there's seasonal work at the packing plant, but that's about all. Nothing too steady." She paused, then added, "I do sewing when I can get jobs. I got told that you can count that against me."

Yvonne put down her pen. "How much do you make?"

"Two dollars a piece for darning and patching, three

dollars a piece for making them up whole." She coughed. "And that's the truth; I don't fib about what I charge."

"And how much do you do in the way of sewing?"

"Oh, maybe ten pieces a week," said Missus Russell.

"Then you can make twenty to thirty dollars in supplemental income?" Yvonne saw the resistance in the woman's eyes and rephrased. "You pick up twenty to thirty dollars from sewing?"

"On a good week. Most times it's less." She hesitated, then said, "Maybe fifteen to twenty is closer, most weeks."

"I see." Yvonne thought of Lauri Palmer, who babysat for her and earned more. "I'll have to put it on the form, Missus Russell, but I promise you, we don't want to deprive you of the food stamps your children are entitled to have. I'll have to review your case with the clinic and find out if there are any special circumstances that might make a difference for you. Do you mind?"

"I was kind of hoping we'd have the food stamps for this week," she said, and the blow to her pride that this admission cost her was painfully visible.

"I tell you what," Yvonne said, against all her better instincts, "I'll let you have twenty-five dollars; my own money, and you can get food for your kids. You can pay me back, if you want, over the next months, as much as you can afford at a time." She had never made such an offer before.

"Why'd you do that?" Leona Russell asked. "Why'd someone like you do that?"

"You mean why would a Vietnamese lend a West Virginia woman enough money to feed her children? Is that what you're asking me? I was twelve years old when we left my country, Missus Russell, and we had been living near the fighting most of my life. I know what it is not to have enough to eat, and I know what it is to be worried about children, since I have a ten-month-old daughter of my own. Now, if that makes any sense to you, Missus Russell, I suggest you take the money."

Missus Russell picked at the sleeve of her sweater.

"That's not what I meant. I thank you kindly for your offer, but my family takes charity from no one."

"It isn't charity. I told you, you can pay me back at any rate you wish. If you want to make certain your children eat, then I'd recommend you take the money. I hope you won't mention this to anyone; we might both get into trouble for it."

This warning seemed to restore Leona Russell's spirits, for she nodded once in agreement. "My kids'll thank you, too, Miz Quok."

"Now, let's get the rest of this form taken care of," said Yvonne after she had taken two tens and a five from her purse and handed them over to Missus Russell.

"Fine," she said, less guardedly than before.

In fifteen minutes, the relevant information was in place and Yvonne went down the hall to the supervisor's office. "Here's something for Ralph," she said, holding out the form.

Her supervisor, a bullet-shaped woman in navy-blue polyester, took the form and glanced through it, initialing it at the bottom and saying, "Supplemental sewing income."

"Not much," Yvonne pointed out.

"Still it has to be considered." She snuffled, part of her constant battle with sinus congestion. "Hand it on to Ralph and take your lunch break; it's almost one and I'll need you back here for the two-o'clock review meeting."

Yvonne took the form down to the end of the hall and handed it to one of the clerks. "Better run a check on her husband. She says he has occasional work, but there might be something else on record."

"Sure thing," said the clerk, snapping her chewing gum. "Ralph'll get right on it."

A little ashamed with herself for her eagerness to leave the office, Yvonne vowed to cut her lunch short by fifteen minutes so that she could be back at her desk well before the meeting. Perhaps she could use the time to come up with some relief for Leona Russell and her six—soon to be seven—children. As she backed out of the small parking lot, she regarded the cinder-block building with a pang of emotion that she could not identify. Then she was on her way toward the main part of Wheeling, bound for her apartment and a few minutes with her baby.

In spite of all her good intentions, Yvonne Quok was a little late returning to the office, and was preoccupied enough not to notice the commotion until she was within half a block of the welfare office, where she was stopped by a policeman at a barricade.

"Sorry, lady, you have to go around."

"Around where?" Yvonne asked. "I'm late back to work."

"Just two blocks up, that's all you have to do," the officer said, trying to wave her on.

"But I work at the Welfare Agency office," Yvonne protested and saw the policeman's face turn very still. "What is it?"

"Maybe you better pull over, ma'am," he said in a much different voice. "There's . . . been a fire."

"A fire?" she repeated, refusing to comprehend.

"The Welfare Agency office. I'm sorry. You were real lucky, ma'am. I don't think anyone else made it out." He paused. "Look, why don't you park the car here by the barricade. No one'll tow it, I'll see to that. The Fire Chief'll want to talk to you. Will you do that for me, ma'am?"

"Yes," Yvonne whispered. "All right. Yes." It was simply impossible. No matter what she had read in the paper or seen on television, the fires that were in the news never happened to anyone she knew or cared about, certainly not to the people she worked with.

As she was fumbling with the keys, a tall, sooty fireman came up to her car. After a few, swift words with the policeman, he leaned over and spoke to Yvonne.

"I'm sorry; what did you say?" Yvonne requested, for suddenly everything around her was a jumble, and nothing seemed to make sense.

"If you don't mind," the policeman said, speaking

slowly and distinctly, "Jack here'll take you to the Fire Chief."

"Oh. Fine. All right." Like an automaton, she got out of her car and locked the door. As she trudged after the tall fireman, she kept thinking back to her last days in Vietnam, and the ruin she had left behind. She never again wanted to see destruction like that, or suffering.

The building was now little more than a shell, most of it black. Fire engines gathered around it, and there were hoses still criss-crossing the street and the little parking lot. A few gutted cars were left next to the building, most of them cracked and broken.

Yvonne stood utterly unmoving as she looked at this horror. And then, from some part of herself she had thought was forgotten, she began a low, wailing chant to mourn the dead.

PART VI

October 23, Cleveland, Ohio

"This is Nina Foss, and we're in the home of Inga Peschovsky, whose three children were killed in the random fire that claimed the lives of over six hundred patrons of the Melton Mall Cinemas." She turned away from the fascinating eyes of the camera to give a sympathetic look to the thirty-five-year-old woman with the ravaged face and dark clothing. "Missus Peschovsky, everyone shares your terrible grief over your tragedy. As you know, many of our viewers have suffered similar losses."

"It's been hard," the woman said in a muffled voice.

"And you've been very brave. We're grateful that you're willing to share your sorrow with all of us." Nina's expression was not quite a smile, but there was not the degree of sadness that she might have had if she had not been offered the national morning-news anchorwoman position by her network the day before. All her work was paying off. She had to make an effort to concentrate on what Missus Peschovsky was saying.

"They were good kids. They were real good kids," their mother said as she began to weep.

Nina put her hand on Missus Peschovsky's. "There's no shame in showing your loss. We're all with you, Missus Peschovsky."

"Marilyn was up for head cheerleader," sobbed Missus Peschovsky. "My... former husband called. He said it was my fault. He said I should never let them go to a public place, not while the fires are still going on." She leaned her head forward to hide her face.

"Missus Peschovsky, don't blame yourself. There's no way you could have known."

"Ted was right; I should never have let them go. They're dead because of me."

Nina signaled to Lenny to stop the taping, and as soon as the camera was off, she did her best to restore Missus Peschovsky's composure. "Inga, Inga, come on. Do what you can, will you? Don't let this throw you."

"I'm sorry, I'm sorry," said Missus Peschovsky.

"Now, get yourself together, Inga," Nina said, doing her best to keep her voice soft and her pace unhurried. "Lenny, will you bring us a cup of coffee?" As she asked, she made a gesture indicating that Lenny should add something to the coffee.

Lenny nodded and signaled one of the others in the five-person crew to supply the coffee. "You okay, Nina?"

"Sure; it's Missus Peschovsky who needs the help," Nina snapped, then added, "Sorry, Lenny. It's been a long day."

"Yesterday was a long day. Tomorrow's gonna be a long day. They're all long days, Nina," Lenny said. "You can't let it beat you, y'know?"

"Of course," Nina said. "I count on it." She got up from the flowered sofa, making a place for Billy Corral to give Inga Peschovsky some of his doctored coffee. "What did you give her? Brandy?"

"Valium. She'd smell the brandy." Lenny shoved his soft brown hair off his forehead. "You think we're still going to make that public meeting in Cambridge this evening? It'll take another hour here at least, and even if we can get tape on the way at once, we'll still be running almost an hour late."

"We'll make it," said Nina.

"If you're certain," Lenny said doubtfully.

"Just make sure that Inga can finish this interview so that we can get on with this." She had to resort to heavier makeup these days in order to keep the fresh look that the network executives had praised. Lately, she had found herself feeling slightly dizzy in the early morning, and it took her longer to gather her thoughts for interviews.

"In another ten minutes she'll be okay," said Lenny, "what about you?"

"I'll be ready. And get my notes for Cambridge. Can we get in to Logan at a good time?"

"We're set," he said, then added, "I know how important all this is to you, Nina, but make sure it doesn't cost too much."

"No way," she promised him. "Has the network come up with any more likely fires or talkative survivors?"

"That'll be waiting in Cambridge." He left her to check the lights and signaled Billy to move so that Nina could take her place next to Missus Peschovsky. "How're you doing?"

Inga Peschovsky had wiped her face and there was a smudge of mascara at the corner of one eye which Nina wiped away.

"Now, do you think you're ready?" She was solicitous, but as much as she wanted to show concern, she was also trying to be practical.

"I think I can manage now," said Inga Peschovsky. "It's just what happens when I think of the children. It was so recent."

"Yes." She gave a little nod to Lenny. "Do you think you can do the rest? We don't want to distress you."

"Yes. I think it's important." She had straightened up and forced her voice to steadiness.

"Then if you're ready, let's get it done." She flicked her tongue over her lips to make them shine, and said, "If you're willing, we'd like to have you share your thoughts with us. Do you think enough is being done to stop these terrible fires?" It was a loaded question, one she had asked in various disguises at every interview, knowing that it always brought the strongest response in her interview subject as well as the audience.

"I don't like to criticize the government, and I think they're trying to do all that they know, but I don't think they're being careful enough. If there's a danger, they should let us know so that we can do something about it. If I'd known what the chances were, I would never have let my children go to the theatre. There must be hundreds of other parents who feel like that." She swallowed hard twice, but this time she did not burst into tears.

"And what would you like to say to the other families who have suffered similar losses to yours?"

"Only that my prayers are with them and I hope that they'll remember me and my children in theirs. It's so difficult, you don't realize how fragile everything is."

This was wonderful, thought Nina, already imagining how it would look on the evening news tomorrow night as part of her continuing series of interviews. "Missus Peschovsky, we thank you for letting us intrude in your hour of grief and we thank you for your generous concern for others that makes it possible for you to talk with us."

Lenny gave her the old speed-up signal, and Nina did her closing at once. "This is Nina Foss in the home of Inga Peschovsky in Cleveland. Thank you all and good-night."

"Great," said Lenny. "We might have to trim a second or two, but you did great. You, too, Missus Peschovsky."

"Thank you," she said automatically. "I hope I've done the right thing," she added, not looking at Nina directly. "My brother said this was good, but Ted... When we separated three years ago he was furious that the court limited his visits, and now he'll say that he was right and the courts were wrong." She was starting to work herself up again, and Nina stopped the spiral.

"You're a very brave woman, Missus Peschovsky, and anyone who thinks differently is a callous boor." She gave her attention to Billy. "I want you to buy Missus Peschovsky dinner. Catch up with us in New York tomorrow morning."

"Okay," said Billy with a sigh, even though squiring the interviewees was part of his job. He had started to feel drained and the enthusiasm that had pushed him at the first was fading.

"Good," Nina said. "You take a load off my shoulders."

Billy nodded; she said that to him every time he did his job and it had ceased to mean anything to him.

"We're almost ready to roll," Lenny said from the doorway where the rest of the small crew had piled the equipment before loading it in the van. On the street below a dozen or so neighbors were gathered, trying not to stare too obviously.

"Fine," Nina said, going back to the sofa one last time. "We'll send you a copy of the interview if you want it, Missus Peschovsky."

"Oh, yes, please," she said in an emotional rush. "Yes, I'd like that." The gratitude that shone in her desolate eyes astonished Nina. What was it about people?

"We're waiting," Lenny called to Nina.

"Be right there," she responded, and held out her hand to Missus Peschovsky. "You know that your grief is shared," she said before she hurried out of the very ordinary house.

Lenny was holding the van door open for her, but he waited while she waved to those in the small crowd who recognized her. "Come on, hotshot. Next stop Cambridge, Mass."

"Fires," said Myron Bethune with exaggerated patience and simplicity, "are not supernatural phenomena. They are ordinary physical manifestations of energy."

The interviewer pursed his lips and stared hard at his subject. "You won't deny, though, will you, Inspector Bethune, that these fires have not been like most fires? Most fires leave evidence of what caused them, and as Fire

Marshal Rountree has already told us, these fires are conspicuous for their apparent lack of cause."

"That's the word," Bethune insisted. "Apparent. There is no reason at all to suppose that because we haven't yet been able to identify the cause that there is none, or that the cause has to be something supernatural."

"From what I understand, Professor Howard Li, who worked for the NSA and was himself a victim of one of these so-called random fires, was of the opinion that the origin of the fires was outside the normal causes. Some have suggested that the Professor's unfortunate death only serves to confirm his theory. Would you care to comment on that?"

Bethune took a deep breath: what he wanted to say was that Howard Ro-jin Li had been an overeducated, underbred arrogant son-of-a-bitch whose family ran a small chain of fabric and tailoring shops in Los Angeles. What he did say was, "No, I wouldn't care to comment at this time."

"But are you investigating this possibility?" persisted the interviewer annoying as a mosquito.

"The various investigatory agencies are exploring many avenues of inquiry at this time," Bethune said stiffly. "No reasonable area of inquiry is being neglected."

"Does that include the so-called supernatural?" The interviewer leaned back smugly, determined to get Bethune to answer the question one way or another.

"It includes anything that the investigators feel is valid. We're trying to take as wide a view as we can and still stay within the bounds of good sense." He glowered at the interviewer. "I don't have immediate up-to-the-minute information on what every single one of the investigating teams are doing—if I did," he went on, forestalling the objection he could sense was coming, "they wouldn't be doing their jobs well."

"I see." The interviewer made a show of examining his notes on the clipboard resting on his knee. "Tell me, Inspector Bethune, how you think these fires began?"

"I am already on record on that issue. I believed then

and still believe that these fires are the work of terrorists aimed at disrupting and destroying the country. I think that the terrorism is aimed primarily at industry, but educational institutions and such companies as banks and insurance companies are also likely targets. Which is why we've recommended extra precautions for these businesses."

"Do you think that there will be demands to be met, a way to ransom the country?"

Bethune took a deep breath. "Over twenty different organizations and individuals have taken credit—if that is the right word—for these fires, but none of them have so far been able to say how the fires are caused or have been able to predict accurately when and where the next will occur. Until such a test is met, this country will pay no money or make any other bargain with those who contact the Bureau or any other agency of the government." He had a dull ache in his shoulder, and he moved testily, trying to ease the cramp he felt coming.

"Inspector Bethune," the interviewer said in his most considered way, "there are constant rumors of efforts on the part of the intelligence community to stop or to influence the coverage given these fires by the news media. Both papers and television journalists have complained that they have been under pressure. Would you care to comment on this?"

"I wouldn't say that it's pressure, exactly," Bethune began. "We believe that we have an obligation to present our perceptions of what the specific risks are in these instances, and the press in all its forms does not always agree with the perceptions of the intelligence community. We do think that it would be best to keep coverage to a minimum and to avoid the sensational, but that is part of our job." He folded his arms, but the cramp in his shoulder was still there.

"What would you call it?" the interviewer persisted.

"It's part of our job. It's part of our responsibility to make certain that the security of the country is safeguarded."

The interviewer nodded sagely. "There are many who

suggest that your time might be better spent trying to discover the causes of the fires than in attempting to block legitimate reporters trying to do their jobs, as you try to do yours."

Bethune coughed. "It must appear that we're wasting time, at least to some of the people who have been following the fires. But let me assure you that every government agency with even the most tenuous connection to our work has put its resources at our disposal in this terrible emergency, and that we are very appreciative of all that has been done through this effort. We have had detailed reports from all the companies and individuals hurt by these fires—"

"That you know of," interjected the interviewer.

"Yes; that we know of, although we believe that we have been able to discover all the fires successfully. If there are others, we are sure to learn of them in time."

"But you will allow that there may be some you have not yet learned of and may never accurately identify."

The cramp was worse and Bethune tried to move his fingers carefully; his right hand responded, his left hand was cold and awkward. "There may be some, of course. For example, a warehouse used by organized crime might have a fire we never get the statistics on, but since most people are law-abiding and eager to have these fires a thing of the past, it is our contention that our files are almost one hundred percent complete."

"Inspector Bethune," said the interviewer in a gentler tone, "are you all right?"

"Just a little sore," said Bethune. "I haven't slept much, and the couch in my office is not the most satisfactory bed in the world." He was embarrassed that he had been caught showing weakness, but he tried to make light of it. "There are many agents in the same position."

"Commendable," said the interviewer, not entirely satisfied. He studied Bethune and then resumed his questions. "You indicated earlier that you felt that the scientific community has not provided the assistance it might."

"Yes, and I stand by that remark. In such an emergency

as this one, our scientific and academic communities might be more willing to divert their attentions and abilities to this problem."

"But most universities have said that they're willing, but with the long periods of funding cutbacks and tight grant money, most of them have neither the time nor the equipment necessary to do the sorts of experiments you require."

Bethune squirmed. "I'm not responsible for the funding problem. Those cutbacks in educational monies were approved by Congress and by the people. To say that this has backfired, as I understand some academics have, is irresponsible and petulant."

"They also point out that defense spending, while at an all-time high, has not resulted in the defense community being diverted to deal with the fires except where they have been directly involved. Would you care to comment on this?"

Squinting against the studio lights that suddenly seemed far too bright, Bethune struggled to come up with the most appropriate answer. "Since many of us assume that these fires are the work of terrorists, we believe that it is most prudent to let our defense forces be kept at the ready to do just that—to defend the country."

"Don't you think that it would do more good to have some of the military personnel made available to fight and investigate the fires?"

"No." Bethune hated being needled. "It isn't my decision to make in any case; it is the decision of the President and the Joint Chiefs, and so far as I am aware, no such change is currently being considered."

"Do you regard that as responsible? Isn't it strange that there has been so little assistance provided by the military?" The interviewer leaned forward and lifted his eyebrows, implying that he and Bethune shared a secret.

"I resent the implications of your remark," Bethune said, and felt the cramp tighten. It was a dreadful feeling, almost nauseating.

"What implications are those, Inspector? I'm asking a

question, and you are making assumptions about its intent."

"You're implying that the military is shirking its responsibility in this difficult time, and that in so doing, we are being exposed to more, not less risks. You ask your questions as if you suspect the Joint Chiefs of wanting the fires to continue."

"It wouldn't be the first time that the armed forces have taken sides by not taking sides," the interviewer said in his most philosophical manner.

"That is the most unconscionable lie!" Bethune started to rise, but the effort was too great. He broke out in a clammy sweat.

"There *is* something wrong," said the interviewer, signaling the director to stop the cameras. "Where's the doctor? I think the Inspector is having a heart attack."

Bethune took a deep breath to protest again. It was bad enough that he had been accused of dereliction of duty, but now the fool was trying to throw him off the subject by this cheap trick. He wheezed out a few syllables of indignation while the interviewer loosened his tie and unbuttoned his collar.

"Hang on, Bethune," he said, his formidable interviewing manner gone and replaced with the look and demeanor of the history professor he had been six years before. "The ambulance is on its way. You'll make it."

The doors burst open and three men rushed into the studio. The oldest shouted orders to the others.

Bethune did not hear them clearly, but to his amazement, he felt grateful to them for arriving.

Even with the electricity on and her five pieces of furniture—a platform bed in her room, a table and two chairs in the kitchen and a love seat in the living room—set up, Carter continued to feel like an intruder, someone trespassing on the Corvin house. "It's the Milne house now," she said aloud as she lugged her sleeping bag up to her bed. Her household goods, all of them new, would start arriving tomorrow morning around ten and she was still trying to decide where she wanted everything to go.

Winslow padded up the stairs behind her, content to be in the house, his curiosity satisfied for the time being.

"There's so much to do," she said as she opened her sleeping bag. She spread it out, thinking that she was wrong to have turned down Cynthia's offer of a pillow. Tomorrow she would have her own pillow, and she could do without one for the night.

The overhead light had been augmented by three wall fixtures that Carter thought were indescribably ugly, but the small pools of light they cast were convenient to the head of her bed. She would be able to read in comfort, which pleased her.

"Damn," she said, reaching out to pat Winslow where he had curled up near the bed. "I didn't bring a book." It had been so long since she had not had easy access to books that now it seemed inconceivable that she would not be able to find something to read. But she could not simply turn off the lights; for one thing she was too keyed up and for another, her habit was too deeply ingrained. She went to rummage in her purse and portfolio; there were two big reports on the most recent fires, a magazine aimed at computer programmers, and a pamphlet on housing insurance. None of it was very promising.

After hanging up her clothes and pulling on her bathrobe, Carter made her way up to the turret. There were books there, she remembered. She could not believe that they would hold her interest for very long, but it was better than having nothing.

As she reached the turret room, she could not at first locate the light switch. Only the pale moonlight fell on the stack of books she had left against the wall, and she reached for them, taking the two on top. As she started back to the second floor, she noticed the light switch, and stretched out her hand to turn it on. Then she changed her mind and went back down the stairs, her two finds held close against her chest. She was pleased to discover she had taken *Computations of the Spirits* and *The Catalogue of Spirits, Angels, Demons, Elementals and Ethereal Beings.* Both seemed to be unlikely subjects, but she was sure they'd bring on a stupor.

Once back in her sleeping bag, she selected the smaller book, *The Catalogue of Spirits*. She glanced over the table of contents, finding the chapter headings baffling and amusing. What on earth was a Cobold? What was the difference between an Angel, an Archangel, a Throne, and a Dominion? Shaking her head, she opened the book at random and started reading at the first paragraph that caught her eye.

> *In the matter of malign spirits of every sort, it is merely the opportunity to do mischief that attracts such beings, for to bring about confusion and disorder is their delight, and the more comprehensive such disorder, the greater the satisfaction the spirit derives from the evil done. Those creatures of the devil who go through the world in the service of chaos and despair take their greatest satisfaction from destruction and death.*

Carter read the paragraph over again, comparing the comments of the nineteenth-century occultist with her own sense of the random fires. "If I were the credulous type," Carter said to Winslow, "I could be persuaded that these fires were demonic in origin."

She turned the pages, running her eyes over the text in a desultory way.

> *There are four sorts of spirits, spirits of nature which are the essence of earth, air, fire and water, and in these forms at their most pure do these spirits manifest themselves. They are called Elementals, for the elements they represent. These Elements are: of Earth, gnomes which are called by some cobolds; of Water undines; of Fire salamanders; of Air sylphs. While belonging neither to the blessed or malignant spirits, they are none-*

> *theless manifestations of great power and those with the occult virtue to call them forth do so at considerable peril, so great is the force of the manifestation of these Elementals.*

The next three chapters were from a treatise by someone named Agrippa, and there were references to occult virtues and the methods employed by the occultist to use these virtues. The language seemed stilted to Carter, even given the style of Agrippa's era, which the introductory notes indicated was the sixteenth century.

> *Whereas the greatest of sorcerors and alchemists have held safe congress with various spirits and beings of the realms beyond nature, such ventures are fraught with hazard and those who venture beyond the realms of ordinary power do so at their peril. Even the most blessed of spirits, by their nature, have great power and they cannot be called without full protection to those who have summoned them; should the magister do otherwise, there is nothing that can protect him from the might of the spirit, and in no way can the magister render himself safe once the manifestation has occurred. All protection must be afforded by the magister prior to the summoning, or his very soul may be forfeit.*

"Sounds delightful," Carter said, feeling sleepier. Reluctantly she put the book aside, thinking that she would probably never look at it again; in fact, she ought to turn the books over to Mister Corvin. She would remind Stephanie of the crates tomorrow, after her furniture arrived.

Half an hour passed, then a second. Carter shifted her position inside the sleeping bag, then shifted again, but the sleep she had thought near continued to escape her. At last, when it was well past midnight, she turned on the light again. With an indignant shake of her head, she reached for the other book, hoping it would be soporific enough to do the job that the first did not.

"I'll say this, Winslow," she muttered as she thumbed through the first five pages, "the style is certainly dense enough."

> *In the annals of the erudite Arabs, there are many references to the numerical significance of combined numbers. Those who have marvelled at the structures of alchemy will find the cognitions of these great scholars a most worthwhile perusal.*

What followed were several pages of diagrams and symbols that left Carter more puzzled than before. Some of the diagrams were in the form of sigils and devices and cartouchelike seals. The names of demons and angels were under these. There followed another block of text on Arabic theories in regard to benefic and malefic numbers.

> *In their deliberations these magi determined that the most malignant of numbers is five and the beginning of a sequence of numbers in units of five with the number five can bring nothing but harm and disaster to those invoking spirits and demons through the vibrations of numbers as assessed in their philosophical sense. It would appear that there were many instances when demons were summoned through the inscription of series of numbers beginning with the malignant five and consisting of multiples of five, such as ten and fifteen. Most malignant of all were twenty-five numbers, which could only be used to summon Shaitan himself, whereas other spirits were brought forth by lesser multiples of five, and in this way, the Arab mathematicians of the time far surpassed the summonings and skills of their European brethren. It is an area of study which has been abandoned by most philosophers in recent centuries in part due to the increase of Rosicru-*

cian and Bavarian Brotherhoods each of whom employ their own rituals and methods for their spiritual and occult advancement.

There are many who have claimed to have experimented with the methods of the Arab mathematicians, but there are no concrete results that are sufficiently reliable for any final judgement on our part. To invoke any spirits through the means of number and numbers alone is inconsistent to the practices of Western occultism and therefore the ritual tested by time and experience continues to be that most often employed by those eager to summon spirits for their knowledge or to bind them to their bidding. It is often regarded as too hazardous to limit a spirit by mere numbers and their vibrations in place of the more respected and powerful pentagrams and similar forms used in the binding of spirits and demons.

When Carter realized she had read most of the last two paragraphs three times and made no sense of the text and could not understand the words, she put the book aside and turned off the light, this time confident that she would sleep.

J.D. Patterson waited to hear what Randall Whiting had to say. "If you tell me I'm too old for this," he warned, "you're fired."

"Hell, J.D., we're pretty much the same age," said Whiting with half a smile. "But maybe we're both too old. I won't admit it if you don't."

"You're a great diplomat," J.D. said wryly. "But that doesn't answer my question. Is my blood pressure a problem?"

"J.D., *everyone's* blood pressure is a problem sometime." He fixed his eyes on an abstracted seascape on the far wall. "You're under a great deal of stress. You know that and I know that. It takes a toll, which I don't have to tell you, because you know it and you can feel it. Yes, your blood pressure is up, and that's not good, but given the circumstances, it doesn't surprise me. In fact, I'd be more concerned if your blood pressure weren't up, because then there'd be something seriously wrong with you. As to what to do about it, to anticipate your question, I'd suggest that you find out what's behind the fires and then take a long vacation. It's no earthly good trying it before the fires are taken care of, because you'll only worry about them in another location."

"Sounds like you've anticipated everything I was going to ask," J.D. said with his humor still unimpaired.

"However, so long as I have you here, I think I'd better tell you that Scott Costa is on the verge of a real breakdown, and I can't guarantee that it will hold off until the fires are over." He looked more serious, more worn.

"Is it worth giving him a leave?" J.D. asked.

"I don't know. He's likely to think you're firing him. He already talks as if you're looking for an excuse."

J.D. shook his head. "If I needed such an excuse, I would have had it six weeks ago. I want to keep Scott going if I can. He has good instincts, when they're working and when he gets that fucking chip off his shoulder." He stopped. "Well? Is there a good way to handle it?"

"Probably not. I've recommended a therapy group for him, but so far he's refused. If you can find a way to take some of the strain off him without being too obvious, then it might buy him some time. If he guesses what you're doing, he's going to resent it." He fell silent, his eyes still on the painting.

J.D. got up from the chair and reached for his jacket which was slung over the arm. "Have you heard anything about Bethune?"

"Speaking of stress, do you mean?" Whiting asked with more sadness than humor.

"Something like that."

"He's alive, and they're guarded in their optimism. They've made McPherson temporary head of the investigation in partnership with an Inspector Godwin, who also thinks that this is all a clever terrorist plot."

"Yeah." J.D. buttoned the jacket and made sure his tie was straight. "That's their party line all right. I guess we ought to contact him for form's sake."

"More speaking of stress?" Whiting gibed. "What about letting Frank or Rountree take care of that for you?"

"Rountree is leaving this afternoon, and Frank has troubles with the FBI guys already," J.D. said. "They sent him out to us to punish him for not going along with their terrorist theory. He was supposed to get buried with us." He chuckled.

"I'd say that he does better here with us than they'd let him do with the FBI breathing down his neck, especially if they don't want him to disagree with them." Whiting watched J.D. walk to the door. "You want something to help you sleep?"

"Nope. Then I'd just need something to help me wake up." He started out the door, and then looked back. "I want you in all the meetings now. Some of the seams are starting to pull. I don't want anyone unraveling on us."

"I know what you mean. I worry about my own seams now and again." He tapped his desktop three times, as if giving a code or signal. "All right. I suppose the topic this morning is the fire in the BART yards?"

"Yes," said J.D. heavily. "Among other things. They're calling it arson for the moment; there was some kind of timing device found—there wasn't much left of it—in the wreckage." J.D. looked at the clock on Whiting's desk. "Gotta run."

Whiting waved his boss away and sat for a few minutes collecting his thoughts, trying very hard not to feel paranoid.

Two secretaries sat across the lunch table from Lois Hillyer, both of them having the soup and sandwich offered by the cafeteria. Lois herself was toying with an uninspired salad of iceberg lettuce and red cabbage. Her mind was wandering, but now and then something one of the women said penetrated her mental haze.

". . . but with the fire destroying most of their stock, and all the costs, Hannah said they might lose the business entirely. Roy's in terrible shape and his partner wants to sue him for having stored their stock in an unsafe place."

"Terrible."

"... not sure how many people got burned..."

"I hear that morgue attendants call burn victims crispy critters."

"That's sick."

"... up on nine ordered all the computers and electronic typewriters disconnected. Said that he wouldn't feel safe unless that was done, and he's taking the stairs; he won't use the elevators."

"How does his staff feel about that?"

"They aren't happy, but as Lillian said, they're all still alive."

"Yeah. These days it sure is. . . . Grace's family. The funeral is tomorrow."

"I'm getting sick of funerals."

"So am I. But so far it's been no closer than my uncle and his family; they were in the airport at Atlanta, coming back from Paris."

"You told me."

"... and you know what's happened to the postal service. It's a week to get a letter from here to Dallas."

"You can't blame them for not using the sorting machines, considering."

"But still."

Lois tried to keep from eavesdropping, but the attraction, the fascination was too great. These people are what the statistics are all about; they're what the company insured.

"... Henry O'Brian's mother was in that Helena fire, at the rehab hospital? She was taking treatment for a stroke. Just shows you."

"Henry was furious about it. He told Mimi that he wanted to take legal action against the center."

Lois thought painfully of her own brother's family being burned, of all the losses that had been suffered and were continuing. She wanted to scream or cry or run away where the fires could not reach her, nor the anguish of grief.

"... when they pulled the plug on Danny. I was glad. The way he was burned, there wasn't any way he could have lived, and he was in such agony. A twelve-year-old kid shouldn't have to go through that kind of pain."

"How'd your stepmother feel?"

"Worse than any of us. I didn't like her much when Dad married her, but since Danny—"

"It's real sad. "They've got two other kids, haven't they?"

"It's not the same."

Lois stared at her plate, unable to touch the food. She tasted bile on the back of her tongue. Before she became sick, she got up and left the table.

Almost half an hour before the movers had left, and Carter stood surrounded by her new possessions in her new house.

"It's going to be real nice," said Cynthia as she and her two girls prepared to leave. "Ben's putting the last of the bedding upstairs. Your washer and dryer will be here on Monday, and the curtains and draperies will be here next Friday. That should get you off to a great start."

"I hope," said Carter, who, now that she had actually moved in, was starting to feel frightened.

"I think the idea of knocking out the wall in those two little bedrooms and making it one big guest room is great," Cynthia continued.

"I hope Stephanie can recommend someone to do the work. And I'll have to find someone to help me with the yard. I love it, but it's huge. And those trees will need pruning. From what I can see, Corvin's nephew let them go wild."

"Hey, Carter," Cynthia said, "don't worry about that now. You'll have a long time to get that sorted out. Enjoy your house."

Ben came down the stairs, his thinning hair messy and a big grin on his face. "This is a great place. If we were looking for something new in this area, I'd want it for us. I like the view and that turret is terrific. I like the wicker furniture you put up there. Reminds me of all that stuff I read about the Raj." He wiped his hands on his sweatshirt. "Is there anything else?"

"I was going to take you out to dinner," Carter said.

"Not tonight," said Cynthia. "We've got a meeting with Barry and Scott."

"How's Scott doing?" Carter asked, remembering the way he had acted during the last briefing.

"Terrible," Cynthia said. "If it were up to me, I'd insist he take a leave of absence, but J.D. won't do it. He told me that Scott wants to stay at work, and so he's having Randy keep an eye on him."

"Poor man," said Carter in an abstracted way. "We're all feeling the pinch, but Scott's the worst of all."

Ben folded his arms. "Want me to call the girls? They're outside looking at the trees."

"You'd better," said Cynthia. "It'll take ten minutes to get them into the car." She leaned over and kissed the corner of his mouth. "You're a treasure, Ben Harper."

"Glad to know I'm appreciated." Ben grinned, then ambled off toward the kitchen. "Pammy! Fiona!" he called as he opened the back door.

"I can't thank you enough for everything you've done, and I don't mean helping me move. I couldn't have got through the last couple weeks without you." Carter wandered over to the window. "I can't help thinking about Greg. I have all sorts of things I wanted to say to him; there were things I wanted to straighten out between us, if they could be. It won't happen now, but I have to catch myself to keep from phoning him."

"You don't have to say anything, Carter." Cynthia sprawled back on the burnt-orange sofa that had been left more or less in the center of the living room—the front parlor—with a brass-and-oak butler's table near the fireplace. "If you need help getting things arranged, just call."

"I can't do that until Tuesday. No phone till then." She laughed. "It's funny, to think of being without a phone."

"Just tell yourself it's out of order." Cynthia looked around. "Did you see where I left my sweater?"

"In the kitchen, on the chair," Carter told her. "I wish there were something I could do to thank you, really thank you."

"You don't have to," said Cynthia. "And don't worry about it. What are friends for?"

"All you have to do is ask, if you ever need anything. Okay?" There was an anxious smile on Carter's lips, but her eyes were troubled. "Promise?"

"Sure, if it makes you feel better," said Cynthia as she went to the kitchen.

"It does." Carter followed her, pausing in the back parlor to wonder again what she was going to do with this room, once she had the rest of the place under control. She had the uneasy sensation that she had taken on more than she was up to.

"Well, what say, if you want to go for dinner in a big way, that we go into the city some night and find a very special restaurant and just pig out?" Cynthia paused to listen to Ben talking to the girls out in the overrun garden.

"Sounds fine to me," said Carter, who had not been into San Francisco in over a year.

"I'll tell Ben and we'll think of something. Let's think about after Thanksgiving." She had pulled her sweater on and was fussing with the leather buttons.

"After the fires," said Carter.

"Yeah," Cynthia agreed somberly. "Let me know when you want me to come back for another workday," she went on, trying to dispel the gloom that had gathered around them at the mention of the fires.

Ben pulled open the back door. "We're ready to go, honey."

"So'm I," Cynthia called back.

"I'll walk you out to your car," Carter offered. "That way I can thank Ben and the girls."

"You don't have to," Cynthia said.

"Yes, I do," Carter corrected, following her friend out

onto the enormous porch. "I guess I should get a swing or something for this."

"A couple little tables, maybe," Cynthia said, going down the stairs.

Ben had already started the car, and the girls were buckled in in the back seat. "It was fun, Carter," Ben said.

"Can we come back when you've got fruit?" Fiona asked.

"You can come back any time, and you can have all the fruit you want." Carter was searching for the right words; she had no way to express her gratitude.

"You don't have to say anything, Carter," Ben told her kindly. "Hell, we all needed the exercise."

Carter nodded. "All right. I appreciate everything you've done. I always will." She stepped back so Ben could turn the car around. She stood and waved as the Harpers drove away, and then she went back into the house, thinking that she would need to go shopping soon and at least get the basics for the kitchen.

She was wrestling with the sofa around sunset when there was the sound of a car in the driveway. Winslow, who had been sleeping on the shaggy area rug in front of the fireplace, raised his head, listened, gave a desultory bark and went back to drowsing. Carter waited, glad for the excuse to stop work.

When there was a knock on the door, she left her work and went to the door, expecting to see Stephanie.

"Hi," said Frank a bit self-consciously. "Could you use a hand?"

Carter sighed. "I could use a reason to stop," she admitted.

"Happy to provide that, too," Frank told her, than added, "Can I come in?"

"Oh," Carter said, stepping aside. "Sure. Sorry. I must be more worn-out than I thought."

"Maybe I should have got here earlier." He stood in the entryway, looking around. "You've certainly changed things since the last time I was here."

"Yeah," Carter said, surprised at the satisfaction his approval gave her. "Thanks to Cynthia and Ben and Pam and Fiona. They were here from ten-thirty till about an hour ago."

"Good. You had help." He strolled into the living room. "I like the sofa. The color's wonderful." Now that he was with her, he began once again to feel awkward. He never knew what to say to her beyond pleasantries, and he often chided himself for his own complex feelings about her. For God's sake, he reminded himself, they were trying to find an answer to the fires, not to flirt. She'd been a widow for less than a month, and no matter what kind of marriage she had had, she could not be interested in someone like him. Carter Milne had a Ph.D. in statistics and that was damned daunting.

"Something wrong?" asked Carter.

Frank shook off his nagging doubts. "No, I'm just sorry I wasn't here to give a hand. Have you had supper yet?"

"Don't tell me you brought another pizza?"

"No, I didn't, but I'll be glad to take you to one of those fish places in Santa Cruz if you'll let me." He saw her hesitate, and hurried on. "I'll work with you tonight," he offered. "I'll do everything but wash windows. I'm the worst window washer around."

"Window washing isn't on the agenda," said Carter with a single giggle. "Okay, Fire Marshal, you're on. I hate to admit it, but I'm hungry and I welcome any opportunity to get out of these jeans. They're disgraceful."

Half an hour later, they drove in Frank's rented car to a restaurant in Capitola. It was getting foggy and so the ocean was nothing but a muffled sound. Over swordfish—Frank—and scallops—Carter—she caught up with the latest on the fires.

"Sid Rountree had a briefing today with the Task Force and the NSA; about the only thing they're fairly convinced about is that whatever it is, it isn't terrorists."

"At last," Carter said. "It took them long enough."

"McPherson was furious; Sid told me he stormed out of the meeting and refused to endorse the latest release, and prepared one of his own. There was another fire in Wilmington, and they're listing it with the others."

"Wilmington as in Delaware?" Carter asked.

"Yes. In a phone-company installation, one of those that handle calls within the same area code. They were having trouble with one of the prefixes and were using alternate routing. At least that's what the company said, and it seems that it's the best idea."

"How bad was the fire?" She had half a scallop on her fork, but she held it, waiting for his answer.

"The building was a total loss, and the dry-cleaning plant next to it went, too. All those flammable chemicals." He stared down at his plate. "Sixteen people killed, another dozen injured, mostly smoke inhalation."

"That's better than some of them have been," she said after a little consideration.

"I suppose so," said Frank, then deliberately changed the subject. "Look, I want to suggest you get some insulation into that attic. I know that the house is well built, but it could make quite a difference in the heating bill. Even your California winters can get cold, can't they?"

Carter went along with his change. "You're probably right. There's so much to take care of with a new house."

By eight-thirty they were back at the house and they spent a hectic and companionable evening moving furniture. By eleven the main floor was almost satisfactory to Carter.

"I'll be getting a stereo eventually and I thought I'd put it and a TV in the back parlor; that gets them out of the living room without sticking them in a bedroom somewhere." She had made them coffee—decaffeinated because it was so late—and they were sitting in the living room, Frank on the sofa, Carter in the deep chair that had a hassock for her feet.

"It's good to see you're planning ahead. I had trouble doing that when Barbara died. It was hard because of my daughter."

"Melinda," Carter said, hoping she remembered the name right.

"That's right. I had to keep thinking for her, but it wasn't real." He looked at her. "You're tired."

"So are you," she said. "I know that feeling; nothing is quite in focus, nothing makes much sense. The fires make that worse. I can't quite imagine how much damage they've done, and that includes Greg."

"You're convinced he figured something out, aren't you?" For all his intentions to keep off the subject of fires, they had come back again.

"Yes. Maybe there was something to his system theory. He always looked for the method, for the trick. He was convinced that there was a system to everything in the world and all you had to do was learn the odds and play them." She breathed deeply. "The house looks good, doesn't it?"

"Sure does," he said, relieved to have her change the subject. He looked at his watch. "It's getting late."

Carter started to yawn. "Excuse me; it's the hour, not the company."

"I know the feeling." Frank got up.

"Frank," she said impulsively, "would you like to stay over? I've got oodles of room and you could take your choice. It might be easier, not driving back at this hour." She flushed. "I'm not suggesting... anything."

"I didn't think you were," said Frank. "I ought to leave," he said, not wanting to go.

"Please. The house seems awfully... empty tonight. I know I'll have to get used to it, but just for now, it would be great to have company." By now her cheeks were scarlet.

"Carter..." He was mildly flustered. "Do you think it's wise?"

"Yes, please," she said in a small voice.

He let her persuade him. "All right. But we're back to the old problem."

"No razor and no toothbrush," she said. "We'll pick some up tomorrow, but you can use my razor if you don't mind a pink one. I'll put in a new blade."

"All right. Which room?"

"There's only two with beds and you know which one is mine," she said. "I've got a couple extra blankets and a second set of sheets." She got up. "It means a lot to me, your staying like this."

Frank could think of nothing to say. He shrugged. "I'll make it up if you'll tell me where the bedding is."

"Linen closet, second floor, next to the bathroom," she said. She went toward the stairs. "I'll show you."

When they had the guest bed made, Carter brought in towels and an oversize shirt. "This isn't the same thing as pajamas, but it ought to do for tonight."

Frank accepted these things from her and diffidently asked, "Do you mind if I take a bath?"

"Go ahead; that's what the towels're for." She took care not to stand close to him or to touch him.

When Carter left, Frank undressed, enjoying his own discomfort. He bathed in the long, deep tub with old-fashioned ball-and-claw feet. Coming out of the bathroom, he found Carter coming up from the first floor where she had been turning out lights and locking the doors. She was wrapped in a terry-cloth robe and had removed what little makeup she had worn.

"Sleep well," Frank said.

"Thanks, you too."

Frank got into bed and noticed that the light was still on in Carter's room even after he had turned off his. He lay back, looking out into the night through the tall windows. A little fog was blowing across the stars, and Frank thought at first it was restful, though he failed to be lulled to sleep.

"Frank?" Carter called from her room.

"What is it?" He was startled to hear her voice.

"I—"

"Is something wrong?"

"No."

He waited for her to speak again, and when she remained silent, he called her name. "What is it?"

"Nothing."

Against his better judgment, Frank got out of bed and

padded down the hall to Carter's door. He stood there, watching her.

She was huddled in her bed, her covers pulled tightly around her. Winslow lay beside her bed, mostly asleep.

"Carter?"

"What?" She twisted around and Frank could see that she had been crying.

He stepped through the door. "What's wrong, Carter?"

"Nothing," she said, her voice shaking. "It all caught up with me. It just—"

He went and sat down on the edge of the bed. "Want to talk about it?"

"Not really." She wiped her eyes. "It doesn't matter."

"Sure it does." He ran one finger cross her cheek. "Sure it does, Carter."

"Frank?" She caught his hand in hers. "Frank, would you sleep with me? I don't mean have sex, if you don't want that, but would you sleep with me?"

"And if I want sex?" He was amazed at how calm he sounded, at how easily he asked.

Carter made a complicated gesture. "I don't know if I'm ready yet. I might not be."

"Don't worry; if you're not, we won't." He watched her lift the edge of the covers, and slid in beside her.

They lay side by side, neither making a move toward the other.

"I don't know what to do," she confessed after a short while.

"Why not turn out the light for a start?" Frank suggested. He blinked at the darkness. "Sleepy?"

"No." She reached out for his hand, and once she had it, she held it as if she was unsure what to do next. "Greg and I were married a pretty long time. I was used to him. I was a faithful wife, and I just don't know..." She faltered and became silent.

"Well, since Barbara died, I haven't exactly been Don Juan. I've had a couple of flings, but that's about it." He was quiet. "I don't think of this as a fling."

"What do you think of it as?" Carter sounded anxious.

"Oh, I don't know. Friendship, maybe. Or affection." He wanted very much to be honest with her.

"I like you, Frank," Carter said, sounding less apprehensive.

"I like you, Carter."

When another several minutes had passed, Carter rolled onto her side. "You're very comfortable." Then she took a short breath. "I hope you don't mind that. I didn't mean anything—"

"I'm flattered," Frank said, slipping his arm around her shoulder and pulling her closer.

"I don't mean you're not attractive; you are attractive." She was tense; her shoulders were rigid and her arms were stiff.

"So are you."

"Even though I'm older than you?"

He chuckled. "How old are you?"

"Thirty-nine. I'll be forty in May."

"Well, I'm thirty-seven. Two years aren't that much, are they?" He kissed her forehead. "Or do you think I'm too young?"

"Oh, no," she said hurriedly.

"Carter, I'm joking," he said gently.

"Oh."

Frank pulled her closer, and now he could feel her body through the shirt and nightgown they wore. She was lean and her muscles were firm. It was a good feeling, lying in the dark like this.

"Maybe it's the fires," she said after a while. "It makes us afraid that we'll never have another chance for anything. It drives us to taking chances we wouldn't take otherwise."

"I wouldn't be here if it weren't for the fires. And neither would you." He said the last as kindly as he could, and he felt her shiver against him.

"I guess..."

He kissed her, their lips still closed, and was surprised at how soft her mouth was.

"Frank," she whispered.

He bent and kissed her neck. "You're okay, Carter. Don't worry."

"I don't know what to do."

"Whatever you feel like doing." He moved so that she could rest her head on his shoulder.

"I don't know what that is." She touched his face. "I don't know what you like."

"Try something and I'll tell you." He opened her nightgown. "How do you get out of this thing?"

She laughed with her nervousness. "I'll take it off." It was not as simple as she had anticipated, and it was only after tugging and wriggling that she was able to pull the thing over her head and toss it aside.

"Want to unbutton my shirt?" Frank asked.

"It's my shirt," she corrected him, her sternness ruined by a giggle.

"Do you want to unbutton it?" He had reached for the top button but she moved his hand aside. "I'm ticklish, sometimes."

"I'll remember that," she said as she concentrated on the buttons. "You're not as hairy as Greg." She bit her lip. "I'm sorry. I didn't intend to say anything like that."

"It's okay," Frank told her, feeling her fingers move over his chest. "You're taller and thinner than Barbara was, and chances are I'll notice, whether I say anything about it or not."

"Thanks," Carter murmured, and kissed him again, this time touching his tongue with her own. "You taste good."

"Swordfish and white wine'll do it every time," he said, only partly joking.

"Tell me if you like this, okay?" she asked before she licked his nipples.

"It's nice, but I think I like it better when I do it to you." Her breasts were small and soft, flattening almost to nonexistence when she lay on her back. Her nipples, taut now, were large for her breasts, and they were sensitive. She shuddered as he teased them, and her head rolled back.

"Frank, that's good," she whispered, drawing air in through her teeth. "That's wonderful."

"Good," he said as he started to stroke her hips. He was enjoying himself, and he was proud of how well he was doing with her. For a first time, they were pleasantly compatible. His hands moved lower. She trembled as he finally slid one hand between her thighs.

"Not too fast," she said. She was breathing more deeply and the pitch of her voice was lower than he had ever heard it before. "Don't rush."

"Fine with me," said Frank, who felt he was going too fast for his own satisfaction. He kept his hand in place, but gave his attention to kissing her—her mouth, her eyes, the lobe of her ear.

She slowly became more pliant, her long legs opening and her arms moving more easily. She was less afraid of touching him, more willing to find her way over the unknown territory of his flesh. "I like your smell, too," she said as she drew him closer to her.

"What's your hurry?" he asked her, taking time to touch her gently before probing more deeply. As he felt the warmth and the wetness on his fingers, desire washed through him, so intense that he was dizzied by it. Who would have thought that Carter would stir him this way? The luxury of her body delighted him, and the tenderness of her response.

"You're so good," she whispered, rolling him over her and bringing her thighs around his.

He slid deeply into her, balanced on his elbows and her hips. It was tempting to press her, but he sensed she would be disappointed if he did. He moved slowly, feeling her rise to the prompting of his body. It felt more delicious than he had thought possible; he wanted to prolong it, to relish, to revel in their union. He felt her breathing change again and her hands slid over his buttocks, pressing him as he moved into her. Neither of them could hold off much longer.

She did not so much come as release all the tension that had built up in her body. One moment she was taut as a violin string and the next she had gasped and gripped and let go.

Frank plunged twice more, then shuddered into her.

"Frank?" She had been still beneath him as he came back to himself.

"It's okay, Carter. Everything's fine." He rolled off her, his arm around her so that she could not move far from him in sleep.

"Yes," she agreed, her mouth near his.

"Oh, yes," he seconded.

As Sidney Rountree handed over the report, he regarded Simon McPherson with contempt. "I have to tell you that there are other copies of this report and everyone involved in the investigation is being provided with a copy. Nothing you can do will change that."

McPherson took the thick binder gingerly, as if he had been handed a live ferret. "You've made your point, Rountree."

"No, I haven't, or wouldn't still be arguing about the fires. You're determined to pursue phantoms, and that's your prerogative, but the rest of us are striking off in other directions, and you'd better remember that." He was tired, irritated, and his headache was now three days old. More than anything else, he wanted to be on a Wisconsin lake fishing with his wife.

"The White House has said that some positive results are expected." It was not a direct confrontation, but close enough to one that both men were ill at ease.

Rountree heard this out with a glower. "Fine. Let us off the leash and we'll move heaven and earth for the White House and the rest of the country. Give us the chance to do it our way."

"I wish we could, but where national security is involved, we don't have much choice in how we proceed." McPherson made no attempt to look sorry about this. "You understand our position, I'm sure."

"No I don't," Rountree said with heat. "I understand that you're blocking some avenues of investigation that might provide us answers. You haven't been able to demonstrate sabotage of any kind, have you? And still you won't let us try other lines of inquiry. That's not only shortsighted, it's criminally irresponsible. If you were anyone but the FBI, we'd have a court order lifting your restrictions."

McPherson rubbed his chin as if he had been struck with a fist, not accusations. "I'm going to do my best to forget you said that, or I'd have to request you be removed from the investigation. I know you're under stress—we all are. But that doesn't excuse your behavior. Watch it, Rountree."

"Oh, yes," Rountree said with excessive civility. "Certainly. We can't go intruding on sacred FBI territory, can we? Let another two or three thousand citizens get burned in more random fires rather than cause the Bureau possible embarrassment. What kind of priorities have you got?"

"The same as you," McPherson said, becoming defensive.

"I doubt it. You're determined to make these things your fiefdom, and the hell with anything else. Don't try to argue, McPherson. Actions speak louder than words, and yours have been shouting from the rooftops since the fires began." He did not wait for the reprimand that was certain to come; he turned on his heel and slammed the door on his way out of the office.

Carter sat at the breakfast table, a foolscap pad in front of her. She gazed out the window, her thoughts in pleasant turmoil. Frank had left an hour ago, promising to return that evening after work. She had gone from being angry with herself to a curious sort of fragile joy. She doodled on the page, hoping to convince herself that she was not wasting time or daydreaming.

When she finally got up, determined to do some food shopping before noon, she glanced at the pad.

The most malignant number is five, she had written—where had that come from?—and circled it several times. She stared at it, as if that would make sense of it. Then she shrugged and went off in search of her jacket.

While she was shopping, that phrase kept coming back

to her. *The most malignant number is five.* She must have read that in one of those old books, she decided as she stood in front of the spices and tried to select the ones she needed most. There was something in the book about summoning spirits with combinations of numbers. After the spices, she went for tea and coffee, then for flour and sugar and the other staples she knew she would have to have. Eggs, milk, chicken, hamburger, a couple of steaks to splurge, and three bottles of wine—one red, two white— as well as an assortment of cheeses.

The most malignant number is five.

Although his physician had left strict instructions that he was not to be bothered with such things, Myron Bethune did his best to keep up with the investigation through Simon McPherson.

"Any new developments?" he asked on the phone.

"New fires or new theories?" McPherson wanted to know.

"Either or both."

"Two possible fires, one in Saskatoon, one in Cardiff, Colorado. They're being checked out now. As to theories, you should see the nut mail. The wrath of God is very popular with many of the letter writers, but so are the Russians, the Chinese and the Arabs."

Bethune wheezed his appreciation. "How's the Task Force?"

"Impossible and getting worse," McPherson declared. "I wish you were still able to work with us." He sighed. "They're going pretty far afield for solutions, and that's wasting time and money when we can't afford to do either."

"I'll get back as soon as they let me. I know how difficult they can be."

"And the press is getting completely out of hand. Do they let you see the news or read the papers?" Before Bethune could answer, McPherson hurried on. "You can't believe how determined they are to make us appear like fools. They have to have a scapegoat and we're it. You'd think we were trying to keep the fires going, to read what most of them are saying." His indignation was so strong that he had to take three deep breaths to control himself.

"Don't let them railroad you, Simon." Little as he wanted to admit it, Bethune was already exhausted. Even this short conversation had leeched out what small amount of strength he had gathered.

"Are you all right, Myron?" McPherson asked, hearing the other man's voice grow faint and his breathing sharpen.

"Sure, sure," said Bethune. "I'm just tired. I'll try to call again tomorrow."

"Only if you're up to it," McPherson warned.

"I'll be up to it," Bethune said with false confidence.

McPherson hesitated, as if he was not certain what to say. "If anything happens, I'll leave a message with the desk. You get some rest."

"I'm doing fine," Bethune insisted.

"Good," McPherson said as heartily as he could. "That's what we like to hear."

"Thanks for giving me the news," Bethune said, struggling for air. He felt a dull ache in his chest and was annoyed at his own weakness.

"Well, talk to you later," said McPherson, and hung up.

Bethune lay back in his bed and wished he could see the monitor mounted above his bed. He wanted to know what kind of display his heart was putting out. It infuriated him that no one would tell him and that he was too weak to get out of bed and look. He felt the ache in his chest grow sharper, but refused to ring for a nurse. It was humiliating enough to be in the hospital at a time like this, but to summon a nurse seemed to him to be complete capitulation. If he waited, the pain would pass.

"Does the idea sound crazy?" Carter asked Frank as she showed him her notes and the books she had been pouring over most of the afternoon.

"Yeah, but then everything with this investigation sounds crazy." He read over the notes she had shown him and had to admit he could not make much sense of them. "Malign numbers. Who came up with that idea?"

"Some Arab mathematicians, about a thousand years ago," said Carter. "It's all in the book. I know it sounds like mumbo jumbo, but it might be worth checking out, just in case. We don't have any more promising lead, do we?"

"No," Frank allowed. "And this makes as much sense as anything. Why not give it a try?"

"You'll back me up when I ask J.D. to get me those figures?" she asked, still uncertain.

Frank nodded. "Okay. Yeah. Why not?"

"Thanks." She had been trying all afternoon to get up the nerve to call PSS and talk to J.D. "I'll give him a ring at home. That way we can work on it first thing tomorrow."

"Aren't you expecting a delivery tomorrow?" Frank asked.

"Uh-huh, but I called Stephanie, and she said she'd come by the house and let the men in. She's glad to get this place off her hands."

"From what you said, I'm not surprised. I gather the house has a peculiar reputation." He had heard a man at the hardware store say that the Corvin family was up to no good and that they had done things in the house that weren't proper.

"That's what everyone says," Carter said, unperturbed by the history of her new home. "And if the books are any indication, the old man must have been pretty strange. Still, what if they're right? That's what keeps coming back to me—what if it's right, and it's malign numbers, and only that, that are responsible for the fires?"

"You're serious about this, aren't you?" Frank asked.

"Why not? It makes as much sense as anything we've tried." Carter read over the notes she had made. "Do you think that J.D. will go along with it?"

"Call him and find out. I'll back you up." He patted her hand. "Try it out."

"Yeah. I'll have to go out to the service station to call."

"I'll drive you. J.D. will accept a collect call, won't he?" Frank started to get up and he held out his hand to Carter. "Come on. Let's get it over with."

"You're with me?" This seemed to surprise her more than anything else.

"Yeah. I'm like that." He went to the door. "Tell me, how do you think he'll take it?"

"Who knows with J.D.?" she said as she went onto the porch with him. "Winslow's out, so we'll have to close the gate. I don't want him running loose."

"Okay." He led the way to his car and held the door for her.

"Thanks," she said as she got into the car. "I'd forgotten what it's like to have doors held for me. I like it."

He got in on his side. "It's a habit." He paused to close the gate as she'd requested, then drove to the Chevron station. "Need a quarter?"

"I've got one; thanks anyway." Now that she was going to make the call, she was worried. What could she say that might convince J.D.? Did she really believe it herself? Before she lost her nerve, she dropped in the quarter and punched in J.D.'s home number, then waited for the operator to come on the line and take her name.

Luckily J.D.'s wife answered the phone and said that she would accept a call from Dr. Milne. "Hi, Carter," she said when the operator clicked off. "I'll get Jerry. Wait a sec, will you?"

It was almost two minutes before J.D. picked up the phone. "Hi, Carter; this is a surprise. I didn't know you had a phone yet."

"I don't. I'm at a service station."

J.D.'s manner changed at once. "It's important?"

"Very. Maybe." She took a deep breath. "I think I might have stumbled onto something that could help us. I don't know if it means anything, and it could be another blind alley, but it might be the answer, too."

"You think it has possibilities?" J.D. inquired in a neutral tone.

"Possibilities, yes. But it's weird, and that could be a problem."

"I'm listening; try me."

"I found some books at my house," she began, "old books, on occult subjects. One of the things I found in them, by accident, was something about malign numbers, numbers that could be used to summon supernatural beings—unfriendly supernatural beings." She paused, and when J.D. said nothing, she went on. "I think there might be something to the notion. Maybe not supernatural, but oddball physics, causing resonances that bring on fires. So I want to find out all the numbers I can for every one of the buildings that have burned."

"That's a tall order. And the fires destroyed a lot of the evidence," J.D. pointed out.

"That's right. It is, and it might not mean a damn thing, but it's the only possibility I could come up with that makes any kind of sense, given what we know about the fires, and assuming they aren't part of some gigantic terrorist conspiracy." She was talking much too fast, but she could not make herself slow down.

"Numbers. Sequences of numbers," said J.D. quietly.

"Yes. Numbers that in some way cause things to happen." She paused again. "It's not totally crazy, J.D."

"Hell," said J.D., "even if it were, I might give you the go-ahead. The fires are crazy."

"I agree," said Carter, feeling suddenly very relieved.

"Okay, as many numbers as you want, you'll get. I'll sent them over with Frank tomorrow evening, if that's soon enough."

"I was planning to come in tomorrow morning," Carter said, wondering how J.D. knew Frank was staying with her.

"Better yet. You can put the staff to work on it."

"With graph paper and pencils," said Carter. "No computers; not until we know one way or another what is going on. We don't need a fire at PSS to prove a point."

"Assuming you might be right, that's a reasonable precaution. I can't help thinking about Howard Li."

"Yes," said Carter, thinking of Greg. She was about to hang up when J.D. surprised her.

"Carter, whether you're right or wrong, you're the only person who came up with any kind of original thinking. Right or wrong, you're doing fine."

"I'm clutching at straws." She hated to say it out loud, as if the words would make the theory more tenuous than it already was.

"Go for it," said J.D. as he hung up.

"Well?" asked Frank as Carter opened the door.

"We're on," she said over the sound of the starting engine.

William held the phone in his hand and wished he were home in Lansing. "Elinore, I'm sorry."

"Sorry doesn't help," she said with bitter anger.

"If I could restore the funding, you know I'd do it. As it is, I'll do everything I can when I get back to change it." He had seen editorials turn public support around before.

"The trouble is that there have been too many fires," said Elinore. "Your precious fires are what lost us our funding. Most of the state emergency money is going to fire rebuilding and there are relief grants being given to families of victims, and those who've lost jobs." She was crying again.

"Listen, Elinore, we'll find a way. Your work is too important to let it stop. We'll work something out, I promise you." He put all the warmth he could into his voice. "Do you want me to cut the trip short? I could be on a plane by this afternoon."

"What's the point? They'd keep you on the fires, and that wouldn't change a damn thing." She sniffed. "The hell with it."

William swallowed hard once. "We'll come up with something. I promise you."

"Fine," she said, weary and defeated.

"I mean it, Elinore. We'll change things. We will."

"I know you mean it, but . . ."

"Listen to me, Elinore: we'll find a way to get your

funding back: we will. The fires are going to stop and we'll be able to readjust. You'll see."

"Right." Her voice was flat. "How's it going out there?"

"I've got another briefing at PSS tonight. That can be interesting." He did not want to talk about what he was doing, but about Elinore. "Are you all right?"

"Just great," she said in that same fatigued voice that she had used when he first called.

"I'm going to call Charlie and have him come over. You shouldn't be alone right now."

"Your brother's out of town. My family's out of town. They're all going to funerals. Ain't life grand." She said nothing more before she hung up.

"Elinore?" William said to the dead phone line. "Damn it, Elinore."

Scott Costa was the first to scoff at Carter's theory. "It's ridiculous! Tell her, J.D. Or are you as loony as she is?"

"Oh, loonier; I've okayed her project," said J.D. in his best humor. "And I expect everyone in the company to cooperate with her. Unless you can come up with a better suggestion." He looked around the conference table. "Anyone?"

This challenge was met with silence, but Cynthia whispered to Carter, "Where'd you come up with such a cockamamie idea?"

"I read it in a book." She looked down at her notes.

"I'm instructing everyone to follow what Carter does, and if you have anything to contribute, you better make sure she hears about it promptly." J.D. rubbed his eyes and stifled a yawn.

"Witchcraft," said Dave Fisher. "What is this, the fifteenth century? What's come over all of you? Are we that desperate?"

"In a word, yes," J.D. told him.

"If you think I'm going to tell McPherson about this, you're nuts," said Sid Rountree to Frank late in the day. "You can call him and tell him that you're trying to figure out the mathematical address of some kind of supernatural fiend that's causing the fires. That makes less sense than his terrorist theory."

"I know what it sounds like," Frank said cautiously.

"If you knew what it sounds like, you wouldn't say it," Rountree corrected him.

"I don't ask you to endorse it. I only want you to get us the assistance we need—mainly the figures we want, all of them—and the access to everyone who might have information that could help us."

"Frank, do you believe this shit?" Rountree asked incredulously.

"I don't know what I believe. I don't believe in fires that start by spontaneous combustion all over the country with no rhyme or reason. I don't believe in terrorists who start fires without leaving a trace and who make no demands. I don't believe in little green men from Mars who are starting fires to make offerings to their gods—"

"How did you know about that one?" Rountree inquired sweetly. "That was after you left."

"I heard about it. And about the theory that this is some kind of government plot to make the population accept a military dictatorship and put all the computers into military hands." Frank spoke crisply.

"No one working on the investigation believes that." Rountree was sounding defensive now.

"Don't think about it; just get me numbers and I won't mention it again." Frank chuckled.

"What about McPherson? He won't like it at all."

"Then don't tell him anything," Frank said. "Or if you have to have a reason, blame it on me; say that PSS is trying to run down anyone, any business that has had dealings with more than two of the victims of the fire. You can suggest they're looking for a cover for insurance fraud, something like that."

"Some cover," Rountree said.

"The Bureau loves conspiracies. This'll make them very happy. Especially McPherson; he's been conspiracy-shopping since this began." He laughed mirthlessly.

"Okay, I'll do what I can, but I sure hope you know what you're doing."

"So do I," said Frank as he rang off.

"There's been an earthquake in Tokyo. Want to cover it?" The producer of the morning news was a man made up of angles, his face made of planes and his eyes hard as marbles. He regarded Nina with an expectant air.

"Earthquake? Tokyo?" It was four-thirty in the morning and although Nina had been up for almost an hour, she was not yet awake.

"That's it. Do you want it? You're Our Lady of Disasters." He scowled at her. "Make up your mind quick. We have to have someone on a plane right after the news. You or Teddy will have to do it."

Nina took a deep breath. "What about the fires?"

"People are getting used to them. They're not the kind of news they used to be. This earthquake is the biggest since Mexico City. Are you going to take it?"

She wondered if her hands were trembling. "If I can take Lenny with me, sure I'll take it."

"Good." Her producer produced a rictus twitch that he had said was his way of smiling, though Nina had often thought it was nothing more than the gas-produced grimaces of babies carried into adulthood.

"I have some information on the latest briefing on the fires." She cocked her head to the side. "How much of it are you going to use?"

"Maybe thirty seconds," said the producer with a marked lack of interest.

"Is that all?"

"We wouldn't do that much if the Bureau hadn't insisted." He poured himself his third cup of coffee of the morning. "They're getting strange."

"How strange?" asked Nina, thinking that perhaps she could take advantage of this turn of events.

"They're trying a new tack: the fires are being caused by American conspirators who've paid for the secret of causing these fires from the foreign terrorists and are using them to shift the marketplace to their advantage. That's why there's been so little success in tracking them down, McPherson says. Some of the biggest corporations are using this to strengthen their places."

Nina's thoughts returned to Tokyo. "How bad is bad? Is there any place I can stay? Will they let me cover the damage, or will it be strictly release footage?"

Again the grimace. "We'll provide a translator, there is a place for you to stay—that's been arranged. You'll have the handouts from the government, but we're trying to make arrangements for you to talk to victims, just as you've been doing with fire victims. We want a usable ten minutes every day for five days while they find out how much damage was done."

"Okay," said Nina, covering a yawn.

"It's likely to be rainy and there's a storm on its way. Dress for it. Not too bright; some of the Japanese won't like it."

"Fine. I've got some navies and a bitter-green outfit, and a tan-and-brown plaid. Think that'll do?" She'd have to call her apartment and ask her cleaning lady to pack her bag for her. She had never had to do that before, and it made her feel a bit odd.

"Better go over the morning guest list; there's another analyst on to talk about the fires and the stock market, and a psychiatrist. The psychiatrist is talking about long-term effects of the fires on the country, particularly children."

"We should have expected that, I guess." Nina sighed. "First the fires, then all the books."

"Just hope that the guy can talk."

Nina thought of several doctors she had interviewed over the last three years and she could only agree. "What tack do you want me to take?"

"Informative, if possible. If not, then just the facts about who's publishing it, the price, the title, the fires it carries." Her producer made a gesture of dismissal. "Make sure you're ready to go to the airport and fly to Japan by ten-thirty. The limo will pick you up."

"And Lenny," Nina reminded him.

"And Lenny."

As she left the producer's office, Nina was already thinking of what she would tell Lenny; she needed him more than ever now, and she had to be sure he was convinced of that before she told him about Japan.

The Task Force members sat in their conference room, stacks of papers and photographs in the center like bizarre dinner dishes waiting to be served. Simon McPherson got to his feet and said very sternly, "We haven't any progress to report. We know nothing more now than we did when these fires started. We're as much in the dark as everyone else. They are looking to us to find answers."

Sidney Rountree said, "I've already told you about this new area of inquiry that PSS wants to undertake. If you'd give your approval, it might make things easier. It's no worse than any of the ideas that we've come up with."

"They're talking like medieval wizards," McPherson accused.

Lois Hillyer, who had been attending these meetings for the last week, spoke up suddenly. "The company I worked for, the insurance company, has recommended that the PSS proposal be pursued. They believe that this survey of accounts and similar records might show things we haven't learned before."

Simon McPherson stared at her as if she had put a loaded gun on the table. "How can you endorse such a ludicrous proposition?"

"How can you not?" she countered. "How can you just turn away from any possibility of a solution?" She spoke with such conviction that the others seated around the table stared at her and McPherson looked embarrassed. "I don't know why any of you would reject this idea just because you didn't come up with it yourselves."

Sidney Rountree did his best to smile. "On behalf of those investigators away from here, I thank you, Ms. Hillyer."

"I'm not finished," Lois said, as amazed at her outburst

as anyone else in the room. "I want to go on record as being opposed to those policies and decisions that have made it difficult or impossible for many of those investigating the fires to follow through on their own areas of inquiry, and I want to request that all restrictions be lifted. If this is a matter of national security, it is so for reasons of hazard, not politics, and in requiring a political response, the officials directing the investigation have hampered those who have been trying to determine the cause and methodology of the fires. Withholding information, for any reason whatsoever, must be regarded as irresponsible at best and criminal at worst." She stopped abruptly. "I'm sorry, Simon. I don't mean this to distress you, although I suppose it will. I just... I just have to say what's on my mind."

While Simon McPherson was still trying to find words to express his indignation and sense of betrayal—he was the one who had brought Lois Hillyer into the case—Horace Turnbull, who had been loaned to the Fire Marshals' Task Force by MIT, rose. "I want to say, on behalf of those struggling to deal with a political bureaucracy, that Ms. Hillyer has done every single investigator a service. She has more courage than anyone else in this room, and I personally want to thank her for having the guts to say out loud what so many of us have been feeling and were afraid to speak."

"What is this?" McPherson demanded. "Are you all so stressed out that you can't see insanity when it's under your noses? Are you going to indulge anyone with crackpot notions? Are you all so scared that you can't think straight and all you can come up with are these Twilight Zone ideas?" He slammed the flat of his hand down on the table and shouted, "I won't have it!"

"Excuse me, McPherson; we haven't voted on this yet, and if the rest of us agree then"—Rountree shrugged philosophically—"I don't see what you can do about it."

"I can stop us from making asses of ourselves!" McPherson's face was flushed and his voice cracked with emotion. "What is *wrong* with all of you?"

Horace Turnbull, whose manner was usually mild and remote, spoke up with uncharacteristic vigor. "If you don't mind my putting my two cents' worth in, I'd have to say that I think that the mathematics behind the theory just might be sound, if you remove all the words that bother you. We know that we manipulate the world with numbers all day long—computers wouldn't work if that weren't the case, would they?—and we have no proof one way or another if perhaps the numbers manipulate right back. There are areas of physics that certainly suggest that might be possible, whether it is convenient for us to believe it or not. The laws of physics don't exist for our convenience; they exist because they exist."

"Before this gets out of hand," said the Fire Marshal from Portland, Maine, "I move that we take a vote on the question. Do we or do we not supply the information, without condition, to PSS, and what laws, if any, would we be breaking if we did."

"I second," McPherson said with heat. "This lunacy has gone far enough."

"Call the vote," said Sidney Rountree.

"All in favor of giving the information requested by Patterson Security Systems without prejudice, signify by raising hands," said Michael Frost, who was Simon McPherson's nominal assistant.

All but two hands rose.

"For the record, those not in favor please raise your hands."

Simon McPherson raised his hand; Horace Turnbull did not. "I am not allowed to vote in this," Turnbull reminded the young FBI officer. "If I were allowed to vote, I would be in favor."

"I protest," McPherson said.

"Noted," Frost stated. "For the record."

"Will someone order the information sent?" Rountree asked. "Since we have discretionary powers in these matters, there's no reason to delay, is there?"

"I wish there were," said McPherson. He looked squarely at Lois Hillyer. "Why don't you do it, since it was your good idea?"

Lois turned bright red, but her voice and manner were composed. "Thank you; I'd consider that a privilege."

With a little sigh, Sid Rountree opened his notebook and checked off one order of business.

"I think that we ought to find out if other governments want their information processed with ours," suggested Turnbull. "It's useful to us and to them. The Canadians especially are apt to want to share information with us."

"That's not responsible," snapped McPherson.

"Do you want us to call a vote?" asked the Fire Marshal from Maine.

"No," grumbled McPherson.

"All right; who should draft the letter? We won't ask you to do it, Simon, knowing your attitude on this." Rountree was looking around the table at the eleven exhausted faces when their attention was caught by the ringing of the phone. Since the meeting was not to be interrupted except in an emergency, all of them stared at the instrument as if they expected it to explode.

Michael Frost answered it, and after the briefest of salutations, became silent.

"Another fire?" asked Lois, her apprehension making her pale.

"Thank you for telling us." Frost hung up the phone. "I'm sorry to have to tell you," he said to the room at large. "Myron Bethune died twenty minutes ago."

Most of those at the table looked saddened but not shocked; Simon McPherson was the most affected. He tried to speak twice before any words would come.

"I'd like . . . I'd like to dismiss the . . . meeting. Until tomorrow morning . . . unless . . ."

The Fire Marshal from Maine rose. "I move we dismiss for the day and that we observe a moment of silence in respect."

"I second," said Lois at once.

"Carried." Rountree got to his feet, and the rest followed his lead. The conference room was very quiet. Finally the Fire Marshal from New Orleans crossed himself and McPherson cleared his throat.

"Thank you; I'll see you tomorrow."

Watching him leave, Lois thought she had been given a stay of execution.

"Okay," Carter said to the three assistants she had been provided, "according to what I've read, we're looking for a sequence of numbers beginning with five, one, six, which summons a Fire Elemental, which is called a Salamander, for a malign purpose. The sequence of numbers must be at least fifteen numbers long and not contain a break or a zero. Anything with a break or a zero is automatically out, because according to what I've read, either the break or the zero interrupts the... uh, vibrations of the numbers. You don't have to go along with the philosophy, just use it as a guide."

The youngest assistant, a woman with a brand-new Ph.D. in math from Cal Berkeley said, "What convinces you that the philosophy is correct? Couldn't there be a purpose to spaces and zeros?"

"I'm not convinced of anything," said Carter. "But we might as well play by the original rules before inventing our own."

The young woman shrugged.

"We're dealing with concepts that are foreign to us," Carter went on, "and that makes our work doubly difficult. Neither you nor I think that Fire Salamanders are real, but we're up against something that looks suspiciously like one. So, for the sake of convenience, we can say that it's what we're dealing with. All right?"

"If you say so," Jimmy Gall said dubiously.

"And for that reason," Carter continued, determined not to be sidetracked, "we are not—I repeat *not*—going to use the computers for this search. Because just in case there really is such a thing as a Fire Salamander, we don't want to find it out the hard way, do we?"

"What about running a search for all the account numbers that contain a zero. You said zeros are safe."

"They are, according to what I've read," Carter said with a strong sense of caution. "All right, we can give it a try. Also, we can eliminate those numbers with dashes or spaces. That might cut some of the work down to size. Anything that begins with the number five, do by hand and by hand only. I don't want any of us taking chances."

"Even if it contains a zero?" asked Jimmy.

"Yes; anything that begins with five, we do by hand. Period. For the time being. Once we have a profile of the key, then we can start using a more specific sort. Okay?"

"How the hell are we supposed to get through all these figures?" asked Andi Reed, the other assistant Carter had been given.

"I'll work with you; we can simply go down columns of figures." Carter looked from Jimmy's eyes to Andi's to Cora's. "If we get it right, it means the end of the fires. That's worth a little tedium, isn't it?"

"You put it that way, I guess it is," Jimmy allowed, "but this sounds a little like the Middle Ages, you know what I mean?"

"Yes; I do," said Carter. "But so far, it's the only explanation anyone's come up with that fits what we know about the fires and is consistent." She held up her pen. "Let's get to work, okay?"

"Ick," said Cora succinctly.

Horace Turnbull sat in the very uncomfortable chair the members of the House of Representatives had provided for him, and regarded the fifteen-person committee that had summoned him to tell them about the progress of the Task Force.

"Are you satisfied, Professor Turnbull, that everything that can be done is in fact being done by the Task Force?" This question came from the Republican Representative from Illinois with the long nose and the receding chin.

"As much as I can be, given the circumstances of the investigation and the nature of the problem." Turnbull folded his arms across his chest, a posture that made him look even more like a walrus than he usually did.

"Would you care to elaborate?" Gordon Kirk, Democrat from Oklahoma, asked the question.

"Congressman Kirk," Horace Turnbull said as if addressing one of his feistier graduate students, "I'm sure you understand that since the Task Force has no power of subpoena or similar legal force, we are left with the goodwill of the people who have been involved with these fires. I'm not suggesting that a change is necessary, but it would help us if there were stronger incentives for cooperation."

"Are you aware of the FBI's assessment of the problem?" The question came from the Chairman of the committee, a sour-faced seventy-one-year-old from Vermont.

"How could I not be?" Turnbull asked sharply. "At every meeting, McPherson reiterates it for us."

"Is that meant as criticism?" the Chairman demanded.

"Yes, since it interferes with our inquiries. I know that the FBI is concerned with the security of the country and is eager to carry out its task; that's not my quarrel. What has been a thorn in the side of all the members of the investigating bodies is that the Bureau has insisted that the investigation reflect its understanding of the problem and no other. I'm sure you can see how this could inadvertently hamper our various procedures."

"That's an interesting choice of words, Professor Turnbull," said the Democratic Representative from central Florida. She was very lean and very blonde and maintained a spectacular tan. Her mind was as sharp as her manner was feminine. "How do you mean 'inadvertently hamper'?"

"I mean that because the FBI wants to protect the country from what it thinks of as terrorist activities, it has required certain restrictions in the investigation that have, among other things, made it difficult for various of the investigatory groups to obtain the information they need for their work. It is not the intention of the FBI to interfere, I'm certain"—he gave the Bureau the full benefit of the doubt here—"but their conduct has had that effect for many of the agencies working on behalf of the Fire Marshals' Task Force."

"What are the risks you see from this, if any?" asked the Representative from Spokane, Washington.

"It may delay an accurate appreciation of the true nature of the fires, thus making it more difficult to arrive at the means to stop them. From the time I was called in as a consultant in this case I have been convinced that the greatest latitude in investigation should be encouraged and the most varied inquiries supported. Unfortunately, not everyone agrees, and this has created more misunderstandings than most of us would like to see." Turnbull cleared his throat. "I cannot help but think that it is important for us to encourage the most extrapolative experiments and methods. More traditional techniques have been shown to be inadequate in this instance."

"FBI Special Agent Simon McPherson does not agree with you," said the Chairman severely.

And now we get to the heart of it, thought Turnbull as he answered. "I am aware of that."

"In fact, he sees what you are doing just short of subversive," the Chairman went on.

"That's his privilege, just as it is mine to regard him as shortsighted and pigheaded." That would certainly draw the battle lines, Turnbull told himself.

"It's been suggested that you are actively attempting to divert the investigation from a reasonable course and encourage the most extreme and irresponsible areas of investigation rather than those that are more in keeping with the scientific method." This was the Representative from Illinois again.

"McPherson sees it that way, no doubt," said Turnbull. "I don't. I'm a physicist, not an FBI agent, and that probably gives me a different perspective."

"Are you saying that you know better than McPherson how to proceed?" challenged the tan Floridian.

"I'm saying that my perspective is different, and that's why I was asked to join this investigation. It is apparent that the standard theories don't apply here, and therefore some of the more... far-out areas of physics are being considered, which I think is necessary, given the lack of progress we've seen in most of these pursuits." He used his most intimidating frown as he spoke.

"How much progress do you think has been impeded?" asked the youngest member of the committee, an attorney from Memphis.

"There's no way of knowing, sir. But to reply to your implied question, do I think that progress had been impeded, the answer, sadly, is yes."

"Professor Turnbull, a man of your reputation has a certain moral obligation to support his country," said the Representative from Washington.

"That does not mean that I'm obliged to rubber-stamp procedures that are not in the interests of successful investigation." He tried to find a position that was more comfortable without any real success. "You've asked me to report to you on how I view the activities of the Task Force, and I am attempting to do that in the most dispassionate way I can. I have no vested interest in the Task Force other than my sincere desire to see the fires stopped. If anyone has suggested otherwise, I have been done a disservice, and so has this committee."

"You are on record as saying you do not believe that the fires are the work of terrorists," pointed out the Floridian.

"That's true."

"Then what do you think they are?" she demanded.

"I don't know. That's why I want to see the widest possible investigation undertaken. I think we will discover that the cause is quite outside the usual explanations and that we will have to approach the whole problem as unique."

"Professor," said the Chairman with great skepticism," isn't that a trifle extreme?"

"Good God, I hope so!" Turnbull said, surprising the members of the committee. "The circumstances call for extremity, wouldn't you say?"

"Order!" the Chairman said as he pounded his gavel in response to the buzz of conversation Turnbull's outburst had created.

"If you have any other questions, let me answer them. If

you don't, I'd like to get back to work," Turnbull said at his most unperturbed.

"You're excused for the time being, Professor, but the committee reserves the right to recall you for further comment."

Turnbull lugged himself to his feet. "Thank you."

J.D. Patterson stopped by Carter's office on his way out the door. "It's almost seven," he told her. "Your assistants went home over an hour ago."

"I know," she said.

"How's it coming?" He indicated the enormous stack of paper on her desk.

"It's coming. It's slow, but it's coming." She sighed. "I didn't realize how much I'd come to rely on the computer until now. I feel like I'm trying to knit while wearing steel gloves."

"You okay?" J.D. did not sound as if he doubted her, but there was concern in his eyes.

"I'm tired. I'm confused. I'm puzzled, but I'm okay." She started to rise, then changed her mind. "I want to work for another hour or so."

"Don't rob Peter to pay Paul. I need you working tomorrow as well as tonight." He paused briefly. "Everything okay at home? Is the new house going to work out?"

"Yes," she said with more animation. "I think it is. I like the place. It grows on me."

"Carter, I'm going to offer Frank Vickery a job. How do you feel about that?" J.D. had the knack of being tactful without appearing to be, but in this instance his intent was clear.

"So long as you aren't trying to do me a favor, it's fine," she said, her attitude becoming reserved.

"No, actually, I think of it as doing me a favor. We've needed someone with his background and experience for some time, and I'd want to hire him if it didn't cause any trouble for you. It's tricky when there's romance at the office."

"I don't think it's romance, I think it's something else,"

said Carter. "And I don't think it would be a problem in any case. It isn't that kind of relationship." She did not want to bristle, but she disliked having her private life dragged into her profession. "Talk to Frank if you've got questions about it."

"I talked to Frank yesterday," said J.D. "He told me it wasn't a good idea to press you."

"He's right," said Carter, amused in spite of herself.

"Okay. Then the job offer goes through and I'll count on both of you to be able to handle things as they develop." He took a step back, then added, "By the way, good luck. You're doing a very good job so far."

Carter laughed ruefully. "You mean we haven't burned the building down yet."

"Something like that," J.D. said as he left Carter to her task.

October 26, Winnipeg, Ontario

Alexander Metcalf had read the memo that had been circulated through the Axelrod Company, but he did not think it applied to his staff. It was true that they worked with computers, but most of what they did was work out exchange rates with various European currencies for the four major magazine publishers in the area. He was already thinking about the Christmas rush which would be upon him and his department shortly, and he wanted to have all the figures ready for John Axelrod on Monday.

"I don't like working on weekends," his secretary told him as he went for a refill of coffee.

"I'm not crazy about it myself," said Alex. "I'd rather be out fishing, but you know what John said about the French market. We ought to be selling more over there than we have been, and that means we have to hustle." He added powdered milk—which he did not like—and sugar to his coffee. "Want some, Annie?"

"No, thank you, Mister Metcalf." She was being prim, which was her way of showing annoyance. "There aren't many exchanges we can work with until Monday."

"Yes, but we can have all the Friday figures current, and that's what John wants, both for orders and for exchange rates. If we work at it, we'll be out of here before noon. That's not such a bad deal, is it, at double-time salary?"

"David and I were going to go shopping this morning," Annie said, not quite sulking.

"Come on, Annie, let's get the orders run up, and then tie them in with the exchange rates. It won't take that long." He had got used to cajoling her in the last year. It was now a habit and neither of them paid much attention to it anymore.

"Should I start with the French figures first?" She had taken one of the stacks of paper and was giving it an off-handed study.

"Yes, then the German, then the Italian. I don't want you to overlook the seasonal orders, either. They're some of the most important for the company."

"What about the magazines? Do you want foreign-language print-runs included with the orders and exchange rates?"

Alex thought this over. "Sure, why not? It will help determine the cost-effectiveness, won't it? Good for you, Annie. I wouldn't have thought of that."

"Well, remember who thought of it when they pass out the bonuses, Alex," she said, not quite making a joke.

"I will." He knew he would have to make a note to himself or he was likely to forget. He often made memos to himself, and he kept lists of things he had to do. He had gained a reputation for efficiency with this device and he was not eager to have it known that his memory was, in actuality, poor.

"Thanks. I'll get to work on the figures. Is it okay if I put them in the computer and let it do the work? That could get me out of here a few minutes early." She was looking at the screen of the monitor and her attention was more on it than on him.

"Of course. I'll stay and take care of the wrap-up." He smiled at her; it was his way of showing goodwill.

"Thanks. I'll give this as long as I can." She had softened a little and Alex thought that he had done as well as he could expect. "Do you have the orders?"

"Certainly," said Alex. He went and got them and brought them out to Annie. "While you're feeding this in, I'm going to work on the breakdown of this year's orders as compared to last. Call me if you need anything." He took his coffee and went back into his office, listening to the very soft clicks of the computer keyboard.

Less than two hours later, Annie stuck her head in the door. "All done; I'm going, okay?"

"If you're done, of course it's okay," said Alex. "I'll see you Monday. Remember, you and David are expected on the sixth. We want you to be there."

"It's on the calendar. It's nice of you and Missus Metcalf to host the office party." She was much more like herself now that her work had been done and she was able to put the office behind her.

"We enjoy it," Alex said, and it was no less than the truth. "See you Monday. Have fun shopping."

"Thanks. By the way, all you have to do is enter the merge program. That's push down the shift key and hit function-four key. Got that?"

"Shift and function-four key. Right you are. And thanks again." He was relieved, knowing that in less than an hour he would be able to go home and spend part of the day with his kids.

"Have fun." With that cheery call, she was gone.

Alex went over the comparison figures, hoping he could put the discouraging statistics in the best possible light. He decided to run the merge program while he made a few difficult decisions.

Following the instructions Annie had given, he set the computer to work, then busied himself with another set of memos.

Somewhere between the figures for Germany and the orders for Italy, a sequence of numbers triggered disaster: the terminal exploded into flame, trapping Alexander Metcalf in his office and setting the whole office ablaze in a matter of seconds. Alex had barely enough time to be surprised before he lost his consciousness and then his life.

October 28, Studio City, California

Stan Price's special-effects laboratory was little more than a twenty-foot-square section of a cavernous warehouse, but there with his specially modified camera and his computer-enhanced graphics, he was able to create low-budget wonders. His particular brand of wizardry had brought him enough clients now that he had moved from an apartment in Van Nuys to a house in Tarzana. For some that transition would not seem like much, but for Stan, who had been the weirdest kid in his high school class fifteen years ago, it was a triumph.

Today the project was a torpedoed spaceship flying apart, and he had been working for three days developing the sequence and the technique he was going to use. He went over his plan one more time, checking the lighting and the track he had built for the camera that would allow a corkscrew turn around the spaceship as it came apart, an effect that promised to be dizzying on the screen.

"What do you think, Stan?" asked his assistant Ursula.

"I think we're almost ready, Silly," he said, using the nickname she had been stuck with for most of her life. Ursula Euphronia Owen was named for both her grandmothers and she had yet to forgive her parents for saddling her with all that.

"What about the camera?" She knew better than to touch it; the camera was Stan's baby and he pampered and adored it more than he pampered and adored his two Japanese wolfhounds.

"I'll check it out. I want you to run through the lighting cues. What about the breakaways?"

"They're the same as yesterday. I think that Julio will be delighted, and that he won't have any idea what a bargain he's getting." She prided herself on having better business sense than her boss, who often priced himself at marginal levels for the fun of doing the project.

"Julio wants a spaceship that comes apart. We'll make sure that the explosion is matted in just right. It doesn't have to be very big. I already have footage we can use and the computer will take care of the enhancements on that, too, once we set it up." He walked under the spaceship and looked up at it. Who would guess that it was made primarily out of packing material and plastic toys? He loved building these things, and he only regretted that he did not get to do it more often.

"How long do you think it will take us to get the whole sequence on film this morning?"

Assuming the computer does its job and there's no problems with the lighting, not much more than an hour, he decided. "Not too long," he answered her. "We ought to have most of it done by lunchtime."

"Good," said Ursula, automatically doubling the time to allow for a retake; no matter what Stan said, he always ended up doing a thing twice, just in case.

"And we can run footage for Julio tomorrow. Call him and tell him, won't you?" Stan was grinning to himself. For him the anticipation was almost everything, and the filming merely a verification of what had gone before. "I want him to be here first thing after lunch. He's always easier to talk to after lunch."

"You mean after three drinks," Ursula said at her driest.

"Hey, that's not fair. I know that most of the time Julio only has mineral water."

"And nose candy," added Ursula. "Okay, tomorrow afternoon at one-thirty. Julio can have a look at the rough film, that's assuming we can get an answer print out of the lab by then."

"That's no trouble. I called them first thing this morning and set it up." Stan grinned again, his face looking very young.

Half an hour later, he was very nearly angry and his eyes were harsh. "Silly, we've got to make a couple adjustments. All that film fucked!"

"We usually have problems," Ursula said at her most laconic, which was her usual pattern as pressure increased.

"Not once the film runs. Damn! Shit!" He climbed up the scaffolding to check the corkscrew track. "Why is this getting in the picture? The angle isn't supposed to let that happen. What's going wrong?" He addressed the model as if the plastic could answer him. "What's wrong? It was all worked out."

Ursula, who had been in watching the monitor, said, "Look, what if we change the degree of the camera by just a degree or a degree and a half? That should be enough of a shift of the view field that no part of the track will be seen."

"That's a lot of calculations." Stan sulked.

"I can take care of it. Why don't you go get a sandwich?"

He merely glared at her. "We've got work to do."

"Okay, stay here and fret while I do the work. I don't care, but let me get this figured out, okay? That's part of what you pay me for." She grinned unexpectedly. "You know models and cameras and computers, but I, old buddy, know math." She pulled her pocket calculator out and started to figure adjustments.

Stan filled the time pacing while Ursula scribbled a few notes and continued to adjust the sequence of camera positions in relation to the model.

"I think I'm almost ready. Just let me make a few modifications and we can roll again," Ursula said, feeling very pleased with herself.

It was going much better the second time, and Stan was becoming almost euphoric. "Hey, Silly," he said as he reached the beginning of the ship-destruction sequence, "this is going real good."

"Uh-huh," said Ursula, watching the monitor.

"Get ready; breakaway coming up." He braced himself, determined to get the perfect illusion of destruction. "Coming up!"

It was spectacular, far more spectacular than anything Stan had ever done, and more destructive. One moment the model was starting to fly apart, and then fire mushroomed through the little effects studio, spreading far beyond the space that Stan and Ursula worked in, a ball of such utter ruin that by the time the fire department reached the building, most of the roof had collapsed and one of the walls had crumbled to unrecognizable shards.

October 30, Racine, Wisconsin

One of the machines was down, but the other two were able to handle most of the billing. The repairmen, used to working on smaller installations, grumbled at the extra work that was required to put the computer back in operation.

"I bet they don't know what's wrong with this," Bernard Reville complained to his two partners, Jack Siggerson and Luke Winters. "I bet that old Murdoch never did more than glance at the specs for one of these babies."

Neither man paid much attention to him. "I'm going to need to check the cables. I have a hunch that we might have a short there that's responding to the surges. It's the only thing that makes sense."

"It happens every so often, and that's all. How much money do you think goes through here in billing, say in a month?" Siggerson asked Winters.

"With fifty-eight boutiques and salons? Who knows? My wife bought an outfit at their downtown store, just slacks and a jacket, over four hundred dollars. I mean, it looks great but four hundred dollars?"

"How many of those do you think they sell in a month?" Winters pursued.

"I don't know. They wouldn't have to sell too many of them. She got a pair of shoes there, too, that was a hundred thirty dollars, and a purse that cost over a hundred. She's a great-looking woman, my wife, and I know she needs to look good in her work, but there are times—" He broke off with a gesture of exasperation.

"My wife spends most of the money on furniture. But she doesn't work full-time like your Gladys does." He pulled one of the cables and examined it as if the outside might show him something. "What do you think? Murdoch says that we're dealing with surges on the line and they're ruining the billings. I thought they were shielded from that kind of thing."

"That don't mean it can't happen," Reville muttered. "Murdoch hasn't had enough hands-on experience with these to know what he's doing. Billing computers. If you ask me, this is the kind of thing that ought to be burning up, not those computers in colleges and radio stations and God knows what other things."

"Hey, Reville, don't even think that," said Winters.

"Sure, sure. But don't you think billings like this would be a logical target? If there's any sense to those fires at all, it's places like this that would be in ashes. They'd never be able to figure out who owed what for what. Je-sus, what a great free ride!" He laughed out loud.

"Want to see what a new cable will do?" Winters suggested, ignoring Reville.

"Sure: why not?" Siggerson said with a shrug. "You got your end hooked up?"

"Yeah. Yours?"

"Yeah. Why don't we see what happens. Start the thing."

"I'll do it," Reville said, and flipped the switch.

For five minutes the huge billing computer ran swiftly

and excellently, and the three men were starting to think they had completed their repair job.

Then there was an ominous pop and the machine faltered. It started once again, but almost at once there was an acrid smell on the air.

"What the hell's that?" Winters asked.

"I don't know," Siggerson admitted and for once both men looked to Reville, for although he was an obnoxious bastard, he was first-class at repairs and he had a sense about computers that some people had with dogs or horses.

Reville reached for the nearest cable, swearing ripely and comprehensively.

"Shit!" Reville yelled as he dropped the hot cable.

The other two exchanged looks just before the flames welled around them, consuming the repairmen, the computer and the two smaller computers and all the billing records that Reville thought made such an irresistible target for destruction.

PART VII

November 1, Felton, California

Frank Vickery read through the notes Carter had been making, leaning over the back of her chair to do it, and to kiss the nape of her neck. "How much longer are you going to keep at this? You've been working since nine and it's after two."

"I'm still trying to find out what you're supposed to do to get rid of a Salamander, and it isn't very encouraging. So far as I can tell, it's no big thing to summon one, but getting rid of it's another matter. Once it burns up everything it can, it just waits to be summoned again so that it can burn up more."

"Great," said Frank sarcastically. "I thought all you had to do was work out the numbers to get it to go away."

"So did I, but so far as I can tell, there aren't any such numbers. You can't send it back to where it came from, because it really came from here, as a distillation of the very essence of fire, or at least that's what the Arab mathematicians imply in their works, and from what these books say, the Arabs were the definitive summoners of Elementals." She folded her arms and leaned her head forward on them. "Frank, I can't think anymore. Everywhere I turn, it's a blind alley."

"Come on, Carter; let's sleep on it. What can another three or four hours do if you end up—" He removed the notebook from under her hands. "Carter, please. You worry me when you wear yourself out like this. And don't tell me you do your best work when you're worn-out, because I don't believe that and neither do you."

"You're right." She started to get to her feet. "I feel so . . . so *frustrated*. What good is knowing what we're up against if we can't do a damn thing about it?"

"Isn't that the human condition?" he asked, hoping to make a joke of it.

"I suppose so," she said, and let the yawn she had been resisting grab her.

"Okay. Now, upstairs. I'll run a bath for you and I'll come scrub your back. How's that?" He was always surprised at how these minor gestures—nothing more than courtesies, really—moved her.

"You don't have to," she said uncertainly.

"No, but I want to. Unless you'd rather bathe all by yourself." He was teasing her, letting his suggestion come as banter so that she would not be troubled by it. He still found her sensitivity unnerving and difficult to anticipate. Occasionally he would say something in jest that would strike her where she was still most tender, and other times he would make what he thought was a simple observation and she would laugh and exclaim at his wit. One day he would figure her out, he promised himself, realizing that it truly did not matter so long as their feelings continued to grow.

He left her to undress and went to the bathroom. In the last few days, he had picked up a brush and a large natural sponge, as well as some herb-scented bubble bath. He poured a little of this into the water as he filled the tub.

"Luxury of luxuries," Carter said as she came in the door. Her terry-cloth robe was tied around her and she carried one of the bath sheets she had purchased on impulse when he got the sponge. "What did I do to deserve this?"

"It isn't a question of deserving. It's a gift, a treat." He adjusted the water to a higher temperature. "Come on; get in."

"Maybe if we suggest that any sequence of ten numbers must have a space or a zero, that would stop the worst of it." She dropped her robe on the floor and went to the bath. "I'm still . . . I don't know how to act with my clothes off when you're around. Funny isn't it? It's not like we're strangers." She got down into the water. "I'm not sure how I should act."

"Any way you want to," said Frank. "I'm not used to this, either. I find that there are times I ask myself what am I doing here? On Labor Day—and it wasn't that long ago—I didn't know you. When we first met, your husband was still alive."

"That bothers me. Does it ever bother you? What if this is just my way of getting over Greg's death? I think about that, too. Maybe I'm using you as an escape. I'd hate to think that was so, but it might be, mightn't it?"

Frank had taken the sponge and was soaking it. His knuckles brushed her back and he liked the feel of it. "Don't worry about it, Carter. If it works out, it works out; if it doesn't, it doesn't."

"What about you?" she asked quickly, in a rush and very quietly. "How do you feel about it."

"I don't know yet. I'm not ready to figure it out. It takes a while." He did not add that he was already thinking of himself as being with her.

"That bubble bath smells good," Carter said. "What are Undines like, I wonder?"

"Undines? Water Elementals?" He stopped sponging water over her shoulders. "Lie back. Let it heat you."

She did as she was told. "I was trying earlier to imagine a Water Elemental and an Air Elemental. How could you get them to manifest? They're not like Salamanders, that burns. They're like the weather. That was all I could think of. What do you do? Send radio signals with the right numbers to make the air different? Hotter? Colder? Windier? What is the problem with a Sylph? I can't come up with anything. And yet the same microwaves are going through the air all the time that summoned the Salamander. Or whatever it is that it does. It's the strangest physics."

"I don't even know how to do that kind of thinking." This admission returned his insecurities. "Do you manage that kind of thinking all the time?"

"Hell, no," she said, laughing gently. "I haven't the least notion about what any of this means and most of my colleagues would think I'd gone round the bend if they knew what I'm up to. But I'm not a physicist, I'm a statistician with a knack for cryptography. I'm good at codes. The way some people are good at chess or at blackjack." There was a trace of bitterness in these last words, but she was too tired to linger with them. "Where's Winslow?"

"Out in back. He didn't want to come in. He likes his doghouse." He now had the brush in his hand and was rubbing soap over the bristles.

"I hope he doesn't get too used to it. When you're... not here, I'll want him inside." She leaned forward and he began to scrub her back. "You know, Barbara used to say that she wanted me to do this for hours. That was before she got sick."

"What did she have?" Carter asked, as she had wanted to do for more than a week. "You don't have to tell me if you'd rather not."

"I can never remember the name. I can tell you what it did; it made parts of her intestines become infected and then develop necrotic tissue, which had to be removed. After a while, there wasn't much left, and she got very thin and weak, and then she got an infection that she couldn't fight off, and it spread, and then it was all over. Her doctors really tried, I'll give 'em that." He discovered that talking about her was not as painful as it had been even three months ago, and as he continued to scrub Carter's back and arms, he went on in a different voice, "I hated seeing her change—she did change. She'd been active and vital and full of laughter and she took care of Melinda like a captain of a soccer team of one. They had great times."

"It was hard on Melinda," Carter said, not needing to ask.

"On all of us. I think the worst was that Barbara stopped laughing—it hurt or it reminded her of hurting." He had stopped wielding the brush and let it dangle in the water.

"How do you think Melinda would feel about me?" She hesitated. "Assuming that she ever has to feel anything about me."

"Maybe we can find out when the fires are over. She likes where she is, and it might be that she'd want to stay there for a while. Her psychologist told me that she might feel more secure being with her mother's family than isolated. But she'll grow out of that. She's been close to me, even before Barbara got sick." He stood up. "How did I get off on this?"

"I asked you," Carter said. "It's my fault." She started to get out of the bath, but Frank put his arm across her.

"Hey, don't rush this. I'm sorry I got distracted. Let me finish this up for you. It's pleasant, isn't it?" He picked up the sponge and began rinsing her off.

"It's wonderful. Thanks. Thanks so much." She moved with the motion of his hand. "Can you do this and not turn someone on?"

"I don't know. I never tried." He started to laugh. "It's nice to know that you feel this way. I can keep it in reserve for later. At two-thirty in the morning, I don't think we're going to be spending a long time in the sack tonight, at least not doing much more than sleeping. It might have been different when I was twenty-two, but not now."

This time Carter chuckled at some length. "A nice friendly quickie?"

"Sounds great. You ready to dry off?" He put the sponge aside and reached for the bath sheet.

"Mmm. I didn't think anything could get my mind off those books and figures. I wouldn't have slept at all if you hadn't done this."

He held the towel for her and wrapped his arms around her as he enveloped her in it. "There's a method in my madness, you see."

"I never doubted it," she said, leaning back against him and grinning at the sensation of his hands through the nubby cloth.

"You're so terrific." He kissed her shoulder where he had dried her.

"I'm so... It makes me happy. You make me happy." Since she admitted this, she felt so vulnerable that she wanted fleetingly to joke or to deny what she had said.

"Good," said Frank, using the towel to turn her around and pull her close against him, still moist, still warm and languid from the bath. He kissed her slowly, pleasurably, very thoroughly. "How can I tell you?"

"You're doing a great job so far." Her questions faded, her hesitations and doubts were put aside in favor of Frank and the marvelous sensations they roused and shared.

J.D. read through the report that Carter put on his desk, going quickly through the pages. "You're sure about this number sequence? Absolutely sure? Sure enough to risk lives on it?"

Carter ground her teeth, but nodded. "Yes. I am. There may be more numbers, but I didn't want to test them, and I'm sure you can understand."

He gave a tight grin. "Discretion and prudence are the better parts of valor?"

"Yeah," she said. "Jimmy wanted to try more, but I didn't like the chance. We don't know how many numbers there are in the sequence, only that these are the first nine of them. In case it's a ten-number sequence, I thought it would be—"

"—playing with fire?" J.D. suggested with no trace of laughter.

"At the very least," she said.

"All right, I'm going to release this, but with a number of reservations and qualifying statements. Glen would take my hide off if I didn't, just in case this isn't the answer at all. Do you understand this?"

"Of course. Jimmy already said that he didn't want the report to be too certain, so we'd be protected. I took responsibility for the wording, and I made it clear to my assistants that I did."

"You're that confident about your results?" asked J.D., showing more interest.

"Yes. I'm that confident. If I'm wrong about this, I have no business doing the kind of work I do for you, and the sooner this is settled, the better." She folded her arms, trying to keep down the panic that she felt well within her. She had just bought a house, a very expensive house, and there was new furniture in it, and here she was putting her job on the line, which was the only thing that stood between her and the world.

"And you plan to test further?" asked J.D.

"I'd like to, but I don't know how safe it would be." She paused. "According to what I've read, it's supposed to take fifteen numbers in sequence, without dashes or zeros, in order to make one of those things manifest. That's the theory, and it might well be true: most of the figures we have do indicate that there were sequences of numbers at least fifteen numbers long, some without dashes or zeros, or entered without dashes or zeros. It requires something more, though, to test it out, like a controlled environment with a limited vacuum or some means of stopping the fire once it starts before it consumes the entire building. And from what the records indicate, these manifestations tend to continue until the target building is in ashes. I don't know what causes the limitations, and I don't have any plan for a safe way to experiment with the thing. What do you suggest?"

J.D. sat back, fingering the pages of Carter's report as if he might be able to absorb the information through his fingers. "All right, suppose we can find a safe way to run some experiments, are you willing to supervise them?"

"I'm willing to try. I'm willing to work with the Task Force in any capacity they think is sensible, and I am willing to turn over every scrap of data we've been able to assemble. I would rather not have to deal with officialdom because of the official attitude toward these theories. I doubt they'd get a fair hearing. What do you think?" She moved her hair off her face and waited.

"Suppose we could manage something here? How would you feel about that?" J.D. did not make the question sound loaded, but Carter sensed that it was.

"I'd like to stay with a staff I know and with people who respect what I do and what my assistants have done. I'd rather not have to convince everyone all over again that this is worth trying. If that means that working here would be the best approach, I'd like it." She paused. "And just now I don't want to take any chances where Frank is concerned."

"I thought that was a factor. I'm glad you admitted it." He opened the report again. "Five, one, six, nine, four, three, three, six, seven. So that's what's been causing the fires," he mused.

"I think it is, yes," she said. "It's part of it, anyway. I think we'd be safe in issuing a warning about those numbers. I think it could make a difference. If people avoided using those numbers in that order, the fires should stop, and that would prove something, wouldn't it?"

"It would go a long way to proving something. By the way, Randall tells me you have an appointment with him at four: do you mind telling me why? Ordinarily I wouldn't ask, but since we're going to try to convince some of the most serious skeptics and detractors that this theory is worth testing, they're going to want to know why you're talking to the in-house shrink. I should give them an answer."

"Isn't the fact that my husband burned to death, that I've just bought a new house, that I have a roommate who's my occasional lover, and that I've been getting an average of five hours sleep a night thanks in large part to work enough reason to want to talk to Randall?" She brought her chin up and her expression was defiant. It was a look that J.D. had never seen her wear before and he was pleased that she was managing so well.

"It's more than enough for me, Carter. In fact, it's not the kind of question that in general I think is any of my business." He paused, then confessed, "Actually, that's not quite true. I worry about Scott Costa and Randy tells me what he can without going too far. Scott's case is special and there's no way that I'd be tending to my responsibilities if I didn't make the effort to keep track of his condition, given its severity."

"But it's not the same with me," she said cautiously.

"Not at all. You're surprising only in your... durability." He finally put the report down. "I want to talk to a few other people, particularly some of the engineers over in the systems wing, to see what they might be able to come up with. You have my word that we'll try to find a way to check this out. I can't make a better offer, Carter." He held out his hand to her and waited for her to take it. "I'm proud of you."

"J.D.?" She was amazed at how readily he had agreed with her, and how little she had had to say to convince him.

"I try to keep an open mind," he said with a hint of a smile. "When the standard solutions don't work, you must try those that are not standard, and if you are not willing to take a chance, you might never have another." He let her think about this before saying, "Whether this works or not, you deserve a bonus for the work you did and for all you've been through while you've been doing the work. In Navy Intelligence, we occasionally got special citations. I don't have that, but I can pass out bonuses; and in this case, I think that might be the better choice anyway."

"If I get a bonus, everyone who worked with me on this, including Frank—most of all Frank—ought to have one, too."

"No argument," said J.D. "Now get out of here while I rile some of the engineers."

Cynthia Harper caught Carter by the elbow and pulled her into the ladies' room. "So tell me all about it."

"Well, I don't know all about it yet; J.D. didn't argue about the report and I think the next stage is a—" Carter began only to be interrupted.

"Not about the project, about Frank. About the house. Tell me all about it. I've been dying to find out what's going on there." Cynthia had lost a few pounds and there were circles under her eyes that looked dark as bruises. Her dark hair, usually very neat, was not quite as ordered or shiny as usual.

"Cynthia!" Carter protested, half flattered and half scandalized by these questions. "How's it going with you?"

"Terrible," said Cynthia. "We're all being driven mad. So tell me something new and exciting and wonderful. I don't think I can stand hearing about fires or deaths or astronomical damage figures for the next ten minutes. Come on; give!"

Carter turned her back on the mirror over the sinks, as if in doing that, she could be more private, more confidential without losing her sense of dignity. "Frank is a... very sweet man."

"Oh, for heaven's sake! Get to the good part. I'll give you that Frank is good-looking and minds his manners and has a nice way with people. A regular grown-up Boy Scout. What's he *like*?"

"Like?" Carter stalled.

"In bed! As a lover!" Cynthia tugged at Carter's sleeve. "I've been waiting for you to get the phone installed, but since we can talk now... well, let me know."

It was difficult for Carter to answer. "He's attentive and considerate and I like him. And he likes me."

"That's good, but what about details? Does he know what to do for you?"

Carter felt heat mount in her face. "Yes, he knows what to do. In fact, the thing that's best is that he knows without having to be told or without indulging me. He likes what I like and I like what he likes and neither of us has to accommodate the other in any way that isn't fine for us, too. I didn't have to tell him how or what or where; it was all fine. He says that it's the same way with him. I hope it is. I'd hate to think that he was... fibbing about something this important, but I don't think he is." Carter grinned suddenly and hugely. "I don't know what this is or how it's going to turn out, but frankly, I don't care. Why the hell is everyone suddenly interested in my sex life?" She had not intended to ask the question, but it came out before she was able to stop it.

"Because it's about the only good news any of us have had in the last couple months. By the way, are we still on for Thanksgiving, or are you doing something Romantic, capital R, with Frank?" She stared into the mirror. "God, I look like a haystack. I haven't had my hair cut in almost two months."

"Are you worried about how you look?" Carter asked.

"Naturally. If I go into court looking harried—and if I went into court today, that's ex*act*ly how I'd look—I work at a disadvantage. I have to do something about the way I look. It's part of the job, especially for women, and never let them tell you any differently. You either have to look like something the cat would never think about dragging in, or you have to look as polished as the best Florentine leather." She fiddled with her hair and squinted at her face, regarding her reflection closely. "Oh, well. All I have to do today is finish collecting the facts about that fire in Helena, to show that it wasn't a failure of our equipment. It's really pro forma, because most courts these days recognize that nothing can make much difference with these random fires, and that even the very best security system isn't going to do much against the..."

"The Fire Salamander. It might not be that, but it's the best shorthand we've got." Carter managed to make her tone light.

"Okay, the Fire Salamander. It doesn't respond to security systems. It just goes in and burns down buildings and takes countless lives and keeps it up no matter what anyone does." She started to cry, putting her hand over her mouth so that all the sound she made was something like rapid-fire hiccoughing.

"Hey, Cynthia," Carter said, surprised at how much her friend was affected.

"Don't," said Cynthia.

"What's going on with you? Is it really that bad?" Carter reached over and put her arm around Cynthia's waist. "Do you want to know anything more about Frank?"

Cynthia gulped hard. "Does he smell good? I don't mean cologne or aftershave or that kind of thing; does he—he—smell good?"

"Yes, as a matter of fact, he does," said Carter, trying very hard not to laugh. "He smells a little bit like new-mown grass or fresh-cut wood."

"Good. That's very good." Cynthia moved away from Carter, her eyes looking as if she was suffering from a cold. "It's important that he smell good."

"I guess," said Carter, wishing she knew why Cynthia was so upset. "I think we might have a key to the fires, something that we can do something about. Does that interest you at all?"

"I don't know anymore. I've been hoping that someone would wave a magic wand and there would be only a few forms and suits to take care of, not lives in terrible trouble and losses that cannot be calculated or understood."

Carter nodded. "Well, there's a chance—it's more than a chance, I think, but for the time being, J.D. is hedging his bets—there's a chance that we've got a handle on it now."

"God, I hope you're right." Cynthia sobbed. "I'm losing heart, Carter. I keep reading and reading and reading and all there is to read says that everyone stands a chance of being burned to death in the next ten years."

"I think we've got a chance," Carter said with more certainty. "I think that maybe we can win."

* * *

William read over the report Frank had shown him. His expression was inscrutable. "Let me get this straight," he said at last. "You think that there is some combination of numbers that causes the fires? Is that what this says?"

"That's it," said Frank.

"Uh-*huh*," said William as he set the report aside. "And how much of this farrago is for public consumption?"

"If farrago means what I think it means," Frank said cautiously, "this isn't one of those easy answers. We're trying to find a workable answer, and no matter how peculiar this looks, it does fit the problem and it has been taken from the accessible evidence."

"Accessible means that it wasn't burned to nothing," William said, watching Frank with real dismay.

"That's all we've had to go on," Frank responded. "Tomorrow J.D. Patterson is going to be discussing this theory and its ramifications with the Task Force. You're the only newsman who's seen a copy, and I'd appreciate it if you didn't blow the story."

"Don't worry. I'm not going to talk about something this crazy until I have some information that's a bit more acceptable to the public." William sighed. "Do you think —honestly, Frank—that there's anything to this?"

"Carter Milne is a very good statistician and she isn't given to flights of fancy," Frank began only to have William hold up his hand to stop him.

"Carter Milne was widowed not long ago and now she's shacking up with you. She might have a good brain, but no one thinks clearly at times like these." William regarded Frank evenly. "And your endorsement isn't exactly unbiased, is it?"

"That has no bearing on her ability with statistics, or her integrity. I know the woman, and I tell you—from my biased point of view, of course—that she isn't going to try to make use of this or any other theory cynically. If you think that there are questions about it, she would agree. She is very much aware of how most people would react to this kind of thing and she's being doubly circumspect for that reason."

"Good for her," William said with fatigue.

"Stop that," Frank warned him cordially. "If you start taking that stance, we might as well give it all up right now. So long as there is any kind of chance at all, we're going to give it a try. We might as well. We don't have much to lose, do we?"

"Is that what you're going to say to the Task Force?" William asked ironically.

"Luckily, I don't have to talk to the Task Force about this; that's J.D.'s job, and he knows how to do it."

"They're going to ask your opinion; you know that, don't you, Frank?" William folded his hands and stared at his friend. "What will you tell them?"

"That it can't hurt to try." Frank paced the length of the motel room. "Nothing we've done so far has worked; this isn't hard to do and it might, it just might, be the key. If it does, then we're ahead of the game. I'd hate to think that we overlooked a solution because of superstition."

"Superstition?" echoed William.

"What else can you call it, when something is rejected because it is philosophically distressing? No one wants to admit that perhaps the old Arab mathematicians were on to something and that what they did was outside of what we call science now. They thought of themselves as scientists, remember."

"All right," said William. "Suppose they find a way to make it work: who's to say that there aren't things even worse that might happen the same way? If all it takes to burn down the world is the right sequence of numbers, what does that do to the arms race? It'll get to a point that no one will want to turn on the TV because the whole place might explode."

"Hey, it's not that extreme, Will. Even assuming that numbers're all it takes, it has to be the right numbers and there have to be enough of them."

"Wonderful; that calms me right down," William said nastily. "Look, I gotta tell you, Frank, this makes me feel real unsafe. I think I'd rather have the fires be the result of terrorist activities instead of a series of numbers. That scares the shit out of me." He caught his lower lip with his teeth. "Yeah, it scares me."

"It scares me, too," Frank admitted. "I don't like to consider the possibilities too much."

"Really?" William asked.

"Really," Frank said. "When Carter first came up with the theory, I was relieved, you know? I thought that at least the bad part might be over. I was proud of her, and I still am. But today, while I was going over the report, I started to think about how it might all backfire. No pun intended," he added morosely. "It wasn't the arms race that got to me, or the thought that this might be the kind of thing that could crop up anywhere, but that it was the kind of tool that might be used politically—you know, a pressure group that isn't touting the popular line and, gee whiz, their headquarters goes up in smoke. That troubles me."

William gazed at Frank in horrified silence. "That couldn't happen, could it?"

"I hope not; but it bothers me." He attempted a rueful smile but it was not successful.

Randall Whiting looked up from his notes and regarded Carter with an intense stare. "Would you repeat that?"

"I'm afraid," she said simply. "I feel that my life has got away from me. That bothers me, you know? I think about Greg and the house and then about Frank, and all I do is dither. I've never dithered before."

"Does it surprise you? Given what's happened to you and around you? Do you think there's anything unusual in . . . dithering?" When she didn't answer he went on with remarkable smoothness, "If this had happened to anyone else and he or she had come to you and said that they were afraid and that they felt at odds with the world and didn't know what to do about it, what would you say to them?"

"I suppose . . . I don't know." She twisted her hands in

her lap. "Most of the time, I stay right on top of it. I almost feel guilty because it's so easy, because I can cope so well."

"What do you think you ought to do instead of cope?" Whiting asked in his most neutral tone.

"What's wrong with me that I don't grieve? Greg hasn't been dead that long and I already have a lover. That's the right word for it isn't it? I have a lover, a man who shares my bed and body."

"If that's what you call it, it's the right word," Whiting said.

"Stop it, Randy. I don't want those nice, easy professionally glib answers that slide off your tongue like chocolate." She waited.

"Nice image," said Whiting. "I think it's a mixed metaphor, but still, a nice image."

Carter was getting angry. "Listen to me, Randy; I want you to talk to me about what's going on in my life; I don't want you to sound like you're getting paid to not answer."

"But that's what I am getting paid for," he reminded her gently. "You're saying you don't want me to do my job so that you can feel better about doing yours?"

"Randy, if this were the Second World War and I came in, stressed out and confused, you'd handle it differently, wouldn't you?"

"Forty years ago, we handled everything differently," Whiting reminded her. "Forty years ago there wasn't as much known about the brain and chemistry, and in the middle of a war we didn't have a lot of time to find out, and none to experiment." He looked at her closely. "But what's your point?"

"It's like being on the edge of a war, with this fire code causing so much damage. It's like cleaning up after a bombing raid, or something like it, or so it seems to me. One minute everything's fine and the next the whole building's fallen down around you and almost everyone in it is dead. That's not a bad description of a bombing raid, is it?" Her face was starting to look haggard again.

"It's not quite the same, but there are similarities, I'll give you that. Go on."

"People do strange things during a war, things they wouldn't do under more... normal circumstances. People make sudden decisions during wars, and they do things with less weighing of alternatives or preparations, because there's always the knowledge that this might be the only chance you'll get at it. That's a factor, isn't it?" She faltered, hoping he would say something. When he did not, she gave a little shake to her head and went on. "I tell myself that's what happened to me; because of the fires, I think I'm in a war and I have to act now or I might not be able to again. I have to take hold of what's here and real because that might be all there is. And I have to look for solutions as pragmatically as possible, since that's all that counts."

"And in a way you're equating your relationship with Frank Vickery and your theory about the fires, is that it?" Whiting often found himself mesmerized by the way his clients perceived themselves and never more compellingly than when they were trying to create order where little or none existed.

"In a way," Carter answered cautiously.

"You think that you've come to your theory as pragmatically as possible." He had only read a couple of pages of her report and so reserved his judgment intellectually as well as psychologically.

"What else was there to do? What else made any sense? Think about the way the fires happen and find the commonality, that was what J.D. wanted me to do. The only commonality other than the high level of destruction was that almost all of the places—and I say almost because in some instances we have no more evidence to go on—is that at some time within a three-hour period before the fires broke out, a specific sequence of numbers was used in conjunction with the electronic devices."

"But why these numbers? Surely there were other numbers that you might have chosen that could also be assumed to be the cause? Or are you troubled because the source of your theory is so . . . questionable? Is that at the base of your questions?" Whiting had been told about Carter's delving into old occult texts for part of her inquiries and he shared the doubts that J.D. had expressed about that area of research. "Carter, you're a bright woman, and the bright ones are always the ones who spend half their time looking in off-the-wall places for their answers. That means that some of those answers are going to be as off-the-wall as the questions, but is that any reason to avoid them?"

"It is if it doesn't save lives, if it jeopardizes the company and raises hopes for no good reason."

He heard the despair at the back of her words and tried to think of something to say. "You said that you think it will work, this theory of yours, and from what I understand, there's little or no cost to implementing it. Even if it turns out not to be correct, the methodology isn't so time-consuming or expensive that it is apt to be a burden." He looked at her with renewed concern. "Is that part of it, too? You're afraid what you're offering has no real value except to make some people feel that they are protecting themselves when they're not?"

Sudden tears slid from her eyes. "Um-hum," she nodded.

"How long would it take you to run the series of numbers you're worried about, assuming you could do it in reasonable safety?" He could tell she felt pressured by this question, but he decided not to modify it.

"Not long, if there were a way to do it safely."

"That's the catch, isn't it? the safety." He narrowed his eyes, calculating how much she would accept before rejecting anything he said to her. "Short of a vacuum, you can't take that risk with any confidence."

"Not really. We know the fires are hot, fast and lethal, and even with all the controls in the world, it could get out of hand. I think that's what happened to that NSA mathematician. You know, Professor Li. I think he was testing out his version of a theory and he forgot how exposed he was."

"It's a legitimate factor," Whiting said. "And short of outer space, you can't test your theory in a completely protected environment." He gave a little smile. "And it isn't easy to test things off the planet, is it?"

"I'm not even sure you could test this off the planet. It might be that it has to have a connection to the world in some way, at least at first."

"But J.D. said that you might be correct in your assumption about radio or microwaves."

"And the operative word there is 'might'." She looked away, out the window at the first rain of the fall. "Might."

"The trouble is that we're not getting anywhere," complained Simon McPherson to Sidney Rountree. "You tell me that your Task Force is continuing to gather evidence and to investigate, that you have now classified seventy-eight fires as being legitimately part of these random fires, with another eighteen possibles. That's a lot of fires and not nearly enough answers or hard information." Since he had assumed command of the FBI branch of the investigations, he often used his position to push others to more activity.

"I can't and I won't make guesses about something like this. You're a policeman, not a fireman. Most people are worried when they see a policeman and they're relieved when they see a fireman. You're trying to get us to act like policemen and I'm telling you right now, McPherson, that we won't." He indicated the door to his office. "Go talk to the other Fire Marshals if you doubt me."

"I don't know if that's necessary," McPherson growled.

"Go ahead. Find out from them how they feel. Don't take my word for it. Indulge your suspicious mind." He was enjoying this opportunity to prod McPherson, since that was all the FBI Special Agent had been doing to him for over a week.

"I've got men I have to deal with; leads to follow. You might not accept the idea that this is a conspiracy, but we haven't rejected that notion yet, and we won't until we're absolutely certain that it isn't a factor in the fires." He held out a file folder. "Have you reviewed this load of horseshit out of PSS?"

"I've glanced at it. I'm going to read the whole report tonight."

"Don't bother. It's straight out of a fifties movie. They must be flying on crack out there in Silicone Valley to come up with something as idiotic as this."

Rountree cleared his throat. "Nothing we've come up with so far has turned out to be right; maybe this is. Recreational chemicals or not, maybe they're on to something. It might not be an answer, but it might give us a key." He wanted to make McPherson squirm and he had the satisfaction of seeing the man waver.

"Malign equations?" McPherson suggested. "Every kid in high school'd like to know about that. They could burn down the building and claim that it was an accident caused by the numbers. Think what they could do to arson cases. You'd have to go to court every time any electronics were involved. Nothing would ever get settled. The insurance companies would wiggle out of every claim for a fire, because they could duck the responsibility for a number sequence. Loony tunes, Rountree."

"It's a possibility and it might stop the fires. If we can show that fires can start this way—"

"They can prove it by burning PSS to the ground. That would be quite a coup." McPherson did not remain to argue further. He remembered to laugh as he left Rountree's office.

Now that the phone was installed, Frank called Anne Bragondette to give her the number where he could be reached when he was away from his PSS office.

"Are you staying with a friend?" Anne asked, unable to hide her anxiety.

"Yes. The phone is listed in the name of Carter Milne. It's in the 408 area code, if you lose the number. Remember to say it's a new number." He wondered how Anne would feel if she knew that Carter was a woman.

"Melinda really misses you, Frank," Anne told him. "She's been asking for you a lot recently. Her teacher called me and said that she's worried about the fires, because she's afraid that you'll be hurt by them."

"It isn't likely," said Frank, thinking about the trouble Carter was having in coming up with a safe way to test her theory.

"I know you're very busy and that your work is important, but I really hope you can see your way clear to getting here for a few days very soon. It would mean so much to Melinda. She wants to see you again, Frank, so she can be sure that her father is still okay." There was real worry in her voice, and it was so unlike Anne that Frank was more concerned than he might have been otherwise.

"Is there something you're not telling me?" he asked his sister-in-law.

"Not really," she said in a resigned way. "We're having more problems than usual. Melinda's psychologist told me that many kids are feeling more apprehensive because of the fires. They see the coverage on the news and they think that they might be next. In Melinda's case, she's worried about you. Right now, that's very bad for her, because she keeps coming back to what happened to Barbara, and nothing we tell her seems to help."

"I ought to talk with her myself, help to reassure her," Frank said, as much to himself as to Anne.

"Pardon my saying so, but you ought to be here to spend some time with her. It's been a long time, Frank, and she has enough worries about being abandoned without this." She made no apology for this outburst. "You belong with your daughter."

"I know that," Frank said.

"And it would help if you could spare her a few days. Never mind the fires, just give your daughter a few days of your time. That's all she's asking right now, a day or two, so she won't be so afraid. I don't want to see her disappointed again."

"Okay, I'll find out if I can take a couple days off. If

they can spare me, I'll get there as soon as possible." He felt angry with Anne, but he knew she did not deserve his anger.

"I won't say anything to Melinda until you're certain you can come. It would make such a difference to her, Frank."

"I understand." He wondered how Melinda would feel about visiting California. Perhaps at Christmas, if everything went right, if the fires were under control, if there were no problems with Carter.

"Frank?" said Anne.

"I'm here. There's a lot on my mind and I was trying to think of the best way to arrange for some time off. I can tell them that Melinda needs to see me. Most of the time they understand such things." He hoped Carter would. Sometimes people without children could not comprehend the bond that parents felt.

"You'll call as soon as you know?"

"Yes, don't worry about that. I'll make sure that we've set up the whole trip before I leave." He knew he would have to talk to Carter that evening. Worried about whether or not her theory would work, she might be upset that he wanted to see Melinda. "Anne, I'll talk to you tomorrow, as soon as I've had a chance to find out how things are out here. If they're willing to let me take a couple days, I'll be there as soon as a plane can get me there. Now, will you let me talk with my daughter?"

J.D. came out of his office, his expression angry and his tone sharp. "I'm getting very tired of Special Agent Simon McPherson. I know he's been concerned about the role the Bureau is playing in the investigation, and he thinks that we ought to be more secret, but, Phylis, he's driving me nuts."

Phylis pushed back from her desk. "Is there anything I can do? I can always say you're not available or that you're in conference and can't be interrupted."

"Tempting, very tempting," he said. "He's against testing Carter's theory, in part because his team didn't think of it. He keeps saying that it isn't safe and it can't possibly work."

"That sounds mutually contradictory," Phylis pointed out with a trace of amusement.

"Don't let that bother you; McPherson doesn't." He ran his hand through his hair. "I think I'll authorize the experiment anyway. He wants to say no to someone, so he can keep his control. We happen to be the easiest target."

"You mean because we have the least respectable theory." This plainly caused Phylis no distress.

"Why not? This is the most anyone's come up with, and that makes it a target." J.D. started back into his office but was stopped by Phylis.

"Frank Vickery wants to talk to you. He wants a few days off to go to Canada—Toronto, I think—to visit his daughter. She's staying with family, I gather."

"Toronto?" J.D. repeated. "What makes him think that we can spare him right now?"

"I don't think he's worried about that. He's concerned about his daughter. Frank's a widower, remember." She waited while J.D. thought about this.

"How long would he be gone?" J.D. asked. "I don't want to run any of these fire experiments without Frank here. He's had the most practical experience and I don't want this experiment compromised."

"Three days?" suggested Phylis. "I said that it would take us at least that long to work out the protocols and he'd be back by the time we started anything concrete."

"Okay, three days, but no more. We can't spare him longer than that." J.D. shook his head. "You're the most persuasive woman I know. I can't help but feel glad that you don't like guys."

"Why?" Phylis said, only mildly interested.

"I don't think I know a single man who could stand up to you and that includes me."

"Coming from you, that's almost a compliment." Phylis indicated the door to J.D.'s office. "You going to be for a while? I want to tell Frank where to find out."

"Sure; why not? I have to get together with Cynthia to go over the legal responsibilities we have testing out this theory. Since we're going to be playing with fire—"

"To coin a phrase," interjected Phylis.

"Yes; to coin a phrase. We've got an obligation and I want to be certain it's all spelled out for the sakes of everyone involved and that includes PSS."

"I'll say this for you, J.D. You do take your responsibilities to heart." She added more briskly, "Shall I ring Frank for you?"

"Go ahead. Why not?"

"And McPherson?"

J.D. made a gesture as if to shoo away a bothersome insect. "I think I'll have to persuade Frank to come to work for us, at least for the time being. That'll get him out from under McPherson and the rest of the bureaucratic logjam. I've already offered him work, and they know it back in Washington."

"They'd insist on sending another member of the Task Force to observe," Phylis warned him.

"So long as it's Sid Rountree, that's fine with me. As usual, you've wrapped it all up for me. Do I pay you enough, Phyl?"

"I wouldn't say no to a raise, if that's what you're hinting at," she said.

"Okay; you work out what you think is reasonable and let me see it. Don't bother padding it; I'm not going to haggle with you." He went back into his office and got ready to have a long, serious chat with Cynthia Harper and with Frank Vickery.

Security at San Jose Airport was more stringent than ever, and Carter pointed out the number of guards who had replaced machines. Many of them held guns.

"They're afraid," said Frank. "That's why it looks like an armed camp. Everyone's worried that they might be next for a fire, and so they do what they can for protection —not that guns will do much against a fire." He handed his bag to a uniformed woman and waited while she opened and inspected it. "Remember, I'll be back in three days, the nine-fifteen flight from Chicago. I'll expect you to pick me up, okay?"

"I'll be here," she promised. "And I'll miss you, Frank."

"Good." He put his arm around her while her purse was examined. "I'll miss you. I'll call you tonight when I get in and before I leave from Chicago. If anything comes up that you think I should know about, give me a call at my sister-in-law's place and tell her that it's urgent."

"You told me that four times already." As they walked toward the gate, Carter asked the one question that had been lingering unspoken between them. "Are you going to tell her about us? Are you going to tell your daughter?"

"I think so. Certainly I'll have to say something to Melinda. I don't know how she'll take it." He indicated a row of uncomfortable-looking plastic chairs.

"Sure," said Carter, sinking into one of them and looking toward the gate where the flight number was posted. "What if she doesn't like the idea of you and me?"

"Well, we'll have to work it out. I'm not going to give you up because she has doubts. But she is my daughter, Carter, and I have to do something to make her understand that you aren't an insult to Barbara's memory." He took a deep breath. "It might mean that if she comes out here with me, I'll have to stay in a motel with her while she's here, until she gets more used to the idea."

"Do you think you'll bring her back with you when you come?"

"I doubt it," Frank said, frowning a bit. "Anne and her psychologist have both said that she ought to finish out the school year where she is, so the earliest would be next summer. Unless I arrange for her to come for Christmas. That's assuming the fires are over and I've still got a job with PSS." He stopped talking as the public address system announced through static that his flight would begin boarding in a few minutes.

"When you get back, you can review the protocols we

come up with for the test. There's bound to be some way that it can be tested. If we get the entire sequence, we'll be fine." She stood with him as he got to his feet.

"Have you noticed? They entirely outlawed smoking in planes since these fires started. Not that I think it's a bad idea, but it won't make any difference if your theory tests out." He grabbed his ticket and boarding pass, leaned over to kiss Carter and started toward the open gate. He looked back and waved, and then he was gone.

Carter stayed long enough to watch the plane take off, for although she did not want to admit it, she was afraid that something might happen to Frank if she could not watch over him.

Sidney Rountree was in need of a shave and his rumpled suit attested to his attempt to sleep on the plane from Washington. He was thin and haggard, and he carried himself like an old man. He recognized Cynthia as she came toward him. "We were delayed in Denver, of all places," he said.

"Three hours," Cynthia agreed. "J.D. would appreciate it if you'd come by his place before I take you to your hotel. He asked me to pick you up so that he'd have his legal staff represented while he explains his position to you. That's for your protection as well as his own so that no one on the Task Force can say that we railroaded you, although that's what J.D.'s apt to want to do."

"And you do work for him, attorney or not," Rountree said, trying to make a quip and failing at it.

"Naturally, but that should make it clear that I'm not going to let my boss put himself at a disadvantage." She indicated the way to the parking lot and asked if he had any more luggage than the garment bag slung over his shoulder.

"This is it. I'm getting good at traveling light." He walked in silence until they were almost at the pickup Cynthia was driving this evening, when he said, "You look as tired as I feel."

"We're all exhausted. And it shows," said Cynthia without any apology. "I've been trying to get an hour for the hairdresser for more than three weeks, and it hasn't happened. I think I'll have to ask for an emergency trim at home one evening." She held the door open for Rountree, then went around to get into the driver's seat. "How's everything with the Task Force?" she asked as they drove out of the lot.

"Terrible. One of our members is popping so many pills he might as well open his own chemistry supply and another one is too tired to think straight. McPherson's still clinging to his conspiracy theory and his terrorists no matter what the evidence indicates to the contrary. And we're getting more and more nut mail all the time. People are so frightened that they want to have their own personal demons responsible for the fires." He had not realized until he heard himself speak how upset he had become in the last two months.

"Sounds about right," Cynthia agreed. They were on Route 280, heading north. "How long do you think it might take to turn them around and get them to listen to this theory that we're getting into order?"

"I don't actually know." He yawned. "I don't mean to be rude, but is there anything to this theory of yours? It looks more like wishful thinking than anything real to me." He saw the hard line of her jaw. "Oh, shit. Look, Cynthia, you're not looking at this from my point of view."

"That makes us even; you're not looking at it from ours." She brought her temper under control. "I don't think you're paying much attention. We could be right—Carter isn't the sort of woman to going off on tangents—and it would seem to me that we're the best chance you've got."

She signaled for a right turn off the scenic freeway. "We had rain this morning and there's supposed to be another storm on its way in; that's a little early for this part of the world, but we can use the water."

Rountree accepted the change of subject. "They say all

the signs are for an early winter. You don't have the weather extremes here that we do back east, but it doesn't change the patterns, does it?"

"Probably not," Cynthia said, feeling less irritated. She drove a few more blocks before saying, "I'm sorry I jumped on you like that. It's because I'm so damned tired. Most of the time I can deal with pressure a little better than this."

"Very tactful, barrister, and I can see why J.D. values you. I hope the head of your legal department is as competent as you are in these matters."

"Now you're resorting to flattery," Cynthia said, but she smiled as she said it. "After this next turn, it's the fourth house on the left, on the knoll."

Rountree nodded appreciatively and watched with anticipation as J.D. Patterson's house came into view.

"I miss you," Carter said to Frank when she heard his voice on the phone.

"I miss you, too. We went to visit friends in Fort Gary today, and they have a Chow. I kept thinking of Winslow and it made missing you worse."

"Even Winslow?" laughed Carter. "Isn't Fort Gary a long way from—"

"Toronto? A fair distance. Barbara's brother lives in Fort Gary." He cleared his throat. "He's a priest, and it isn't often that he travels, so..."

"No joke, but the mountain and Mohammed?" Carter suggested. "Oh, I'll be glad when you get back. We're almost finished with the protocols and I think we've got a reasonably safe way to experiment on the code without too much danger to us. It was that comment about off the planet that did it. We're establishing a double vacuum chamber, one within another, enough oxygen in the first to support a small fire, but not for very long. By containing the whole thing in a second vacuum chamber, we think we can stop any tendency to break out of the initial chamber. Also, the only thing we're likely to lose is one computer, so we'll be using a small one. We'll program it so that the tandem computer is two digits behind the one being tested. That way we won't be taking the kind of risk that might happen if both were running at the same time." She said this all in a rush. Her voice got higher as the words tumbled out of her and by the end of her explanation, she was breathless.

"Show me first thing day after tomorrow," he said. "I'll be headed for Minneapolis tomorrow—"

"I thought it was Chicago," she interrupted.

"I'm taking a later plane and changing in Minneapolis. I'll be getting back at four-ten, just in time to think about dinner. You can choose the place and I'll catch you up on my kid."

"How is she?" Carter had meant to ask about her first thing.

"She's doing pretty well. I don't want to run up the phone bill telling you about it when we can talk tomorrow night. It's going to be okay, I think. It'll take some work, but it's not impossible."

Carter heard the reservations in his tone but decided to ignore them. "That's good news. I want to hear all about it." She stopped. "Cynthia is at a meeting with J.D. and Sidney Rountree. He flew in yesterday and they spent most of this afternoon going over all my research and now they're trying to outline a testing standard that will satisfy the Task Force and the FBI."

"Easier said than done," Frank said, feeling glum.

"They're working on it. I don't know whether or not Rountree believes we're all 'round the bend or not, but he has said that he thinks we ought to test this out, and I gather that's a change from when he arrived."

"That's something, I guess." He made himself express an enthusiasm he did not and could not feel. "If he's convinced, we can get the rest to pay attention, and that ought to be sufficient to win most of them over."

"I hope to God you're right," she said. "I won't keep you, Frank; see you tomorrow, at four-ten, coming in from Minneapolis. Have a safe flight; I love you."

"I love you, Carter. See you tomorrow." He did not realize until he hung up what he had said.

"Is that the lady you told me about?" asked Melinda.

"Yes," said Frank.

"*Do* you love her?" she asked softly.

"Yes, I do," said Frank, vaguely surprised at the strength of his emotions.

"More'n me?" She spoke so quietly that she was almost inaudible.

Frank turned to her, reaching out to hug her. "No. I could never love anyone more than you, Pumpkin. But I love her very much—differently than you and very much."

Nina Foss picked up the telephone and dialed the number of Patterson Security Systems. She tapped her fingers nervously as she waited for her call to be answered. These days she usually left these calls to her assistants, but this time she knew that she had to do the phoning herself, if she wanted to get to Jeremiah Dermott Patterson himself.

When Phylis Dunlap came on the line, she was polite but not impressed. "Is there some number where Mister Patterson can reach you in an hour or so, Miss Foss? I'm afraid he isn't in his office just now and I don't expect him back for another forty-five minutes. He often runs a little late."

"Perhaps if you can tell me where he is, I can reach him there," said Nina who was no longer used to being put off.

"Oh, I don't think I can do that; he has several stops and I don't know for certain where he is likely to be until he returns to the office." Phylis said this smoothly, with the ease of long practice. She knew, in fact, precisely where J.D. was—he had been called to give a provisional identification of Scott Costa's body, which had been discovered that morning. Since his family were not in the area, the police had asked for J.D., as his employer.

"It's really rather urgent that I speak with Mister Patterson," Nina said, deliberately pressuring Phylis. "We want to give fair coverage in our stories, but we need cooperation in order to do this. If he won't speak with me, then we'll have a problem. You understand, I'm certain."

"You mean that if he doesn't answer your questions you will do your best to discredit his work. I understand that, and so will he. If you will let me have a number where you can be reached I will see that he has it as soon as he arrives. I'm afraid that will have to do, Ms. Foss." She kept her tone even and cordial. "Let me recommend that you not put too much pressure on Mister Patterson; he has something of a temper when pressed and these last few weeks has tried it to the limits; I'm sure you understand."

"You can reach me at 714-555-8250. I'll be here for another hour or so and then I have to catch a shuttle back to New York. If he tries, I'm sure he'll reach me before I have to leave. It really is urgent, you understand." She was nastily sweet. "If we don't talk I'll have to use the information I already have on the state of his research, based on what the Task Force has released, and I don't believe that Mister Patterson would appreciate that."

"I'll see that he has your message," said Phylis, and when the phone connection was broken, she added, "What a bitch," in an emotionless way. "God."

"We're getting a longer number sequence to test," Carter told J.D. with excitement. "It's from the research we've done in coordinating records from all the sources that have supplied them. It's a chain of over ten numbers, we're sure of that. No spaces, no zeros, which means that we're looking for a sequence of fifteen numbers most likely."

"How much of a risk was your checking?" J.D. inquired, mildly preoccupied. He was glaring at the notes he had made to himself on his legal-size pad.

"It's easy; there are plenty of sequences with ten

numbers that are used almost daily and nothing has happened to those who have used them. We ran an analysis curve on them and decided that a fifteen-number sequence was probably the best bet. Not many codes are twenty numbers long, and there are enough fifteen-number sequences in the figures we have on hand to make it likely. That narrows our search a great deal, don't you think?"

"It could be," said J.D., then changed his tone to a more aggrieved one. "Did you see the Foss coverage last night? Did you?"

"No," said Carter. "I was working on statistics. But we've all heard about it. I'm sorry she took out after you."

"I returned her call and talked to her; she wanted to know what we were doing, and I tried to give her direct answers without causing any problems for the company, and she made it sound like we were wasting the taxpayers' money, bilking the government, and that our projects were nothing but cynical attempts to profit from tragedy." His outburst was all the more distressing because it was spoken in a reasonable, level tone.

Carter sat and listened, not knowing what to say to restore his confidence in what his company was doing. Finally she said, "Frank'll be back this afternoon and he's going to be on hand tomorrow when we go over the design for the testing facility."

To her amazement, this information seemed to restore some of J.D.'s equilibrium. "Fine. It's good to have him back. I'm relieved that he's decided to take a job with us, at least for the time being. I want him to stay with us if it works out. . . . What do you think?"

"I want it to work out, too," said Carter, almost embarrassed by the question and her answer.

"Good. I'll keep that in mind. If this investigation goes the way I hope it might, we'll all have reason to be proud." He stopped, then confessed, "When you first brought this theory to me, I accepted it because I wanted us to have something—anything—to work on. I could see how much trouble we all had because there was nothing we were able to do, and the frustration and sense of failure were eroding most of what was left of our sense of purpose." He met her eyes reluctantly. "I wanted us to have something to work toward. Do you see? We had to have a project other than cataloguing our failures, and you were the first to come up with an idea. So we took it, not because it made sense or because we thought it might work, but because it was—"

"There?" she finished for him, in part proud that he had been so candid with her and in part infuriated that he had had so little confidence in her work.

"Yes; there. I don't mean to offend you. That's the last thing I want to do. Because, you see, I've come around to thinking that whatever it is you're onto, it looks like you could be right. The more I follow your work, the more sense it makes. I'm a little put off because of the occult aspect of what you've done—it doesn't seem scientific, but the fires don't respond to any of the scientific methods others have tried, and maybe what you're doing can make a difference. Mind you, if it doesn't pan out, that won't bother me as much as it might, because no one has succeeded. If you're right, and we can prove it, you'll never make a house payment again for as long as you work here, and that is a bottom-line promise. I'll give it to you in writing."

"J.D.?" said Carter, perplexed at this outpouring.

"I want to thank you for everything you've done, and for keeping at this no matter what people have said to you and no matter what doubts you may have had." He folded his arms. "I guess that crap that Foss was spouting got to me more than I'd like to think." He cleared his throat. "Coming on top of Scott's suicide, it threw me."

"Poor Scott," Carter murmured. She could think of nothing more to say.

"I didn't know how much pressure he was under. If I had, I'd have insisted that he take a leave of absence and pride be damned." He stood up and began to pace. "His sister arrived this afternoon and she's supposed to take charge of everything. She said that she didn't know what they'd do about burial, since he killed himself. I didn't realize—though I probably should have—that the rest of his family is very strict and old-fashioned Catholic. It's too bad."

"J.D., would you rather put off this talk until tomorrow?" Carter suggested. "It's late and there's no reason to review the protocols until Frank's here. You look like you could use a little rest yourself." She knew she was out of line saying this and ordinarily she would never have done so, but it was clear that J.D. was not concentrating on what they were doing.

"Oh, fuck it, I hadn't meant to dump all that on you. Hell, I didn't want to tell this to Whiting. But you're undoubtedly right. I'm not paying you the kind of attention you deserve. And you're being very patient with me. Tell me the chain of numbers we're going to be checking out."

"Oh." She did not need to consult her notes, having reviewed them so often that she was afraid she could recite them in her sleep. "Five, one, six, nine, four, three, three, six, seven, two, three. When we get the others, we'll let you know."

"Don't take any chances." J.D. picked up the sheets of paper that she had handed to him when she first came in. "I'll go over this, I give you my word, before we confer tomorrow. I might not do it tonight. Part of me would like to go home and get smashed, but I'll probably end up taking a swim, a pill and a very hot bath."

"Sounds great," said Carter, noticing how drawn J.D. was looking. The lines that bracketed his mouth had deepened in the last weeks and his cheeks had sunk.

"Doesn't it?" He shook his head. "Don't worry, Carter; I can manage, I really can. There are days it gets to me more than other days and this was one of them, but I haven't given up yet, and because of what you've done, I don't think it's likely."

"What do you think about the rest of the company?" She had not intended to ask the question, but the words were out before she was aware of them, and she discovered that she wanted to know the answer.

"Can't you tell? The whole feel of the place has

changed in the last few days, thanks to your theory and the chance to make a difference and the tests coming up. You've given us all a shot in the arm when we needed it most."

"Oh," whispered Carter, not able to believe it.

"Don't let it go to your head," recommended J.D. "If this doesn't work, we'll be back at square one, and you can bet that we'll have more trouble."

"Thanks," Carter said brusquely.

"I don't mean to put everything on your shoulders; forget I put it that way, I didn't mean it." He stared out the window. "I make it sound like I expect you to carry the whole thing, and I don't, believe me, I don't."

"But, J.D." she began and then said, "What if this doesn't work after all? You brought it up; that means you've thought about it and you have some idea about what it might mean, don't you?"

"Anyone in my position would," J.D. said, making this as matter-of-fact as he could. "Okay, let's talk about what could happen if your theory doesn't test out. First is that it might point in a related direction and more workable. That's what would be best. If it doesn't work because we can't make the test work, then we have to restructure the experiments to test it; that's not good, but it's not bad. If it just washes out—nothing is proven except that we're wrong and there's no hint of a new direction—then we'll be under pressure. Continuing pressure, like nothing we've had before, and that's going to put intolerable strain on some of the people who work here."

Carter cleared her throat. "Because of me?"

"Not really; because they work for Patterson and Patterson is testing the theory. You're the one who came up with the theory, but now it's Patterson's concern, and all of us are—"

"But this is the direct result of the theory I came up with." She rose. "And no matter what you say, the results will be mine, really, and I'll have to live with it if it doesn't work out." She took a few steps toward the door and then stopped. "Everyone knows that it's my baby. If it doesn't work and it doesn't provide any kind of key, I'll offer my resignation."

"You can offer anything you want; I won't accept it." J.D. gave Carter a narrow look. "We're not here just to back proven winners. We provide industrial security, but that hasn't stopped our clients from being robbed or sabotaged, it's merely reduced the number of incidents and the severity of them, which is what's expected. Think of the number of times that the government has tested theories at enormous cost and they've been wiped out."

"We're not the government," Carter reminded him.

"Thank goodness." J.D. flung up his hands. "Tell you what—let's hold off this discussion until after we've tested the theory and find out where we are in the scheme of things."

"Okay." Carter was more relieved than she wanted to admit.

"And on the positive side, Frank's pal, that William Riddour, or however his last name goes, has done three quite favorable reports on what Patterson and the insurance companies are doing. It might not reach everyone the way the morning news does, but it's balanced and it has impact." He rose and headed toward the door with Carter. "Come on, it's about time for a cup of coffee, wouldn't you say? And you can still get to the airport on time."

Carter allowed herself to be persuaded.

November 5, between Hawaii and San Diego

Captain van Schuyler lowered his binoculars and peered out into the worsening weather. The *Lowell Cassiopia* wallowed in heavy seas as it plowed east by northeast toward the United States and the marketplace for the woolens, leather and suede goods, and in the refrigerated hold, New Zealand lamb.

"What do you think?" the navigator was a generation younger than the Captain, who was over fifty and looked it.

"I don't like the way it feels. It's all wrong." The Captain came from a long line of seafaring men and had grown up on the water. "The wind's wrong and I don't like the color of the water."

"Want me to check for storms ahead? We can plot a course around the worst of it if we take precautions."

Captain van Schuyler disliked the electronic devices the Lowell company had installed on all their ships. He felt it made for sloppy sailors, but he could not deny that there had been fewer losses and better times between ports since the links to the weather satellites had been set up two years before.

"Captain?" Navigator Welsh said when he had no immediate answer. "What do you want me to do?"

He could sense the storm the same way a hunter could sense a prowling animal. "Well, it's out there."

"You want to change course, to go around it?"

"You might as well, Mister Welsh. So long as we have the things, we might as well use them." He recalled the long arguments between his father and grandfather over radar and wondered if he were being as obdurate and unreasonable as his grandfather had been. Was the reason he disliked all the equipment only his resistance to something new.

When Bruce Welsh had finished getting his information about the extent, direction, and speed of the storm, he notified the Captain. "I'm going to send our coordinates ahead to San Diego and our change of course."

"Do you think it's necessary... yes, of course you do, and doubtless the company needs to know what we're doing. All right; relay information and get back anything you can." He lifted his binoculars and gazed out at the brass-green clouds. "They may have some instructions."

It was difficult for Navigator Welsh to conceal his impatience with Captain van Schuyler. Privately he thought that his superior was old-fashioned and indecisive as well as paranoid about anything of later than World War Two vintage. He accepted the instructions as neutrally as he could and went to carry out his orders.

Somewhere in the middle of the verification sequence, the crucial fifteen numbers passed through the air. Both the Lowell office in San Diego, which was on the ninth floor of a glass-and-steel office building, and the *Lowell Cassiopia* far at sea were suddenly and devastatingly invaded by fire.

The office building was a complete loss, and it was never determined how the *Cassiopia* was lost at sea, but it was assumed that it was a victim of the storm that raged through the Pacific in waters west of Baja California.

November 8, Greentrees Farm, Kentucky

Kathleen Runcinan went into the stall, her toolchest in one hand. "I haven't seen a case like this," she told the anxious owners hovering outside the stall door.

"But Collins Bright Marigold... we paid a fortune for her, and now this." The woman was near fifty, she wore too much makeup on her lined features and Kathleen was reasonably certain that the woman had not been in a saddle for more than twenty years. Her husband, a decade older, had weathered his years better, and aside from deep laugh lines, he had the look of a much younger man.

"Look, Doc," said Booth Stirling, "we don't know what's wrong with her, but we aren't in a hurry to have any of our other horses take sick. We don't expect miracles—"

"Oh, yes we do," interrupted Gloria Stirling. "We can't afford any rumors that there is anything the least wrong with our Saddlebreds. There are more than sixty horses here. Do you have any idea the investment they represent?"

"I have an excellent idea," Kathleen said steadily. "Now let me tell you that by the sound of it, whatever is wrong with this mare seems more like a bad reaction to an injection. You can see the site of an injection there, on the base of her neck—it's swollen and oozing fluid." She went down on her knee by the mare, smoothing her neck. "That's what it looks like. Who gave the injection?" She was afraid she knew the answer, but she had to ask.

"Your senior partner," said Booth. "We had Doc Mitchell out for routine vaccinations."

"How long ago?" Kathleen inquired, knowing it would be in the office records."

"Teddy Ward, our head groom, took her temperature. It was one hundred and three at two this afternoon." Gloria said this as an accusation.

"What did he do, other than take her temperature?" asked Kathleen.

"That's about it," said Booth. "He and Brewster, our trainer, suggested we ask for you."

"I see." She had to find out what her senior partner had done to cause the mare to become so ill. "I'm going to take some fluid samples from the infection site, and then I want to find out if there are records of what this mare was given. You've owned her less than five months, haven't you?"

"Yes, just over four," said Gloria. "We had a problem when we bought her, but now she's in foal to Jet Stream."

That would certainly increase the amount of damages the owners could ask, if they decided to pursue the matter, thought Kathleen as she checked the glossy chestnut neck. The mare whimpered, and her breathing got heavier. Her eyes were glazed and her breath smelled almost fishy. "You're sure a sick lady," said Kathleen.

Booth watched her. "We've got records in the office; you can check them if you want."

"Let me see them, will you? I might be able to find out some worthwhile information. I appreciate how cooperative you're being." She had to be polite, for these breeders were some of the most important clients her business dealt with, and the approval or disapproval of the Stirlings of Greentrees Farm could mean the difference between a success and failure as an equine veterinary doctor.

"Mari's a good mare," Booth said with that touch of sentimentality he always revealed for horses, even the most difficult ones. "She's a little high-strung"—Kathleen translated that as meaning that Collins Bright Marigold was crazy as a loon—"but you should see her single-foot. Just like a ballet dancer."

"With any luck, she'll be back on her feet in a little while, and you can show me how well she moves. I tell you, Mister Stirling, I do think that this is some kind of allergic reaction to the vaccines used. If there's anything in her records, we can get to work on it at once. In the meantime, I'm going to give her an antibiotic that will lessen the infection." She knew that as long as she appeared to be doing something, Booth Stirling would suspend his doubts about her.

"Tell me," Gloria asked, showing her lack of confidence in Kathleen, "what do you plan to do if you don't find anything in the records or any history of allergy?"

"First, I'll check with her old vet and see if there was any history of infections or allergies of any kind, and then I'll try to treat what is wrong." Kathleen looked at the mare. "Something has made her sick, and since she can't tell me, I have to use everything I can to make her well again."

"Let me get Brewster. You can find out from him what's in the records."

"Thanks," Kathleen said to Booth, hoping that her irresponsible senior partner had remembered to make a note of the vaccine batches he used, in case there was any pattern of trouble from the pharmaceutical company that made the vaccines.

Brewster was a squat, muscular man who knew more about horses than almost any trainer Kathleen had met. He regarded Kathleen with measured curiosity and said, "She's still running a fever and I'd bet that the infection is getting worse, judging from the sweat on her coat and the way her eyes look. She's delicate; it's the overbreeding."

"Brewster!" objected Gloria Stirling.

"That's what makes her delicate," Brewster insisted, not the least intimidated.

"Brewster's right," Booth said with obvious affection for his overbred mare. "She's a fine lady, and that means she has to have special treatment."

"Look, Doc," said Brewster, "I'll get the batch information and anything else you need. There's a PC in the Farm offices, and you can use it to contact the drug company, if that might make a difference. I wouldn't be surprised if her old vet has records about sensitivity that they... forgot to pass along."

"No one would do that," Gloria said.

"This is horse-trading, Missus Stirling, no matter what else you call it," said Brewster with veiled contempt. "You got a mare with good lines and good papers, who happens to be just a tiny bit allergic to the vaccine for... oh, anything. It's easy to forget to mention that when deciding on a price, since that might lower her market value, which is all that matters to some of the men in this business."

Kathleen's opinion of Brewster went up several notches. She said, "If there's a way to get ahold of her old vet, I'd like to do that."

"I'll make some phone calls for you," said Brewster, and left.

It was almost two hours later that Kathleen was able to break away from the mare to get to the office, and there she found, in a neat, square hand, the number of Collins Bright Marigold's prior vet as well as a copy of the vaccination records. She sat down and began the slow process of phone calls and comparisons.

She was trying to find the records on the batch of rabies vaccine the mare had been given when she was aware that there was a scent of charring on the air. Knowing how much fire could panic horses, she rose, looking for an alarm and hoping that the smoke detectors were in good working order.

A popping noise caught her attention, and she saw that the PC was smoking; in the next instant, it had burst into flame. The smoke alarms blatted and shrilled, and Kathleen rushed toward the door, only to find her path blocked by a sheet of flame. Her fear and anger gave her strength to push toward the door as the flames licked her clothes, and then, as if fed up on the game, fastened on her flesh. As she fell, screaming, she heard the terrified screams of the horses and the shouts of those trying vainly to save them.

November 11, Philadelphia, Pennsylvania

Walter Horne was definitely a Walter; not a Wally or a Walt. He took his work very seriously and he was meticulous in making sure his job ran smoothly, which was not always easy to do, especially in the early morning: he was in charge of traffic control in the commuter train yard. He reported to work at four-thirty every morning, and remained until one in the afternoon. At that time, being methodical and organized, he went to Murphy's Grill where he had either a pastrami sandwich with a bowl of soup or corned beef and cabbage, when it was available. He had been doing this for more than fifteen years and everyone who worked near the yards knew him. They knew also that he was married, that he and his wife had three children, one of whom was seriously retarded, and that Walter was very proud of this afflicted child's limited abilities.

For the last several weeks, Walter had been dissatisfied with the way the new night man was handling the trains, letting them get piled up in a haphazard order that slowed down the orderly progress in the morning. He had even gone so far as to make his dissatisfaction official, which was very unlike Walter. Everyone said that there was bound to be trouble between Cabbot and Horne, and it seemed to be building to a head as the weather grew steadily worse and the commuter trains had narrower margins in their schedules.

"What did Cabbot do last night?" Walter asked Tony

Escobar as he came into the offices located above the train yard where he could see all the tracks.

"He left early; said he had an errand he had to take care of. Me, I think that it had something to do with Martha Roman, but that's just a guess." He winked brashly. Walter did not share the humor of the situation.

"How many trains have come in since then?" Walter asked as he looked around the office as if he expected to see alien invaders in the corners. "How long ago was that?"

"Cabbot was out of here a little before three. I've done what I could since then. I only got here a few minutes before he left, so he didn't have much time to tell me. I've been trying to sort it all out." Tony Escobar liked his work and he had great respect for Walter—though he had thought him a wimp at first—and knew that Cabbot's lackadaisical attitude was driving Walter nuts.

"How much have you got done?" asked Walter, scowling out into the darkness.

"A little. It's... pretty confusing. I don't know how long it will take to get things running smoothly this morning." Escobar thought that he had never seen Walter look more annoyed.

Walter sat down at the large console that showed the location of every train in the yard. "What did that fellow do?"

"I don't know, Walter," Escobar admitted, feeling that he was letting down a man who put great stock in dependability. "I can't figure it out. It looks like he just let them come in any way they liked and never gave a thought to how they'd get out of here."

"You may be right," Walter said as he glared at the board, shaking his head at the disorder he found there. It was bad enough when Cabbot was on duty all night, but leaving early as he did only served to compound the problem. He wished he had the chance to talk to Cabbot right at this minute; he would tell him precisely what he thought of these irresponsible and slipshod methods as well as letting the directors of the company know how much time and money had been lost because Cabbot had decided he needed to get laid.

"Walter?" said Escobar, coming to look over his shoulder. "How bad is it?"

"It's a mess," said Walter without any modification. "I only hope we can make it less chaotic by the time the trains have to roll. Commute starts pretty soon, and we're nowhere near ready for it." He began to work out a switching plan for the yard that would minimize the hassle of getting the trains moving. "We have at the most forty minutes before the demand will get beyond our ability to handle it. That means we have to start the switching right now, and get the sequence adjusted. I want you to take care of the south side of the yard and I'll take the north. See what the status of the trains are and start them moving."

Escobar shrugged. "I'll give it my best shot," he promised, and set to work on the smaller board at the other side of the office.

Walter sat by himself, studying the board for a little time. It was not unlike chess, he thought as he started to work. One move implied the next, and the next. It was a question of the right sequence. Where over sixty trains were involved, the plotting was very complicated, but Walter was determined to do as much as he could. He was also certain that he had to do something about Cabbot. The more he grappled with the confusion, the angrier he got.

Finally he had a sequence established, one that would be a start if not an ending to the movement of the trains—and not a minute too soon, he realized—that would give him a chance to keep up with the schedules if he were lucky.

"Ready?" Escobar asked as he checked the clock. "The first run's got to roll."

"Yeah, let's start. We're going to have to work like hell to keep on top of it."

"You go first." Escobar knew that the north side rolled before the south. He leaned back and lit a cigarette and watched while Walter started the switching. He loved to watch Walter work, for it seemed to him that what his boss

FIRECODE

did was a lot like music—not that he knew too much about music—and the grace of the movement of the trains delighted him.

Because of the cigarette smoke, neither paid much attention to the burning smell. Then the whole board leaped with fire, and the insulation of the wires sizzled. Both men coughed and scrambled, and Escobar made it as far as the door before he collapsed. He caught sight of Walter lying unmoving over the burning board. Below in the train yard, the first collision was already starting.

PART
VIII

November 13, McLean, Virginia

"Do you mean that this witch-doctor solution might work?" Simon McPherson demanded. He was alone in his office but the speaker phone on his desk was holding his attention.

"It looks that way," came Horace Turnbull's amiable growl. "They're going to be testing it tomorrow. The preliminary information indicates there's a very good chance. Little as any of us might like to admit it, this could be the answer."

"Does that mean that a sequence of numbers can actually cause a fire to break out?" McPherson's voice went up almost half an octave.

"It appears that it could," said Turnbull.

"How do we convince the general public of this? And if it checks out, how the hell do we avert panic about numbers?" McPherson was growing infuriated.

"A simple announcement to the press should do the trick, as well as a sensible and reasonable report to the various major companies in the country that might reasonably be in danger from these incursions. You're anticipating an outcry I don't think you're going to get; the country is tired of all these fires and most of the people would welcome a workable solution no matter how outwardly absurd it may be." Turnbull coughed once, more from tact than any feeling in his throat. "If you're troubled about how the Bureau might be seen, you have only to say that you were exploring many areas of investigation and that you support the findings of Patterson Security Systems and congratulate the company for its diligence and success."

McPherson wanted to object but he had one more question to ask. "Is there any... application of this technique we might want to investigate?"

"Do you mean," began Turnbull in a markedly less cordial tone, "you're curious if there might be a way to use this as an offensive weapon?"

"I... I was wondering because once we release the sequence, anyone might use it," said McPherson.

"And the most likely would be us?" Turnbull guessed. "I have been told forever and ever that this government condemns terrorism of any and every kind all over the world and as policy would never practice terrorism. Were you planning to change this? Mister McPherson? Did you have something in mind for this equation?"

"Of course not!" McPherson forced himself to speak with righteous indignation. "Our use of this terrible force is the furthest thing from my mind or from anyone else in government."

"Oh, come now," said Turnbull with exaggerated patience, "how naive do you think I am? Of course some of you are thinking about this. You'd be falling down on the job if you didn't. And you would be worse than criminal if you did not decide never to use this weapon in any way at any time." His voice had become steely. "And in case one of your zealots gets any frisky ideas about using this unofficially, I have written out everything I have learned about this equation and I have included a full report on the research to date and the nature of the fires for arson investigation. I have sent eight copies out to colleagues of mine to release to the press should anything happen to me, my family or any other member of the investigatory team—"

"We don't do that!" barked McPherson.

"Of course you don't. It's always a lone loon, isn't it? Never anyone with connection to any branch of government. Still, if any terrorism of this sort crops up elsewhere, my colleagues will blow the whistle. Oh, they are not all in this country. And I included very specific instructions. These colleagues are quite trustworthy and respected in their various disciplines—oh, yes, I have not limited myself to physics—and they will not hesitate to act." The purpose was strong in his voice. "I mention this to you so that you can pass it on to some of the more . . . determined members of your profession who might not be as . . . prudent as you are."

"You're paranoid," McPherson scoffed.

"Then none of us have a thing to worry about and my documents will moulder in safe-deposit boxes," said Turnbull, then added, "Keep in touch; we'll know the results on the tests by tomorrow night, and then we can discuss the next step, can't we?"

McPherson listened to the empty line for the better part of a minute, hating the fact that he had been hung up on. One of the worst things about Turnbull, he thought, was his knack for getting the last word. Then he broke the connection and began a necessary and unpleasant duty. He dialed a number that few people possessed and that not even his secretary was allowed access to, and waited for the required four rings. "Hello," he said to the curt answer. "This is McPherson. You'd better hold off on those plans."

"Why?" asked the voice.

Reluctantly, McPherson outlined all that Horace Turnbull had told him.

Frank watched Carter's face in the bathroom mirror. "You nervous?"

"Aren't you?" She was brushing her teeth and there was foam on her lips.

"Keep that up, and you won't have any teeth left by the time you're forty." He came up behind her and kissed her on the nape of the neck. "It'll be all right," he assured her.

"If it's not, I told J.D. I'd quit." She said this very quietly and her eyes flicked away from his in the mirror.

"You won't have to; for one thing, no matter what happens, J.D. won't let you quit. You've done too much work for him." He went and got her bathrobe and pulled the towel she was wearing aside.

"You mean his pride would keep me on?" She turned and looked him square in the face. "Is that it?"

"He has a very strong sense of loyalty. You've delivered and he feels under obligation to you. Don't fault him for that, Carter. It's really one of the nicest things about him." He kissed her and then moved back from her. "Come on, let's get dressed and head for PSS. You won't stop feeling jumpy until you see how the test goes."

"You're right," she said. "I want to hide under the bed, too, almost as much as I want to get this test over with."

"I think using the two computers to monitor was a great idea," he told her as he watched her dress. "It does cut down the chance for another fire."

"It seemed sensible," she said distantly. She was searching for her shoes and buttoning her blouse. "Have you seen my tweed jacket?"

"In the closet, right where you put it day before yesterday," said Frank. "We can get breakfast in Los Gatos, can't we?"

"I don't think I can eat a thing," said Carter as she stepped into her shoes.

"You'd be surprised. I used to think that, when there were official functions to attend. And then I found out that I was more hungry then than at any other time." He got her jacket for her and held it as she slipped it on. "You look very good, Doctor Milne. And I can't for the life of me figure out what a pretty, brainy lady like you sees in a fireman like me."

He had asked it teasingly but she answered it without a trace of bantering. "I see warmth and kindness and friendship and love; I see insight and compassion and caring." She kissed him.

Another time her candor might have disturbed him, but now he grinned. "Okay; I figure you've got brains enough to know what you want."

"It took me a while to figure it out," she said. "But, oh, Frank, thank you for being there when I came to my senses."

When Sidney Rountree reached his office, he found a message from Horace Turnbull to call him, with three different phone numbers and the note that it was urgent. Rountree sighed and wished he was feckless enough to hold off on the call until he had had his cup of coffee and read the first three pages of the *Times*. Reluctantly he called the first number on the list and was told that Professor Turnbull was at the second number. With gentle resignation, the Fire Marshal called the number and waited while a graduate assistant went to bring Turnbull to the phone.

"Horace, this is Sid; you wanted to talk to me."

"Oh, yes; I'm glad you called. Do you mind if I transfer the call to my office? I have some figures I'll need at hand."

Rountree sensed trouble, and had to hold himself in check while he waited for Turnbull to gain some privacy. He found that he was hoping the line was secure; when had that happened? Secure lines were things in spy novels.

"Sid?" said Horace.

"What is it? What's happened?"

"I'm not sure, but I think we have a serious problem developing. I think that some of our pals have to all intents and purposes gone over to the other side—but they don't see it that way, of course."

"How do you mean?" asked Rountree, fighting the coldness that had gathered in his chest.

"I had a very disturbing conversation a little while ago,

and I think you'd better know about it." For the next ten minutes, he explained the conversation he had had with Simon McPherson and his own contingency plans. "What is crucial here is how the tests turn out, how PSS gets this theory of theirs to work. If I were you, I'd get in contact with them immediately and ask to be kept informed of every stage of the testing, how it goes, and what the results are, otherwise we might find a lid has been clapped on the whole thing."

"But we're the Task Force, this is our baby." Rountree wanted to believe that Turnbull was being alarmist, but that nagging cold that spread through him warned him otherwise.

"Just let Patterson be right and you know damned well that this could lead to a potential weapon that would be unspeakably effective, and that means a total blackout on information of any kind about the fires."

"But that would mean the fires would continue," Rountree pointed out. "And what would the press have to say?"

"Not as much as you might think; coverage of the fires is decreasing all the time, and it could become one of those acceptable hazards, like the freeway death statistics or the problems with toxic dump sites." He cleared his throat. "Rountree, I serve on nine separate commissions about such things as hazardous wastes, nuclear power, and all the rest. We make our reports, and many of them indicate dangers so serious the link of cigarettes to lung cancer looks tenuous by comparison. Do these reports get any attention? No. Why not? Because there is a lid put on them, since they don't reflect favorably on this or that agency of the government. And don't kid yourself, Rountree, the government is in business to perpetuate itself and nothing else."

"But what's the point of stopping this?" Rountree was more baffled than he wanted to admit. "It's not as if we're—"

"Look, this fire thing is the stuff that terrorism is made of. Officially we do not approve of terrorism and we like to point a righteous finger at those who do. But the fact remains that we play the same rough game that the others do, only we're not willing to be the bad guys to the public."

"Turnbull, don't you think that you may be overreacting? The strain of the last weeks—"

"Bullshit. I'm trying to give you a warning, Rountree, and I'm telling you that you'd better take charge right now, make sure that there is plenty of coverage of this test and plenty of explanations. Otherwise we'll all have inadvertently added another hideous weapon in our clandestine arsenal." Turnbull sounded more world-weary than angry, and for that reason was more convincing than he might have been otherwise.

"Okay, I'll call Frank and tell him to make sure there's press there. He won't like it; they're worried about what happens if it doesn't work out."

"I, for one, would heave a sigh of relief," said Turnbull.

"Turnbull, I don't say you're right, and I won't say that I agree with you, but I'll pass on the warning. What PSS does about it is up to them. Do you agree?"

"Possibly, if they haven't had orders already."

"Come on, this isn't a James Bond script, or one of those end-of-the-world thrillers." His stomach hurt and he wished he knew where he'd put the tablets his doctor had prescribed.

"No, this is real," said Turnbull. "Make that call, Rountree. A little embarrassment if it doesn't work is better than having this turned into something unthinkable."

"I'll call," he promised, and was relieved to be able to say good-bye to the massive Bostonian.

Although he wanted to have a few minutes to himself to digest this latest information, Rountree had said he would call, so he picked up the phone and dialed PSS.

"Is Patterson there? This is Sid Rountree," he said, and had the oddest notion that there was someone on the line. He attributed the sound to the long-distance relays, but he was nervous and it still bothered him.

"Just a minute, I'll connect you. Mister Patterson arrived about fifteen minutes ago. He's still in his office."

This gentle reminder of the time difference from East to West Coast was taken in the spirit that it was given.

"Thanks. I'm glad I caught him before they started their tests." He waited, and then heard J.D. Patterson greet him.

"I hope we can call you in a couple of hours with good news," said J.D., doing his best to keep his enthusiasm in check.

"Look, J.D.," said Rountree, "I've just had a very disturbing call from Horace Turnbull. I want you to listen to what I have to say." He took less than five minutes to outline what the physicist had said to him. "Anyway, little as I like to think it, there might be something to his worries, and for that reason, I'd suggest you do as he recommends and have a member of the press there, someone who can be counted upon to use good judgment about what and how the tests are represented to do."

"I'll ask Frank if that black reporter from Lansing is still in town. He seems to have pretty good sense, and he respects Frank; I don't think he'd go out of his way to make things difficult for him." J.D. did not seem as disbelieving as Rountree had thought he would be, and he said so. "It's the years in Naval Intelligence. There were always some yahoos who wanted to get out there and settle everything once and for all, cost and lives be damned. This is probably more of the same."

"You mean you think it could happen?" Rountree said, and the cold in his gut became suddenly worse.

"Well, it's not completely impossible," said J.D. in a measured way. "It all depends on where the buck stops. It's something to think about. I appreciate the warning. We can do our best to make sure it's okay at this end."

"Fine," Rountree said dully. "Glad to be of help."

"I'll call you back when we know what the results are," said J.D. "We should know by the time you're getting ready to go home. Maybe before then, if Carter's called it right all down the line."

"I hope she has," said Rountree, his mind working very slowly. He wondered if he had finally got in over his head. Maybe he ought to take a few days off, as his physician had suggested. Maybe it was time for him to get away.

"Hey, great," said William when Frank called him less than half an hour later. "Yeah, I can get there pretty fast." He could not quite believe his luck.

"Okay; we'll have a pass and a secretary waiting and they'll hold off the first test until you get here. We've got three Fire Marshals attending the tests and two insurance investigators as well as most of the staff who've been on the assignment."

"Good, I'll need names and all that, but we can do that later. I'm going to bring my notepads and if it's allowed, my tape recorder. Can you clear that for me?"

"Sure. Consider it done." Frank knew that there would be videotaping for the whole test and that one more piece of equipment should make no difference.

As soon as he hung up, William let out a whoop and hurriedly gathered up his material and rushed toward the door of his room, almost forgetting the key in his rush.

He drove quickly, right at the edge of the speed limit, and once he arrived at PSS, he rushed into the reception area of the atrium and identified himself to the guard on duty.

"Just a minute," said the guard and called for his contact.

William was surprised when he saw Phylis Dunlap coming out of the elevator, a visitor's badge in her hand. "Mister Ridour, how good of you to come on short notice." She was, as always, self-possessed and unflappable.

"We're in the next building, in the development labs. We're set to begin shortly." She led the way through the halls and out along a winding path into the largest and least-windowed of the PSS buildings. "We're on the third floor," she explained as she ushered him into the elevator.

William tried to conceal his excitement. He had to keep reminding himself that there was a good chance that the whole experiment could fail, and if it did, then there would be another search for the cause of the fires, and this time more of the investigators would be disheartened.

"Good morning, Mister Ridour," said J.D. Patterson, coming to welcome him to the testing facilities. "When we're done here, I hope you'll join us for a celebration."

"You're sure that's what it'll be?" asked Carter, looking very nervous as she stood beside one of three computers set up in room. The largest was enclosed within what appeared to be a double half-egg made of glass or plastic.

"I'm sure that we'll be celebrating something," said J.D. loudly enough that the dozen people in the room heard him plainly.

William gave him full points for tact and diplomacy. If the test was successful he would mention the encouragement and support J.D. provided; if it failed, he would find a way to show that J.D. had faith in his staff. "I'll be proud to do that. I'll take it as a personal honor."

Dave Fisher was at one of the consoles on the outside of the egg and Carter was at the other. Two technicians were with them, and they were making a number of last-minute checks.

Frank Vickery was with a blocky man in a fireman's uniform who was examining the sealing on the eggs. He came at last to J.D.'s side. "Yeah, Coppard said that the seals meet his standards. He isn't sure how much tolerance something like this requires, but he's certain that this is up to more strain than most of the vacuum setups he's seen."

"What do you think?" asked J.D., adding, "Remember that we go up in smoke if you're wrong."

"I think that it's going to work, smoke or no smoke, and I think that the seals, since it's a double chamber, will hold. I wouldn't trust a single chamber." Frank looked at William. "I hope you know we can't promise absolute safety."

"Understood," said William, and found it hard to swallow. He wished he could think of some kind of joke that would put them all at ease, but it escaped him.

"Let me explain what we've done," said Carter in a clear, loud voice. "That's so you'll know what is supposed to happen, as opposed to what is not supposed to happen." She waited while all the people in the room fell silent. "We have two computers set up out here, and one in the vacuum shell. That barrier of vacuum is for our protection, I hope, if the theory turns out to be right. To express the idea as succinctly as possible, it appears that there is a sequence of numbers that are able to generate spontaneous combustion. We believe that the sequence is fifteen numbers long and that it has no spaces or zeros in it. We've come across account numbers and similar codes that fall into this pattern, and those are the ones we'll run first. This computer here"—she indicated the nearest one—"will run the first five numbers, the second will run the next five numbers, and the computer inside the vacuum shell will run the last five, going through numerical patterns until it has used all possible combinations or until the inner chamber, which is only partially a vacuum, shows fire. That's what we're trying to do. We will also be able to run all sequences and combinations of numbers, if the first sets are not accurate." She had been speaking faster and faster, and now forced herself to slow down. "We'll keep testing until all the possible sequences and combinations have been exhausted before we abandon this area of inquiry."

"The method is unorthodox," J.D. said, picking up from her, "but since orthodox methods have failed, we believe that it is sensible to try this, if only to eliminate it as a possibility." He looked over the people gathered around him. "You've all worked long and hard on this project, spending many more hours than your records show trying to unravel this mystery, and you have all been under more pressure than this company has ever experienced. And all of you have been touched in some way by these dreadful fires. All of you have lost someone you loved and valued to the fires. That's a very high price to pay for ignorance, and your dedication is a credit to your care. I want to thank every one of you for what you've done." He made a point of making direct eye contact with everyone in the room, including William.

"When do you want to get started?" asked Dave Fisher

with an anxious look at his watch. He had taken two pills half an hour ago but they had not made much difference in his taut-strung nerves.

"There's no time like the present," said J.D. affably. "Go ahead; start the test."

The first computer hummed and the technician tapped onto the screen:

51694

"What made you choose that series of numbers?" asked William, directing his question to Frank.

Carter answered, "It fits the curve. The sequence is on the records of every company that had a fire that we know of."

The second computer came to life:

33672

"Let me guess," said William with a quizzical glance at Carter. "It fits the curve."

She made an edgy gesture. "Now it's up to the computer in the shell."

"What do you think will happen?" asked William, hoping that they might actually have stumbled on the solution.

"I don't know," she admitted very softly.

The machines continued to run, and those standing around the double shell did everything they could to conceal or disguise their tension. Even Phylis, normally cool under the greatest stress, started to suck on cough drops.

"Is it okay to smoke in here?" asked one of the computer technicians.

"No," said J.D.

Gradually even this desultory talk stopped; now they stood silently, waiting for something to happen, each aware that if they were right, and their precautions were not adequate, they would realize their success as they burned to death.

The numbers flashed on the screen of the enclosed computer, like a series of secret addresses.

More than ten minutes had gone by—and the room seemed to ring like an invisible gong with the pressure of waiting—before there was a quiver in the vacuum chamber, and a bright feather appeared at the back of the monitor where the cable attached to the electrical power.

"Oh, my God," one of the technicians whispered.

The feather expanded, flared, grew, now becoming a small banner of flame. It flapped against the computer terminal, growing larger again, and those who stood watching, all but mesmerized, started to grow frightened.

"We got fire engines standing by," Coppard announced, not quite as calmly as he would have liked.

The flame fingered the computer greedily, and the plastic began to surrender to the caress as the monitor visibly drooped.

"If this gets any larger, perhaps we'd better leave the building," J.D. suggested, staring at the flame.

Finally the low oxygen content did its work, and the fire shrank and faltered, sagging against the machine as if seeking support before it withered away.

It was very silent in the room.

Then Frank let out a whoop and the others joined, giddy with victory and relief.

Coppard was making a lavish third toast when William managed to pull J.D. aside.

"What is it?" J.D. asked, showing more goodwill and bonhomie than he usually expended.

"I want to know when I can file the story," he said, coming directly to the point. "Am I going to have any trouble with this exclusive, and is the FBI going to try to stop me?"

"Hey, hold up there," J.D. said, holding up one hand to stop William's torrent of questions. "So far as I know, there isn't a real story yet in any case."

"What do you mean, no real story? You just demonstrated that you've found the key to the fires, and—"

J.D. cut William short. "We found what *may* be *a* key,

not necessarily the only key, and not necessarily an infallible method of calling up one of the fires." He looked around the room and gestured to Carter to join him. "Besides, this is Carter's doing."

Carter, flushed with satisfaction and Schramsburg, smiled warmly at William. "With a lot of help and a tremendous amount of luck," she said and put her arm around J.D.'s waist, something she had never done before and would not be likely to do again.

"Help is good sense; luck is luck," said J.D.

"So, how much of this are you going to let me print?" William pursued.

"Print?" Carter repeated.

"I'm a reporter, remember, and it's my job," William said with an apologetic grin.

"That's not for me to say," she began, but as he started to speak, she went on. "It doesn't seem sensible to me to release anything yet."

"How do you mean?" William asked, doing his best to remain polite.

"Well, we've only got the most preliminary results and it could be that there are problems we don't understand yet. To release any information prematurely could cause more problems than what we've already encountered." She set her champagne glass aside. "For all we know, there are those who might try to test out this demonstration for themselves and in doing it, cause another fire. And there are those who would want to see for themselves that the method works and then..." She shrugged.

"Don't you think that's a little extreme?" William suggested, looking to J.D. for support.

Carter was the one who responded. "Look, if you think that I'm overestimating the problem, you haven't thought about it; I haven't done anything *but* think about it for months. If this code really works, then we'll test it out. Once we have the code demonstrated, then we'll have to make up our minds how to handle it."

"Feisty, isn't she?" J.D. said proudly.

"Think about my position, Doctor Milne," William said. "I have an obligation to report this. What you've done can effect the safety of millions of Americans."

"But this is still in the developmental stage," Carter protested.

"She has a point, Ridour," J.D. said, some sternness coming into his courteous expression. "What you've said about your obligation is true as far as it goes, but how would you feel if you released this information and a flock of new fires broke out because of it, because a hacker had to find out for himself if his computer could get the right code, or because someone was mad at his boss or his doctor or his relatives and found a way to feed the code into their bank accounts or telephones or God knows what else?"

"And think what it might do if people knew what to avoid," William said with asperity.

"As far as we know," J.D. said, "we have to assume that this works very well, but we don't know if it's repeatable. It may be that the number has to change in some minor way each time. There may be not one code, but a sequence of codes." J.D. looked to Carter for support.

"From what I've read," she said carefully, "there's just the one sequence of numbers for fires, but there are other sequences to summon other... manifestations." She faltered, then went on. "If that's the case, I think we'd better tread very carefully."

William nodded, but said, "You know, you can't keep me from reporting this. I have the First Amendment to stand on."

"Yes," J.D. said seriously. "And if it came to that, we aren't going to stand in your way. But give us a little time, won't you? Let us have a chance to check this out and come up with a way that will satisfy both you and everyone else involved." He signaled for the champagne. "If this tests out, you won't lose much by waiting a couple of days to file. And in the meantime, you can say that you're watching a series of experiments that look promising, if you wish."

"Big of you," William said, adding, "I'll be calling my paper this evening."

Carter stepped away from J.D. and put her hand on William's arm. "Please, don't be hasty. I know everyone wants a magic solution, and I know . . . it's hard to wait for an answer, but if you let us have a little time—"

"A stay of execution?" suggested William.

"Yes," Carter said, very somberly. "Until we can be certain that our methods will contain the fires, and until we can rule out any number sequences but one in particular, it might be best for everyone to hold off." She stared at him. "William, think about what might happen. We've had enough suffering already."

"But we could have more," he said, more firmly. "And that's what I want to prevent."

"So do we all," J.D. agreed.

"Please," Carter said to William. "Let us have the time to make sure. So that we can spare everyone false hope or . . . worse risks than we face already. We have to establish that there is one and only one way to summon these fires, and then find a way to keep it from happening ever again."

William nodded slowly. "I'll wait two days, and if you've got some sign of progress, we'll talk again." It was the most he was prepared to offer.

"Great," J.D. said, visibly relieved.

"Thank you," Carter told him before turning to accept a third glass of champagne.

"The claims of Patterson Security Systems are being checked now by scientific teams at MIT and the NSA," said Nina Foss with all the earnestness she could muster. "Patterson Security Systems announced yesterday afternoon that after extensive testing they have worked out the source of the unexplainable and tragic fires that have plagued the country and parts of Canada and Mexico for the last several weeks. Should this procedure indeed turn out to be the key plans will soon be under way to stop or control these fires more reliably than has previously been the case." She did her best not to sound sour, but she was annoyed that the end of the fires should be so anticlimactic. She had wanted at least a major international confrontation out of them, perhaps the result of an admission from the Russians or Iranians or Chinese or Libyans or South Africans that they had come up with a marvelous and undetectable weapon that they could use to demand ransom from the U.S., Europe or any other country they chose. She had fantasized the role she would play in such a confrontation and the subsequent negotiations, and she was still upset that she might be deprived of the opportunity she had imagined for herself.

On the screen, the smoothest of the Presidential advisers fielded questions from a roomful of excited reporters.

"I'm sorry, gentlemen; that's all I can say for the time being. We really don't know any more, and we want to stress at this time that until the experiments are confirmed, we will not be in a position to act in any way."

"Mister Smith," a reporter in the first row demanded, "is there any truth to the rumor that this is merely a stopgap attempt to quell panic?"

"The President has too much respect for the tenacity and determination of the American people to do such a cynical thing."

Another reporter made himself heard. "What role has the government played in this? How much help and funding was provided?"

"The Fire Marshals' Task Force has administered their funds and allocated them according to their judgment," Smith dodged expertly.

"But wouldn't you agree that Patterson has been regarded as a maverick in the fire investigation?" demanded a loud-voiced woman with a strong Texas accent.

"Patterson Security Systems is an independent, private-sector company and is not expected to act in the same way as government agencies. If this is seen as being a maverick, then there's perhaps some misunderstanding about the nature of the relationship between the private sector and the government." Smith gave his stern-but-friendly expression. "Patterson has pursued the same goals as all other investigators working on the problem—to find the cause of these terrible fires and put a stop to them."

There was a mad clamor, but Smith had had enough. He held up his hand and indicated that he had to attend another meeting and was already late.

"Mister Smith, what do you see as the most important development in this latest discovery?" This was the reporter from *Newsweek* and he had a moral advantage over some of the others, since one of the main offices of his magazine had been gutted by fire less than a month ago.

"That depends on whether it tests out or not. Assuming it does, then we have the means to control the incidents of fire, and that, you will agree, is of primary importance." It was more of a description than an assessment, but he knew it was enough to satisfy the reporters until he had something more concrete to offer them.

"Mister Smith—"

"I am late, gentlemen. Thank you for your attention." He made good his escape and hurried to the door, signaling his escort.

"Little as I like to admit it," Horace Turnbull said to Sid Rountree not long before lunch the next day, "the Patterson people appear to have it. We've run their experiment here and the results are just as described. These fires start with a specific sequence of numbers. Apparently that is the only workable sequence; we've tried the full range of variations on the fifteen-digit sequence. I suppose we ought to think ourselves lucky in that there is only one sequence that has this effect." His voice was rough with fatigue and when he attempted to laugh, he coughed instead.

Rountree, who had caught the shuttle flight to Boston, was still mildly dazed by what he had been shown. "So it's just a matter of fifteen numbers? Nothing more than that?" He shook his head. "That's what this was all about? Just that?"

"Surely you were told?" Turnbull said, making it sound almost insulting.

"I was told, but . . . I didn't—"

"Believe it?" Turnbull prompted. "I share your reaction, but pragmatism requires that we acknowledge the validity of the results and accept that ridiculous as it may be, those numbers in that specific order, create fires."

"All right, I accept it, but I still . . . Horace, how does it work? What makes it work?"

"That is apt to keep me and a good number of my colleages busy for some time to come." Turnbull found his pipe and made a great production of loading it and getting it started. "There was something very unsettling about the tests. Watching that fire start out of nothing, for no reason other than that it had been . . . summoned."

"You're starting to sound mystical," Rountree chided him.

"Have you read any theoretical physics? There are times that they look more like philosophy or even theology than physics. Science doesn't have the hard edges we'd like it to have, Sid. It is often difficult to get a workable definition of any phenomenon that satisfies science. In this case, we must accept that there is some property in this series of numbers that when transmitted electronically brings about spontaneous combustion. Whether you or I like it, whether science provides for it, we have proof that it happens, and that, as they say, is that."

Rountree rubbed his face. "I hope you figure out why. I wouldn't want this to happen again."

Turnbull smoked in silence, staring fixedly into the wraiths of smoke. "You know, I had a talk with Milne—that statistician at Patterson who came up with this whole notion. She admitted that she originally got the notion from some obscure occult texts she found in the attic of her new house. She's concerned that there may be similar sequences of numbers that might influence other phenomena. She said that it made very little sense in terms of science, but she had the feeling that this would indicate that it might be wise to experiment in other areas."

"Come on," said Rountree in disgust.

"I'm not sure that I don't agree with her. She's been right so far. And I'd rather find out that we're wrong than attempt to deal with other disasters." He squirmed around to face Rountree. "Don't you agree?"

Rountree got up and paced down the cluttered office. "It sounds absurd," he said. "It sounds like something out of a grade-B movie. It sounds like the worst kind of sloppy thinking."

"So it does. But the fact of the matter remains, fifteen numbers in the right—or wrong—order will burn your house down."

"Don't you think we ought to find out how to get rid of this thing first, before we tackle any other possible problems?" Rountree stopped by the window and looked out into the sleety drizzle.

"I'm not sure we can get rid of it. That's one of the reasons I think we ought to check it out, if nothing else." Turnbull heaved a massive sigh. "Whatever the case, I don't think we can afford to neglect any possibility, not after what we've already experienced."

"Does that mean that you want to present a united front? Is that what this talk is all about?" Rountree folded his arms.

"Not precisely," said Turnbull. "You understand that this may not gain much public acceptance. They will want to forget the fires, put the whole thing behind them."

"But why do we have to set up a project? Don't you think that Congress will want to continue the investigation?"

"No," said Turnbull. "Not unless we're willing to turn over everything we learn to the military, and I for one could not have that on my conscience." He waited while Rountree continued to pace. "You know that this is a possibility, don't you?"

"I see your point, but I think you're borrowing trouble and we still have plenty on our plate as it is. I'm willing to suggest that we establish guidelines as part of the Task

Force's operation but I don't think that it would serve any purpose to require that certain actions be undertaken, not yet."

"If we don't do it right now, we may never have the opportunity. Don't argue about this with me; think it over and we'll talk again in a day or so. Humor me, Sid."

Rountree gave him a searching look. "You've done more with those clowns than I have, and you know more about the way they think and how they operate. Okay. I'll suggest to the Task Force that we make stringent guidelines in this, and that we make sure that there are means of access for getting the resultant information. Since it is still in our laps, we have that power."

"For a while," cautioned Turnbull. "I'll be glad when this is over. I promised my wife we'd take our two oldest grandchildren to Scotland for ten days, and even in the winter, that sounds like fun."

So Horace Turnbull was a man with the usual kind of family. Rountree thought that very astonishing, for he had always assumed that Turnbull was just...a physicist, a man living and working at the university, dedicated to thought and teaching and very little else. Rountree tried not to gawk. "I know the feeling," he was able to say.

"We lost family in that fire in New York, and you can understand why Hannah wants to take time for those who are living. After all, as she keeps reminding me, we're not going to last forever." He sighed. "If only I could be easy in my mind about what the feds might do. If I was convinced that none of this would be abused, I'd make reservations for Edinburgh tomorrow, but I have this nagging sense that unless we get rid of this thing completely, we'll be haunted by it forever."

"The Task Force has authority to make sure there's no abuse of the information we've gained."

"For the time being," Turnbull warned him.

As much as Rountree wanted to dismiss the professor's worries, he could not think how to do it. "I suppose so."

* * *

Nina Foss waited while she was transferred within the phone system of PSS, spending the anxiety-ridden minutes in nibbling the bright red polish off her tipped nails. She had not bitten her fingernails since she was ten, but now it was more and more difficult to resist them, and when she had resorted to tips to keeping them acceptably long and shiny, she had sensed an inner failure that puzzled and frightened her.

"Miss Foss?" said a crisp woman's voice on the end of the line, very clear for a cross-country call.

"Doctor Milne." Nina was at her most cordial, pouring on her charm like hot fudge on ice cream.

"No; this is Cynthia Harper of the legal department of Patterson Security Systems." The tone was less receptive than it had been a moment ago.

"I was waiting to speak with Doctor Milne. As you can imagine, there are a number of questions I'd like to ask her." She had the list of them written on her pad in front of her.

"I'm sorry, Miss Foss. Doctor Milne is not at liberty to discuss the recent tests carried out here. If you wish an official press release, the Fire Marshal's Task Force has issued one, and I'm certain they'd be willing to answer your questions." Cynthia resisted the urge to tell Nina Foss what she thought of her ambulance-chasing journalism.

"Oh, come, Ms. . . . Harker?"

"Harper," corrected Cynthia. "Missus, actually."

"How quaint," said Nina, and could have bitten her tongue a second later for this lapse.

"You may wish to speak with our man in charge of operations. He can tell you what the current position of the Task Force is on the experiments we've been running." Cynthia kept her temper by a major effort of will. Alienating a woman who appeared on a national news program every morning, no matter how satisfying, might ultimately work against her and her company as well as her friend.

"I want to speak to Doctor Milne," Nina persisted. "And barring that, to whoever ran the experiments."

"That's not possible," Cynthia told her.

Nina gnawed more of her nail polish. "All right, is it possible to make an appointment to speak with Doctor Milne?"

"I'm sorry, not at present, no."

"I see. I suppose I ought to call William Ridour. It seems he's the only journalist to gain your favor. Maybe I should ask him what his trick is." This was meant to be nasty.

"He's given fair coverage and he's been concerned mainly with experiments in prevention and research instead of the fires themselves." She had been told to take this line, and although she felt it was not really adequate, she held to it, as instructed. In fact, she had doubts about the exclusive coverage they had granted William, but she understood the wisdom of the decision, and never more than now with Nina Foss on the line.

"When do you think I might be able to arrange some sort of interview with Doctor Milne?" Nina inquired, less pleasantly than ever.

What Cynthia wanted to say was "when hell freezes over," but she answered, with only a slight hesitation, "Doctor Milne will be available for comment when the Task Force has indicated the results of its tests and come to a recommendation about what is to be done next."

Against all her training and better judgment, Nina slammed the phone down, and then, all training aside, pulled one of the expensive tips off her nail with her teeth. She was still seething when the door to her luxurious corner office opened and Lenny came into the room.

"Don't want to disturb you, Nina, but we got to have a talk." His expression was earnest and it surprised Nina that he sounded worried about her.

"What is it?"

"I know you don't want to, but you have to slow down, honey. You're wearing yourself ragged. And I don't mean that mess you've made of your manicure. This morning there were circles under your eyes and if you think makeup will take care of them, you're kidding yourself." He had taken one of the chrome-and-leather chairs and was lounging in it because it forced him to.

"I didn't know you cared," Nina said flippantly.

"You're my meal ticket and I'm yours. I can film you anywhere and with anyone, but you got to help me, Nina. You can't go on running yourself into the ground, not if you and I are going to last for the long haul. I don't know about you these days, but that's what I want. If it's still what you want, we have to talk."

What had she been expecting, she asked herself. A declaration of undying passion? As unexpected tears stung her eyes, she recognized that part of her had always assumed Lenny's devotion sprang from unacknowledged adoration. It galled her to know that he was so formidably pragmatic. Then her good sense and ambition exerted themselves and she took a deep breath. "You're right. I have been getting carried away with this fire thing. I ought to ration myself a little better."

"Good you think so," Lenny said with a nod. "Now, I think it might be a good idea if we have dinner tonight and work out a long-term strategy for you, so that they won't want to kick you back downstairs when the fires come to an end—which seems to be coming up. Think about spiking their guns; you could do a series of special reports on women who were given the shaft at work because of age. You do two or three of those, and they won't dare let you go for at least a year, and by then, we can build up a following that will keep you on top. And me along with you." He smiled at her. "What do you think? Does it sound good?"

In spite of the last pangs of disappointment, Nina had to admit that Lenny had made several good points. "Dinner sounds good. Not too late, though, since I've got to be up so early."

"Right," Lenny agreed with a toothy smile. "What say I meet you in the lobby at five-thirty?" He did not wait for an answer as he hoisted himself out of the chair. "Also, it's time we thought about finding the right man for you. A few words in the gossip columns about now wouldn't hurt, especially if the man has some headlines already attached to him. We'll discuss that, too." With a vague wave, he ambled out of her office.

Nina sat and stared at the little pile of nail tips on the polished surface of her desk.

From his office, J.D. Patterson could see the traffic on the distant expressway moving at a slow crawl as the drizzle slowly changed to rain. He held the receiver close to his ear and listened to the computer-generated ersatz Bach that had been bleating for well over three minutes. His patience was wearing thin, but he did what he could to contain it by doodling on the yellow pad by his elbow and guessing how many fender benders there would be in the next two hours. Finally he heard a click and a polite but very distant voice informed him that Admiral Haeverson had been located and would speak with him directly. J.D. grinned in anticipation.

"Hey, Jerry!" boomed the jovial voice as he came on the line. "How's it going? I saw about your breakthrough on the news. Great going!"

"You don't have to hype me," J.D. responded, beaming in spite of himself. "How's Hawaii?"

"It's paradise, as they keep saying in the ads. You ought to bring the family out here for a couple of weeks now that this fire thing is under control."

"That's what the company shrink tells me," J.D. said, as he tried not to chuckle. "And maybe when it's all over, I will."

It was typical of Admiral Haeverson that he recognized the reserved tone in J.D.'s voice at once. "What's the problem, kid? Is there something they aren't telling us?"

"I'm not sure," J.D. said. "There are a lot of lids being clamped on this investigation all of a sudden. I've had two official calls from Simon McPherson with the FBI warning me not to discuss the methods of testing the theory, or the actual numbers involved. He has also insisted on delaying the warnings we recommended be issued that, wherever possible, number sequences be kept to under fifteen digits, and where more than fourteen digits had to be used, that the sequence contain at least one zero or one space. We can all but guarantee that this will stop the fires altogether."

"You sure you want to be telling me this on a regular phone connection, kid?" asked the Admiral. "Isn't this just a touch sensitive?"

"Not to me," J.D. answered with purpose. "But it seems that others regard it so, and that, pal, troubles me. I keep thinking that someone wants this fire thing all for himself, and that scares the shit out of me."

"Yeah," said Admiral Haeverson, his tone much more thoughtful than it had been at first.

"We think we've come up with a plan that could get rid of this thing altogether, but no one is giving us a hand with it, and we've got a subtle hint that there are those who would appreciate it if we'd just turn our records over and go home." He did not want to reveal his anger, but he could keep it out of his voice entirely.

"I wonder whose fine Italian hand is behind that?" Admiral Haeverson said.

"Stop fishing, Eric," J.D. recommended. "I don't know, but I've got a pretty good idea you could find out. That's one of the reasons I'm calling." He waited for Admiral Haeverson to ask the question, since it was up to him to decide if he wanted to get into the picture.

"What's the other?" asked the Admiral when he had taken a moment to think things over.

"I need an in at NASA. I need someone who can make certain arrangements." This was far more speculative and as a result his manner was less forceful.

"What arrangements?" This time Eric Haeverson was suspicious.

"My staff here is working on a method to get rid of the thing, but we're not in a position to do it ourselves, or we would." He paused. "To be frank, I don't know if it will work, or even if it *can* work, but if we can pull it off, then we can be certain that this will never plague us again." He knew that his voice was once again confident and emphatic.

"You've got a lot of faith in your staff," said Admiral Haeverson.

"I have reason to," J.D. reminded him.

"True," the Admiral concurred. "Okay, tell you what. I'll take a day or two and I'll come over and poke around as much as I can. I'll see what's causing the problem at the Bureau or wherever and I'll do what I can to get you out of this blockage."

"That's more than I asked," said J.D., so relieved that he felt very nearly light-headed.

"So I volunteered. By the sound of it, you need a little clout, and you're entitled." He cleared his throat. "Want to come with me to Washington?"

"Maybe you'd better wait until you see what's going on here before you ask me that," J.D. suggested. "Figure on a day here, and then on to the snake pit."

"Lordy, Lordy, kid, that sounds pretty dire." Haeverson paused while a loud splash in the background told J.D. that the Admiral was out by his pool.

"Sorry; I'm fed up with the—"

"I know what you mean," the Admiral interrupted him.

J.D. took the implied warning to heart. "We'll arrange for your plane tickets and we'll arrange for housing. It's the least we can do."

"Thanks. I'll make a point of doing whatever I can to deliver the goods. We'll discuss the whys and hows when I get to San Jose. Would it be better for me to fly in and out of San Francisco?"

"I'll check. I'll have Phylis leave the departure time for you and your tickets will be waiting at the airport." He made a few more notes to himself.

"Sounds good," said the Admiral. "I'm glad you called, Jerry. You're the only one from the old group who's never asked me for a favor, and you're the only one I've actually owed one to." He paused and then added, "You know, we lost some family and lots of friends to these fires. It's hard to think of so many being lost. I want to do my part. I don't think I have." He coughed. "I'll see you soon, Jerry."

"My regards to the family," said J.D., wishing he could think of some consolation to offer.

"Yeah, and to yours. Later." With that, Admiral Haeverson hung up.

J.D. was just about to buzz Phylis when he noticed that on the expressway, three cars were stopped, and he could tell that they had been part of a rear-end collision chain. He decided to regard it as a favorable omen—he needed some sign to buoy up his spirits. Knowing that Eric Clifford Haeverson would be on his way soon was the first break he had encountered since Carter's experiment had paid off.

As Carter finished putting the groceries on the shelves, she was frowning, and at last Frank could stand it no longer.

"What's the matter?" he asked as he put the cheese in the refrigerator.

"It's bothering me and I don't know why," she replied in a distant voice.

"'It'?" he repeated. "What 'it' are we talking about?"

"The idea about the satellite. The more I think of it, the trickier it sounds. It's too complicated, and that means that things could go wrong too quickly and too easily. When there are so many factors, it makes it too tricky. There's got to be a simpler way." She slung her leg over one of the kitchen chairs and sat down, her chin resting on the back.

"Expound; get it out of your system or figure out what's wrong," Frank recommended as he drew up the other kitchen chair.

Across the room, Winslow lifted his blunt black head from his food bowl and regarded them in the steady, aloof manner of Chows.

In spite of the generous offer, Carter sat for some little time, her eyes almost blank. Her face was almost expressionless and when she broke her silence, it was in a dreamy, half singsong way. "If we code the numbers into a satellite, who's to say that there won't be some poor bastard keeping track of this, in America—North and Central and South—or Europe or Asia or Africa who won't have just the wrong frequency going, and we'll be stuck with the thing. How do we explain to the French or the Saudis or the Thais that they've bought themselves their very own Fire Elemental? They might think that we're being irresponsible to send something like that into space without making damned sure no one could snag it before the vacuum ended it. The trouble is, I'd agree with them, and I'm the idiot who came up with the idea."

"So what's left?" asked Frank. "You said yourself that Whiting hit it on the head when he told you that something like that has to be off the planet to be safe. We can't use it to set up a base on the moon, or Mars."

"That's part of the problem, isn't it?" She met his eyes fleetingly before glancing away once more. "How to get it out there without risking bringing it back here."

"Send it with a space probe," he suggested.

"But how to trigger it," she said, taking his suggestion more seriously than he had intended it.

"What?" he said. "Why trigger it? Why not simply wish the fucking thing bon voyage and happy landings out near ... Alpha Centauri."

"Because it might still be viable. The sequence could still be activated, I'm afraid. How the hell do you know about Alpha Centauri?" She was able to make a sound that was not quite a giggle.

"High school. And *Star Trek*. Like everyone else, I guess. I always liked the sound of it." He got up and went to the refrigerator again. "Want a beer?"

"Sure. I want an answer, too." She let out a long, slow sigh. "A beer and a little popcorn. Will you get the stuff out? I'll set up the pan." She had risen and had gone to the stove. "Where'd you put that wok lid?"

"Second cabinet on the right," he said as he got the beers. "Wok lids and paella pans. Now that's Californian for you."

"How would you know?" she asked, entering into the spirit of his banter.

"All us Easterners are great experts on California. I thought you knew that."

"Sure." She had poured out the hard yellow kernels and was putting the lid over them, when she stopped and turned on the gas, then stood mesmerized by the flame. She turned the gas off and then on, all her attention on it, and her face registered a strange sense of recognition.

Frank had opened two bottles of Anchor Steam and had been about to pour the dark beer into mugs when he noticed her behavior. "Carter?"

"I was just thinking," she said as she got back to the business of making popcorn.

"About what?" He filled the mugs as he waited for her answer.

She shook the paella pan slowly, the corn rattling inside. "When the *Challenger* blew up, all that fire. The fuel tanks going like that. It was so dreadful."

"It was," he agreed, knowing that she had not reached the core of her thoughts.

"The rocket separates at least once, sometimes twice on a launch, and when it fires, there is a burst of flame from the next stage." She sounded like a child reciting in class.

"And?" Frank encouraged her.

"I should find out how that do that, how they trigger the separations."

The first of the kernels popped, and the sound was so sudden, so loud that both of them jumped. Another few little bursts came from under the wok lid. "Keep shaking it," Frank advised.

Carter laughed, more loudly than the situation deserved, but with real amusement. She reached for a potholder and increased the movement of the pan.

"Don't forget what was on your mind," Frank reminded her as the corn popped. "Want me to melt the butter?"

"Sure." She kept at her task. "I won't forget. I just need to let it develop a while. Something's there. It's that separation process, that's the key. It's simple and it doesn't have nearly as much risk."

"I'll try to remind you. If I can understand what you're saying."

She turned on him. "Will you stop that?"

"What?" He was truly startled.

"That 'poor dumb me' act you do. I don't give one tinker's damn whether or not you can string degrees after your name, or have all the jargon right. Hell, I don't have *any* of your fire-fighting jargon, and I don't know anything about crowd control and how to save lives. But I've got a couple of pieces of paper that say I have a serious knack with numbers. But that doesn't mean I trust me with a fire hose, or a scalpel, for that matter. Okay?" She had very nearly thrown the popcorn at him and they both knew it.

"So long as I've got the butter, go ahead," he offered, indicating the pan. "How's your aim?"

"Rotten. I'm terrible at team sports." She started to laugh and no matter how she worked to stop and return to her indignation, it poured out of her, becoming a happy, crowing torrent.

Frank put the butter back on the stove, taking care to make sure the handle of the pan was pointed away from them, and then he went and wrapped his arms around her. They kissed once, twice, and between hiccoughs and chortles, the upset was over. "Come on," he said at last, "let's do the popcorn and beer, okay?"

"Fine. Fine." She kissed his chin. "Is it silly to fall in love like this?"

"O' course it is. But it's sillier not to." He grabbed the mugs and pointed to the paella pan with its fluffy contents. "Toss the butter into that. I'm hungry."

"To hear is to obey," she teased, but did the job.

Just as some men run to fat in middle age, Admiral Eric Haeverson had run to lean. He had always been tall and rangy; at thirty-two when J.D. had first met him, he had been trim and athletic, hale as the captain of an old clipper ship. Now, twenty-six years later, he was more than thirty pounds leaner and had he not retained that glow of health, he might have seemed cadaverous. He got off the plane in a lightweight gabardine suit, looking like a successful businessman returning from a Hawaiian holiday. As he stepped into the terminal, he looked around and was pleased to see J.D. himself waiting for him a few steps away.

"Eric!" J.D. called out with an off-handed wave.

"Jerry," Admiral Haeverson acknowledged, coming toward his former colleague.

"I see you're traveling under wraps," J.D. said, indicating the neat civilian dress.

"I don't see any reason to advertise my visit just yet. They'll know soon enough what we're up to, but there's no reason to let them have a running start." He held up the garment bag and the small suitcase he carried. "This is it. We can go."

J.D. indicated the proper direction and they started toward the front of the airport. "I've set up a meeting with my staff."

"It's almost three," said the Admiral. "This could go late."

"They know that; they're prepared and willing." J.D. had the ability to get through a crowd without appearing to push, and the two men made fast time to the parking lot.

"Have you worked out your strategy yet, or is that part of the reason for this meeting?" Admiral Haeverson spoke in the matter-of-fact way that J.D. remembered from his days in Naval Intelligence, when the then-Captain Haeverson would discuss almost anything in that same down-to-earth manner.

"It's part of it. We know which methods won't work with Washington. We're trying to find something that will, yet won't read like blackmail to the Bureau or other agencies."

"That's not going to be easy. How does the Task Force see this, or is it staying neutral?" They were almost at the main part of the terminal when there was an announcement over the public address system.

"Mister Patterson, Mister Patterson, please come to a white courtesy phone for a message. Mister Paterson to a white courtesy phone."

With half an oath, J.D. looked around for one of the white telephones and at last spotted one on the wall near the men's room. He went and picked it up, identified himself and waited. As he listened, his expression changed. When he hung up, he came back to Admiral Haeverson. "Sorry about that."

"Bad news?" He knew it was already.

"My company shrink's just been picked up for drunk driving. That was one of the legal staff telling me that they'd sent someone down to arrange for bail." They had resumed walking, not quite as rapidly as before.

"Is that a pattern with him?" Haeverson reached the automatic doors first and went through them ahead of J.D.

"A habit? No. In fact, so far as I know, it's never happened before. I think that all this pressure caught up with him at last. He's had to tend to all of us and I'm not sure there's been anyone taking care of him. You know the statistics on docs and drugs." He indicated the Mercedes parked near the terminal. "I'll put your things in the trunk."

"Thanks," said Haeverson, handing them over. "Is this going to make for problems?" he asked as J.D. got into the car and opened the doors from the console between the front seats.

"Nothing too drastic. I suppose I'll have to find out if this is the beginning of a pattern or just the pressure of the moment. Randy Whiting's a good man and he does his job well. He's not one of those superior bastards who think people are interchangeable with white mice. Which is probably why he was drinking. We've had a suicide in the company not long ago, and I think it was harder on Randy than he could admit." They were starting out of the parking lot, but the line to the toll booth was long and it crept.

"Was the suicide connected with the fires?"

"Yes and no. Costa was under pressure already and I think that this caught up with him. I did my best to keep his pressure to a minimum without being too obvious about it. Hell, last summer Randy suggested that he might want to take a couple months' disability leave. That made Costa more stressed than before, and so Randy dropped it and warned me that Costa wasn't in good shape. I knew that, but I hadn't any idea how serious it was until Randy talked to me. He was doing everything he could to keep Scott Costa going, and then the suicide came." At last he reached the booth, paid their fees and headed out toward the freeway.

"You mean on top of the fires," Haeverson said.

"Certainly the fires accentuated the problem, but, yes, it was additional to all the pressure about the fires." He drove steadily, changing lanes only when necessary, and with turn signals.

"I can see why a man might want an extra drink or two," Eric Haeverson said. "You and I had a week of that, after that fiasco with Maggiore and Gorvic."

"But we weren't driving that week, and certainly not where the California Highway Patrol could spot us." He was nearing his exit, and he signaled and changed lanes almost without thinking.

"What does this do to your current plans?" As always, Eric Haeverson brought matters back to current issues. He was as pragmatic as he had ever been.

"I don't think it does very much, although it might deprive us of a good head. Randy's good at assessing group behavior. If this hasn't shaken him up too much, I hope we can have him join us tomorrow." They were off the freeway and onto the expressway.

"Maybe you can go over things with him on the phone," Haeverson said, paying little attention to their surroundings. "How much farther?"

"Ten, maybe twelve minutes," said J.D.

"Is there anything you want to tell me that you don't want the others to hear? We'd better do that now."

J.D. considered the offer. "You have a better sense of these things than I do, but it seems to me that there's something going on here. Someone on the Task Force is playing footsie with the Congress or the military or the Bureau or someone like that. I had a talk with Sid Rountree last night, and he's been convinced of it for more than a month. I thought he was being a little paranoid at first, but not anymore."

"And what does that mean, do you think?"

"It means that we've got to watch our steps, or they'll throw their national-security cloak over us and the next thing you know, nothing we've learned will do a bit of good." He moved into the left-hand lane, preparing for the turn two miles ahead.

"From what you've said, the process has already begun."

"You know, at first I thought it was simple resistance on the part of the FBI to let the Fire Marshals' Task Force handle the problem. You know what territoriality is in Washington. And then I found myself wondering if someone might be weird enough and irresponsible enough to view this series of disasters as a potential weapon. That's when I began to pay more attention. I don't know where Special Agent McPherson stands on that aspect of the issue, but I know he did not want to have the Task Force take over what he saw as his job." They had almost reached the turn and J.D. began to signal again.

"Those buildings on the left are yours?" asked Haeverson.

"That's PSS, you bet. And please spare me all the jokes you can make with those letters—I've heard all of them." He waited for a break in the oncoming traffic to make his turn.

"Many times over, I suspect," said Eric Haeverson with a chuckle. "How large a meeting is this going to be?"

"Carter Milne—she's the one who figured out the code—Cynthia Harper—she's from legal—Barry Tsugoro—he's been my main troubleshooter all through this. Very sharp man, is Barry. Dave Fisher—I wooed him away from one of the big insurance companies about four years ago. He's a tenacious investigator and he's done some work with the feds in the past. Frank Vickery is on loan to us from the Task Force, and he's got a job with PSS anytime he wants it." He drew into his parking space and set the hand break before turning off the ignition.

"Is he going to take it?" asked the Admiral, "or could he be your mole?"

"I don't think so. He's got something going on with Carter, and for what it's worth, he was sent out to us originally because of clashes with the Bureau." He opened the door, but hesitated getting out.

"That could be his cover," Haeverson reminded him.

"Don't think that didn't occur to me at first," J.D. said quietly. "But that's changed. He's either the very best amateur I've ever encountered anywhere—I say amateur because he's been a fireman and a Fire Marshal for most of his adult life—or he's precisely what he appears to be." He was out of the car now. "Besides, judging from the kinds of problems the Task Force has had, I'd guess that the problem was closer to the Task Force home. My guess is that one of the Marshals or one of their advisers is working both sides of the street, and that is one of the reasons I called you in—you have clout and you are the wildest of wild cards."

As they entered the atrium of PSS, they stopped to pick up a visitor's ID for Admiral Haeverson from which his rank and service were missing. For the time being, he was simply E. C. Haeverson.

Three people were waiting in the conference room on the third floor when J.D. and Haeverson walked in: Cynthia, Carter and Frank.

"Social or professional?" asked J.D. as he looked over the three.

"A little of both. We were making plans for a dinner in San Francisco this weekend. I owe Cynthia and Ben one." Carter had had a haircut that day, at Cynthia's insistence, and she was still not used to the feel of it around her face and against her neck.

Cynthia, looking neater and more rested than she had in more than a week, had also been spruced up that noon, sacrificing lunch for a trim and set. She was dressed in a neat black-and-white houndstooth suit, the pattern in the skirt more than twice the size of the pattern in the jacket. She wore this with a burgundy silk blouse, and Haeverson decided that she would be very interesting to watch in court. "Good afternoon, Admiral, if we're supposed to call you that."

"Eric will do," he said, offering her his hand and approving of the firm clasp she gave.

As soon as the introductions were complete, J.D. brought Phylis into the room and introduced her as well. "I wouldn't get half of the work done I do without her. She's the most efficient woman in the company, and the nice thing is that she knows how to act on her own initiative; she doesn't have to come to me with everything."

Phylis, who had met Admiral Haeverson once several years before, shook his hand. "I'll be sitting in with the meeting, and I've warned my partner that I won't be home until late."

"Thanks. And thank Carol for me, as well," J.D. said. "I hope her horses are okay?"

"Fine. Everyone's been worried that there might be more stable fires since that one in Kentucky, but so far it hasn't happened. One of the big shows was canceled because of the fire, but so far it's only one."

"There's been another fire, incidentally," said Carter as she pulled out her notes from her portfolio.

"Where?" demanded J.D.

"Near New Orleans," she answered. "At a dock where they were unloading a shipment of cars from France. A whole run of order invoices was being matched to engine-block numbers and unfortunately five-one-six-nine-four-three-three-six-seven-two-three-one-eight-nine-eight came up."

"Is that the number?" asked Haeverson, unnecessarily but still awed.

"Yes. There are times I'm afraid to say it aloud, or even think it, because of what it might do." She flushed and shook her head.

"Do you really believe that?" Haeverson had no condemnation, only curiosity, in his voice.

"What else can I believe? You test that number with the double-vacuum chamber and you get a fire every time. No other series of numbers we have run—and we've run every combination several times now—produces that effect."

"Fifteen digits," said the Admiral, taking a chair next to the one at the head of the table. "Is that significant?"

"If you're a tenth-century Arab occultist, it is," said Carter, defiance coming into her voice; she lifted her chin.

"Is that where you came across this idea?" Haeverson gave her an encouraging smile. "Back when I was still working actively in Naval Intelligence—where I met Jerry, incidentally—we used to look everywhere for material. Sometimes those occult writings are very persuasive."

"And sometimes they're right," said Carter.

"True enough; sometimes they're right."

Lois Hillyer blinked in the bright sun as she stepped out of her hotel. She had arrived in Kingston the night before and had not seen much of the place but the lobby of her hotel. Now, dressed in a light linen suit with a long jacket and an open neck—she felt out of uniform without her neat silk bow tie—she was about to do something she had not done in more than six years: interview for a job.

The doorman helped her into the cab and wished her good luck in the musically accented English spoken in Jamaica.

"Where to, Missus?" asked the cabbie and moved off as soon as she had given him the address.

Underwood Assurance was located in the business section of Kingston, in a stucco-and-glass building. Lois entered it at her usual brisk pace, and then forced herself to slow down; here such briskness was not expected.

The man interviewing her turned out to be one of the vice-presidents, a fellow in his late thirties named Jared Fox.

"Pleasure, Miss Hillyer," he said as he indicated the chair on the opposite side of his desk.

Under other circumstances she might have objected to the "Miss," but she had been warned that the British influence in Jamaica was old-fashioned, and so she let it pass and simply shook hands. "Thank you." She sat down and smoothed the linen of her skirt, thinking that the one problem with the fabric was that it wrinkled so quickly and so easily.

"I see here that you did some work for the Task Force in regard to those dreadful fires," Fox said as he lifted her résumé from one of the stacks on his mahogany desk. "Quite an alarming series of disasters."

"Yes. Part of my family died because of them," she said very quietly.

"Ah. Most unfortunate. Accept my condolences." He looked at her, his head a little to one side. "You must pardon me, Miss Hillyer, but I am at a loss to know why you've sought employment here. There's no question of qualification, aside from the differences with British procedures and law, we welcome someone with experience in the United States, since there is a great deal of cross-pollination, as it were." He intended this to be witty and gave her the chance to smile. "When someone with your background contacts us, we're really most pleased." There was a hint of puzzlement in his tone.

"You're wondering why I decided to look for work here," she said, knowing that she would have to deal with that question eventually.

"Well, yes, as a matter of fact, I am." He sounded very British now, and his reserve did not surprise her.

"It's difficult to explain," she said, and had to stop herself from pleating the fabric of her skirt. "When my brother and his family were killed, I inherited their house, and that was a place to stay until I was called in as a consultant for the Task Force. I ended up feeling rootless, and everything I was doing reminded me of all the loss. That's all there seemed to be in the world—loss and grief and suffering. I had to get away from it. It wasn't just a matter of depression, it was more than that. I wanted to do some good instead of patching things up after the bad."

"But all assurance schemes ultimately are arranged for . . . um, patching things up, Miss Hillyer." As always he was delicate about the underlying proposition of insurance.

"What we're... gambling on is that the patching up will not have to be done very extensively or very often."

"Yes," she said with asperity, "I am aware of that, Mister Fox, but your company is not caught up in the kind of all-encompassing disaster that was the pattern working with the Task Force." She modified her tone a little. "I'd like to feel that there was at least an element of constructive worth in my work; I'd lost sight of that in the States. I'd been interviewed by other companies, but what they wanted was the skills I had gained in the Task Force, and I'm discovering that I can't keep going, not in such work. So"—she tried to grin but was not able to manage it—"here I am."

"Very commendable." He added another of his standard witticisms. "Considering your previous experience, how do you feel at the prospect of working right in the middle of the Bermuda Triangle?"

For the first time Lois actually smiled. "I'll take my chances."

She leaned back and directed her gaze toward the window. "It was almost winter in the States when I left, and all the trees were bare. I had to wear boots and a heavy coat in order to be comfortable when walking on the street and the heat was on all night long at the building where I had a condo. Who wouldn't rather be here?"

"We have very severe storms, Miss Hillyer, and there are other disadvantages of living here. This *is* an island, and there is a degree of political unrest here. There is a level of poverty you might not find acceptable, and there are amenities that you probably expect as a matter of course that are not automatically available here if they are available at all." He lit his cigarette and looked down at her speculatively. "Our salaries, while reasonable, are not comparable to what you were receiving, and the working conditions will not tend to lead to as rapid promotion as you have experienced to date. We are a British company licensed by the Jamaican government: we are not as enlightened about women, and being an American, you will find that there are certain areas of the company that are simply not available to you."

"I expected something like that," she said, but not as confidently as before.

Fox gave her a crooked smile. "I realize it is very tactless of me to ask, and in your country it wouldn't be permissible, but the circumstances here are different, and since you are not—"

"Go ahead; you've already been asking personal questions that you would not be permitted to ask in the States." She sat a little straighter in the chair.

"Very well, then. Is there perhaps some reason other than the fires and the unfortunate loss of your family that contributes to your decision? For instance, romantic reasons." He studied her as she gave her answer.

"No, no other reason. Yes, I had a man I was seeing, but that wasn't a factor in my coming here, at least not in the way you mean. I'm not running away from a broken heart or anything like that." She almost wished she were. Once she had made up her mind, it was all so easy. No one had tried to talk her out of it, and there was nothing holding her, not even the house; it had sold two weeks after it had been put on the market.

"Miss Hillyer," said Jared Fox, "I'm reasonably certain that your application for work here will be approved. In a very real sense this interview is something of a formality, and it has the effect of allowing one of the vice-presidents —in this case, myself—to check you out, as it were."

"Does that mean that I'll be getting the job?" She had not been aware of how much she really wanted it until she asked the question.

"If you want it. We'll send you a formal letter outlining such things as salary, benefits and requirements, since you're an American citizen. You need to send us back a signed agreement which we will enclose. I would advise you to consult a solicitor to review the contract and negotiate any points you feel are open to alteration or limitation."

"I'll do that," said Lois, feeling very happy.

"Then assuming that all works out, we can assume that

you will start here in six weeks. We move at our own pace here, and you might find that you need the time to complete your living arrangements."

"Thank you," she said, starting to get up.

"One more thing; we will expect you not to continue in your advisory capacity in regard to the fires, unless you are recalled to your country by subpoena or similar orders." He said this sternly, but it was apparent that it was more for form's sake than out of inner conviction.

"That's fine with me," she said, getting to her feet and holding out her hand.

He took it. "We'll be very pleased to have you as part of our company, Miss Hillyer. May I say that we count this as a fortuitous development? A woman of your background and experience, as I've said before, has unusual talents and capabilities and we understand how to appreciate these—"

"Please, Mister Fox, let me earn your opinion of me." She was more confident now than she had been in months, and it gave her a sureness that astonished her.

"If you like; although it is only fair to say that you're off to a running start on my . . . our good opinion." He indicated the door. "If you have any questions, don't hesitate to ask them of me. You know the number; don't hesitate to use it."

Suddenly Lois was bashful. "Thank you. I . . . I will."

When Eric Clifford Haeverson dressed for his flight to Washington D.C., he donned his full uniform and carried his peaked cap under his arm, as imposing a figure as any in the Navy.

"Planning to scare the shit out of them just standing there?" J.D. said when he arrived at Admiral Haeverson's hotel.

"Kid, we need all the guns we can mount for this one."

"First-class seats too, of course," said J.D. "Might as well go in style."

"There's a taxi waiting for us. I took care of the bill

and all they want is your key." J.D. indicated the room. "Sorry it wasn't a full suite."

A parlor and bedroom is more than enough. What do I want a second bedroom for, anyway?" He picked up his luggage. "I've been going over the material we've assembled, and I think that unless there's more unity in Washington than I've usually seen, we'll be able to get the hearing we need."

When the plane landed at Dulles, it was evening, and the huge empty preserve around the isolated airport had sunk into deep and angular shadows where the bare branches scratched at low clouds. The limousine, arranged for by Phylis, sped them to their hotel and the driver assured them that there would be another one waiting for them in the morning to take them to the hearing. Both men acknowledged this with little more than nods.

"What do you think?" J.D. asked that evening over dinner in a restaurant so discreet and expensive that the waiters were practically invisible.

"I think that those people who notice such things have noticed them. We have not come to beg for anything; we are coming to make a point and we intend to be heard." He poked at his squab. "They have gall to charge this much for a little bird."

J.D. recognized this as a deliberate change of subject and lightening of tone. "Yeah, but look what they charge for snails. That's even worse; snails are just a garden pest."

"Aren't they. Snails and bugs." He said nothing more and J.D. took the warning to heart.

Simon McPherson had gained more than fifteen pounds in the last six weeks. As pressure had mounted, so had his appetite and he was beginning to be uncomfortable in his clothes, which was almost more embarrassing to him than the infuriating position he was in, thanks to those Granola bars out in Silicone Valley. They probably had coked up to come to their malign-number scheme, and now this! wanting to launch the second stage of a rocket with the malign sequence. If he hadn't been warned in time, this would have dropped on him in the morning like a proverbial falling safe. He pushed away the midnight sandwich he had been munching and read over the memo again. He had no idea who it was within PSS who was leaking information to Norman Haley, who had been persuaded to share it with the FBI, but at the moment Simon McPherson was convinced that if he had any future in his work, it was because of that person.

McPherson thought of himself as a simple man, a little brighter—well, perhaps quite a bit brighter—than average, from a good middle-class home, with an expensive education and a sense of obligation to his country, which he had been taught to love all his life. Only recently had he thought to question any of these assumptions, and that had been when Lois Hillyer had left over a week ago.

He forced himself to read the memo again to keep from being distracted by the memory of that last conversation—it was not an argument—he had had with her. He had gone to her, assuming that her plans for travel were merely a ploy to get him to make their relationship more regular. He had realized almost from the moment he met her that she was the right kind of wife for him. She was bright—not quite as bright as he, but brighter than average—and very pretty without being beautiful. She came from a good background, and had checked out perfectly. Her work gave her some understanding for his work and was an excellent background for a wife of a rapidly rising Special Agent. Her manners were excellent and he knew he could fill the void in her life by proposing.

But when he had said that he knew she was the woman for him, she had had the unmitigated brass to say that he was not the man for her, and when he had pressed her, she had rattled off a list that included such words as "narcissistic", "pompous", "chauvinistic", "overbearing", "insensitive", "self-aggrandizing", "tyrannical", "a moral coward" and several others that made him squirm as they flitted through his mind. She had refused to listen to anything he had said to explain, and had added "self-deluding" and "puerile" to her uncomplimentary list.

"All you've told me, Simon," she had said in that maddeningly cool manner of hers, "is what I can do for you. I can be an ornament and a means to enhance your prestige. I can take care of you and minister to your wants and run your house and show myself to be a good example of an FBI wife. You've never said what you can do for me, or even what you want to do for me."

"Well, damn it, Lois, you haven't been listening. I just did tell you all that," he had countered, more baffled than angry at her lack of response. "I dote on you."

"Dote? Not love or care for or even like?" Her blue eyes were suddenly very sad. "Do you know that I like Impressionist art?"

"Does that mean a Paris honeymoon?" he had joked, having no idea what Impressionists had to do with their conversation.

"Do you know that I was a track star in high school? Do you know that my favorite flower is the iris, not the rose or the orchid or even the gardenia? Do you know, or even care, that I'm allergic to milk products, or that I like to listen to Vivaldi in the bathtub?"

"Now, how could I know—"

She had interrupted him. "You could have asked." When he had not spoken, she had continued, "Simon, you've got a cutout in your mind, and a list. It's your profile for the right wife for you. When I came along, I more or less fit the profile, and that was all you cared about. It might surprise you to know that I don't tint my hair—some ash-blondes are natural. But all you wanted was a woman who filled the bill. Well, I don't fill the bill. You see, I am not a cardboard cutout. I like to giggle in bed and I'm a sucker for having my toes licked, but you don't know that, either."

"I'll remember it; wait until we're engaged." He had been desperate then.

"You're still not listening; we aren't going to be engaged. I am leaving for Kingston just as I planned, I am going to work there and maybe, if I'm very lucky, I'll have a lover or a husband who will know who I am in the dark, and will like me for the person I am as well as love me."

In spite of all his good intentions, Simon McPherson gobbled down the last of the sandwich and shoved the plate aside. He studied the memo and ended up shaking his head. It read:

> McPherson:
> My contact informs me that PSS has come up with a new idea about getting rid of the fire number. Since they have demonstrated that there is such a thing, they might well get something through. They need the cooperation of NASA and some funding, but if they are correct, that would eliminate all current strategic use.
> Haley

Which, Simon McPherson thought as he reviewed his plans for the future, would never do.

November 18, Cancun, Mexico

Every year Kostas and Irene Satraki took two weeks for their vacation and came to this Mayan treasure of a place, delighting in the beauty, the slow pace and the heat. Kostas spent part of the time fishing, and Irene took her camera everywhere, using up two or three dozen rolls of film. Neither she nor her husband of twenty-eight years knew she was a very good photographer, or cared.

The last two years, Kostas had brought along his portable computer to check in with the office, or so he claimed. Irene regarded the thing—hardly bigger than a good-size purse—as a toy and thought that her husband deserved to indulge himself.

They stayed at the same hotel, and for the last three years in the same room. The view delighted them both, for they looked out at the shining stretch of incredibly blue water that was the southern end of the Gulf of Mexico.

"You go take your pictures," Kostas advised on this morning halfway through their vacation. "I want to do a little work. No sense in dragging this infernal machine along if I don't use it."

Irene thought that it was more likely he would play games with it, as he did with their two grandchildren at home, but she only smiled.

"We are getting that new inventory, and I want to find out how it's going." He had pulled out the portable computer, and was reaching for the phone.

"Don't stay on too long. You know how unreliable the phones are here, and those computer calls cost a fortune," she warned him, her only comment against the machine.

"We're doing okay; we can afford a couple of minutes to Nebraska."

"Whatever you say." She picked up her camera and went out to the marketplace.

It was warm, the sun drenched the world in light so intense it was almost liquid. It clung to the buildings and the people, turning all of them burnished, golden, artifacts of the ancient civilization that once thrived here. Irene strolled past makeshift booths featuring all manner of things for sale, from food to leather goods to toys. Her Spanish was not good enough to haggle in, but she had mastered the technique while still a little girl in Greece, and it amused her to bargain in pantomime.

She had bought some fruit—Kostas was always warning her about the fruit, but she always ate it—and was looking for a shady place to sit when she noticed the great cloud of smoke spreading over the marketplace.

Shouts and cries from others caught her attention, and she found herself taking pictures of the faces around her, which most often were stoic, now showing alarm, consternation, distress and fear. It reminded her of some of the faces she had seen on the news when that Foss woman—Irene thought she was pushy and unsympathetic—talked to survivors of the terrible fires.

Only after she had taken most of a roll of thirty-six pictures did she realize that the smoke was coming from the general direction of the hotel, and the first icy finger of dread touched her. Without realizing what she was doing, she started to run.

Then she encountered the police cordons and saw the few, outmoded fire engines and ambulances, and without understanding Spanish or the local dialect babbled around her, she knew that it was her hotel that was burning, and that Kostas was gone.

November 23, Concord, New Hampshire

Retirement, even early retirement, suited Loring Wygand. Between the insurance settlement and his university pension and the small but regular royalties from his textbooks, he managed quite well. Living frugally and in comparative isolation helped him to make the most of what he had as well as give him the benefits of privacy and solitude. For the first time in his life, he had almost enough time to study his favorite enigma, the baffling so-called Roger Bacon manuscript brought to America in 1912 by the rare-book dealer Wilfred Voynich.

Wygand was certain that most of the borders and all of the designs on the cypher-written pages were part of the puzzle and contained as much if not more information than the writing; he knew that if he could figure out the code in the designs, he could break the code in the text.

Two days ago, he had finally received full-size photostats from Yale and was determined to work on all the borders, designs, illustrations and all other shapes represented on the pages. He had worked with his computer mouse long enough that he was certain that he could work out the proper interrelations that would finally and incontrovertibly break the code.

Not often given to levity, Wygand actually whistled as he set himself up in his study, selecting the first page with all deliberation. He looked at it, the old-style writing so in contrast with the shiny photostat paper. He wished he could use the actual manuscript, but that was certainly impossible. To think that it had survived from the twelfth century, if all the records were right! He was overjoyed for this chance to work on it.

He took more than an hour to set himself up, and to review the information garnered by Brumbaugh and D'Imperio which had been his main reading for well over a year. Now he was going to have a chance to add to the vast speculation and scholarship surrounding the manuscript.

Very carefully, Wygand began to trace all the forms with his mouse, and to record and compare the similarities. For many hours, he worked contentedly, happily, absorbed in what he was doing.

Whether it was the old Franciscan friar Roger Bacon who wrote the manuscript or another, the fire that devastated Loring Wygand's house proved that the Arab mathematicians were not the only ones to use malign numbers to bring about fire; had Wygand had the opportunity, he would have seen the fatal series of numbers 516943367231898 in the analysis of angles and rings in the cosmological folios. The author of the manuscript had been determined to protect his work from uninitiated eyes.

November 27, Muncie, Indiana

Thanks to the Thanksgiving weekend, the arcade was jammed with kids—mostly boys—playing on the various games that had been set up. It was the first weekend of serious Christmas shopping and the publicity director for the mall, Jamey Soleil from Hutsville, Alabama, had come up with the idea of installing the arcade and only charging a dime for the games instead of the usual quarter. He had also got the idea of dressing the arcade attendants as elves, which the parents thought was cute and the kids thought was silly.

"Look, Mister Blair," Jamey Soleil—pronounced "*sol-ee-ill*"—was explaining as the Christmas music blared over the speakers, "you don't have to worry about it—the kids are in the arcade, most of 'em. The only others are either too young or too old to cause much trouble, and they're sticking close to their parents. And the parents are happier and they'll stay longer and buy more because the kids are off playing Space Pirates or whatever is their favorite game."

"I'm not objecting to that, but this business of having prizes coming out of the arcade, that bothers me. We're apt to be giving away a brand-new car to a kid who decides it's his, not his family's." He was a nondescript man with a pallid complexion and a dandruff problem.

"Mister Blair, I won't say that isn't a factor. We all know what the psychologists say about kids that age"—both men nodded, although both had only the vaguest notion of what was meant—"and it's a risk, no doubt about it. But think of what it can do for the mall, and for the store. You're going to get publicity, and a lot of it will be free, because we can serve it up as news. Keep that in mind." There was also the matter that Jamey's brother-in-law ran the largest Chrysler dealership in the city and had donated the prize.

"I know what the advantages are, never fear, but it's the disadvantages that worry me, Mister Soleil. I'm very pleased with the sales and the—"

"Body count?" suggested Jamey, indicating the crowd milling its way through the covered mall.

"That's not a flattering way to speak of it, but it's accurate I guess." He rubbed his hand over the clean surface of his desk and indicated the window. "I'm concerned about those kids. We've never had so many of them here at one time. Most parents leave those kids with sitters or neighbors or someone—they don't like having to bring them shopping any more than we like them here."

"That's true for everything except Christmas shopping. I've shown you the figures, the demographics on this. We're gonna have those kids all over the place for Christmas whether we like it or not, so we might as well make the most of it. The dimes will more than pay for the rental of the machines, and having those elves around to make change is a great way to have security without making it obvious that we don't trust the little buggers an inch."

"Mister Soleil," Mister Blair rebuked him without a trace of conviction.

"Well, you got another word for 'em?" He laughed. "You're having your best year since this place opened, you admit that yourself, you've had more coverage and paid for less of it than ever, and you know that's true, and still you're afraid that something's gonna backfire. God's truth, Bob, I don't know what to do with you. Don't you know when you've been handed a miracle? Well, maybe a small one and not very mystical, but this place is making money like it wasn't legal tender, and you're bitching about it." Jamey put his hands on his hips, a gesture that had been left over from his childhood.

"That's not the point," said Robert Blair, his face more lugubrious than ever. "We're really not adequately insured for crowds of this size, and if anything should happen, it would be a disaster."

"Boy, you don't waste any time looking at the silver lining, do you? Here's the best deal going in town, and you sit around like you think all the money's gonna turn into straw or something."

"I can't help it. With all the terrible disasters we've seen these last few months . . ." The words trailed away.

"Hey, those are slowing down, haven't you noticed? The government's got it all under control. They figured out how to handle it, just like we all knew they would. Tell you what: come on down to the arcade. Talk to some of the parents. Let 'em know how glad you are to see all the family here for a change."

"I'm not," Blair stated.

"Then lie," Jamey Soleil instructed. "And smile."

That was the reason that one of the first victims of the fire that consumed more than two-thirds of the Blair-Tyler shopping mall from its point of origin in the added video-game arcade was one of the partners who had developed the mall and who had been managing it and its principal store for the last five years. The video games, hooked up three and four together, had arrived at a fatal score as three of the machines tallied the fifteen-digit sequence.

PART
IX

November 28, Oxon Hill, Virginia

Norman Haley got up from his desk and started toward the door before it occurred to him that he was not satisfied with what he had to offer. He almost got back on the telephone to California, but didn't. He had asked for the information as part of his Task Force duties, and so far he had not used anything that had not been made available to the Task Force members. But if he asked for more, if he pressed his position to take advantage of it, then he would be something more than a Fire Marshal who had protected his position; he would be seen as an informant, and one who was working to compromise the Task Force effort instead of doing his best to see that it accomplished its ends.

"Maggie," he said to his secretary, "I want you to call McPherson for me."

Maggie Gunderson nodded and mumbled a few words, then did as she was told.

"What have you got for me, Haley?" McPherson sounded bleary, as if he had just awakened.

"Nothing we haven't already heard. I talked to my... connection. I still think that there's no understanding on that end of our conversations." He had made it a point to establish the fact that it was his decision to pass on information to the FBI, not his contact within PSS.

"I know; you're the one who's the informant, and if push comes to shove, your source is protected." He was not in a good mood, that was obvious.

"If the hearing goes well today, we're completely ready to move on our end. They're doing the studies now at PSS with help from all those aerospace companies out in Silicone Valley. Whatever they have to say about the plans, it isn't pie in the sky."

"You mean that it won't be easy to debunk it or shunt it off into defense industries for study and development." Now he sounded more disgusted than anything else. "Okay, any more good news, or is this it?"

"That's about it. They have the methods and the means."

"And all they lack is opportunity." McPherson snorted. "You made my day, Haley."

"Look, you were the one who asked me to keep you informed so that you could manage this for the good of the country." Recently he had found that the smooth replies he got from McPherson worried him, and that this would aid America was no longer as apparent as it had been. "When is the public going to be given the chance to deal with this? When are we going to release the number sequence to our allies?"

"When it's safe; when we're sure the information won't be abused." It was the same reply McPherson had provided before.

"But there have been more fires. Don't you think that there's some reason to make requirements along the lines already recommended so that the sequence can't be triggered accidentally?" He knew he was pleading, but even he could not have said precisely why or for what.

"It's unfortunate," McPherson said.

"All those people, that mall. It could have been prevented." He wanted some assurance that he had made the right decision when he had joined forces with McPherson.

"It could have been, but at what cost?" McPherson asked. "Sure, we save a couple thousand, but we expose untold millions, even billions to the threat of these fires from our enemies."

"Yeah," said Haley, unable to shake off the guilt that had its hooks in him.

"It's almost over, Haley, and you've done your part. You've shown you're a responsible and concerned citizen, no matter what those misguided colleagues of yours think. You're the only one with guts enough to face the hard facts of security; the others are ostriches. Vickery is the worst. If it were up to me, I'd see him dismissed and I'd never allow him access to any kind of sensitive work, not even fire fighting."

"Hey, Frank Vickery's a good man. He cares about the country and he cares about the people. I won't listen to this about Frank." Haley felt even more distressed because he had the sense that some of Frank's difficulties had come through him. It was inadvertent, because he had not realized that McPherson and—at the time—Bethune would take his opinion and use it against Frank's legitimate questions. McPherson had explained the decision and Haley had tried to find the same commitment in himself that he discerned in the men from the FBI. At first it had been possible, but now that was not the case. "Look, McPherson, unless there's some reason for you to contact me again, I think that this is all I ought to do for you. I can't see, with the hearing today, that there's anything more I have to offer. It'll all be out, almost in the open, and my contribution won't be necessary."

"You can't be sure of that," said McPherson. "You can never tell when you might happen onto something that we need to know. If you'd rather keep your name off the records, that's fine; I'm willing to do that, but it could be that you'll want to have credit when we've worked out all the ramifications of this project."

"What project?" Haley demanded.

"Stopping the fires, of course. Thanks for the call. We'll talk again soon, okay?" Before Haley could bring up anything else, McPherson hung up.

Norman Haley sat by himself in his office, thinking of the hearing that was about to begin. He thumbed through the Rolodex on his desk, searching for a number. It was early in California, not yet seven in the morning. That would mean he could not yet reach Frank at the office; he would have to call the house.

Frank hung up the phone and looked at Carter in dismay and anger. "That was Norman Haley."

"Who's that?" she asked as she finished setting up the coffeemaker.

"He's a Fire Marshal in Virginia; he's been a consultant to the Task Force since the first of these fires. I went on an inspection with him in Virginia, in September. He's a good man."

"Then what's the matter?"

"I . . . Norm just told me that he's been giving information from the Task Force to the FBI."

"Shit," she said.

"Yeah, and that's not all of it; he's been passing on what we're doing here at PSS to the FBI, as well." He cleared his throat and moved away from her. "He said that he's had information from the first and he thought it was his duty as a citizen and a responsible investigator to keep the Bureau informed."

"Do you believe him?"

"Yes. Norm's a good man. He wouldn't do this if he didn't think it was necessary, and he wouldn't do it out of spite or petulance or politics, but out of genuine concern. He tried to tell me, but he didn't have to."

Carter came and put her hand on his arm. "What now?"

"Now we go to the office. There's someone I have to talk to before we call J.D. Not that we could reach him, anyway. He's got that hearing this morning and he's already left his hotel for it."

"What do you think his chances are, under the circumstances."

"You mean because of leaked information? You're being delicate, Carter. Very delicate." He leaned over and kissed her. "Coffee ready?"

"Not quite. I gather from your silence that you know who the leak is, and I also gather that you want to handle it your own way. That's fine with me, but if you change your mind and want to talk, I want to listen; okay?" She leaned against him briefly, then said, "How do you want your eggs?"

"Poached," he answered. "On English muffins, if you can. I know we got some when we were shopping." He smiled at her. "Thanks."

"For what?" she asked as she went to get the omelette pan she used in place of a poacher.

"For your good sense and forebearance and all that good stuff." He went to the refrigerator and got out the muffins. "Want me to toast one for you, too?"

"Yes, please," she said, filling the omelette pan with water and then adding a dash of sherry.

Before the eggs were ready, he had put the split muffins into the broiler and got the tops browned. While he put them on plates, he said, "I don't know, Carter. This whole thing has me . . . I've never had to deal with a situation like this."

"I'm listening," she reminded him.

"Listen to me a little while, then." He put the plates on the counter by the stove, then got out their coffee mugs and filled them. "I . . . I've known Norm Haley for, oh, twenty years. I never had any reason to question him about any decision he made, because he's the four-square type, as dependable as a good workhorse. I can see that he wanted to do the right thing, and I can see that he probably got . . . rooked by someone at the Bureau, probably Bethune, before he died. But you see, he continued to do this, and he asked . . . someone at PSS to report to him, and that puts a different light on it. It isn't simply passing on his information now, it's a question of enlisting someone else without telling them what the information was to be used for, and that's different, somehow, that's another level of action, and it troubles me, because I don't know that Norm would do that of his own accord, and if he didn't, the person responsible has a lot to answer for. Using the best intentions of an honest man that way is... it isn't just wrong, it's underhanded and scheming, and I don't like to think about—"

He was interrupted by Winslow whining to be let out.

"Now there's a dog with the right idea." Carter went to open the back door, and when she came back the eggs needed her attention. "Here's your plate," she said, handing it to him, and then she got her own.

"Thanks." He sat down, but did not start to eat. "Carter, what if the... person at PSS did know and understand what was going on all the time; what if it was deliberate and all the rest of it."

"You're borrowing trouble, aren't you? You just said that your poor friend Norm told you that this person at PSS didn't know what it was about or who the information was going to. Are you certain you know who got the information from Norm?"

"Oh, yeah, I know that. He told me that McPherson has been pumping him regularly. And he was convinced at first that it was for the security of the country. Maybe the person at PSS thinks the same thing."

They were through with breakfast before he said anything more. "If things don't go well with... the person, I don't know what it will mean in terms of my staying on at PSS. I thought I'd better warn you." He barely looked at her as they gathered their things for leaving. "It could change things for us, couldn't it?"

There was no inflection whatever in her voice. "Yes, I suppose it would, if it came to that."

"And?" they were almost at the door.

"If you won't borrow trouble, I won't borrow trouble," she said, "I've had my life turned upside down twice in the last couple months, and I don't know what I'd do if it happened again. We'll manage, don't doubt it, if that's what we want to do. If we don't, then—"

"Would you want me around if PSS didn't keep me on?" She had just locked the front door as he asked this.

Carter looked at him in amazement. "Is that a serious question? Of *course* I'd still want you around, no matter what PSS did or didn't do. We're not living together for the convenience of Jeremiah Dermott Patterson, or hadn't you noticed."

"But wouldn't it be awkward for you?"

"It would be a hell of a lot more than awkward to have you gone," she said as they got into the car.

"Then we'd better do something about my daughter, don't you think?" It was a problem they had skirted several times, and most of the time it was not an issue because neither of them had discussed their remaining together.

"I guess so," she said, and started out of the driveway, pausing to lock the gate so that Winslow would be confined in the enormous yard.

J.D. Patterson wore a dark suit, very deep blues flecked with grays, and the most subdued and impressive shirt and tie in his wardrobe; Admiral Haeverson was in uniform. They faced the committee from their place at the table and did their best to present an air of confidence.

"What makes you think that this . . . proposal could succeed?" the oldest member of the committee asked, his tone loaded with unspoken derision.

"I think it would work, Senator, because of everything we've learned about the nature and control of these fires," said J.D. at his most urbane. "All our research has shown that this sequence of numbers will cause spontaneous combustion when linked with electronic equipment and the microwave system. Therefore, the triggering of a second stage of a rocket launch would inevitably cause the fire to be started in the manner outlined, and then the vacuum of space would essentially bring the thing to an end."

"And what makes you think," began a Congressman

from Tennessee, "even assuming this notion has any basis in fact, that this would actually get rid of this... firebug?"

Some of the committee members chuckled and the chairman rapped sharply with her gavel.

"We assume it will work because it has worked in laboratory tests consistently. There's no reason to suppose it won't work in practice." J.D. opened his portfolio. "I have copies of our tests and the results with supporting documentation for you, and I have already provided the committee staff with the material, so you can study it."

"So you want us to spend all that money to launch a rocket just to get rid of this... what did you call it?—malign number?" This was from the Floridian, and she had the look about her that suggested that she was closing in for the kill.

"I don't see that a launch would be so great a problem. There is a space probe scheduled to go off in two weeks, and there is no reason it cannot be programmed to do the job for us; in fact, Admiral Haeverson is here to press just that use of the project, so that the officials of NASA can deal with the Navy instead of with an industry they have no prior contact with."

Eric Haeverson took up the theme. "I am impressed with the quality of research and documentation provided by Patterson Security Systems in their work with this problem. It is my opinion that there is a good deal of sense to their plan, and it can be carried out with minimal expense if we adapt current projects to the use as outlined in the material already provided to the members of the committee."

"And how do you think the public would feel?" demanded the Congressman from Oregon who had recently joined the committee. "They all remember the *Challenger* disaster. Do you think they would support a deliberate use of fire in a launch?"

"I don't see how they can help it, given the rocket fuel we use," said Admiral Haeverson. "And I respectfully remind the committee members that this launch is not manned, that the probe is a deep-space photographic probe with fly-bys for Jupiter and Saturn as well as possible enhancement of the photography we already have of Neptune and Uranus."

"These space probes are frigging expensive, Admiral: what if this malign number of yours blows the whole thing up, what then?" The feisty Texan asking this question peered at the two witnesses as if they were suspected of grand larceny at the least.

"Let me say this," J.D. answered. "I would submit that even if the malign number proves to be detrimental to the probe launch, it has already cost more in lives and material than a dozen space probes. I believe that the risk is worth the potential return, and if it were a matter of business, such as what is done by my firm, and it were my decision to make, I would not hesitate to authorize this expenditure and assume the risk."

"Easily said, Mister Patterson," the Senator from New Hampshire accused. "It isn't your decision or risk, is it?"

"Senator Pace," said Admiral Haeverson, "I have known this man more than twenty years, I have seen him work under great pressure and I have watched his company grow from little more than a two-man shop to what it is now, with branches in six cities and a reputation that is enviable. If this man says that he believes the risks to be tolerable and the expenditure reasonable, I would accept his word and I would support him."

A great white polar bear of a man who sat at the far end of the committee table and who had appeared to be asleep now rumbled into life. This was the legendary Hank Marchek from Ohio and his thirty-eight years in the Senate had made him a master of infighting and treachery. His grumble seemed to come from the middle of his body and not his throat. "Mister Patterson," he said, "do you seriously expect us to endanger the security of the entire United States of America on a whim? Do you expect us to leave ourselves open to enemy action on a whim?"

"With the Senator's permission," J.D. said calmly. "I

would not describe our proposal as a whim. We've been working very hard and for many weeks to come up with something that might work. I know that this is true of many others in the country and I do not underestimate their dedication or purpose, but we were fortunate enough to be the first to identify the nature of the problem and the triggering sequence of numbers. Why these numbers should cause this reaction is a matter we can solve later; it seems to me that the first order of business is to be rid of the thing."

Representative Neil Hoag from Wyoming had the next question. He was something of a Western-style dandy, given to suit jackets with brightly studded yokes, as if this could camouflage the bright trap of his mind. "Admiral, would you mind my asking why you're lending your prestige and support to this . . . farfetched project?"

"For one thing, Congressman, I don't see that this project *is* farfetched. It's only because there are those with vested interests who had other ideas about these fires that you would take this stance. We have every reason to believe that there are those who would like to see this number-invoked fire be kept, under lock and key, as it were, and used as part of our military arsenal." He had opened the door now, and he looked ready for the fray. "I think that as a responsible member of the Navy and as a member of Naval Intelligence, I am under obligation to protect this country, and I cannot see that retaining any vestige of this fire can promote the safety of this country or its people."

"That's a fine show of patriotic fervor," rumbled Hank Marchek. "And naturally we applaud you for it." He shoved a massive hand through his thatch of white hair. "But don't you think that this might be to our advantage in the long run? Don't you think that there may come a time when we'll need this fire and the number that brings it? I don't know about you, Admiral, but I am convinced that there are enemies of this country who would not hesitate to use this, if they had it."

"And we're to become like our enemies in order to

protect ourselves from them?" Admiral Haeverson asked. "That's like saying that we should test a hydrogen bomb by dropping it on a major American city in order to make adequate preparations in case the enemy drops a bomb on a major American city. It is at best irresponsible, and at the worst, it moves a very major hazard away from the scrutiny of Congress and into the area of the covert and clandestine, where the checks and balances of our system cannot reach it except with great difficulty." He leaned forward and folded his hands. "I am not one to advocate the dismantling of necessary weapons, nor do I favor standing unprepared and defenseless in the face of our enemies, but this is not in the same area as our weapons. This is a thing that was wished upon us by a force or forces unknown, and it behooves us to return it in the same manner. This serves many purposes, not the least is that it shows our country and the world that where something as potentially disastrous as a sequence of numbers causing spontaneous combustion is concerned, we will stop at nothing to ensure the safety of this country and the world. How long do you think it's going to be before someone in Europe or Asia makes a call or a computer connection to the U.S. and in some context or another triggers that sequence? The cat will be out of the bag then, and we will have much to answer for. It may be true that we did not deliberately call that thing into being, but it is certainly accurate to say that once we have the means to be rid of it—and we do—we have a moral obligation to free our population and the population of the world from this threat. We are all subjected every day to threats to our lives and well-being that most of us have little or no power to change or stop—the hazards of nuclear waste and nuclear war, the problems of pollution and environmental toxicity, the hazards of physical health, the state of our financial well-being related to the larger economy—but this thing, this *one* thing we can influence. We can indeed rid the country of this threat, this well-demonstrated danger, and we can do it without further hazard or risk. If you choose not to act, then every one of you will be personally accountable for the loss of lives and property that come after this time because of that malign sequence of numbers. Thank you; that's all I have to say."

J.D. leaned back in his chair and resisted the urge to pat Eric Haeverson on the back.

Frank had opted for Carter's office as the setting with the supposed informant. He was restless with misery and when Carter offered him coffee and a kind word, he snapped at her. "Sorry, honey; I hate this."

"I know," she said. "But it will be over soon."

"God, I hope so." He stopped and picked up a piece of paper from her desk. "What do I say? Do I start out with what I know or do I let—"

Carter took the paper out of his hand and put it back on the desk. "Sit down and relax a minute, Frank. You're getting too worked up, and that won't do any of us any good, including—"

Dena came to the door, saying, "Phylis Dunlap's here."

Both Frank and Carter turned, almost guiltily, as if surprised in something wrong. Carter nodded. "Please send her in, Dena."

Like everyone at PSS, Phylis was looking tired; her face showed lines like fissures from her nose to the corners of her mouth, and there was a deep crease between her brows that had not been so pronounced at the end of summer. Her pant suit was neat, camel-colored and worn with a navy-blue blouse with only one gold chain for jewelry. She looked from Carter to Frank. "You wanted to see me? You've heard something from the East?"

Now that the inevitable was under way, Frank no longer felt nervous. He regarded her steadily. "Yes, you could say that."

"Is it good news? Do we have the support and the funding? Are they going to okay the launch?" Her questions were not guarded, and this alone encouraged Frank.

"Phylis, how much do you know about what's been going on?" It was an easy question to ask.

"I've tried to keep up with whatever comes across J.D.'s desk." She looked from one to the other again. "Carter, what's this about?"

"We've got a problem," she said, hating to be dragged into the matter, but not knowing how to avoid it.

"Something *is* the matter," Phylis said, and took the nearest chair. "Tell me what's happened. Is J.D. all right?"

"So far as we know, J.D.'s fine," said Frank. "I had a talk this morning with Norm Haley."

"How is he?" asked Phylis without a trace of embarrassment.

"He's got a couple problems," said Frank, puzzled by her response.

"Oh? What?" She reached for her purse and her notebook. "Is it anything I'm going to need later?"

Frank was certain now that he had misjudged the situation, but he knew he had to find answers. "I don't think so, Phylis. But there are some developments that are... difficult."

"Norm's okay? He was sounding pretty strange the last time I talked with him." She opened her notebook and held her pen ready.

"Uh, listen Phylis," said Frank, searching for the right words, "how long have you been... dealing with Norm?"

"J.D. told me to make our material available to anyone in the Fire Marshals' Task Force who needed it. Norm contacted me, oh, six, seven weeks ago, I think, and wanted to get updates." She hesitated. "I've got a note of it in my files somewhere, if you'd like me to get it."

"Did you talk with J.D. about this?" Carter asked.

"Not specifically. He'd already outlined the policy and said I should use my own judgment. Now"—her manner shifted subtly—"will you tell me what this is all about?"

Frank answered her question reluctantly. "When Norm called me this morning, it was to tell me that he's been giving your information not to the Task Force, or not exclusively to the Task Force members, but to the FBI as well, which is one of the reasons J.D.'s had the hassles he's had, and why so much of what we've been doing here was being misrepresented and debunked on the other end."

Phylis was shocked; she said nothing for almost a full minute. "That bastard," was her first, soft response.

"Don't be too hard on Norm," said Frank, compelled to defend his friend. "He was pressured into it."

"That's no excuse," Phylis snapped. "We're all being pressured and that doesn't mean we've been handing reports around in an irresponsible way." She closed her notebook. "How much damage did he do?"

"We don't know yet. I'm still waiting to hear from J.D.," said Carter. "We're hoping that it wasn't so bad that we can't fix it."

"How good are the chances?" Phylis kept her voice pleasant, but her patience was getting thin. "If it's my actions that brought this about, even accidentally, then there are aspects of this I have to answer for. Tell me, please, how serious the damage might be?"

"We have reason to believe that there are those persons in the military and intelligence communities who want to keep the Fire Elemental number on hand as part of the weapons available for—"

Phylis interrupted Carter. "So that's the game. Our Elemental is at our mercy, or something along those lines, right?" Phylis was growing more angry with every word she spoke. "It isn't enough that this thing should have ruined lives and property by mischance, now we have to plan to use it deliberately. That's *obscene*. It makes me feel sick."

"I know," Carter said with deep sympathy. "I hope that J.D. can make them all see good sense. It's bad enough having the bomb hanging over our heads, I don't want the Fire Elemental there as well."

"What makes you think that it has to come to that?" asked Phylis in a manner that revealed she had already considered that herself.

"I think that if someone is dumb enough to try to put that thing under wraps, we'll have it with us a long time," said Carter. "I've been thinking about that since this morning, and it bothers me more than... Look, Phylis, I knew that there was always the chance that there might be a military use for this, but I didn't think that we'd be the ones to try to have it, or we'd be the ones stupid enough to try to keep it."

Phylis shook her head. "I think I'd better make a phone call. I'd better tell J.D. about this. He'll have to decide how he wants to handle this. If he wants it, he can have my resignation."

"Phylis!" Carter protested.

"It's only right," said Phylis. "I love the job and J.D.'s the best boss I've ever had, but after something like this, well, I wouldn't blame him for letting me go. I didn't do my job properly."

"Why don't you leave that up to him," Frank suggested gently.

"I suppose you're right," said Phylis. "Oh, God." She put her hand to her eyes and started to cry, to her acute embarrassment. "I'm sorry," she tried to apologize. "I... I don't..."

Carter rose and put her arm around Phylis's shoulders. "Go on, let it out. If it's not for this, it's for everything else we've all been through."

Phylis brought herself under control. "Look," she said as she wiped her eyes, "I'm going up to the office to call J.D., and then I'm going to call Carol, so she won't have to try to pick up the pieces without warning." She wiped her tears away again, and moved her hands as if to shove them and everything else away. "How could I have done something so... inexcusable?" she demanded of the air.

"We've all been under stress," Carter said again, thinking of Scott Costa, dead; Glen Lewis on medical leave because of heart trouble; herself widowed and living with another man in less than a month; Randall Whiting, for the first time in his life arrested for drunk driving. "We've all paid the toll."

"Thanks," Phylis whispered before she left the room.

"What do you think?" Carter asked Frank when they were alone again.

"I don't know. If it were me, I'd keep her on and chalk this up to pressure and the assumption that Haley was using the information in the manner he implied. It wasn't an unreasonable request and Phylis had no immediate reason to suspect that everything wasn't kosher." Frank managed a rueful wink. "Hey, you know this was supposed to be my ordeal, and you fielded most of it."

"Do you mind?" Carter asked, troubled as she realized he was right.

"Christ, no. I can't tell you how glad I was that you could do it and that Phylis wanted to talk to you. I haven't had to handle many of these confrontation things, and it sure as hell makes it easier to have a backup." He leaned over and kissed her.

"Are you sure? There were times Greg would get furious because he said I took over when—" She was becoming more distressed with each word, and he cut her short.

"I'm not Greg," he said very gently. "You try sitting back when I need help, and then you'll find out what makes *me* mad. If you don't mind my speaking ill of the dead, let alone my . . . rival, there were things about Greg that he should have outgrown in high school."

"Frank . . ." She was not certain what to tell him.

"And sometimes—just another little thing about me—I'm a boor, and I'm socially clumsy and I can be an ass. That doesn't change that I love you, it just means that I'm not Prince Charming."

Finally she laughed.

When J.D. got off the telephone, he found his old friend watching him with veiled curiosity. "Troubles?" the Admiral inquired.

"That was my secretary," J.D. said. He had been back from the committee hearing for almost an hour but was still in the full suit, vest and tie that he disliked and normally avoided. "It seems there is a problem with the Fire Marshals' Task Force. Do you happen to know if a Norman Haley is going to appear before the committee?"

"Tomorrow or something like that; I had a look at the list of witnesses they're hearing. Why?" While the Admiral was not precisely pushing, he was determined to know what had given the hard set to J.D.'s mouth and the glitter to his eyes.

"Because it appears that for whatever misguided, misbegotten reason, the man has been passing out information to the FBI. He told Phylis he needed it for the Task Force, and then gave it a double run; for the Task Force and for the special use of McPherson. I don't think that's just FBI, either," J.D. mused. "McPherson has carried on about terrorists from the beginning, and I wouldn't be surprised to learn if he still thinks that there are some kind of organized crazies behind it." He looked toward his friend. "Any recommendations?"

"One or two, but you won't like them." Admiral Haeverson had the gift of being able to think in double-time when it was necessary and his mind was moving with that strange, rapid clarity that always impressed J.D. There was a change of expression on Haeverson's face, almost a blankness, as if he were looking at something a long way away, and a deceptive laziness about him. His speech slowed down and he moved little. Twenty-five years ago when he had first seen this, J.D. had been perplexed by it; now he recognized what was happening and watched with interest.

"Suggestions?" J.D. asked.

"One or two, one or two," Haeverson repeated distantly. "I'm going to make a couple phone calls myself, one to the Deputy Director of the FBI." His tone of voice made this sound like he was trying to remember where he had left his cuff links.

"You know him?"

"You are not the only person who ever worked in my old unit," Haeverson reminded J.D. with a ghost of a chuckle. "I know him and he'll listen to me. He's a little like an old Inquisitor—only he really is righteous and his sense of duty is unfailing."

"Is that all?" J.D. wanted to arrange for a late lunch or early supper; he was very hungry and that was turning him testy.

"Not quite. Why don't you go down to the restaurant? The hotel's food isn't half bad." He had that same, distant air about him and J.D. accepted the man's need for privacy.

"Can I bring you anything?" It was his one concession to the strange situation they were in.

"I'll call room service. Now go down there; it's important that at least one of us be visible. In this town, that's part of the game and if we want to win, we have to keep to the rules." Haeverson leaned back on the little sofa and looked toward the windows. "Give me about forty minutes, if you can. Don't eat the way you usually do. Buy a paper and read it or... something. Make sure they know you're there and not worried. That's what we're after."

"Okay," J.D. said, recalling all the coaching he had had on the plane. As he left the suite, he heard Eric Haeverson punch a series of numbers into the phone.

Within the FBI the Deputy Director inspired a kind of awe that the more powerful and more polished Director did not. While the public was fascinated and repelled by the force of the man who ran the Bureau, few of them were aware of the soft-spoken fellow with the 170 IQ who served as his executive officer. Those who worked for the Bureau found Taylor Ville every bit as imposing as Samuel Overton.

Simon McPherson sensed trouble in the summons to Ville's office, but hastened to obey, damning the timing of the order and hoping that it was nothing more than coincidence.

Taylor Ville kept his office at sixty-eight degrees in the winter and seventy-four degrees in the summer, and dressed accordingly. His vest was knit and his shirt was a heavy silk broadcloth. He was surrounded by books, and unlike most of the other officials of the Bureau, Ville's office was always a bit cluttered, showing the stage of his various projects in progress.

McPherson entered the room as soon as the secretary indicated he could, and he went right up to the square oak desk where Taylor Ville waited for him.

"I had a telephone call a little while ago, McPherson, and it—oh, sit down if you like; this may take a while—troubled me." He paused to give McPherson a chance to speak. "Does that interest you at all?"

"I guess it must because I'm here," said McPherson carefully. The few times he had been in the Deputy Director's office, he had the sense that he was entering a particularly elegant minefield.

"Very astute. But you have a reputation for being astute, haven't you?" Again he waited.

"I really don't know," McPherson said.

"This is hardly a time to be modest, but let that pass. I've been going over your reports, the most recent ones, on the investigations of the Task Force and your part in it. I'm sorry to say that it appears that you made a point of trying to extend your authority in a very inappropriate way. I don't think it serves the cause of the country or the function of the Bureau to use those scare tactics you've held to throughout this whole thing." He folded his arms and stared at McPherson. "Or perhaps that was a ploy, a deliberate maneuver."

"A ploy?" McPherson said, not quite able to keep from shifting in his chair. "I don't understand."

"I warned you against false modesty," Ville said conversationally. "Would you like me to be more blunt?"

"Deputy Director, I—" McPherson began, but was not permitted to continue.

"I realize that this is in part our fault. When you and Bethune were first assigned, you were given your instructions, and from what I can tell, gave them a loose interpretation that has led to some unfortunate abuses of your position at a time when it was most essential to hold to the line in as strict a manner as possible." He fell silent again, his gray eyes fixed on McPherson's face.

Does he ever do that to his wife? McPherson speculated in order to keep control of himself. "That wasn't our understanding," said the Special Agent when he was sure he could keep the right demeanor.

"And it was to your advantage to continue this way. I'm sorry I wasn't asked to review the matter before now. A great deal of unpleasantness could have been avoided if this had been brought to my attention months ago, but then—" He shrugged. "I see that you have continued to state in your reports that you are convinced that the fires are the work of terrorists even though it has been consistently demonstrated that they are the result of spontaneous combustion brought about by a sequence of what has been called malign numbers. In bald terms, the number sequence summons a Salamander, a Fire Elemental—you ought to read some of these old alchemical writings, McPherson; it would tell you a thing or two about terrorism—and we know what the results are, don't we?"

"You don't think that's the real reason." McPherson could hardly bear to hear Ville speak this way. "You sound worse than Professor Turnbull."

"And speaking of the good Professor, you have been alienating his good opinion, and that is not to anyone's advantage except possibly yours. I've spent the last twenty minutes trying to determine what you can get out of this, and I assume that it must be the ego gratification of power."

"As if you don't find it gratifying," McPherson was stung to retort.

"You won't understand it, but no, I don't. I find it necessary, and for that reason I use minimal amounts of it when it is needed, but it is not for the satisfaction of my ego. Solving a problem satisfies my ego; catching fish satisfies my ego; even playing second fiddle in an amateur string quartet satisfies my ego: scaring people into obeying me does not satisfy my ego. And certainly it does not please me the way it does you. You would seem to take pleasure in the fear you evoke, and the manipulations you can perform as the result of the fear. I don't have to tell you, I suppose, that this is not what our participation in the investigation was intended to accomplish. Your fellow-officers participating with the Fire Marshals' Task Force have said that you preferred to work alone. They did not make an issue of it because of Myron Bethune's unfortunate death. But I am of the opinion they ought to have been more inquisitive."

"That was part of it," McPherson admitted. "But we were up against it. I passed on my reports as well as Myron's so that they could study what we'd already done, but with all the fires and all the questions, I thought that backtracking, as I would have had to do, would waste time we didn't have." He hated the self-defensive tone he heard in his voice; if he heard it, he knew that Ville also was aware of it, and that grated.

"So you carried on as you thought best, is that it?" asked Ville.

"I sent a series of memos to the Director, in case he wanted a change in policy."

"But you neglected to send one to me," said Ville gently, and both men knew that this went beyond mere oversight. "You know that Director Overton has been under intense pressure from the White House, from Congress and from the press, to come up with an answer to these disasters, and to find a means to contain and prevent them. It is within the purview of the Bureau to do this, and along with the officials at the NSA, we have all been working diligently, relying on those Agents participating in the investigation for the most dependable, accurate and comprehensive information possible to obtain. Would you assess the situation differently?" He asked the question as if this were a class examination in tactics and strategy.

"Perhaps a little differently," McPherson said. "In the view of the Task Force, it was most important to identify the source and cause of the fires, and then to deal with the agency behind them. It's in their second report."

"But you disagreed."

"Well, yes. I couldn't say that stopping the fires wasn't important; of course it was. But to ignore what was behind the fires was simply irresponsible. That's the difference between cops and firemen, I think. Cops know that there are bad guys out there and firemen only think about putting out fires. I said at the beginning that it was an oversight not to involve police in the investigation."

"McPherson," said Ville in gentle rebuke, "*we* are the cops for them. The FBI was put on the case to be the cops. In that sense, you performed some of the function properly in that you kept in mind that there could be... bad guys out there. What you decided that was against our best interests was that you *insisted* that there be bad guys out there. You *required* villains. And that, McPherson, has caused you to make some very poor decisions and act on some most unwise assumptions. As a result, you methodically hindered the investigation of the Task Force and gave priority to those areas that supported your theories instead of encouraging every area of investigation. You gave preference to those who agreed or appeared to agree with you and you selected your facts to fit your assumptions. All of that is poor procedure. You chose to act upon those data that encouraged the public and the investigators to suppose that the fires were the result of terrorism, which increased the level of panic in the country and hampered the efforts of investigation. If the fires had indeed been the result of terrorism, your climate of hysteria would have made their apprehension more difficult and their chance of greater damage significantly affected."

"I think that's a bit unreasonable," McPherson said, smarting.

"I am not yet finished. By attempting to discredit the work of those unwilling to support your theories, you guaranteed that the time required to discern the cause of the fires was greater than it might have been without such interference, and you used this not only to promote your position, but to strengthen your credibility with the public, the news media and with Congress in a way that others now regard with serious concern. Your behavior was, at the least, opportunistic."

"That's not so!" McPherson insisted.

"If it isn't, then your behavior is simply irrational, and that is not a quality that is useful in an agent." He folded his hands.

"I did my best!"

"For all our sakes, I hope not. If hampering legitimate inquiry in the name of witch-hunting is your notion of doing your best—"

"But the fires didn't just happen!" McPherson protested. "I don't give a fuck what they say is the cause, you know and I know that unless there was someone doing it, this simply could not happen."

"No, McPherson, this is what *you* know; it is your dogma. It is not mine. If it can be demonstrated—and it has been—that these fires originate with a sequence of numbers, nothing more and nothing less, then that is the cause, and there are no villains waiting in the wings." He stared hard at the younger man. "Because you decided that there were bad guys doing this, you felt justified in exceeding your authority in a number of ways, and in doing this, you have done a great deal of damage: do you understand that?"

"What damage?" He was frightened of what was coming next; Ville knew much more than McPherson had assumed.

"I trust that part of the question is rhetorical." He lifted his brows. "You frightened one of the assistants of the Fire Marshals' Task Force into providing you with material that ought not to have been given to you except with the knowledge and consent of the Task Force and you used that information obstructively. Because of that, the man in question, one Norman Haley, put others into the position of having to work in ways and to ends that were contrary to the work in which they were already engaged. Think about that, McPherson. You have been supposing that you can drop a stone in a pond and only have one ripple because that is convenient for you. The ripples are spreading and they are going to bring embarrassment—at the least—to the Bureau."

"I didn't order anyone to do this," McPherson objected.

"Oh, of course not," said Ville. "You merely hinted at the dire things that might happen if they didn't, suggesting that if they loved their country and were concerned for their loved ones, they would have to do this for the protection of everything that mattered to them. That is the usual way, isn't it."

"I didn't insist." It was going to be worse than he had anticipated, and that was bad enough.

"Naturally not. You only said that without their help your hands could be tied at a time when that might make the difference between another fire occurring and not." He let his breath out slowly. "McPherson, what *are* we going to do with you?"

"I'll resign," he said stiffly. "If you insist, I will resign."

"Don't be crass, old man," Ville recommended. "That would be worse for all of us, leaving a blot on all sorts of copybooks, and since we didn't precisely cover ourselves with glory in the first place, we will have to finesse—isn't that a dreadful thing to do to a perfectly innocuous noun? —our way through."

"I'll be willing to claim health reasons." He hated Ville at that moment, and wanted nothing so much as to have the profound satisfaction of slamming his fist into the older man's jaw.

"I think not, unless you insist. I think we are going to do a little reassigning. Sadly, you are not the only zealous man in this organization, or woman either, and for that reason it is important that everyone understands that such oversteppings will be noticed and dealt with."

"In other words, you're going to make me an example." He had decided that was impossible, that it could never happen to him, not with all the good he had done, and yet...

"I am afraid we are, yes." He tapped some papers on the cluttered desk. "You're being reassigned. If, after a year you wish to resign, the resignation will be accepted with thanks for service. If you insist on resigning now, then there will be a problem, because we will feel it incumbent upon ourselves to call certain witnesses to the committee to explain why they took the actions they did, and at whose behest they did so. Am I making myself clear so far?"

"You'll blow the whistle, as you see it." McPherson had to make an effort not to shout.

"A mixed metaphor, but that about sums it up. You are being reassigned to the Tucson area. There are many problems we deal with there, especially drugs and illegal aliens. You will have something to do with your time and you can leave yourself a good record for later, if you are diligent. Are you following me?" He read McPherson's vitriolic gaze. "No doubt you would like to boil me in oil just now, but believe me, this is preferable to anything that would happen if Norman Haley appeared before the joint committee on fires. You would end up in very hot water indeed."

"That could be another mixed metaphor," McPherson said, putting all of his contempt into his words.

"I'm glad you're learning to divert your anger into humor. It can stand you in good stead while you go through these next very awkward weeks." He indicated another series of papers. "For what it may be worth, neither the NSA nor the CIA, nor for that matter, the DIA has been able to find any foreign terrorist groups that had anything to do with these fires. Most of them are worried that the fires were being developed to be used against them. And from what I've learned, they were not entirely incorrect. He folded his hands. "All right, Mister McPherson, you may say whatever you want. It will be kept in confidence and it will not go into any part of your record. I'd rather you vented your spleen now, in private, than waited for an ill-considered moment when the press or other news media might hear you."

"I have nothing to say," growled McPherson.

"Don't be silly. You're bursting with venom. For God's sake, spew it out. It will poison you if you don't."

"I have nothing to say," McPherson repeated.

Ville shrugged. "That's your privilege, but let me urge you to reconsider while you may. You're in trouble and your current attitude can only make it worse."

"I did my job the best way I knew how. You're shitting on me now, but you waited until you could do it without getting caught with your pants down, and that makes it all fine and okay, and you can get rid of me with a clean conscience and the perfect sense of having stayed pristine. Well, that's peachy keen, Ville. That's just real hunky-dory."

"That's a start," Ville approved.

"Don't bother with this phony act of letting me speak off the record. There's no 'off the record' at the Bureau, and don't try to kid me with saying there is. So, if you don't mind, I'll go back to my office now. And I'll do what I can to make sure you all are satisfied with my reports in future. No bad guys. Fine."

"That is not what I said," Ville reminded him with steel under his soft words.

"Getting people to talk turns out to be not what you said before. It's going to take a little time for me to get good at the language around here. I thought I understood it, but apparently that isn't the case, is it?"

"As long as you remember the agreement you signed when you joined the Bureau. I'm afraid we're getting very stringent about that."

"In other words, you can say whatever you like and I can say nothing without getting screwed." He had risen from his chair. "No matter what you say, you know I did the right thing. We had to find a way to get the information. The Task Force was sitting on things we needed, and with all the ludicrous theories coming out of some of the investigators, we had to field them before the media got hold of them or we would all have looked like asses, and deserved to. If that means you're going to write me off, then that's what you'll do and nothing I can do will change it. It's a shitty way to treat me, but I'm not the first and knowing you, I won't be the last. Or are you doing this for Overton so he won't need to get his hands dirty on a bit of scum like me?" He had started toward the door, but he turned and pointed his finger at Taylor Ville. "You're shafting me for doing the things that had to be done. If I'd been right, you'd have promoted me and given me a medal and everyone would say that I'd showed initiative. As it is, I'm the scapegoat."

When Simon McPherson was gone, Taylor Ville lifted the telephone and spoke not with Director Overton but with one of several psychiatrists. "I'm afraid that we are going to have a problem."

"Do you have a recommendation?" asked the man on the other end.

"That Philippino agent, the one who lost her hand? See if she's willing to arrange a chance encounter with McPherson. He's feeling very abused and his ego is in dreadful shape. If possible, I want him to avoid thinking he's a Byronic hero. If she thinks she can handle him, I have a feeling it might be best if he has to help someone else for a change. Really help them."

"I'll want to talk to him first," the other warned.

"Naturally. He'll be sent out to Tucson early next week. If you sit next to him on the plane, that ought to work." Ville paused. "I'll send his file over so you can familiarize yourself with it before you take him on. He's insufferable, but I don't like to leave him working without a net."

"If you say so," said the other.

Carter and Cynthia were the first to get to J.D.'s office, and they found Phylis, looking a little strained but otherwise very happy, breaking out the Schramsburg champagne.

"What on earth is this all about?" asked Cynthia as she

saw the cheese and pâté and crackers set out on the conference table.

"J.D. sent that. He had it arranged before he left, just in case. He called ten minutes ago, and—"

"We won?" Carter finished, not able to believe it.

"Thanks to Admiral Haeverson and some high muckymuck at the FBI, they're willing to try it. Two weeks before Christmas, bye-bye to the fires."

Barry Tsugoro had heard the end of this, and as he came into the conference room, he let out a whoop. "Do you mean that they actually pulled it off? Where's Dave? He ought to be here. Where's Frank?"

"Calling Toronto," said Carter. "He's talking with his daughter, making arrangements for Christmas."

Cynthia grinned. "When's she coming?"

"It's more a case of when he's going. He'll be spending the holidays there. It's what her psychologist recommends."

"I see." Cynthia fell silent but this was hardly noticeable because Dave Fisher came in, and on his heels half a dozen of the other employees of PSS who had answered the urgent summons.

Phylis Dunlap went to the head of the table. "It's been confirmed," she said, having to shout to be heard over the voices. "We're getting our launch chance. The committee gave J.D. assurances. And Admiral Haeverson got confirmation from the Navy to use their probe for the test."

There was a general sort of cheer and then the loud bang of champagne corks.

The sound of the conversation was high and excited, the movements quick and eager. People milled around the conference table helping themselves to the food, talking to convince themselves that what they had worked so long for had finally come about.

"Hey," Cynthia said, coming over to Carter with two pâté-slathered crackers in one hand and two filled plastic champagne glasses in the other. "I just had an idea. If you're not doing anything at Christmas, Ben and I would be happy to have you with us. The girls go to Wally and Emily, and there's just the two of us."

Carter took one cracker and a glass. "I don't know. I'm still coming to terms with Frank."

"You could go with him," Cynthia suggested.

"No; it's not time yet." She took a bite of the cracker and said with her mouth full, "It's great to hear about J.D.'s success. And having Admiral Haeverson along must have helped."

"If you think I'm going to get you to change the subject that easily, you've forgotten what I do for a living. Cross-examination is a skill I've done very well with."

Carter was jostled by one of the others, and they exchanged abbreviated apologies. "Cynthia, please, not now. We can talk about this later, when it's more private."

This time Cynthia accepted her response. "Okay; later. Maybe we can go out for a bite to eat later, if you don't mind, or we can work out lunch. How does that sound?"

"Fine." She was a bit distracted, and while she finished the cracker, Frank joined them.

"Melinda sounds well. She's beginning to get better grades again, and her psychologist told me that she has fewer incidents of anxiety. What the hell happened before we sent our kids to shrinks?" He had taken one of the champagne glasses. "French?" he asked after a first appreciative sip.

"Napa Valley," Carter corrected. "Maybe we can go visit the cellars someday. I don't know if they take visitors, but it's a nice excuse for a day off."

"Not at this time of year," said Frank with a meaningful nod toward the window. "It's been coming down like that for almost three hours..."

"Even that Fire Elemental would have tough going against that downpour," said Carter, doing her best to keep their talk away from personal matters. "Any news when J.D. is coming back?"

"He's trying for day after tomorrow if Admiral Haeverson thinks they have all the right bases covered." Cynthia looked around the room. "Too bad they don't have ticker-tape parades in San Jose."

Frank brought them back to more serious matters. "What do you think you'll do about the holidays?"

Carter sighed. "I don't know yet. Cynthia gave me a lovely offer, but for all I know, I'll take off a week and go to Hawaii. I've never been there, and it sure as hell would take my mind off Christmas."

"That sounds like fun," said Frank.

"I just thought of it. What about the rocket launch? Do you think we'll get to go?" She was changing the subject once more and this time neither Frank nor Cynthia tried to stop her.

"From what I was told, it looks like J.D. will be able to go, but not the rest. It is a Navy launch, and even though it's just a space probe, they're being pretty closed about it. You know how jumpy NASA has been since the *Challenger* blew up. J.D. was in the Navy, and that gives him an edge. The Admiral can swing that, but I don't know what it does for the rest of us. If anyone ought to go, it's you, Carter," said Cynthia, making sure her voice carried a way.

One or two of the others nearby agreed, but Carter shook her head. "Maybe old Mister Corvin deserves the thanks, since it was his books that got me on the track. The fact is, J.D. let me try, and that means more than anything else. He's the one who owns the company and who took the chance. If he wants to go to Florida, I'm glad. The fact of the matter is, I'm pretty sure that a launch would make me more nervous than anything else. What if it doesn't work? If I were there I'd have a hell of a lot of explaining to do and I wouldn't like that at all."

Frank knew that a little chortle was expected and he was able to oblige, but he then said, "I'm going to say this once and then we won't talk about it again until we're home, but I'm very sorry that we can't be together here. I'd like to think that Melinda will get used to the idea that I want to marry again, but that will take time."

"Thanks," Carter said softly, giving him a quick kiss on the jaw before giving her attention to Cynthia.

"I've been trying to think how you get a copyright or a patent on the numbers that summon an Elemental. There are still the Elementals of Earth, Air and Water to be accounted for."

Carter nodded and said, "Yes; that's been worrying me."

"Hey, Carter, I was just being funny," Cynthia protested.

"I only wish you were," Carter said before she went to get a refill on the champagne and a gob of the triple-cream Explorateur that was set out on a fake-crystal tray.

Frank watched her. "She could be right," he said softly.

Cynthia shook her head once more. "Don't remind me."

Sidney Rountree walked through the light snow, watching the ghosts of steam each breath made. He had always liked old-fashioned locomotives, and when he was a child, he used to stomp through the fresh snow with his breath steaming while he whistled and chugged. Even now, part of him remembered those days with nostalgic pleasure, and so when he reached the place where Horace Turnbull was waiting, Rountree was smiling.

"Christmas spirit, Mister Rountree?" asked the professor.

"Something like that," said Rountree. "How are you?"

"Much better, thank you. I've had time with my grandchildren, and that always does a great deal to bring me back to earth. When you're lost amid theories and concepts, a four-year-old climbing over your shoulder is marvelous therapy, don't you think?" His face was ruddy and when he laughed, he created his own fog.

"Are you going to the launch?" Rountree asked.

"Yes, as a matter of fact I am. Since we worked on the verification of the number sequence, we're anxious to make sure it all goes according to plan. We've worked the thing out in the laboratory, and for what it may be worth, it's turned out very well. I'm truly looking forward to the launch. I want to wish that thing bon voyage once and for all." He paused, listening to the Christmas carols coming from speakers near the Common.

"I like that one," said Rountree, as the chorus sang "The Holly and the Ivy."

"Yes, so do I; though what it has to do with Christianity, I can't think." He gave a low, rumbling laugh. "Paganism always creeps in the back door, doesn't it?"

The two men walked in friendly silence around one end of the Common.

"Boston's really beautiful in the winter, isn't it?" Turnbull said to Rountree as they stood at the corner, looking away toward the distant towers of Prudential Center.

"Yes, it is," said Rountree. "I'm glad that worse didn't happen here. The way the fires were going—"

"Yes, indeed." They went a little way farther, then Turnbull said, "What was the decision about the Fire Marshals' Task Force? Are they going back to the National Fire Data Center?"

Rountree shook his head. "No. The decision is to keep on in an advisory capacity, and with provision for going on loan internationally if the conditions warrant such action."

"What conditions would those be?" asked Turnbull.

"We don't know that yet; we're leaving the option open to be invited in," Rountree said, then added, "I'm going to be in charge for the first year. I was hoping you might be willing to be one of our advisers, if we need that."

Turnbull beamed. "Of course. Gracious, Sid, I'd be offended if you gave a party and didn't want me to come. I imagine this could be very, very interesting."

"Thanks." His reticence faded. "Where's your favorite tavern? Let me get you a little something for the holidays."

"And I'll get you a little something for your new position. I must say that for once I approve of a government decision. In fact, I approve of two, come to think of it. I think that the launch is the most sensible thing they've done yet where this Salamander is concerned."

"Salamander?" said Rountree, trying his best to sound puzzled.

"Oh, come now. What else would you call it? I know that where the general public is concerned you like to stay away from those old mystic terms, but since it acts like a Salamander and looks like a Salamander, why don't we call it a Salamander and save ourselves a great amount of double-talk." He pointed to a sign down one of the side streets. "There's a very nice pub down that way. I think we'd both find something to our tastes there."

"Sounds fine with me." As they started across the street, Sid Rountree thought that he never imagined himself having drinks with a Nobel Laureate, let alone one he would think of as a friend. He grinned, and as they reached the door to the pub, he chuckled and clapped Horace Turnbull on the back.

Turnbull gave him a thumbs-up and they went into the cozy warmth with the best of good fellowship.

"Stephanie said she'd look after Winslow for me, and I won't be gone more than four days," said Carter as she pulled her hood up against the rain. Aside from her and Frank, the beach was empty and windblown.

"You sure you want to leave him alone?" said Frank.

"Well, I know he doesn't travel well. He likes the new house and he knows Stephanie. Two plane rides in a week would be a bit much for him, don't you think?" She had thrust her hands deep into her pockets, but now she took one out and slipped it into his.

"I just don't want you to be lonely," said Frank.

"Well, I will be, whether Winslow is with me or not. That's why I want to spend part of the time away, so I'll have an excuse to be lonely and so I'll have something to do instead of brood about it." She squinted into the rain, her hair clinging around her face and falling across her cheeks like tendrils of pale seaweed.

"You're being practical, going to Hawaii for Christmas," he said, smiling ruefully.

"Yes and no. I want to go there, I don't want to sit home being depressed, I don't want to get mad at you for spending time with your daughter. And you know, I think I need a little time alone. I haven't had much of that since... since Greg died, and I've been avoiding thinking about it. Whiting warned me about it again just yesterday."

They were almost to the outcropping of rock where they usually turned back. "I hope you enjoy the trip. I don't want you to dislike the place. We might decide to go there together one day."

"This isn't a proposal, is it?" She laughed outright. "If it is, I warn you—"

"I don't know what it is. It's not time to decide that yet, is it?" They walked together out to the first few rocks, taking time to find their footing on the slippery stones.

"You're right. Maybe we can figure it out." She went a few more cautious steps. "I'll probably be all silent and stuffy with you tomorrow when I drive you to the plane. Don't pay any attention to me. It means I'm pouting."

"Pouting? You?" He held out his hand to help steady her. "Okay, and if I talk a lot about nothing, it's because I'm nervous." They reached the crest of the rocks and stood watching the waves contend with the rain. "It's snowing in Toronto. I'll have to get a good pair of boots while I'm there. California's spoiling me for weather."

"Good." She was the first one to start back, picking her way slowly, and taking time to be sure of her footing.

They went down the beach in silence, standing close to each other for tender, lingering kisses before they started back to the car. Each wrapped their arms tightly around the other and held on with unabashed longing.

"I'm going to miss you," Frank said.

"I'm going to miss you," Carter agreed.

"Are you going to watch the launch?"

"Sure; we're getting the closed-circuit coverage. Why not? You'll be on a plane; I might as well." She leaned against his shoulder. "That isn't below the belt, Frank. It's just that I feel... at odds knowing you're going to be away."

"Watch the launch. See what you did. I'm proud of you.

When they show it on the evening news, I'm going to tell Melinda and all Anne's family that you were the one who figured it out."

"You and me together," Carter said forcefully.

"You," he insisted, touching the tip of her nose with his index finger. "The credit's yours and you'll offend me if you don't take your bow."

"Like a man?" she suggested, smiling.

"You betcha," he said, as they started toward the car together.

"Where do you want to have dinner?" she asked as she tightened her seat belt.

"Someplace nice that serves wet people."

They laughed as they drove off, and they were laughing still when they reached a quiet restaurant where they had eaten before. By unspoken agreement, this was their Christmas dinner and they were determined to enjoy it.

"When Melinda comes out at Easter, you two will get along very well," Frank promised her.

"I hope we do. It'll take time, Frank. Let us do it on our own time, okay?"

It was the only time they referred to any future; for the time being, they were content with relishing what they had.

On the viewing platform, Admiral Haeverson had the place of honor, and he enjoyed it with a wicked satisfaction. "It makes them crazy to see me here," he confided to J.D., who was on the seat below him. "They had me safely out of their way in Hawaii and over most of my active service, taking time only to advise and to consult, the rest of the time lolling around. And now, here I am back again on the wildest card in the deck."

"You're enjoying this," J.D. said, getting some of the delight his friend felt.

"Look, when you've been in a backwater..." He slapped J.D. on the shoulder. "You remember what it was like, with all the Cambodian things. You've given me exactly the thing I wanted most, and I will be grateful to you to the day I die, Jerry." He peered at the tall rocket. "I hope that thing flies like angels never could and that fire thing fizzles like a demon in a rainstorm."

J.D. laughed out loud. "So do I, Eric."

They were grinning when Horace Turnbull lugged himself up the steps toward them. "Good morning, gentlemen. While I don't believe we've ever met face-to-face before, I want you to know what a pleasure it is to see you at last. I congratulate you for all your hard work and for that very skillful handling of that McPherson business." He held out his hand to J.D. "Mister Patterson?"

"Professor Turnbull?" J.D. responded, taking the man's hand. "I thought your explanation of the trouble with fifteen-number sequences was brilliant, and the way you were able to protect the actual sequence nothing short of masterful."

"My, what wonderful accord!" marveled Horace Turnbull. "There's nothing like success to bring out the virtues in men." He indicated the seats occupied by J.D. and Admiral Haeverson. "Very choice. You are doubtless enjoying the fruits of your victory, Admiral."

"Absolutely; just as you are."

The three men exchanged conspiratorial smiles and Turnbull went down the stairs back to his less august seat.

"He's the best ally we had," said Haeverson.

"Not quite; Frank Vickery is the best. That's why he's going to work for me. Don't tell me that they sent him to us to get him out of their hair—I know they did. But he didn't have anything to do. It was his determination and his experience that made things possible for us." J.D. looked down over the spectators' stands, and then over to the news-media stands.

"See anyone you know?" Haeverson asked, not quite joking.

"As a matter of fact, yes. There's a newsman from Lansing who spent a lot of time at PSS. That tall black man in the fifth row. That's William Ridour."

"I read some of his stories. They were very good." Haeverson looked at him thoughtfully. "I hope Lansing knows what it has in him."

"I hope so, too. I sent his editor a letter of appreciation. I hope he pays attention. Ridour deserves more than a few kind words and a pat on the back." J.D. took a deep breath. "Maybe one of these days, I'll think of a way to say thank you."

There was an unintelligible announcement over the public address system and Admiral Haeverson consulted his watch. "Another five minutes and then up she goes. I'm pleased that they opened this up to the public the way they did. They're all afraid that this'll go up like a Roman candle, but it's going to be fine. It's going to launch like a dream and the whole thing's going off without a hitch. I'm absolutely sure of it. The way I could feel about missions, sometimes."

"I remember," said J.D.

"This is just like it." Haeverson sat back, grinning.

J.D. stared at the rocket. God, what if he had been wrong, what if their calculations were wrong, what if it didn't work? Cheryl had asked him just those questions before he had left for Florida, and he had reassured her that everything was going to be fine.

"That's what they always say, but you know it's not true." She had the cynicism that only the very young possess.

At the time he had laughed at his daughter, but sitting here in the Florida sun—which was somehow different than the sun in California—he had found himself wondering.

There was another burst of static and then a few words from the speakers on the platform.

"This probe," said the elderly man one rank of seats above Admiral Haeverson, "is an historic launch, and one that will increase our knowledge of the solar system through the pictures it will send back to us here on earth. And to generations yet unborn, it will show more of the universe than we have ever seen before, which is our legacy to our grandchildren and their grandchildren and to grandchildren of generations never dreamed of."

"Say something about the fire code, damn you," whispered Admiral Haeverson.

"The mathematical experiment to be carried out in this probe will reap its harvest in much less time, and can add to the security of the entire world." The accents were less portentous, and the man seemed to be apologizing for this part of his speech. "This aspect of the probe will be assessed within a few minutes of launch, and it will then be more generally applied."

"That man must be their champion waffler," said Haeverson.

"It's politics," J.D. reminded him.

"It's bullshit," said Haeverson, but not very loudly.

Again there was a racket from the speakers of the public address system, and the man on the platform cut his remarks short.

"Let us wish the space probe *Navigator* calm seas and a safe harbor at the end of her long, long voyage."

The crackling speakers took over, and the rocket, like a racehorse in the starting gate, showed the shaking and sweating that marked its prelaunch readiness.

Admiral Haeverson leaned forward and very nearly had to shout into J.D.'s ear in order to be heard at all. "Almost there!"

J.D. nodded, caught up in the tremendous excitement in spite of himself. He crossed his fingers the same way he used to do as a kid.

Then, finally came the noise that was so vast and low that it was more like a movement in the ground than a sound. The rocket quivered and strained, and then, as the flames spurted out at the base, the huge vehicle began to inch its way upward.

Watching it, J.D. thought it absolutely impossible for the launch to get off the ground let alone reach outer space. He could imagine the whole thing toppling or falling back to earth, overwhelmed by its own weight and size.

And then, amazingly, it was climbing, climbing, going straight into the vast blue of the Florida sky, its rocket leaving a trail of smoke to mark its progress.

The first stage separated and the second stage ignited, and those gathered to watch gasped at the sight. No one listened to the static of the public address system, now completely overloaded by the sound of the rocket.

Higher and higher the rocket climbed, and it could only be seen by the trail it left.

J.D. looked into the sky, his fingers crossed more tightly, repeating over and over in a private chant, "Burn you bastard, burn you bastard, burn you bastard." If they had been right, the separation of the second and third stage would be triggered by the fifteen-number sequence, the first half on the ground, the second half in the rocket, preset in the computer that guided the enormous vehicle into space. There would be no oxygen when the separation occurred, and once the fuel was exhausted, the fires would be at last and irrevocably gone.

The sound faded to the roar of a near-by freeway at rush hour and then to landing jet planes.

"The second-stage separation is about to initiate," announced the loudspeakers.

"Do it do it do it do it do it," whispered J.D.

The rocket trail served to obscure the ignition. A hush came over those watching, and they waited for the announcement that the separation had or had not occurred.

"Separation is complete," said the loudspeaker after what felt like far too many minutes.

There was a cheer at this, but in the aftermath of the rocket launch, it was a pallid effort, hardly more than a rattle of toys.

"It worked," Admiral Haeverson shouted to J.D.

For once in his life, J.D. could not say anything. He continued to stare at the exhaust trail of the rocket until the winds smeared it across the sky.

Two Years Later
July 10, Chitral, Pakistan

The radio was battery-powered and worked sporadically, but new batteries had been sent up from Lahore and now for the first time since the guerillas got it, they were able to use the thing properly. The radio, hidden in the shepherd's hut, was never operated for long, and then, always in code.

"There are trucks on the road," the shepherd's son, a boy of nine, told the fighter who found his way to the hut at the dark end of the night.

"There are always trucks on the road," the fighter said, his one eye glistening with fatigue and contempt.

"With Russian soldiers. I have kept track. I pretend to be foolish and they pay no attention to me, but I keep watch and I know what I have seen."

"Be quiet," said the fighter, and then relented. "All right, tell me, and you had better not be incorrect."

So the boy began to read from the tallies he had kept for the last forty-eight hours, answering the occasional questions of the fighter as he strove to recall every detail of what he had seen.

"You have done well," the fighter told him. "I will put this into the code and I want you to keep watch while I transmit the information. They are waiting to hear from me and—"

The boy obeyed, hurrying outside the hut and crouching in the lee of the building, for the winds in the mountains were fierce even in summer. He huddled in his cloak, listening to the strange sounds of the radio and hoping that the Russians would not come in the helicopters while the fighter transmitted his message. He had considered the radio an honor, and now that it worked, he would have to relinquish it to the fighters.

As the numbers of the code completed, the boy could feel the wind change. He thought he knew every form and permutation the wind could take, but this night he could tell that there was something in the air, in the wind, that had never been there before.

FIRST-RATE 'WHODUNITS' FROM MARGARET TRUMAN

__MURDER IN THE WHITE HOUSE
(B31-402, $3.95, U.S.A.)
(B31-403, $4.95, Canada)

A thriller about the murder of a Secretary of State . . . Could the President himself have been the killer? All the evidence pointed to the fact that the murder was committed by someone very highly placed in the White House . . .

"Terrifically readable . . . marvelous . . . She has devised a secret for her President and First Lady that is wildly imaginative . . . The surprise ending is a dandy . . ."
—*New York Daily News*

__MURDER ON CAPITOL HILL
(B31-438, $3.95, U.S.A.)
(B31-439, $4.95, Canada)

The Majority Leader of the U.S. Senate has been killed with an ice pick . . .

"True to whodunit form she uses mind rather than muscle to unravel the puzzle. Ms. Truman's writing is bright, witty, full of Washington insider insight and, best of all, loyal to the style of the mysteries of long ago. She may bring them back singlehandedly. Here's hoping so!"
—*Houston Chronicle*

WARNER BOOKS
P.O. Box 690
New York, N.Y. 10019

Please send me the books I have checked. I enclose a check or money order (not cash), plus 50¢ per order and 50¢ per copy to cover postage and handling.* (Allow 4 weeks for delivery.)

_____ Please send me your free mail order catalog. (If ordering only the catalog, include a large self-addressed, stamped envelope.)

Name _____

Address _____

City _____

State _____ Zip _____

*N.Y. State and California residents add applicable sales tax.